# The Blue Hotel

## And Other Stories

## Stephen Crane

(previously published as
*Maggie and Other Stories*)

WSP

WASHINGTON SQUARE PRESS
PUBLISHED BY POCKET BOOKS NEW YORK

A Washington Square Press Publication of
POCKET BOOKS, a Simon & Schuster division of
GULF & WESTERN CORPORATION
1230 Avenue of the Americas, New York, N.Y. 10020

ISBN: 0-671-46036-6

First Washington Square Press printing December, 1960

19  18  17  16  15  14  13  12  11  10  9

WASHINGTON SQUARE PRESS, WSP and colophon are
trademarks of Simon & Schuster.

Printed in the U.S.A.

# The slum,
# with its lost women
# and forgotten men.

This twilight world found its chronicler in Stephen Crane. He lived among society's outcasts so he could write about them.

All his characters—the New York harlots, Western cowboys, and Civil War soldiers—are as real today as when he created them.

A trail-blazer, Crane brought a new, naturalistic voice to American fiction, a voice no American writer has been able to ignore since these stories first began to appear.

---

**"One of the clearest cases of genius in American fiction. . . ."**

—*Carl Van Doren*

# *Introduction*

## *The Gossip and the Legends*

ALMOST NO AMERICAN WRITER, except perhaps Edgar Allan Poe or F. Scott Fitzgerald, has stimulated as many rumors and legends as Stephen Crane. The Crane myths, which sprang up weedlike during his lifetime and soon after his death in 1900, are indeed fantastic growths, doubtless having their roots in the considerable amount of jealousy and spite that spread around him after the stirring reception of *The Red Badge of Courage* in England in 1895 and its delayed but nevertheless general acclaim in this country not long afterward. Thomas Beer, in the appendix to his delightful memoir of Crane, tells of some of these rumors and the problems they present to a biographer.

In 1903 Mr. [Willis] Clarke began to collect copies of letters and facts for a life of Stephen Crane but was so baffled by conflicting statements that he dropped the work. . . . The mythology encountered by Mr. Clarke may interest readers who have been struck by a note of apology in this most imperfect study. Mr. Clarke was informed by people who had met Crane and admired him that he was the illegitimate son of Grover Cleveland, the outcast child of an eminent family in New York, an Australian sailor, a German actor and an ex-convict. He was gravely assured that the several published statements about Crane in journals, the *Bookman, Leslie's Weekly* and *Scribner's Magazine* were industrious camouflage devised by the late Ripley Hitchcock on behalf of Appleton's [Crane's publisher]. My own contact with the legendary Crane revealed other jewels of rumour. I have, with regret, rejected the tales of Crane's love affair with

v

the lamented Sarah Bernhardt, of his duel in New Orleans, of his attempt to burn James Gordon Bennett's yacht, of his marriage to Australian, English, Spanish and African dancers, of his ninety thousand dollar cablegram to the New York *Journal,* of his death of delirium tremens in Paris and of his murder by an actress still living who happened at the time of his death to be in Chicago. With less pain I have rejected anecdotes of Crane which were in print during his childhood as anecdotes of Mark Twain, Thomas Hood, Abraham Lincoln and Andrew Jackson. There have also been visited upon me stories of his gaieties which are, with probably as much truth, told in regard to Bill Nye, Eugene Field, Clyde Fitch and other celebrities still extant.[1]

Joseph Conrad, who became a friend and admirer of Crane's in England, suggests very plausible reasons for the gossip when he says: "He was surrounded by men who, secretly envious, hostile to the real quality of his genius (and a little afraid of it), were also in antagonism with the essential fineness of his nature."[2]

## The Twenty-eight Wandering Years

Stephen Crane was born at 14 Mulberry Place, Newark, New Jersey, on November 1, 1871, the fourteenth child of the Reverend Jonathan Townley Crane, a Methodist minister. Three years later, the family moved to Bloomington, New Jersey, and then to successive parishes in Paterson, Jersey City, and Port Jervis, where the Reverend Crane died in 1880, when Stephen was nine.

In 1882, the family moved to Asbury Park, where Stephen's brother Townley operated a news-reporting agency. From this time until 1888, Crane attended school in Asbury Park. Then, in the next two years, he went to the Pennington

[1] Thomas Beer, *Stephen Crane: A Study in American Letters* (New York: Alfred A. Knopf, 1923), pp. 243-244.
[2] *Ibid.,* p. 26.

Seminary, at Pennington, New Jersey, and the Hudson River Institute, at Claverack, New York.

In September, 1890, Crane entered Lafayette College, where he joined Delta Upsilon fraternity. He stayed only one term, however, transferring early in 1891 to Syracuse, where he remained until June. That spring, he was regular catcher and then regular shortstop on the Syracuse baseball team. A group picture shows Crane among the nine members of the team.[3] Competing with the likes of Colgate, Union, Rochester, and Hamilton, the Syracuse team won fifteen out of twenty-four games. Crane also reported for the *New York Tribune* and published several sketches in the Syracuse *University Herald.*

The summer of 1892 found him reporting for his brother's news agency in Asbury Park and contributing a number of sketches to the *New York Tribune*. In August, he incurred the wrath of Whitelaw Reid, owner and editor of the *Tribune,* who was also the Republican candidate for vice-president. Crane had reported an Atlantic City parade of a mechanics' organization in such a realistic way that the group regarded his news story as very disparaging. Consequently, they heaped much invective upon Reid's paper, and Reid felt that the whole incident had cost him many votes in the campaign against Grover Cleveland. As a result, Crane was fired.

In 1893, having borrowed a thousand dollars from one of his brothers for the purpose, Crane privately published *Maggie: A Girl of the Streets* under the pseudonym of John-ston Smith. He had previously failed to interest any publisher in it. It sold very poorly, and visitors to Crane's meager room in New York commented about the unsold copies upon which they were invited to sit in the absence of sufficient chairs. This edition of *Maggie* has now become a rare Crane item.

The following year saw Crane contributing sketches and feature articles to the *New York Press* and to several magazines. It was also the year *The Red Badge of Courage* first

---

[3] *Stephen Crane's Love Letters to Nellie Crouse, with six other letters, new materials on Crane at Syracuse University, and a number of unusual photographs,* ed. E. H. Cady and L. G. Wells (Syracuse: Syracuse University Press, 1954).

appeared, running in several installments in the *Philadelphia Press*. It was published in book form in 1895, as was his first book of verse, *The Black Riders and Other Lines*. At this time, Crane was traveling throughout the Southwest and Mexico for Irving Bacheller's magazine syndicate. In 1896, besides contributing to numerous periodicals, including Elbert Hubbard's *The Philistine*, he saw three of his works published: *George's Mother*, *Maggie*, and *The Little Regiment*, the last a collection of Civil War stories, two of which—"Three Miraculous Soldiers" and "A Mystery of Heroism"—appear in this collection.

On New Year's eve, Crane sailed from Jacksonville, Florida, as a seaman aboard the *Commodore* on her tragic and abortive filibustering expedition to aid the Spanish insurgents in Cuba. When the ship foundered off the coast of Florida, Crane spent thirty hours in a ten-foot dinghy. From this experience came one of his finest stories, "The Open Boat," and also some physical aftereffects, from which he perhaps never fully recovered.

Nevertheless, in 1897, he went to Greece to report the Greco-Turkish War for the *New York Journal* and the *Westminster Gazette*. Here he was joined by Cora Taylor, a twice-married woman two years older than he, whom he had met in Jacksonville, where she had been the proprietress of a bawdyhouse. Cora had induced the Hearst office to send her abroad as the first American woman correspondent, and a few scattered articles later appeared in New York under her *nom de guerre*, Imogene Carter. Although Cora took Crane's name and lived as his wife the rest of his short span, they were never, according to Berryman,[4] legally married because she had never been divorced from her second husband. Later that year, they went to live in England, at Oxted, Surrey.

Eighteen ninety-seven was also the publication year of *The Third Violet*, a short novel dealing with a New York artist. Because of the towering critical and popular reception of *The Red Badge of Courage* in England, Crane was well re-

---

[4] John Berryman, *Stephen Crane* (New York: William Sloane Associates, 1950).

ceived in literary circles, becoming acquainted with several established writers of the day as well as with a number of rising ones, particularly Joseph Conrad.

Leaving Cora in England to cope with their precarious financial circumstances, the peripatetic Crane returned to America shortly after the outbreak of the Spanish-American War. He tried to enlist in the Navy, but when he was turned down, he shipped to Cuba as a war correspondent, at first for the *New York World* and then for the *New York Journal*. In those days of the yellow press in America, many papers were sending men to this little war and fanning war feeling into blazelike intensity. Crane, however, rejected this kind of sensational journalism. In many ways his writing anticipated the kind of war-reporting that Ernie Pyle was to do in World War II. It shows a similar interest in the common soldier, a similar sincerity and honesty, a similar eye for striking detail. Although Crane was sick and feverish much of the time, he managed to send back thirty-eight dispatches, nineteen to the *World* and the same number to the *Journal*. One of the best, which Stallman includes in his *Omnibus*,[5] is the report of the San Juan Hill engagement.

Among Crane's Cuban activities during the war, he accompanied a Marine scouting party somewhere near Guantánamo. For his courageous assistance in the course of this mission he was commended in official dispatches by the commanding officer of the Marine detachment. Another time, he slipped into Havana ahead of the official American occupation by posing as a tobacco-buyer. For a short time unaccounted for, he was reported dead, much to the distress of Cora, to whom the rumor had traveled and who wrote a pathetic request for information to Washington. Crane turned up safe, but became so ill toward the end of 1898 that he was sent back to the United States. During this year, *The Open Boat and Other Tales of Adventure* was published.

After failing to persuade Cora to leave England and join him in New York, Crane returned to England early in 1899,

---

[5] *Stephen Crane: an Omnibus*, ed. Robert Wooster Stallman (New York: Alfred A. Knopf, 1952), pp. 399-412.

establishing Cora and himself in Brede Place, a large, ram-
bling, medieval manor in Sussex. Here his hospitality was im-
posed upon by curious acquaintances and celebrity-hunting
strangers to such an extent that often he could not work. However, during the year, a number of his writings were published: his second volume of poems, *War is Kind;* his novel
with a Greco-Turkish War background, *Active Service;* and a
collection of narratives, *The Monster and Other Stories.* He
also contributed to a number of periodicals as well.

Now Crane's health was failing badly, probably from the
effects of a lifelong tendency toward tuberculosis and from the
scars of his open-boat and Cuban hardships. He was moved to
Dover early in May of 1900, and then to Badenweiler, Germany, where it was hoped the baths might help him. He died
there on June fifth. His body was returned to New York and
interred at Evergreen Cemetery, Elizabeth, New Jersey.

## Social Views

Unlike William Dean Howells and Hamlin Garland, both of
whom knew and encouraged him, Crane never became closely
concerned with social issues. It was usually the moral or
psychological aspects of a situation that caught his interest.
Of his Bowery story "An Experiment in Misery" he wrote:
"I tried to make plain that the root of Bowery life is a sort of
cowardice. Perhaps I mean a lack of ambition or to willingly
be knocked flat and accept the licking." [6]

To this might be added a comment Crane once made: "I
was a Socialist . . . but when a couple of Socialists assured me
I had no right to think differently from any other Socialist and
then quarrelled with each other about what Socialism meant,
I ran away." [7]

As shown by the grim description of the sweatshop and its
proprietor in "Maggie," and from the comment about the
Standard Oil Company at the beginning of "Virtue in War,"

[6] Berryman, *Stephen Crane,* p. 141.
[7] *Ibid.*

it would probably be safe to say that Crane's general sympathies were against the capitalist and clearly with the common man.

## The Plan of This Collection

In making the selection of stories here, I have attempted to follow three criteria. First, I have tried to find, generally, the best of Crane's stories. This is not an easy task because, of the nearly ninety pieces of his writing that may be classified as short pieces of fiction, though many of them are hasty, uneven, experimental, financially pressured productions, certain ones may have some particularly vivid human perception or striking image or symbol to recommend them. Secondly, I have tried to include selections that would suggest the range in locale of his stories. Thirdly, I have tried to use materials that would illustrate Crane's principal themes, his method, his diction, and his imagery, and thus help the reader to decide, when these stories by Crane are set refloating on the main stream of reputable American writing, just how high they should ride upon those waters.

## General Criticism

### Themes

The pervading theme in Crane's stories—indeed, in all his work—is perhaps the most ubiquitous theme in all American literature: loneliness. As found in Crane, it is the loneliness of a central honest or innocent character in a situation in which he or she has to deal with worldly or morally weak people, or with an impersonal or indifferent environment. This is the situation, for example, in "Maggie," in "The Bride Comes to Yellow Sky," and in "The Pace of Youth." Maggie's drunken mother is not only a personal antagonist but also a symbol of the whole hostile and depressing world that Maggie never made. In "An Episode of War" and "The Open Boat," the opposition is clearly this indifferent and sometimes inimical world. "The Open Boat" is perhaps the most allegorical of all of Crane's stories, for it suggests that man's natural condition is one of helplessness in an open boat. The captain, the oiler, the cook, and the correspondent seem to stand for mankind, and the universe is represented by the ominous sea, the soaring gulls, the distant clouds and sky, the lurking sharks in the night, and the windmill on the shore:

> This tower was a giant, standing with its back to the plight of the ants. It represented in a degree, to the correspondent, the serenity of nature amid the struggles of the individual—nature in the wind, and nature in the vision of men. She did not seem cruel to him then, nor beneficent, nor treacherous, nor wise. But she was indifferent, flatly indifferent.

The story's famous opening line—"None of them knew the color of the sky"—implies that the overwhelmingness of man's struggle to survive at his own level of existence allows him little hope of any metaphysical help. Like Yeats's wild swans, the gulls become symbols of the aloofness and permanence of nature in contrast with the puniness and impermanence of man. Symbolically, too, all that the men have to help them, outside themselves, is a "thin little oar, and it seemed often ready to snap." The influence of this story, even to the oar business, on Hemingway's *The Old Man and The Sea* seems apparent.

In "An Episode of War," as the young lieutenant is dividing the coffee beans with his sword on the spread-out rubber blanket, he is, ironically, badly wounded by a stray bullet. Here again is Crane's vision of an impersonal and unpredictable world, and once again one thinks of Hemingway, this time of the scene in *A Farewell to Arms* where Lieutenant Henry and his Italian ambulance-driving friends are blown up while eating a cheese lunch. The naturalistic view of the universe in these stories and others constitutes a second major theme in Crane's work.

Another major motif is Crane's almost clinical preoccupation

with the behavior of men in situations of crisis or danger—
both brave men and cowards figure frequently and impor-
tantly. A line-up of the courageous ones would include not
only the group in "The Open Boat," the lieutenant in "An
Episode of War," and Marshal Jack Potter in "The Bride
Comes to Yellow Sky," but also Collins in "A Mystery of
Heroism," Henry Johnson in "The Monster," the gambler in
"The Blue Hotel," the New York Kid in "The Five White
Mice," the Greek child in "Death and the Child," the pro-
tagonists in both "The Price of the Harness" and "Virtue in
War," and a number of others. In "Death and the Child,"
Crane develops a child-is-father-to-the-man theory about
courage, for the crawling child is unruffled by the surrounding
war conditions, whereas the adult correspondent-turned-sol-
dier, Peza, is shaken by uncontrollable fear:

> Palsied, windless and abject, he confronted the primitive
> courage, the sovereign child, the brother of the moun-
> tains, the sky, and the sea, and he knew that the defini-
> tion of his misery could be written on a wee grass blade.

With Peza to begin a list of cowards, one can easily add
some interesting others, such as the Swede and the Easterner
in "The Blue Hotel," and Senator Cadogan's son, Caspar, in
"The Second Generation."

From this presentation of man's conduct under crisis,
however, comes perhaps the only really positive and hopeful
note in Crane's writing. This is not based simply on the argument that the brave men far outnumber the cowards. It rests
mainly on a clear affirmation, which sounds throughout most
of his stories, of man's occasional capacity for courage and
endurance.

A fourth major theme is the very ironic one that generosity
often leads to suffering. This is found, for example, in "The
Monster," when Dr. Trescott's deeply felt moral obligation to
save the life of the Negro hired man Henry Johnson, who
has rescued his son, leads to his ostracism in his home town.
The narrowness and conformity of small-town life and the

maliciousness of feminine gossip, although lesser themes in
this and other of the Whilomville[8] stories, point up the
influence of Crane on such later American provincial realists
as Sinclair Lewis and Sherwood Anderson.

One also finds in Crane variations on the father-and-son
theme, or more specifically as applied to Crane, the mother-
and-daughter or father-and-daughter motif. This occupies a
large place in "Maggie," "The Pace of Youth," and "The
Second Generation." In any of its forms it pivots on the inability of two different generations to understand each other.

A final theme to comment on is the children-are-a-race-
apart one. In this Crane aligns himself with the Mark Twain
of *Tom Sawyer,* and clearly anticipates Booth Tarkington;
indeed, Penrod and his pals seem to be fashioned almost
directly after Jimmie Trescott and his friends in "Angel Child"
and the other Whilomville stories in which they appear.
Particularly, the nauseating Lola Pratt of Tarkington's *Seventeen* seems to be descended directly from the Angel Child
herself.

## Imagery and Symbolism

Of all Crane's qualities as a writer, it is, I think, his
metaphorical imagination that most impresses the reader.
Again and again one is struck by some particularly vivid piece
of imagery. At times the image may lean toward theatricality,
but much more often it will be arresting, perceptive, and
original, yet effectively understated. Here, for instance, is
Marshal Jack Potter riding self-consciously in a Texas railroad
coach alongside his new bride on their way home to Yellow
Sky:

> He sat with a hand on each knee, like a man waiting
> in a barber's shop.

And thus Crane sees the tents of American soldiers in the
Spanish-American War for "The Price of the Harness":

---

[8] *Whilom* means former or sometime.

Here were scattered tiny white shelter tents, and in the darkness they were luminous like the rearing stones in a graveyard.

And the scene in the Bowery tale called "George's Mother," as George Kelcey is reluctantly on his way to the prayer meeting with his mother:

In a dark street the little chapel sat humbly between two towering apartment houses. A red street lamp stood in front. It threw a marvelous reflection upon the wet pavements. It was like the death stain of a spirit.

This juxtaposing of purity and worldliness seems to be a deliberate part of Crane's literary method, not only in such descriptions as this, but in putting side by side such opposite characters as Maggie and her mother, or the timid, newly married Mrs. Jack Potter and the blustering, drunken Scratchy Wilson in "The Bride Comes to Yellow Sky." This is the ironic nature of things, Crane seems to say, and this, one cannot help noticing, is the source of much of the ironic power of his stories. The good and innocent often suffer, and tragedy ensues, continues Crane, because neither Providence nor the guilty bystanders in the world will intercede. This, I think, is the meaning of Crane's direct statement to the reader at the end of "The Blue Hotel."

Often it is the opening description in Crane's stories that strikes the note of the indifference of the universe, and swirling dust, rain, snow, or fog becomes a symbol of this indifference. It is a blizzard in "Men in the Storm," rain in "An Experiment in Misery," fog in "The Little Regiment" (it was fog, too, in *The Red Badge of Courage*), and dust at the beginning of part two of "Maggie":

A wind of early autumn raised yellow dust from cobbles and swirled it against a hundred windows.

Again the Hemingway reader will notice a similarity.

Although Crane changes his color symbolism from time to time, he generally seems to use yellows in unpleasant associations. Here, in "The Second Generation," he uses yellow to emphasize death and revulsion:

> In and out of the ditchlike trenches lay the Spanish dead, lemon-faced corpses. . . .

Stallman has spoken of Crane's extraordinary preoccupation with blue. Beer mentions his "passion for red," and states that his "purple was sinister and repugnant." Berryman has also commented on his colors. In "The Open Boat," gray is the keynote color—in the sky, the gulls, the sea, and the faces—and contributes much to the impersonal-universe theme of the story.

Other symbolic possibilities about which one cannot help speculating are the frequent games of chance in Crane's stories, used as devices for pointing up the absence of moral purpose in the world—the dice game in "The Five White Mice," and the card game in "The Blue Hotel," for instance. Then there is the circus in "The Five White Mice," the carrousel in "The Pace of Youth," and the dime museum with its "meek freaks" in "Maggie." All seem somehow to strengthen the feeling of the world's lack of moral direction or divine organization.

*Allegory*

It is not difficult to see many symbols in Crane's writing. Occasionally these symbols will carry the whole story into the deeper realm of allegory. In "The Open Boat" one has such a story. Perhaps one finds another in "The Pace of Youth," with its symbolic pursuit of the young lovers by the middle-aged father. In this collection there are others, too, which offer intriguing allegorical possibilities.

*Narrative Method*

Crane builds his stories around a single mood, to which, as one can see, his use of colors contributes. In his longer narratives, however, he may have a series of moods, which he indicates by separations in the text. Often his stories end with a small piece of action quietly pointing out the ironic truth contained in the story, as when Dr. Trescott at the end of "The Monster" is shown absently counting all the unused teacups of the ladies who have stayed away from his wife's tea party.

## Style

There are details about Crane's writing style that one would have otherwise: his strong predilection, for instance, for the passive voice, the split infinitive, and the misplaced adverb. Lack of good formal training? Indifference? Haste? In any case, it was part of the man and therefore part of the writer. Regarding his general writing style, perhaps the best comment has come from another professional story writer, Willa Cather:

> When you examine the mere writing in this unorganized material [Crane's war sketches], you see at once that Crane was one of the first post-impressionists; that he began it before the French painters began it, or at least as early as the first of them. He simply knew from the beginning how to handle detail. He estimated it at its true worth—made it serve his purpose and felt no further responsibility about it. I doubt whether he ever spent a laborious half-hour in doing his duty by detail—in enumerating, like an honest, grubby auctioneer. If he saw one thing that engaged him in a room, he mentioned it. If he saw one thing in a landscape that thrilled him, he put it on paper, but he never tried to make a faithful report of everything else within his field of vision, as if he were a conscientious salesman making out his expense-account. "The red sun was pasted in the sky like a wafer," that careless observation which Mr. Hergesheimer admires so much, isn't exceptional with Crane. (He wrote like that when he was writing well.) What about the clouds, and the light on the hills, and the background,

and the foreground? Well, Crane left that for his successors to write, and they have been doing it ever since: accounting for everything, as trustees of an estate are supposed to do. . . .[9]

## Evaluation of Crane's Stories

Originating with Irving and Poe, the short story in America has had some distinguished practitioners—Hawthorne, Bret Harte, Mark Twain, Henry James, Jack London, Ring Lardner, Fitzgerald, Hemingway, Faulkner, Salinger, and a goodly number of others. Curiously, it is difficult to recall more than three to six of the stories of any one of the writers in this genre which are particularly well remembered or to which one can give the highest rating. This situation suggests inconsistency of performance, or a reluctance on the part of readers and critics to recognize much more than each writer's very best. Three of the stories in the group that follows—"The Open Boat," "The Bride Comes to Yellow Sky," and "The Blue Hotel"—have come to be ranked with the best our short-story tradition has produced. I hope that from this collection of Stephen Crane's stories, many of which have been out of print for some time, there will emerge a fresh view of the scope and luminous flashes of power of an enigmatic but engaging literary personality, and perhaps an upward movement of a number of his other stories to the status they deserve.

—AUSTIN McC. Fox

The Nichols School
Buffalo, New York
*May, 1960*

---

[9] Willa Cather, "Introduction," *The Work of Stephen Crane* (New York: Alfred A. Knopf, 1925-1927), ed. Wilson Follett, Vol. IX, p. x, xi.

# A General Bibliography

BEER, THOMAS. *Stephen Crane: A Study in American Letters.* With an Introduction by Joseph Conrad. New York: Alfred A. Knopf, 1923.

BERRYMAN, JOHN. *Stephen Crane* ("The American Men of Letters Series"). New York: William Sloane Associates, 1950.

CADY, EDWIN H. and WELLS, LESTER G. (eds.). *Stephen Crane's Love Letters to Nellie Crouse, with six other letters, new materials on Crane at Syracuse University, and a number of unusual photographs.* Syracuse: Syracuse University Press, 1954.

FOLLETT, WILSON (ed.). *The Work of Stephen Crane.* 12 vols. New York: Alfred A. Knopf, 1925-26.

HOFFMAN, DANIEL G. *The Poetry of Stephen Crane.* New York: Columbia University Press, 1957.

LINSON, CORWIN K. *My Stephen Crane,* edited with an introduction by Edwin H. Cady. Syracuse: Syracuse University Press, 1958.

STALLMAN, ROBERT WOOSTER (ed.). *Stephen Crane: an Omnibus.* New York: Alfred A. Knopf, 1952.

STALLMAN, R. W. and GILKES, LILLIAN. *Stephen Crane: Letters,* with an introduction by R. W. Stallman. New York: New York University Press, 1960.

*Stephen Crane (1871-1900).* An exhibition of his writings held in the Columbia University Libraries September 17-November 30, 1956, arranged and described by Joan H. Baum Foreword by Professor Lewis Leary, Columbia University. With appendixes contributing to the bibliography of Stephen Crane. New York: Columbia University Libraries, 1956.

WELLS, H. G. "Stephen Crane from an English Standpoint" (1900), *The Shock of Recognition*, Vol. II, edited by Edmund Wilson. New York: Grosset and Dunlap, 1955.

WILLIAMS, AMES W. and STARRETT, VINCENT. *Stephen Crane, A Bibliography*. Glendale, California: John Valentine, Publisher, 1948.

# Contents

# The Blue Hotel

## And Other Stories

# *Maggie*

## *- i -*

A VERY little boy stood upon a heap of gravel for the honor
of Rum Alley. He was throwing stones at howling urchins
from Devil's Row, who were circling madly about the heap
and pelting him. His infantile countenance was livid with the
fury of battle. His small body was writhing in the delivery
of oaths.

"Run, Jimmie, run! Dey'll git yehs!" screamed a retreating
Rum Alley child.

"Naw," responded Jimmie with a valiant roar, "dese mugs
can't make me run."

Howls of renewed wrath went up from Devil's Row throats.
Tattered gamins on the right made a furious assault on the
gravel heap. On their small, convulsed faces shone the grins
of true assassins. As they charged, they threw stones and
cursed in shrill chorus.

The little champion of Rum Alley stumbled precipitately
down the other side. His coat had been torn to shreds in a
scuffle, and his hat was gone. He had bruises on twenty parts
of his body, and blood was dripping from a cut in his head.
His wan features looked like those of a tiny, insane demon.
On the ground, children from Devil's Row closed in on their
antagonist. He crooked his left arm defensively about his head
and fought with madness. The little boys ran to and fro,
dodging, hurling stones, and swearing in barbaric trebles.

From a window of an apartment house that uprose from
amid squat, ignorant stables there leaned a curious woman.
Some laborers, unloading a scow at a dock at the river, paused
for a moment and regarded the fight. The engineer of a passive tugboat hung lazily over a railing and watched. Over

1

on the island, a worm of yellow convicts came from the shadow of a gray, ominous building and crawled slowly along the
river's bank.

A stone had smashed in Jimmie's mouth. Blood was bubbling over his chin and down upon his ragged shirt. Tears
made furrows on his dirt-stained cheeks. His thin legs had
begun to tremble and turn weak, causing his small body to
reel. His roaring curses of the first part of the fight had
changed to a blasphemous chatter. In the yells of the whirling
mob of Devil's Row children there were notes of joy like songs
of triumphant savagery. The little boys seemed to leer gloat-
ingly at the blood upon the other child's face.

Down the avenue came boastfully sauntering a lad of
sixteen years, although the chronic sneer of an ideal manhood
already sat upon his lips. His hat was tipped over his eye
with an air of challenge. Between his teeth a cigar stump was
tilted at the angle of defiance. He walked with a certain
swing of the shoulders which appalled the timid. He glanced
over into the vacant lot in which the little raving boys from
Devil's Row seethed about the shrieking and tearful child
from Rum Alley.

"Gee!" he murmured with interest. "A scrap. Gee!" He
strode over to the cursing circle, swinging his shoulders in a
manner which denoted that he held victory in his fists. He
approached at the back of one of the most deeply engaged of
the Devil's Row children. "Ah, what d' hell," he said, and
smote the deeply engaged one on the back of the head.

The little boy fell to the ground and gave a tremendous
howl. He scrambled to his feet, and perceiving, evidently, the
size of his assailant, ran quickly off, shouting alarms. The entire Devil's Row party followed him. They came to a stand
a short distance away and yelled taunting oaths at the boy
with the chronic sneer.

The latter, momentarily, paid no attention to them. "What's
wrong wi'che, Jimmie?" he asked of the small champion.

Jimmie wiped his blood-wet features with his sleeve. "Well,
it was dis way, Pete, see? I was goin' teh lick dat Riley kid,
an' dey all pitched on me."

Some Rum Alley children now came forward. The party stood for a moment exchanging vainglorious remarks with Devil's Row. A few stones were thrown at long distances, and words of challenge passed between small warriors. Then the Rum Alley contingent turned slowly in the direction of their home street. They began to give, each to each, distorted versions of the fight. Causes of retreat in particular cases were magnified. Blows dealt in the fight were enlarged to catapultian power, and stones thrown were alleged to have hurtled with infinite accuracy. Valor grew strong again, and the little boys began to brag with great spirit. "Ah, we blokies kin lick d' hull damn Row," said a child, swaggering.

Little Jimmie was trying to stanch the flow of blood from his cut lips. Scowling, he turned upon the speaker. "Ah, where was yehs when I was doin' all deh fightin'?" he demanded. "Youse kids makes me tired."

"Ah, go ahn!" replied the other argumentatively.

Jimmie replied with heavy contempt. "Ah, youse can't fight, Blue Billie! I kin lick yeh wid one han'."

"Ah, go ahn!" replied Billie again.

"Ah!" said Jimmie threateningly.

"Ah!" said the other in the same tone.

They struck at each other, clinched, and rolled over on the cobblestones.

"Smash 'im, Jimmie, kick d' face off 'im!" yelled Pete, the lad with the chronic sneer, in tones of delight.

The small combatants pounded and kicked, scratched and tore. They began to weep, and their curses struggled in their throats with sobs. The other little boys clasped their hands and wriggled their legs in excitement. They formed a bobbing circle about the pair.

A tiny spectator was suddenly agitated. "Cheese it, Jimmie, cheese it! Here comes yer fader," he yelled.

The circle of little boys instantly parted. They drew away and waited in ecstatic awe for that which was about to happen. The two little boys, fighting in the modes of four thousand years ago, did not hear the warning.

Up the avenue there plodded slowly a man with sullen

eyes. He was carrying a dinner pail and smoking an apple-wood pipe. As he neared the spot where the little boys strove, he regarded them listlessly. But suddenly he roared an oath and advanced upon the rolling fighters. "Here, you Jim, git up now, while I belt yer life out, yeh disorderly brat." He began to kick into the chaotic mass on the ground. The boy Billie felt a heavy boot strike his head. He made a furious effort and disentangled himself from Jimmie. He tottered away.

Jimmie arose painfully from the ground, and confronting his father, began to curse him. His parent kicked him. "Come home now," he cried, "an' stop yer jawin', er I'll lam the ever-lasting head off yehs."

They departed. The man paced placidly along with the apple-wood emblem of serenity between his teeth. The boy followed a dozen feet in the rear. He swore luridly, for he felt that it was degradation for one who aimed to be some vague kind of soldier, or a man of blood with a sort of sublime license, to be taken home by a father.

- *ii* -

Eventually they entered a dark region where, from a careening building, a dozen gruesome doorways gave up loads of babies to the street and the gutter. A wind of early autumn raised yellow dust from cobbles and swirled it against a hundred windows. Long streamers of garments fluttered from fire escapes. In all unhandy places there were buckets, brooms, rags, and bottles. In the street infants played or fought with other infants or sat stupidly in the way of vehicles. Formidable women, with uncombed hair and disordered dress, gossiped while leaning on railings, or screamed in frantic quarrels. Withered persons, in curious postures of submission to something, sat smoking pipes in obscure corners. A thousand odors of cooking food came forth to the street. The building quivered and creaked from the weight of humanity stamping about in its bowels.

A small, ragged girl dragged a red, bawling infant along the crowded ways. He was hanging back, baby-like, bracing his wrinkled, bare legs. The little girl cried out, "Ah, Tommie, come ahn. Dere's Jimmie and fader. Don't be a-pullin' me back." She jerked the baby's arm impatiently. He fell on his face, roaring. With a second jerk she pulled him to his feet, and they went on. With the obstinacy of his order, he protested against being dragged in a chosen direction. He made heroic endeavors to keep on his legs, denounced his sister, and consumed a bit of orange peeling which he chewed between the times of his infantile orations.

As the sullen-eyed man, followed by the blood-covered boy, drew near, the little girl burst into reproachful cries. "Ah, Jimmie, youse bin fightin' agin."

The urchin swelled disdainfully. "Ah, what d' hell, Mag. See?"

The little girl upbraided him. "Youse allus fightin', Jimmie, an' yeh knows it puts mudder out when yehs come home half dead, an' it's like we'll all get a poundin'." She began to weep. The babe threw back his head and roared at his prospects.

"Ah," cried Jimmie, "shut up er I'll smack yer mout'. See?" As his sister continued her lamentations, he suddenly struck her. The little girl reeled, and recovering herself, burst into tears and quaveringly cursed him. As she slowly retreated, her brother advanced, dealing her cuffs.

The father heard, and turned about. "Stop that, Jim, d'yeh hear? Leave yer sister alone on the street. It's like I can never beat any sense into yer wooden head."

The urchin raised his voice in defiance to his parent, and continued his attacks. The babe bawled tremendously, protesting with great violence. During his sister's hasty maneuvers, he was dragged by the arm.

Finally the procession plunged into one of the gruesome doorways. They crawled up dark stairways and along cold, gloomy halls. At last the father pushed open a door, and they entered a lighted room in which a large woman was rampant.

She stopped in a career from a seething stove to a pan-covered table. As the father and children filed in, she peered at them. "Eh, what? Been fightin' agin!" She threw herself upon Jimmie. The urchin tried to dart behind the others, and in the scuffle the babe, Tommie, was knocked down. He protested with his usual vehemence because they had bruised his tender shins against a table leg.

The mother's massive shoulders heaved with anger. Grasping the urchin by the neck and shoulder, she shook him until he rattled. She dragged him to an unholy sink, and, soaking a rag in water, began to scrub his lacerated face with it. Jimmie screamed in pain, and tried to twist his shoulders out of the clasp of the huge arms.

The babe sat on the floor watching the scene, his face in contortions like that of a woman at a tragedy. The father, with a newly ladened pipe in his mouth, sat in a backless chair next the stove. Jimmie's cries annoyed him. He turned about and bellowed at his wife. "Let the kid alone for a minute, will yeh, Mary? Yer allus poundin' 'im. When I come nights I can't get no rest 'cause yer allus poundin' a kid. Let up, d'yeh hear? Don't be allus poundin' a kid." The woman's operations on the urchin instantly increased in violence. At last she tossed him to a corner, where he limply lay weeping.

The wife put her immense hands on her hips, and with a chieftain-like stride approached her husband. "Ho!" she said, with a great grunt of contempt. "An' what in the devil are you stickin' your nose for?" The babe crawled under the table, and turning, peered out cautiously. The ragged girl retreated, and the urchin in the corner drew his legs carefully beneath him.

The man puffed his pipe calmly and put his great muddied boots on the back part of the stove. "Go t' hell," he said tranquilly.

The woman screamed, and shook her fists before her husband's eyes. The rough yellow of her face and neck flared suddenly crimson. She began to howl.

He puffed imperturbably at his pipe for a time, but finally arose and went to look out the window into the darkening chaos of back yards. "You've been drinkin', Mary," he said. "You'd better let up on the bot', ol' woman, or you'll git done."

"You're a liar. I ain't had a drop," she roared in reply. They had a lurid altercation.

The babe was staring out from under the table, his small face working in his excitement. The ragged girl went stealthily over to the corner where the urchin lay. "Are yehs hurted much, Jimmie?" she whispered timidly.

"Not a little bit. See?" growled the little boy.

"Will I wash d' blood?"

"Naw!"

"Will I—"

"When I catch dat Riley kid I'll break 'is face! Dat's right! See?" He turned his face to the wall as if resolved grimly to bide his time.

In the quarrel between husband and wife the woman was victor. The man seized his hat and rushed from the room, apparently determined upon a vengeful drunk. She followed to the door and thundered at him as he made his way downstairs.

She returned and stirred up the room until her children were bobbing about like bubbles. "Git outa d' way," she bawled persistently, waving feet with their disheveled shoes near the heads of her children. She shrouded herself, puffing and snorting, in a cloud of steam at the stove, and eventually extracted a frying pan full of potatoes that hissed. She flourished it. "Come t' yer suppers now," she cried with sudden exasperation. "Hurry up now, er I'll help yeh!"

The children scrambled hastily. With prodigious clatter they arranged themselves at table. The babe sat with his feet dangling high from a precarious infant's chair and gorged his small stomach. Jimmie forced, with feverish rapidity, the grease-enveloped pieces between his wounded lips. Maggie, with side glances of fear of interruption, ate like a small, pursued tigress.

The mother sat blinking at them. She delivered reproaches, swallowed potatoes, and drank from a yellow-brown bottle. After a time her mood changed, and she wept as she carried little Tommie into another room and laid him to sleep, with his fists doubled, in an old quilt of faded red-and-green grandeur. Then she came and moaned by the stove. She rocked to and fro upon a chair, shedding tears and crooning miserably to the two children about their "poor mother" and "yer fader, damn 'is soul."

The little girl plodded between the table and the chair with a dishpan on it. She tottered on her small legs beneath burdens of dishes. Jimmie sat nursing his various wounds. He cast furtive glances at his mother. His practiced eye perceived her gradually emerge from a mist of muddled sentiment until her brain burned in drunken heat. He sat breathless.

Maggie broke a plate.

The mother started to her feet as if propelled. "Good Gawd!" she howled. Her glittering eyes fastened on her child with sudden hatred. The fervent red of her face turned almost to purple. The little boy ran to the halls, shrieking like a monk in an earthquake. He floundered about in darkness until he found the stairs. He stumbled, panic-stricken, to the next floor.

An old woman opened a door. A light behind her threw a flare on the urchin's face. "Eh, child, what is it dis time? Is yer fader beatin' yer mudder, or yer mudder beatin' yer fader?"

- *iii* -

Jimmie and the old woman listened long in the hall. Above the muffled roar of conversation, the dismal wailings of babies at night, the thumping of feet in unseen corridors and rooms, and the sound of varied hoarse shoutings in the street and the rattling of wheels over cobbles, they heard the screams of the child and the roars of the mother die away to a feeble moaning and a subdued bass muttering.

The old woman was a gnarled and leathery personage who could don at will an expression of great virtue. She possessed a small music box capable of one tune, and a collection of "God bless yehs" pitched in assorted keys of fervency. Each day she took a position upon the stones of Fifth Avenue, where she crooked her legs under her and crouched, immovable and hideous, like an idol. She received daily a small sum in pennies. It was contributed, for the most part, by persons who did not make their homes in that vicinity. Once, when a lady had dropped her purse on the sidewalk, the gnarled woman had grabbed it and smuggled it with great dexterity beneath her cloak. When she was arrested she had cursed the lady into a partial swoon, and with her aged limbs, twisted from rheumatism, had kicked the breath out of a huge policeman whose conduct upon that occasion she referred to when she said, "The police, damn 'em!"

"Eh, Jimmie, it's a shame," she said. "Go now, like a dear, an' buy me a can, an' if yer mudder raises 'ell all night, yehs can sleep here." Jimmie took a tendered tin pail and seven pennies and departed. He passed into the side door of a saloon and went to the bar. Straining up on his toes, he raised the pail and pennies as high as his arms would let him. He saw two hands thrust down to take them. Directly the same hands let down the filled pail, and he left.

In front of the gruesome doorway he met a lurching figure. It was his father, swaying about on uncertain legs. "Give me deh can. See?" said the man.

"Ah, come off! I got dis can fer dat ol' woman, an' it 'ud be dirt teh swipe it. See?" cried Jimmie.

The father wrenched the pail from the urchin. He grasped it in both hands and lifted it to his mouth. He glued his lips to the under edge and tilted his head. His throat swelled until it seemed to grow near his chin. There was a tremendous gulping movement and the beer was gone. The man caught his breath and laughed. He hit his son on the head with the empty pail.

As it rolled clanging into the street, Jimmie began to scream, and kicked repeatedly at his father's shins. "Look at deh dirt what yeh done me," he yelled. "Deh ol' woman'll be t'rowin' fits." He retreated to the middle of the street, but the old man did not pursue. He staggered toward the door. "I'll paste yeh when I ketch yeh!" he shouted, and disappeared.

During the evening he had been standing against a bar drinking whiskies, and declaring to all comers confidentially,

"My home reg'lar livin' hell! Why do I come an' drin' whisk' here thish way? 'Cause home reg'lar livin' hell!"

Jimmie waited a long time in the street and then crept warily up through the building. He passed with great caution the door of the gnarled woman, and finally stopped outside his home and listened. He could hear his mother moving heavily about among the furniture of the room. She was chanting in a mournful voice, occasionally interjecting bursts of volcanic wrath at the father, who, Jimmie judged, had sunk down on the floor or in a corner.

"Why deh blazes don' cher try teh keep Jim from fightin'? I'll break yer jaw!" she suddenly bellowed.

The man mumbled with drunken indifference. "Ah, w'at's bitin' yeh? W'a's odds? W'a' makes kick?"

"Because he tears 'is clothes, yeh fool!" cried the woman in supreme wrath.

The husband seemed to become aroused. "Go chase yerself!" he thundered fiercely in reply. There was a crash against the door, and something broke into clattering fragments. Jimmie partially suppressed a yell and darted down the stairway. Below, he paused and listened. He heard howls and curses, groans and shrieks—a confused chorus as if a battle were raging. With it all there was the crash of splintering furniture. The eyes of the urchin glared in his fear that one of them would discover him.

Curious faces appeared in doorways, and whispered comments passed to and fro. "Ol' Johnson's playin' horse agin."

Jimmie stood until the noises ceased and the other inhabitants of the tenement had all yawned and shut their doors. Then he crawled upstairs with the caution of an invader of a panther's den. Sounds of labored breathing came through the broken door panels. He pushed the door open and entered, quaking.

A glow from the fire threw red hues over the bare floor, the cracked and soiled plastering, and the overturned and broken furniture. In the middle of the floor lay his mother asleep. In one corner of the room his father's limp body hung across the seat of a chair.

The urchin stole forward. He began to shiver in dread of awakening his parents. His mother's great chest was heaving painfully. Jimmie paused and looked down at her. Her face was inflamed and swollen from drinking. Her yellow brows shaded eyelids that had grown blue. Her tangled hair tossed in waves over her forehead. Her mouth was set in the same lines of vindictive hatred that it had, perhaps, borne during the fight. Her bare, red arms were thrown out above her head in an attitude of exhaustion, something, mayhap, like that of a sated villain.

The urchin bent over his mother. He was fearful lest she should open her eyes, and the dread within him was so strong that he could not forbear to stare, but hung as if fascinated over the woman's grim face. Suddenly her eyes opened. The urchin found himself looking straight into an expression which, it would seem, had the power to change his blood to salt. He howled piercingly and fell backward.

The woman floundered for a moment, tossed her arms about her head as if in combat, and again began to snore. Jimmie crawled back into the shadows and waited. A noise in the next room had followed his cry at the discovery that his mother was awake. He groveled in the gloom, his eyes riveted upon the intervening door. He heard it creak, and then the sound of a small voice came to him. "Jimmie! Jimmie! Are yehs dere?" it whispered. The urchin started. The thin, white face of his sister looked at him from the doorway of the other room. She crept to him across the floor.

The father had not moved, but lay in the same deathlike sleep. The mother writhed in an uneasy slumber, her chest wheezing as if she were in the agonies of strangulation. Out at the window a florid moon was peering over dark roofs, and in the distance the waters of a river glimmered pallidly.

The small frame of the ragged girl was quivering. Her features were haggard from weeping, and her eyes gleamed with fear. She grasped the urchin's arm in her little, trembling hands and they huddled in a corner. The eyes of both were drawn, by some force, to stare at the woman's face, for they thought she need only to awake and all the fiends would come from below. They crouched until the ghost mists of dawn appeared at the window, drawing close to the panes, and looking in at the prostrate, heaving body of the mother.

- iv -

The babe, Tommie, died. He went away in an insignificant coffin, his small, waxen hand clutching a flower that the girl, Maggie, had stolen from an Italian.

She and Jimmie lived.

The inexperienced fibers of the boy's eyes were hardened at an early age. He became a young man of leather. He lived some red years without laboring. During that time his sneer became chronic. He studied human nature in the gutter, and found it no worse than he thought he had reason to believe it. He never conceived a respect for the world, because he had begun with no idols that it had smashed.

He clad his soul in armor by means of happening hilariously in at a mission church where a man composed his sermons of "yous." Once a philosopher asked this man why he did not say "we" instead of "you." The man replied, "What?" While they got warm at the stove, he told his hearers just where he calculated they stood with the Lord. Many of the sinners were impatient over the pictured depths of their degradation. They were waiting for soup tickets. A reader of the words of wind demons might have been able to see the portions of a dialogue pass to and fro between the exhorter and his hearers. "You are damned," said the preacher. And the reader of sounds might have seen the reply go forth from the ragged people: "Where's our soup?" Jimmie and a companion sat in a rear seat and commented upon the things that didn't concern them, with all the freedom of English tourists. When they grew thirsty and went out, their minds confused the speaker with Christ.

Momentarily, Jimmie was sullen with thoughts of a hopeless altitude where grew fruit. His companion said that if he should ever go to heaven he would ask for a million dollars and a bottle of beer. Jimmie's occupation for a long time was to stand at street corners and watch the world go by, dreaming blood-red dreams at the passing of pretty women. He menaced mankind at the intersections of streets. At the corners he was in life and of life. The world was going on and he was there to perceive it.

He maintained a belligerent attitude toward all well-dressed men. To him fine raiment was allied to weakness, and all good coats covered faint hearts. He and his orders were kings, to a certain extent, over the men of untarnished clothes, because these latter dreaded, perhaps, to be either killed or laughed at. Above all things he despised obvious Christians and ciphers with the chrysanthemums of aristocracy in their buttonholes. He considered himself above both of these classes. He was afraid of nothing.

When he had a dollar in his pocket, his satisfaction with existence was the greatest thing in the world. So, eventually, he felt obliged to work. His father died, and his mother's years were divided up into periods of thirty days.

He became a truck driver. There was given to him the charge of a painstaking pair of horses and a large, rattling truck. He invaded the turmoil and tumble of the downtown streets, and learned to breathe maledictory defiance at the police, who occasionally used to climb up, drag him from his perch, and punch him. In the lower part of the city, he daily involved himself in hideous tangles. If he and his team chanced to be in the rear, he preserved a demeanor of serenity, crossing his legs and bursting forth into yells when foot passengers took dangerous dives beneath the noses of his champing horses. He smoked his pipe calmly, for he knew that his pay was marching on. If his charge was in the front, and if it became the key truck of chaos, he entered terrifically into the quarrel that was raging to and fro among the drivers on their high seats, and sometimes roared oaths and violently got himself arrested.

After a time, his sneer grew so that it turned its glare upon all things. He became so sharp that he believed in nothing. To him the police were always actuated by malignant impulses, and the rest of the world was composed, for the most part, of despicable creatures who were all trying to take advantage of him, and with whom, in defense, he was obliged to quarrel on all possible occasions. He himself occupied a downtrodden position, which had a private but distinct element of grandeur in its isolation.

The greatest cases of aggravated idiocy were, to his mind, rampant upon the front platforms of all the streetcars. At first his tongue strove with these beings, but he eventually became superior. In him grew a majestic contempt for those strings of streetcars that followed him like intent bugs. He fell into the habit, when starting on a long journey, of fixing his eye on a high and distant object, commanding his horses to start, and then going into a trance of oblivion. Multitudes of drivers might howl in his rear, and passengers might load him with opprobrium, but he would not awaken until some blue policeman turned red and began frenziedly to seize bridles and beat the soft noses of the responsible horses.

When he paused to contemplate the attitude of the police toward himself and his fellows, he believed that they were the only men in the city who had no rights. When driving about, he felt that he was held liable by the police for anything that might occur in the streets, and that he was the common prey of all energetic officials. In revenge, he resolved never to move out of the way of anything, until formidable circumstances or a much larger man than himself forced him to it.

Foot passengers were mere pestering flies with an insane disregard for their legs and his convenience. He could not comprehend their desire to cross the streets. Their madness smote him with eternal amazement. He was continually storming at them from his throne. He sat aloft and denounced their frantic leaps, plunges, dives, and straddles. When they would thrust at, or parry, the noses of his champing horses, making them swing their heads and move their feet, and thus disturbing a stolid, dreamy repose, he swore at the men as fools, for he himself could perceive that Providence had caused it to be clearly written that he and his team had the inalienable right to stand in the proper path of the sun chariot, and if they so minded, to obstruct its mission or take a wheel off. And if the god driver had had a desire to step down, put up his flame-colored fists, and manfully dispute the right of way, he would have probably been immediately opposed by a scowling mortal with two sets of hard knuckles.

It is possible, perhaps, that this young man would have derided, in an axle-wide alley, the approach of a flying ferry-boat. Yet he achieved a respect for a fire engine. As one charged toward his truck, he would drive fearfully upon a sidewalk, threatening untold people with annihilation. When an engine struck a mass of blocked trucks, splitting it into fragments as a blow annihilates a cake of ice, Jimmie's team could usually be observed high and safe, with whole wheels, on the sidewalk. The fearful coming of the engine could break up the most intricate muddle of heavy vehicles at which the police had been storming for half an hour. A fire engine was enshrined in his heart as an appalling thing that he loved with a distant, doglike devotion. It had been known to over-turn a streetcar. Those leaping horses, striking sparks from the cobbles in their forward lunge, were creatures to be ineffably admired. The clang of the gong pierced his breast like a noise of remembered war.

When Jimmie was a little boy he began to be arrested. Before he reached a great age, he had a fair record. He de-veloped too great a tendency to climb down from his truck and fight with other drivers. He had been in quite a number of miscellaneous fights, and in some general barroom rows that had become known to the police. Once he had been arrested for assaulting a Chinaman. Two women in different parts of the city, and entirely unknown to each other, caused him considerable annoyance by breaking forth, simultaneous-ly, at fateful intervals, into wailings about marriage and support and infants.

Nevertheless, he had, on a certain starlit evening, said wonderingly and quite reverently, "Deh moon looks like hell, don't it?"

- ʋ -

The girl, Maggie, blossomed in a mud puddle. She grew to be a most rare and wonderful production of a tenement district, a pretty girl. None of the dirt of Rum Alley seemed to be in her veins. The philosophers, upstairs, downstairs, and on the same floor, puzzled over it. When a child, playing and fighting with gamins in the street, dirt disgusted her. Attired in tatters and grime, she went unseen.

There came a time, however, when the young men of the vicinity said, "Dat Johnson goil is a putty good looker." About this period her brother remarked to her, "Mag, I'll tell yeh dis! See? Yeh've eeder got t' go on d' toif er go t' work!" Whereupon she went to work, having the feminine aversion to the alternative. By a chance, she got a position in an establishment where they made collars and cuffs. She received a stool and a machine in a room where sat twenty girls of various shades of yellow discontent. She perched on the stool and treadled at her machine all day, turning out collars with a name which might have been noted for its irrelevancy to anything connected with collars. At night she returned home to her mother.

Jimmie grew large enough to take the vague position of head of the family. As incumbent of that office, he stumbled upstairs late at night, as his father had done before him. He reeled about the room, swearing at his relations, or went to sleep on the floor.

The mother had gradually risen to such a degree of fame that she could bandy words with her acquaintances among the police justices. Court officials called her by her first name. When she appeared, they pursued a course which had been theirs for months. They invariably grinned, and cried out, "Hello, Mary, you here again?" Her gray head wagged in many courts. She always besieged the bench with voluble excuses, explanations, apologies, and prayers. Her flaming face and rolling eyes were a familiar sight on the island. She measured time by means of sprees, and was swollen and disheveled.

One day, the young man Pete, who as a lad had smitten the Devil's Row urchin in the back of the head and put to flight the antagonists of his friend Jimmie, strutted upon the scene. He met Jimmie one day on the street, promised to take him to a boxing match in Williamsburg, and called for him in the evening.

Maggie observed Pete.

He sat on a table in the Johnson home, and dangled his checked legs with an enticing nonchalance. His hair was curled down over his forehead in an oiled bang. His pugged nose seemed to revolt from contact with a bristling mustache of short, wirelike hairs. His blue, double-breasted coat, edged with black braid, was buttoned close to a red puff tie, and his patent-leather shoes looked like weapons. His mannerisms stamped him as a man who had a correct sense of his personal superiority. There were valor and contempt for circumstances in the glance of his eye. He waved his hands like a man of the world who dismisses religion and philosophy, and says "Rats!" He had certainly seen everything, and with each curl of his lip he declared that it amounted to nothing. Maggie thought he must be a very "elegant" bartender.

He was telling tales to Jimmie. Maggie watched him furtively, with half-closed eyes lit with a vague interest.

"Hully gee! Dey makes me tired," he said. "Mos' e'ry day some farmer comes in an' tries t' run d' shop. See? But d' gits t'rowed right out. I jolt dem right out in d' street before dey knows where dey is. See?"

"Sure," said Jimmie.

"Dere was a mug come in d' place d' odder day wid an idear he was goin' t' own d' place. Hully gee! He was goin' t' own d' place. I see he had a still on, and I didn' wanna giv 'im no stuff, so I says, 'Git outa here an' don' make no trouble,' I says like dat. See? 'Git outa here an' don' make no trouble'; like dat. 'Git outa here,' I says. See?"

Jimmie nodded understandingly. Over his features played

an eager desire to state the amount of his valor in a similar crisis, but the narrator proceeded.

"Well, deh blokie he says, 'T' blazes wid it! I ain' lookin' for no scrap,' he says—see?—'but,' he says, 'I'm 'spectable cit'zen an' I wanna drink, an' quick, too.' See? 'Aw, go ahn!' I says, like dat. 'Aw, go ahn,' I says. See? 'Don' make no trouble,' I says, like dat. 'Don' make no trouble.' See? Den d' mug, he squared off an' said he was fine as silk wid his dukes—see?—an' he wan'ed a drink—quick. Dat's what he said. See?"

"Sure," repeated Jimmie.

Pete continued. "Say, I jes' jumped d' bar, an' d' way I plunked dat blokie was outa sight. See? Dat's right! In d' jaw! See? Hully gee! He t'rowed a spittoon t'rough d' front windee. Say, I t'ought I'd drop dead. But d' boss, he comes in after, an' he says, 'Pete, yehs done jes' right! Yeh've gotta keep order, an' it's all right.' See? 'It's all right,' he says. Dat's what he said."

The two held a technical discussion.

"Dat bloke was a dandy," said Pete, in conclusion, "but he hadn' oughta made no trouble. Dat's what I says t' dem: 'Don' come in here an' make no trouble,' I says, like dat. 'Don' make no trouble.' See?"

As Jimmie and his friend exchanged tales descriptive of their prowess, Maggie leaned back in the shadow. Her eyes dwelt wonderingly and rather wistfully upon Pete's face. The broken furniture, grimy walls, and general disorder and dirt of her home of a sudden appeared before her and began to take a potential aspect. Pete's aristocratic person looked as if it might soil. She looked keenly at him, occasionally wondering if he was feeling contempt. But Pete seemed to be enveloped in reminiscence.

"Hully gee!" said he. "Dose mugs can't feaze me. Dey knows I kin wipe up d' street wid any t'ree of dem."

When he said, "Ah, what d' hell!" his voice was burdened with disdain for the inevitable and contempt for anything that fate might compel him to endure.

Maggie perceived that here was the ideal man. Her dim

thoughts were often searching for faraway lands where the little hills sing together in the morning. Under the trees of her dream gardens there had always walked a lover.

- *vi* -

Pete took note of Maggie. "Say, Mag, I'm stuck on yer shape. It's outa sight," he said parenthetically, with an affable grin.

As he became aware that she was listening closely, he grew still more eloquent in his description of various happenings in his career. It appeared that he was invincible in fights. "Why," he said, referring to a man with whom he had had a misunderstanding, "dat mug scrapped like a Dago. Dat's right. He was dead easy. See? He t'ought he was a scrapper. But he foun' out diff'ent. Hully gee!"

He walked to and fro in the small room, which seemed then to grow even smaller and unfit to hold his dignity, the attribute of a supreme warrior. That swing of the shoulders which had frozen the timid when he was but a lad had increased with his growth and education in the ratio of ten to one. It, combined with the sneer upon his mouth, told mankind that there was nothing in space which could appall him. Maggie marveled at him and surrounded him with greatness. She vaguely tried to calculate the altitude of the pinnacle from which he must have looked down upon her.

"I met a chump deh odder day way up in deh city," he said. "I was goin' teh see a frien' of mine. When I was a-crossin' deh street deh chump runned plump inteh me, an' den he turns aroun' an' says, 'Yer insolen' ruffin!' he says, like dat. 'Oh, gee,' I says, 'oh, gee! Git off d' eart'!' I says, like dat. See? 'Git off d' eart'!' like dat. Den deh blokie he got wild. He says I was a contempt'ble scoun'el, er somethin' like dat, an' he says I was doom' teh everlastin' pe'dition, er somethin' like dat. 'Gee,' I says, 'gee! Yer joshin' me,' I says. 'Yer joshin' me.' An' den I slugged 'im. See?"

With Jimmie in his company, Pete departed in a sort of

blaze of glory from the Johnson home. Maggie, leaning from the window, watched him as he walked down the street. Here was a formidable man who disdained the strength of a world full of fists. Here was one who had contempt for brass-clothed power; one whose knuckles could ring defiantly against the granite of law. He was a knight.

The two men went from under the glimmering street lamp and passed into shadows. Turning, Maggie contemplated the dark, dust-stained walls, and the scant and crude furniture of her home. A clock, in a splintered and battered oblong box of varnished wood, she suddenly regarded as an abomination. She noted that it ticked raspingly. The almost vanished flowers in the carpet pattern she conceived to be newly hideous. Some faint attempts which she had made with blue ribbon to freshen the appearance of a dingy curtain she now saw to be piteous.

She wondered what Pete dined on.

She reflected upon the collar-and-cuff factory. It began to appear to her mind as a dreary place of endless grinding. Pete's elegant occupation brought him, no doubt, into contact with people who had money and manners. It was probable that he had a large acquaintance with pretty girls. He must have great sums of money to spend.

To her the earth was composed of hardships and insults. She felt instant admiration for a man who openly defied it. She thought that if the grim angel of death should clutch his heart, Pete would shrug his shoulders and say, "Oh, ev'ryt'ing goes."

She anticipated that he would come again shortly. She spent some of her week's pay in the purchase of flowered cretonne for a lambrequin. She made it with infinite care, and hung it to the slightly careening mantel over the stove in the kitchen. She studied it with painful anxiety from different points in the room. She wanted it to look well on Sunday night when, perhaps, Jimmie's friend would come. On Sunday night, however, Pete did not appear. Afterward the girl looked at it with a sense of humiliation. She was now

convinced that Pete was superior to admiration for lambre-
quins.

A few evenings later, Pete entered with fascinating inno-
vations in his apparel. As she had seen him twice and he
wore a different suit each time, Maggie had a dim impression
that his wardrobe was prodigious.

"Say, Mag," he said, "put on yer bes' duds Friday night
an' I'll take yehs t' d' show. See?" He spent a few moments
in flourishing his clothes, and then vanished without having
glanced at the lambrequin.

Over the eternal collars and cuffs in the factory, Maggie
spent the most of three days in making imaginary sketches
of Pete and his daily environment. She imagined some half-
dozen women in love with him, and thought he must lean
dangerously toward an indefinite one whom she pictured as
endowed with great charms of person, but with an altogether
contemptible disposition. She thought he must live in a
blare of pleasure. He had friends and people who were afraid
of him. She saw the golden glitter of the place where Pete
was to take her. It would be an entertainment of many hues
and many melodies, where she was afraid she might appear
small and mouse-colored.

Her mother drank whisky all Friday morning. With lurid
face and tossing hair, she cursed and destroyed furniture
all Friday afternoon. When Maggie came home at half-past
six her mother lay asleep amid the wreck of chairs and a
table. Fragments of various household utensils were scattered about the floor. She had vented some phase of drunken
fury upon the lambrequin. It lay in a bedraggled heap in
the corner.

"Hah!" she snorted, sitting up suddenly. "Where yeh
been? Why don' yeh come home earlier? Been loafin' 'round
d' streets. Yer gettin' t' be a reg'lar devil."

When Pete arrived, Maggie, in a worn black dress, was
waiting for him in the midst of a floor strewn with wreckage.
The curtain at the window had been pulled by a heavy
hand and hung by one tack, dangling to and fro in the
draught through the cracks at the sash. The knots of blue

ribbons appeared like violated flowers. The fire in the stove
had gone out. The displaced lids and open doors showed
heaps of sullen gray ashes. The remnants of a meal, ghastly,
lay in a corner. Maggie's mother, stretched on the floor,
blasphemed, and gave her daughter a bad name.

- *vii* -

An orchestra of yellow-silk women and bald-headed men,
on an elevated stage near the center of a great, green-hued
ball, played a popular waltz. The place was crowded with
people grouped about little tables. A battalion of waiters
slid among the throng, carrying trays of beer glasses, and
making change from the inexhaustible vaults of their trousers
pockets. Little boys, in the costumes of French chefs, paraded up and down the irregular aisles vending fancy cakes.
There was a low rumble of conversation and a subdued clinking of glasses. Clouds of tobacco smoke rolled and wavered
high in air above the dull gilt of the chandeliers.

The vast crowd had an air throughout of having just
quitted labor. Men with callused hands, and attired in garments that showed the wear of an endless drudging for a
living, smoked their pipes contentedly and spent five, ten, or
perhaps fifteen cents for beer. There was a mere sprinkling
of men who smoked cigars purchased elsewhere. The great
body of the crowd was composed of people who showed
that all day they strove with their hands. Quiet Germans,
with maybe their wives and two or three children, sat listening to the music, with the expressions of happy cows. An
occasional party of sailors from a warship, their faces pictures of sturdy health, spent the earlier hours of the evening at the small, round tables. Very infrequent tipsy men,
swollen with the value of their opinions, engaged their companions in earnest and confidential conversation. In the balcony, and here and there below, shone the impassive faces
of women. The nationalities of the Bowery beamed upon the
stage from all directions.

Pete walked aggressively up a side aisle and took seats with Maggie at a table beneath the balcony. "Two beehs!" Leaning back, he regarded with eyes of superiority the scene before them. This attitude affected Maggie strongly. A man who could regard such a sight with indifference must be accustomed to very great things. It was obvious that Pete had visited this place many times before, and was very familiar with it. A knowledge of this fact made Maggie feel little and new.

He was extremely gracious and attentive. He displayed the consideration of a cultured gentleman who knew what was due. "Say, what's eatin' yeh? Bring d' lady a big glass! What use is dat pony?"

"Don't be fresh, now," said the waiter, with some warmth, as he departed.

"Ah, git off d' eart'l!" said Pete, after the other's retreating form.

Maggie perceived that Pete brought forth all his elegance and all his knowledge of high-class customs for her benefit. Her heart warmed as she reflected upon his condescension.

The orchestra of yellow-silk women and bald-headed men gave vent to a few bars of anticipatory music, and a girl, in a pink dress with short skirts, galloped upon the stage. She smiled upon the throng as if in acknowledgment of a warm welcome, and began to walk to and fro, making profuse gesticulations, and singing, in brazen soprano tones, a song the words of which were inaudible. When she broke into the swift, rattling measures of a chorus, some half-tipsy men near the stage joined in the rollicking refrain, and glasses were pounded rhythmically upon the tables. People leaned forward to watch her and to try to catch the words of the song. When she vanished, there were long rollings of applause. Obedient to more anticipatory bars, she reappeared among the half-suppressed cheering of the tipsy men. The orchestra plunged into dance music, and the laces of the dancer fluttered and flew in the glare of gas jets. She divulged the fact that she was attired in some half-dozen skirts. It was patent that any one of them would have proved adequate for the purpose for which skirts are intended. An occasional man bent forward, intent upon the pink stockings. Maggie wondered at the splendor of the costume and lost herself in calculations of the cost of the silks and laces.

The dancer's smile of enthusiasm was turned for ten minutes upon the faces of her audience. In the finale, she fell into some of those grotesque attitudes which were at the time popular among the dancers in the theatres uptown, giving to the Bowery public the diversions of the aristocratic theatregoing public at reduced rates.

"Say, Pete," said Maggie, leaning forward, "dis is great."

"Sure!" said Pete, with proper complacence.

A ventriloquist followed the dancer. He held two fantastic dolls on his knees. He made them sing mournful ditties and say funny things about geography and Ireland.

"Do dose little men talk?" asked Maggie.

"Naw," said Pete, "it's some big jolly. See?"

Two girls, set down on the bills as sisters, came forth and sang a duet which is heard occasionally at concerts given under church auspices. They supplemented it with a dance, which, of course, can never be seen at concerts given under church auspices.

After they had retired, a woman of debatable age sang a Negro melody. The chorus necessitated some grotesque waddlings supposed to be an imitation of a plantation darky, under the influence, probably, of music and the moon. The audience was just enthusiastic enough over it to make her return and sing a sorrowful lay, whose lines told of a mother's love, and a sweetheart who waited, and a young man who was lost at sea under harrowing circumstances. From the faces of a score or so in the crowd the self-contained look faded. Many heads were bent forward with eagerness and sympathy. As the last distressing sentiment of the piece was brought forth, it was greeted by the kind of applause which rings as sincere.

As a final effort, the singer rendered some verses which described a vision of Britain annihilated by America, and Ireland bursting her bonds. A carefully prepared climax was reached in the last line of the last verse, when the singer threw out her arms and cried, "The star-spangled banner." Instantly a great cheer swelled from the throats of the assemblage of the masses, most of them of foreign birth. There was a heavy rumble of booted feet thumping the floor. Eyes gleamed with sudden fire, and callused hands waved frantically in the air.

After a few moments' rest, the orchestra played noisily, and a small, fat man burst out upon the stage. He began to roar a song and to stamp back and forth before the footlights, wildly waving a silk hat and throwing leers broadcast. He made his face into fantastic grimaces until he looked like a devil on a Japanese kite. The crowd laughed gleefully. His short, fat legs were never still a moment. He shouted and roared and bobbed his shock of red wig until the audience broke out in excited applause.

Pete did not pay much attention to the progress of events upon the stage. He was drinking beer and watching Maggie. Her cheeks were blushing with excitement and her eyes were glistening. She drew deep breaths of pleasure. No thoughts of the atmosphere of the collar-and-cuff factory came to her.

With the final crash of the orchestra, they jostled their way to the sidewalk in the crowd. Pete took Maggie's arm and pushed a way for her, offering to fight with a man or two. They reached Maggie's home at a late hour and stood for a moment in front of the gruesome doorway.

"Say, Mag," said Pete, "give us a kiss for takin' yeh t' d' show, will yer?"

Maggie laughed, as if startled, and drew away from him. "Naw, Pete," she said, "dat wasn't in it."

"Ah, why wasn't it?" urged Pete.

The girl retreated nervously.

"Ah, go ahn!" repeated he.

Maggie darted into the hall and up the stairs. She turned and smiled at him, then disappeared.

Pete walked slowly down the street. He had something of an astonished expression upon his features. He paused under a lamppost and breathed a low breath of surprise. "Gee!" he said, "I wonner if I've been played fer a duffer."

### - viii -

As thoughts of Pete came to Maggie's mind, she began to have an intense dislike for all of her dresses. "What ails yeh? What makes ye be allus fixin' and fussin'?" her mother would frequently roar at her. She began to note with more interest the well-dressed women she met on the avenues. She envied elegance and soft palms. She craved those adornments of person which she saw every day on the street, conceiving them to be allies of vast importance to women. Studying faces, she thought many of the women and girls she chanced to meet smiled with serenity as though forever cherished and watched over by those they loved.

The air in the collar-and-cuff establishment strangled her. She knew she was gradually and surely shriveling in the hot, stuffy room. The begrimed windows rattled incessantly from the passing of elevated trains. The place was filled with a whirl of noises and odors. She became lost in thought as she looked at some of the grizzled women in the room, mere mechanical contrivances sewing seams and grinding out, with heads bent over their work, tales of imagined or real girlhood happiness, or of past drunks, or the baby at home, and unpaid wages. She wondered how long her youth would endure. She began to see the bloom upon her cheeks as something of value. She imagined herself, in an exasperating future, as a scrawny woman with an eternal grievance. She thought Pete to be a very fastidious person concerning the appearance of women.

She felt that she should love to see somebody entangle their fingers in the oily beard of the fat foreigner who owned the establishment. He was a detestable creature. He wore white socks with low shoes. He sat all day delivering orations in the depths of a cushioned chair. His pocketbook deprived them of the power of retort. "What do you sink I pie fife dolla a week for? Play? No, py tamn!"

Maggie was anxious for a friend to whom she could talk about Pete. She would have liked to discuss his admirable mannerisms with a reliable mutual friend. At home, she found her mother often drunk and always raving. It seemed that the world had treated this woman very badly, and she took a deep revenge upon such portions of it as came within her reach. She broke furniture as if she were at last getting her rights. She swelled with virtuous indignation as she carried the lighter articles of household use, one by one, under the shadows of the three gilt balls, where Hebrews chained them with chains of interest.

Jimmie came when he was obliged to by circumstances over which he had no control. His well-trained legs brought him staggering home and put him to bed some nights when he would rather have gone elsewhere.

Swaggering Pete loomed like a golden sun to Maggie. He took her to a dime museum, where rows of meek freaks astonished her. She contemplated their deformities with awe, and thought them a sort of chosen tribe. Pete, racking his brains for amusement, discovered the Central Park Menagerie and the Museum of Arts. Sunday afternoons would sometimes find them at these places. Pete did not appear to be particularly interested in what he saw. He stood around looking heavy, while Maggie giggled in glee.

Once, at the Menagerie, he went into a trance of admiration before the spectacle of a very small monkey threatening to thrash a cageful because one of them had pulled his tail and he had not wheeled about quickly enough to discover who did it. Ever after, Pete knew that monkey by sight, and winked at him, trying to induce him to fight with other and larger monkeys.

At the museum, Maggie said, "Dis is outa sight!"

"Aw, rats!" said Pete. "Wait till next summer an' I'll take yehs to a picnic."

While the girl wandered in the vaulted rooms, Pete occupied himself in returning, stony stare for stony stare, the appalling scrutiny of the watchdogs of the treasures. Occasionally he would remark in loud tones, "Dat jay has got glass eyes," and sentences of the sort. When he tired of this amusement, he would go to the mummies and moralize over them.

Usually he submitted with silent dignity to all that he had to go through, but at times he was goaded into comment. "Aw!" he demanded once. "Look at all dese little jugs! Hundred jugs in a row! Ten rows in a case, an' 'bout a t'ousand cases! What d' blazes use is dem?"

In the evenings of weekdays, he often took her to see plays in which the dazzling heroine was rescued from the palatial home of her treacherous guardian by the hero with the beautiful sentiments. The latter spent most of his time out at soak in pale-green snowstorms, busy with a nickel-plated revolver rescuing aged strangers from villains. Maggie lost herself in sympathy with the wanderers swooning in snowstorms beneath happy-hued church windows, while a choir within sang "Joy to the World." To Maggie and the rest of the audience, this was transcendental realism. Joy always within, and they, like the actor, inevitably without. Viewing it, they hugged themselves in ecstatic pity of their imagined or real condition. The girl thought the arrogance and granite-heartedness of the magnate of the play were very accurately drawn. She echoed the maledictions that the occupants of the gallery showered on this individual when his lines compelled him to expose his extreme selfishness.

Shady persons in the audience revolted from the pictured villainy of the drama. With untiring zeal they hissed vice and applauded virtue. Unmistakably bad men evinced an apparently sincere admiration for virtue. The loud gallery was overwhelmingly with the unfortunate and the oppressed. They encouraged the struggling hero with cries, and jeered the villain, hooting and calling attention to his whiskers. When anybody died in the pale-green snowstorms, the gallery mourned. They sought out the painted misery and hugged it as akin.

In the hero's erratic march from poverty in the first act

to wealth and triumph in the final one, in which he forgives all the enemies that he has left, he was assisted by the gallery, which applauded his generous and noble sentiments and confounded the speeches of his opponents by making irrelevant but very sharp remarks. Those actors who were cursed with the parts of villains were confronted at every turn by the gallery. If one of them rendered lines containing the most subtile distinctions between right and wrong, the gallery was immediately aware that the actor meant wickedness, and denounced him accordingly. The last act was a triumph for the hero, poor and of the masses, the representative of the audience, over the villain and the rich man, his pockets stuffed with bonds, his heart packed with tyrannical purposes, imperturbable amid suffering.

Maggie always departed with raised spirits from these melodramas. She rejoiced at the way in which the poor and virtuous eventually overcame the wealthy and wicked. The theatre made her think. She wondered if the culture and refinement she had seen imitated, perhaps grotesquely, by the heroine on the stage could be acquired by a girl who lived in a tenement house and worked in a shirt factory.

- *ix* -

A group of urchins were intent upon the side door of a saloon. Expectancy gleamed from their eyes. They were twisting their fingers in excitement. "Here she comes!" yelled one of them suddenly. The group of urchins burst instantly asunder and its individual fragments were spread in a wide, respectable half-circle about the point of interest. The saloon door opened with a crash, and the figure of a woman appeared upon the threshold. Her gray hair fell in knotted masses about her shoulders. Her face was crimsoned and wet with perspiration. Her eyes had a rolling glare. "Not a cent more of me money will yehs ever get—not a red! I spent me money here fer t'ree years, an' now yehs tells me yeh'll sell me no more stuff! Go fall on yerself, Johnnie

Murckre! 'Disturbance'? Disturbance be blowed! Go fall on
yerself, Johnnie—"

The door received a kick of exasperation from within, and
the woman lurched heavily out on the sidewalk. The gamins
in the half-circle became violently agitated. They began to
dance about and hoot and yell and jeer. A wide, dirty grin
spread over each face.

The woman made a furious dash at a particularly out-
rageous cluster of little boys. They laughed delightedly, and
scampered off a short distance, calling out to her over their
shoulders. She stood tottering on the curbstone and thundered at them. "Yeh devil's kids!" she howled, shaking her
fists. The little boys whooped in glee. As she started up
the street, they fell in behind and marched uproariously. Occasionally she wheeled about and made charges on them.
They ran nimbly out of reach and taunted her.

In the frame of a gruesome doorway she stood for a moment, cursing them. Her hair straggled, giving her red features a look of insanity. Her great fists quivered as she shook
them madly in the air. The urchins made terrific noises until
she turned and disappeared. Then they filed off quietly in the
way they had come.

The woman floundered about in the lower hall of the
tenement house, and finally stumbled up the stairs. On an
upper hall a door was opened and a collection of heads
peered curiously out, watching her. With a wrathful snort
the woman confronted the door, but it was slammed hastily
in her face and the key was turned.

She stood for a few minutes, delivering a frenzied challenge at the panels. "Come out in deh hall, Mary Murphy,
if yehs want a scrap! Come ahn, yeh overgrown terrier,
come ahn!" She began to kick the door. She shrilly defied the
universe to appear and do battle. Her cursing trebles brought
heads from all doors save the one she threatened. Her eyes
glared in every direction. The air was full of her tossing fists.
"Come ahn, deh hull gang of yehs, come ahn!" she roared
at the spectators. An oath or two, catcalls, jeers, and bits of

facetious advice were given in reply. Missiles clattered about her feet.

"What's wrong wi'che?" said a voice in the gathered gloom, and Jimmie came forward. He carried a tin dinner pail in his hand and under his arm a truckman's brown apron done in a bundle. "What's wrong?" he demanded.

"Come out, all of yehs, come out," his mother was howling. "Come ahn an' I'll stamp yer faces t'rough d' floor."

"Shet yer face, an' come home, yeh old fool!" roared Jimmie at her. She strode up to him and twirled her fingers in his face. Her eyes were darting flames of unreasoning rage, and her frame trembled with eagerness for a fight.

"An' who are youse? I ain't givin' a snap of me fingers fer youse!" she bawled at him. She turned her huge back in tremendous disdain and climbed the stairs to the next floor.

Jimmie followed, and at the top of the flight, he seized his mother's arm and started to drag her toward the door of their room. "Come home!" he gritted between his teeth.

"Take yer hands off me! Take yer hands off me!" shrieked his mother. She raised her arm and whirled her great fist at her son's face. Jimmie dodged his head, and the blow struck him in the back of the neck. "Come home!" he gritted again. He threw out his left hand and writhed his fingers about her middle arm. The mother and the son began to sway and struggle like gladiators.

"Whoop!" said the Rum Alley tenement house. The hall filled with interested spectators. "Hi, ol' lady, dat was a dandy!" "T'ree t' one on d' red!" "Ah, quit yer scrappin'!"

The door of the Johnson home opened and Maggie looked out. Jimmie made a supreme cursing effort and hurled his mother into the room. He quickly followed and closed the door. The Rum Alley tenement swore disappointedly and retired.

The mother slowly gathered herself up from the floor. Her eyes glittered menacingly upon her children.

"Here now," said Jimmie, "we've had enough of dis. Sit down, an' don' make no trouble."

He grasped her arm and, twisting it, forced her into a creaking chair.

"Keep yer hands off me!" roared his mother again.

"Say, yeh ol' bat! Quit dat!" yelled Jimmie madly. Maggie shrieked and ran into the other room. To her there came the sound of a storm of crashes and curses. There was a great final thump and Jimmie's voice cried, "Dere now! Stay still." Maggie opened the door now, and went warily out. "Oh, Jimmie!"

He was leaning against the wall and swearing. Blood stood upon bruises on his knotty forearms where they had scraped against the floor or the walls in the scuffle. The mother lay screeching on the floor, the tears running down her furrowed face.

Maggie, standing in the middle of the room, gazed about her. The usual upheaval of the tables and chairs had taken place. Crockery was strewn broadcast in fragments. The stove had been disturbed on its legs, and now leaned idiotically to one side. A pail had been upset and water spread in all directions.

The door opened and Pete appeared. He shrugged his shoulders. "Oh, gee!" he observed. He walked over to Maggie and whispered in her ear, "Ah, what d' hell, Mag? Come ahn and we'll have a outa-sight time."

The mother in the corner upreared her head and shook her tangled locks. "Aw, yer bote no good, needer of yehs," she said, glowering at her daughter in the gloom. Her eyes seemed to burn balefully. "Yeh've gone t' d' devil, Mag Johnson, yehs knows yehs have gone t' d' devil. Yer a disgrace t' yer people. An' now, git out an' go ahn wid dat doe-faced jude of yours. Go wid him, curse yeh, an' a good riddance. Go, an' see how yeh likes it."

Maggie gazed long at her mother.

"Go now, an' see how yeh likes it. Git out. I won't have sech as youse in me house! Git out, d' yeh hear! Damn yeh, git out!"

The girl began to tremble.

At this instant Pete came forward. "Oh, what d' hell,

Mag, see?" whispered he softly in her ear. "Dis all blows over. See? D' ol' woman 'ill be all right in d' mornin'. Come ahn out wid me! We'll have a outa-sight time."

The woman on the floor cursed. Jimmie was intent upon his bruised forearms. The girl cast a glance about the room filled with a chaotic mass of debris, and at the writhing body of her mother.

"Git th' devil outa here."

Maggie went.

- x -

Jimmie had an idea it wasn't common courtesy for a friend to come to one's home and ruin one's sister. But he was not sure how much Pete knew about the rules of politeness.

The following night he returned home from work at a rather late hour in the evening. In passing through the halls, he came upon the gnarled and leathery old woman who possessed the music box. She was grinning in the dim light that drifted through dust-stained panes. She beckoned to him with a smudged forefinger.

"Ah, Jimmie, what do yehs t'ink I tumbled to las' night! It was deh funnies' t'ing I ever saw," she cried, coming close to him and leering. She was trembling with eagerness to tell her tale. "I was by me door las' night when yer sister and her jude feller came in late, oh, very late. An' she, the dear, she was a-cryin' as if her heart would break, she was. It was deh funnies' t'ing I ever saw. An' right out here by me door, she asked him did he love her, did he. An' she was a-crying as if her heart would break, poor t'ing. An' him, I could see be deh way what he said it dat she had been askin' orften; he says, 'Oh, gee, yes,' he says, says he. 'Oh, gee, yes.'"

Storm clouds swept over Jimmie's face, but he turned from the leathery old woman and plodded on upstairs.

"'Oh, gee, yes,'" she called after him. She laughed a laugh that was like a prophetic croak.

There was no one in at home. The rooms showed that attempts had been made at tidying them. Parts of the wreckage of the day before had been repaired by an unskilled hand. A chair or two and the table stood uncertainly upon legs. The floor had been newly swept. The blue ribbons had been restored to the curtains, and the lambrequin, with its immense sheaves of yellow wheat and red roses of equal size, had been returned, in a worn and sorry state, to its place at the mantel. Maggie's jacket and hat were gone from the nail behind the door.

Jimmie walked to the window and began to look through the blurred glass. It occurred to him to wonder vaguely, for an instant, if some of the women of his acquaintance had brothers.

Suddenly, however, he began to swear. "But he was me frien'! I brought 'im here! Dat's d' devil of it!" He fumed about the room, his anger gradually rising to the furious pitch. "I'll kill deh jay! Dat's what I'll do! I'll kill deh jay!"

He clutched his hat and sprang toward the door. But it opened, and his mother's great form blocked the passage. "What's d' matter wid yeh?" exclaimed she, coming into the rooms.

Jimmie gave vent to a sardonic curse and then laughed heavily. "Well, Maggie's gone teh d' devil! Dat's what! See?"

"Eh?" said his mother.

"Maggie's gone teh d' devil! Are yehs deaf?" roared Jimmie impatiently.

"Aw, git out!" murmured the mother, astounded.

Jimmie grunted, and then began to stare out the window. His mother sat down in a chair, but a moment later sprang erect and delivered a maddened whirl of oaths. Her son turned to look at her as she reeled and swayed in the middle of the room, her fierce face convulsed with passion, her blotched arms raised high in imprecation.

"May she be cursed forever!" she shrieked. "May she eat nothin' but stones and deh dirt in deh street. May she sleep in deh gutter an' never see deh sunshine again. D' bloomin'—"

"Here now," said her son. "Go fall on yerself, an' quit dat."

The mother raised lamenting eyes to the ceiling. "She's

d' devil's own chil', Jimmie," she whispered. "Ah, who would t'ink such a bad girl could grow up in our fambly, Jimmie, me son. Many d' hour I've spent in talk wid dat girl an' tol' her if she ever went on d' streets I'd see her damned. An' after all her bringin' up an' what I tol' her and talked wid her, she goes teh d' bad, like a duck teh water."

The tears rolled down her furrowed face. Her hands trembled. "An' den when dat Sadie MacMallister next door to us was sent teh d' devil by dat feller what worked in d' soap factory, didn't I tell our Mag dat if she—"

"Ah, dat's anudder story," interrupted the brother. "Of course, dat Sadie was nice an' all dat—but—see?—it ain't dessame as if—well, Maggie was diff'ent—see?—she was diff'-ent." He was trying to formulate a theory that he had always unconsciously held, that all sisters excepting his own could, advisedly, be ruined.

He suddenly broke out again. "I'll go t'ump d' mug what done her d' harm. I'll kill 'im! He t'inks he kin scrap, but when he gits me a-chasin' 'im he'll fin' out where he's wrong, d' big stiff! I'll wipe up d' street wid 'im." In a fury he plunged out the doorway.

As he vanished, the mother raised her head and lifted both hands, entreating. "May she be cursed forever!" she cried.

In the darkness of the hallway, Jimmie discerned a knot of women talking volubly. When he strode by, they paid no attention to him. "She allus was a bold thing," he heard one of them cry in an eager voice. "Dere wasn't a feller come teh deh house but she'd try teh mash 'im. My Annie says deh shameless t'ing tried teh ketch her feller, her own feller, what we useter know his fader."

"I could 'a' tol' yehs dis two years ago," said a woman, in a key of triumph. "Yes, sir, it was over two years ago dat I says teh my o' man, I says, 'Dat Johnson girl ain't straight,' I says. 'Oh, rats!' he says. 'Oh, hell!' 'Dat's all right,' I says, 'but I know what I knows,' I says, 'an' it'll come out later. You wait an' see,' I says, 'you see.'"

"Anybody what had eyes could see dat dere was somethin' wrong wid dat girl. I didn't like her actions."

On the street Jimmie met a friend. "What's wrong?" asked the latter.

Jimmie explained. "An' I'll t'ump 'im till he can't stand."

"Oh, go ahn!" said the friend. "What's deh use! Yeh'll git pulled in! Everybody 'ill be on to it! An' ten plunks! Gee!"

Jimmie was determined. "He t'inks he kin scrap, but he'll fin' out diff'ent."

"Gee!" remonstrated the friend. "What's d' use?"

- xi -

On a corner, a glass-fronted building shed a yellow glare upon the pavements. The open mouth of a saloon called seductively to passengers to enter and annihilate sorrow or create rage.

The interior of the place was papered in olive-and-bronze tints of imitation leather. A shining bar of counterfeit massiveness extended down the side of the room. Behind it, a great mahogany-imitation sideboard reached the ceiling. Upon its shelves rested pyramids of shimmering glasses that were never disturbed. Mirrors set in the face of the sideboard multiplied them. Lemons, oranges, and paper napkins, arranged with mathematical precision, sat among the glasses. Many-hued decanters of liquor perched at regular intervals on the lower shelves. A nickel-plated cash register occupied a place in the exact center of the general effect. The elementary senses of it all seemed to be opulence and geometrical accuracy.

Across from the bar, a smaller counter held a collection of plates upon which swarmed frayed fragments of crackers, slices of boiled ham, disheveled bits of cheese, and pickles swimming in vinegar. An odor of grasping, begrimed hands and munching mouths pervaded all.

Pete, in a white jacket, was behind the bar, bending expectantly toward a quiet stranger. "A beeh," said the man.

Pete drew a foam-topped glassful, and set it dripping upon the bar.

At this moment, the light bamboo doors at the entrance swung open and crashed against the wall. Jimmie and a companion entered. They swaggered unsteadily but belligerently toward the bar, and looked at Pete with bleared and blinking eyes.

"Gin," said Jimmie.

"Gin," said the companion.

Pete slid a bottle and two glasses along the bar. He bent his head sideways as he assiduously polished away with a napkin at the gleaming wood. He wore a look of watchfulness. Jimmie and his companion kept their eyes upon the bartender and conversed loudly in tones of contempt.

"He's a dandy masher, ain't he?" laughed Jimmie.

"Well, ain't he!" said the companion, sneering. "He's great, he is. Git on to deh mug on deh blokie. Dat's enough to make a feller turn handsprings in 'is sleep."

The quiet stranger moved himself and his glass a trifle farther away and maintained an attitude of obliviousness.

"Gee! Ain't he hot stuff?"

"Git on to his shape!"

"Hey!" cried Jimmie, in tones of command. Pete came along slowly, with a sullen dropping of the underlip.

"Well," he growled, "what's eatin' yehs?"

"Gin," said Jimmie.

"Gin," said the companion.

As Pete confronted them with the bottle and the glasses, they laughed in his face. Jimmie's companion, evidently overcome with merriment, pointed a grimy forefinger in Pete's direction. "Say, Jimmie," demanded he, "what's dat behind d' bar?"

"Looks like some chump," replied Jimmie. They laughed loudly.

Pete put down a bottle with a bang and turned a formidable face toward them. He disclosed his teeth, and his shoulders heaved restlessly. "You fellers can't guy me," he said. "Drink yer stuff an' git out an' don' make no trouble."

Instantly the laughter faded from the faces of the two men, and expressions of offended dignity immediately came. "Aw, who has said anyt'ing t' you?" cried they in the same breath.

The quiet stranger looked at the door calculatingly.

"Ah, come off," said Pete to the two men. "Don't pick me up fer no jay. Drink yer rum an' git out an' don' make no trouble."

"Aw, go ahn!" airily cried Jimmie.

"Aw, go ahn!" airily repeated his companion.

"We goes when we git ready! See?" continued Jimmie.

"Well," said Pete in a threatening voice, "don' make no trouble."

Jimmie suddenly leaned forward with his head on one side. He snarled like a wild animal. "Well, what if we does? See?" said he.

Hot blood flushed into Pete's face, and he shot a lurid glance at Jimmie. "Well, den we'll see who's d' bes' man, you or me," he said.

The quiet stranger moved modestly toward the door.

Jimmie began to swell with valor. "Don' pick me up fer no tenderfoot. When yeh tackles me, yeh tackles one of d' bes' men in d' city. See? I'm a scrapper, I am. Ain't dat right, Billie?"

"Sure, Mike," responded his companion in tones of conviction.

"Aw!" said Pete, easily. "Go fall on yerself."

The two men again began to laugh.

"What is dat talking?" cried the companion.

"Don' ast me," replied Jimmie with exaggerated contempt.

Pete made a furious gesture. "Git outa here now, an' don' make no trouble. See? Youse fellers er lookin' fer a scrap, an' it's like yeh'll fin' one if yeh keeps on shootin' off yer mout's. I know yehs! See? I kin lick better men dan yehs ever saw in yer lifes. Dat's right! See? Don' pick me up fer no stiff, er yeh might be jolted out in d' street before yeh knows where yeh is. When I comes from behind dis bar, I t'rows yehs bote inteh d' street. See?"

"Ah, go ahn!" cried the two men in chorus.

The glare of a panther came into Pete's eyes. "Dat's what I said! Unnerstan'?"

He came through a passage at the end of the bar and swelled down upon the two men. They stepped promptly forward and crowded close to him. They bristled like three roosters. They moved their heads pugnaciously and kept their shoulders braced. The nervous muscles about each mouth twitched with a forced smile of mockery.

"Well, what yer goin' t' do?" gritted Jimmie.

Pete stepped warily back, waving his hands before him to keep the men from coming too near.

"Well, what yer goin' t' do?" repeated Jimmie's ally. They kept close to him, taunting and leering. They strove to make him attempt the initial blow.

"Keep back now! Don' crowd me," said Pete ominously.

Again they chorused in contempt, "Aw, go ahn!"

In a small, tossing group, the three men edged for positions like frigates contemplating battle.

"Well, why don' yeh try t' t'row us out?" cried Jimmie and his ally with copious sneers.

The bravery of bulldogs sat upon the faces of the men. Their clenched fists moved like eager weapons. The allied two jostled the bartender's elbows, glaring at him with feverish eyes and forcing him toward the wall.

Suddenly Pete swore furiously. The flash of action gleamed from his eyes. He threw back his arm and aimed a tremendous, lightning-like blow at Jimmie's face. His foot swung a step forward and the weight of his body was behind his fist. Jimmie ducked his head, Bowery-like, with the quickness of a cat. The fierce answering blows of Jimmie and his ally crushed on Pete's bowed head.

The quiet stranger vanished.

The arms of the combatants whirled in the air like flails. The faces of the men, at first flushed to flame-colored anger, now began to fade to the pallor of warriors in the blood and heat of a battle. Their lips curled back and stretched tightly over the gums in ghoul-like grins. Through their white, gripped teeth struggled hoarse whisperings of oaths. Their eyes glittered with murderous fire.

Each head was huddled between its owner's shoulders, and arms were swinging with marvelous rapidity. Feet scraped to and fro with a loud, scratching sound upon the sanded floor. Blows left crimson blotches upon the pale skin. The curses of the first quarter-minute of the fight died away. The breaths of the fighters came wheezing from their lips and the three chests were straining and heaving. Pete at intervals gave vent to low, labored hisses, that sounded like a desire to kill. Jimmie's ally gibbered at times like a wounded maniac. Jimmie was silent, fighting with the face of a sacrificial priest. The rage of fear shone in all their eyes, and their blood-colored fists whirled.

At a critical moment, a blow from Pete's hand struck the ally, and he crashed to the floor. He wriggled instantly to his feet and, grasping the quiet stranger's beer glass from the bar, hurled it at Pete's head.

High on the wall it burst like a bomb, shivering fragments flying in all directions. Then missiles came to every man's hand. The place had heretofore appeared free of things to throw, but suddenly glasses and bottles went singing through the air. They were thrown point-blank at bobbing heads. The pyramids of shimmering glasses, that had never been disturbed, changed to cascades as heavy bottles were flung into them. Mirrors splintered to nothing.

The three frothing creatures on the floor buried themselves in a frenzy for blood. There followed in the wake of missiles and fists some unknown prayers, perhaps for death.

The quiet stranger had sprawled very pyrotechnically out on the sidewalk. A laugh ran up and down the avenue for the half of a block. "Dey've t'rowed a bloke inteh deh street."

People heard the sound of breaking glass and shuffling feet within the saloon and came running. A small group, bending down to look under the bamboo doors, and watching the fall of glass and three pairs of violent legs, changed in a moment to a crowd. A policeman came charging down the sidewalk and bounced through the doors into the saloon. The crowd bent and surged in absorbing anxiety to see.

Jimmie caught the first sight of the oncoming interruption. On his feet he had the same regard for a policeman that, when on his truck, he had for a fire engine. He howled and ran for the side door.

The officer made a terrific advance, club in hand. One comprehensive sweep of the long night stick threw the ally to the floor and forced Pete to a corner. With his disengaged hand he made a furious effort at Jimmie's coattails. Then he regained his balance and paused. "Well, well, you are a pair of pictures. What have ye been up to?"

Jimmie, with his face drenched in blood, escaped up a side street, pursued a short distance by some of the more law-loving or excited individuals of the crowd.

Later, from a safe, dark corner, he saw the policeman, the ally, and the bartender emerge from the saloon. Pete locked the doors and then followed up the avenue in the rear of the crowd-encompassed policeman and his charge.

At first Jimmie, with his heart throbbing at battle heat, started to go desperately to the rescue of his friend, but he halted. "Ah, what's d' use?" he demanded of himself.

- *xii* -

In a hall of irregular shape sat Pete and Maggie drinking beer. A submissive orchestra, dictated to by a spectacled man with frowsy hair and in soiled evening dress, industriously followed the bobs of his head and the waves of his baton. A ballad singer, in a gown of flaming scarlet, sang in the inevitable voice of brass. When she vanished, men seated at the tables near the front applauded loudly, pounding the polished wood with their beer glasses. She returned attired in less gown, and sang again. She received another enthusiastic encore. She reappeared in still less gown and danced. The deafening rumble of glasses and clapping of hands that followed her exit indicated an overwhelming desire to have her come on for the fourth time, but the curiosity of the audience was not gratified.

Maggie was pale. From her eyes had been plucked all look of self-reliance. She leaned with a dependent air toward her companion. She was timid, as if fearing his anger or displeasure. She seemed to beseech tenderness of him.

Pete's air of distinguished valor had grown upon him until it threatened to reach stupendous dimensions. He was infinitely gracious to the girl. It was apparent to her that his condescension was a marvel. He could appear to strut even while sitting still, and he showed that he was a lion of lordly characteristics by the air with which he spat.

With Maggie gazing at him wonderingly, he took pride in commanding the waiters, who were, however, indifferent or deaf. "Hi, you, git a russle on yehs! What yehs lookin' at? Two more beehs, d' yeh hear?" He leaned back and critically regarded the person of a girl with a straw-colored wig who was flinging her heels about upon the stage in somewhat awkward imitation of a well-known *danseuse*.

At times Maggie told Pete long, confidential tales of her former home life, dwelling upon the escapades of the other members of the family and the difficulties she had had to combat in order to obtain a degree of comfort. He responded in the accents of philanthropy. He pressed her arm with an air of reassuring proprietorship.

"Dey was cursed jays," he said, denouncing the mother and brother.

The sound of the music which, through the efforts of the frowsy-headed leader, drifted to her ears in the smoke-filled atmosphere, made the girl dream. She thought of her former Rum Alley environment and turned to Pete's strong, protecting fists. She thought of a collar-and-cuff manufactory and the eternal moan of the proprietor: "What een hale do you sink I pie fife dolla a week for? Play? No, py tamn!" She contemplated Pete's man-subduing eyes and noted that wealth and prosperity were indicated by his clothes. She imagined a future rose-tinted because of its distance from all that she had experienced before.

As to the present, she perceived only vague reasons to be miserable. Her life was Pete's and she considered him worthy of the charge. She would be disturbed by no particular apprehensions so long as Pete adored her as he now said he did. She did not feel like a bad woman. To her knowledge she had never seen any better.

At times men at other tables regarded the girl furtively. Pete, aware of it, nodded at her and grinned. He felt proud. "Mag, yer a bloomin' good looker," he remarked, studying her face through the haze. The men made Maggie fear, but she blushed at Pete's words as it became apparent to her that she was the apple of his eye.

Gray-headed men, wonderfully pathetic in their dissipation, stared at her through clouds. Smooth-cheeked boys, some of them with faces of stone and mouths of sin, not nearly so pathetic as the gray heads, tried to find the girl's eyes in the smoke wreaths. Maggie considered she was not what they thought her. She confined her glances to Pete and the stage.

The orchestra played Negro melodies and a versatile drummer pounded, whacked, clattered, and scratched on a dozen machines to make noise.

Those glances of the men, shot at Maggie from under half-closed lids, made her tremble. She thought them all to be worse men than Pete. "Come, let's go," she said.

As they went out, Maggie perceived two women seated at a table with some men. They were painted, and their cheeks had lost their roundness. As she passed them, the girl, with a shrinking movement, drew back her skirts.

- *xiii* -

Jimmie did not return home for a number of days after the fight with Pete in the saloon. When he did, he approached with extreme caution.

He found his mother raving. Maggie had not returned home. The parent continually wondered how her daughter could come to such a pass. She had never considered Maggie as a pearl dropped unstained into Rum Alley from Heaven, but she could not conceive how it was possible for her daughter to fall so low as to bring disgrace upon her family. She was terrific in denunciation of the girl's wickedness.

The fact that the neighbors talked of it maddened her. When women came in, and in the course of their conversation casually asked, "Where's Maggie dese days?" the mother shook her fuzzy head at them and appalled them with curses. Cunning hints inviting confidence she rebuffed with violence.

"An' wid all d' bringin' up she had, how could she?" moaningly she asked of her son. "Wid all d' talkin' wid her I did an' d' t'ings I tol' her to remember. When a girl is bringed up d' way I bringed up Maggie, how kin she go teh d' devil?"

Jimmie was transfixed by these questions. He could not conceive how, under the circumstances, his mother's daughter and his sister could have been so wicked.

His mother took a drink from a bottle that sat on the table. She continued her lament. "She had a bad heart, dat girl did, Jimmie. She was wicked t' d' heart an' we never knowed it."

Jimmie nodded, admitting the fact.

"We lived in d' same house wid her an' I brought her up, an' we never knowed how bad she was."

Jimmie nodded again.

"Wid a home like dis an' a mudder like me, she went teh d' bad," cried the mother, raising her eyes.

One day Jimmie came home, sat down in a chair, and began to wriggle about with a new and strange nervousness. At last he spoke shamefacedly. "Well, look-a-here, dis t'ing queers us! See? We're queered! An' maybe it 'ud be better if I—well, I t'ink I kin look 'er up an'—maybe it 'ud be better if I fetched her home an'—"

The mother started from her chair and broke forth into a storm of passionate anger. "What! Let 'er come an' sleep under deh same roof wid her mudder agin? Oh, yes, I will, won't I! Sure! Shame on yehs, Jimmie Johnson, fer sayin' such a t'ing teh yer own mudder! Little did I t'ink when yehs was a baby playin' about me feet dat ye'd grow up teh say sech a t'ing teh yer mudder—yer own mudder. I never t'ought—"

Sobs choked her and interrupted her reproaches.

"Dere ain't nottin' teh make sech trouble about," said Jimmie. "I on'y says it 'ud be better if we keep dis t'ing dark, see? It queers us! See?"

His mother laughed a laugh that seemed to ring through the city and be echoed and re-echoed by countless other laughs. "Oh, yes, I will, won't I? Sure!"

"Well, yeh must take me fer a damn fool," said Jimmie, indignant at his mother for mocking him. "I didn't say we'd make 'er inteh a little tin angel, ner nottin', but deh way it is now she can queer us! Don'che see?"

"Ay, she'll git tired of deh life atter a while, an' den she'll wanna be a-comin' home, won' she, deh beast! I'll let 'er in den, won't I?"

"Well, I didn't mean none of dis prod'gal bus'ness anyway," explained Jimmie.

"It wa'n't no prod'gal daughter, yeh fool," said the mother. "It was prod'gal son, anyhow."

"I know dat," said Jimmie.

For a time they sat in silence. The mother's eyes gloated on the scene which her imagination called before her. Her lips were set in a vindictive smile. "Ay, she'll cry, won' she, an' carry on, an' tell how Pete, or some odder feller, beats 'er, an' she'll say she's sorry an' all dat, an' she ain't happy, she ain't, an' she wants to come home agin, she does." With grim humor the mother imitated the possible wailing notes of the daughter's voice. "Den I'll take 'er in, won't I? She kin cry 'er two eyes out on deh stones of deh street before I'll dirty d' place wid her. She abused an' ill-treated her own mudder—her own mudder what loved her—an' she'll never git anodder chance."

Jimmie thought he had a great idea of women's frailty, but he could not understand why any of his kin should be victims. "Curse her!" he said fervidly. Again he wondered vaguely if some of the women of his acquaintance had brothers. Nevertheless, his mind did not for an instant confuse himself with those brothers nor his sister with theirs.

After the mother had, with great difficulty, suppressed the neighbors, she went among them and proclaimed her grief. "May Heaven forgive dat girl," was her continual cry. To attentive ears she recited the whole length and breadth of her woes. "I bringed 'er up deh way a daughter oughta be bringed up, an' dis is how she served me! She went teh deh devil deh first chance she got! May Heaven forgive her."

When arrested for drunkenness, she used the story of her daughter's downfall with telling effect upon the police justices. Finally one of them said to her, peering down over his spectacles, "Mary, the records of this and other courts show that you are the mother of forty-two daughters who have been ruined. The case is unparalleled in the annals of this court, and this court thinks—"

The mother went through life shedding large tears of sorrow. Her red face was a picture of agony.

Of course, Jimmie publicly damned his sister that he might appear on a higher social plane. But arguing with himself, stumbling about in ways that he knew not, he once almost came to a conclusion that his sister would have been more firmly good had she better known how. However, he felt that he could not hold such a view. He threw it hastily aside.

- *xiv* -

In a hilarious hall there were twenty-eight tables and twenty-eight women and a crowd of smoking men. Valiant noise was made on a stage at the end of the hall by an orchestra composed of men who looked as if they had just happened in. Soiled waiters ran to and fro, swooping down like hawks on the unwary in the throng; clattering along the aisles with trays covered with glasses; stumbling over women's skirts and charging two prices for everything but beer, all with a swiftness that blurred the view of the coconut palms and dusty monstrosities painted upon the walls of the room. A "bouncer," with an immense load of business upon his hands, plunged about in the crowd, dragging bashful strangers to prominent chairs, ordering waiters here and there, and quarreling furiously with men who wanted to sing with the orchestra.

The usual smoke cloud was present, but so dense that heads and arms seemed entangled in it. The rumble of conversation was replaced by a roar. Plenteous oaths heaved through the air. The room rang with the shrill voices of women bubbling over with drink-laughter. The chief element in the music of the orchestra was speed. The musicians played in intent fury. A woman was singing and smiling upon the stage, but no one took notice of her. The rate at which the piano, cornet, and violins were going seemed to impart wildness to the half-drunken crowd. Beer glasses were emptied at a gulp and conversation became a rapid chatter. The smoke eddied and swirled like a shadowy river hurrying toward some unseen falls. Pete and Maggie entered the hall and took chairs at a table near the door. The woman who was seated there made an attempt to occupy Pete's attention, and failing, went away.

Three weeks had passed since the girl had left home. The air of spaniel-like dependence had been magnified and showed its direct effect in the peculiar offhandedness and ease of Pete's ways toward her. She followed Pete's eyes with hers, anticipating with smiles gracious looks from him.

A woman of brilliance and audacity, accompanied by a mere boy, came into the place and took a seat near them. At once Pete sprang to his feet, his face beaming with glad surprise. "Hully gee, dere's Nellie!" he cried. He went over to the table and held out an eager hand to the woman.

"Why, hello, Pete, me boy, how are you?" said she, giving him her fingers.

Maggie took instant note of the woman. She perceived that her black dress fitted her to perfection. Her linen collar and cuffs were spotless. Tan gloves were stretched over her well-shaped hands. A hat of a prevailing fashion perched jauntily upon her dark hair. She wore no jewelry and was painted with no apparent paint. She looked clear-eyed through the stares of the men.

"Sit down, and call your lady friend over," she said to Pete. At his beckoning, Maggie came and sat between Pete and the mere boy.

"I t'ought yeh was gone away fer good," began Pete, at once. "When did yeh git back? How did dat Buff'lo business turn out?"

The woman shrugged her shoulders. "Well, he didn't have as many stamps as he tried to make out, so I shook him, that's all."

"Well, I'm glad teh see yehs back in deh city," said Pete, with gallantry. He and the woman entered into a long conversation, exchanging reminiscences of days together. Maggie sat still, unable to formulate an intelligent sentence as her addition to the conversation, and painfully aware of it.

She saw Pete's eyes sparkle as he gazed upon the handsome stranger. He listened smilingly to all she said. The woman was familiar with all his affairs, asked him about mutual friends, and knew the amount of his salary. She paid no attention to Maggie, looking toward her once or twice and apparently seeing the wall beyond.

The mere boy was sulky. In the beginning, he had welcomed the additions with acclamations. "Let's all have a drink! What'll you take, Nell? And you, Miss What's-your-name. Have a drink, Mr. ——, you, I mean." He had shown a sprightly desire to do the talking for the company and tell all about his family. In a loud voice, he declaimed on various topics. He assumed a patronizing air toward Pete. As Maggie was silent, he paid no attention to her. He made a great show of lavishing wealth upon the woman of brilliance and audacity.

"Do keep still, Freddie! You talk like a clock," said the woman to him. She turned away and devoted her attention to Pete. "We'll have many a good time together again, eh?"

"Sure, Mike," said Pete, enthusiastic at once.

"Say," whispered she, leaning forward, "let's go over to Billie's and have a time."

"Well, it's dis way! See?" said Pete. "I got dis lady frien' here."

"Oh, g'way with her," argued the woman.

Pete appeared disturbed.

"All right," said she, nodding her head at him. "All right for you! We'll see the next time you ask me to go anywheres with you."

Pete squirmed. "Say," he said beseechingly, "come wid me a minute an' I'll tell yer why."

The woman waved her hand. "Oh, that's all right, you needn't explain, you know. You wouldn't come merely because you wouldn't come, that's all." To Pete's visible distress, she turned to the mere boy, bringing him speedily out of a terrific rage. He had been debating whether it would be the part of a man to pick a quarrel with Pete, or would he be justified in striking him savagely with his beer glass without warning. But he recovered himself when the woman turned to renew her smilings. He beamed upon her with an expression that was somewhat tipsy and inexpressibly tender.

"Say, shake that Bowery jay," requested he, in a loud whisper.

"Freddie, you are so funny," she replied.

Pete reached forward and touched the woman on the arm. "Come out a minute while I tells yeh why I can't go wid yer. Yer doin' me dirt, Nell! I never t'ought ye'd do me dirt, Nell. Come on, will yer?" He spoke in tones of injury.

"Why, I don't see why I should be interested in your explanations," said the woman, with a coldness that seemed to reduce Pete to a pulp.

His eyes pleaded with her. "Come out a minute while I tells yeh. On d' level, now."

The woman nodded slightly at Maggie and the mere boy, saying, " 'Scuse me."

The mere boy interrupted his loving smile and turned a shriveling glare upon Pete. His boyish countenance flushed and he spoke in a whine to the woman: "Oh, I say, Nellie, this ain't a square deal, you know. You aren't goin' to leave me and go off with that duffer, are you? I should think—"

"Why, you dear boy, of course I'm not," cried the woman affectionately. She bent over and whispered in his ear. He smiled again and settled in his chair as if resolved to wait patiently.

As the woman walked down between the rows of tables, Pete was at her shoulder talking earnestly, apparently in explanation. The woman waved her hands with studied airs of indifference. The doors swung behind them, leaving Maggie and the mere boy seated at the table.

Maggie was dazed. She could dimly perceive that something stupendous had happened. She wondered why Pete saw fit to remonstrate with the woman, pleading forgiveness with his eyes. She thought she noted an air of submission about her leonine Pete. She was astounded.

The mere boy occupied himself with cocktails and a cigar. He was tranquilly silent for half an hour. Then he bestirred himself and spoke. "Well," he said, sighing, "I knew this was the way it would be. They got cold feet." There was another stillness. The mere boy seemed to be musing. "She was pulling m' leg. That's the whole amount of it," he said suddenly. "It's a bloomin' shame the way that girl does. Why, I've spent over two dollars in drinks tonight. And she goes off with that plug-ugly, who looks as if he had been hit in the face with a coin die. I call it rocky treatment for a fellah like me. Here, waiter, bring me a cocktail, and make it strong."

Maggie made no reply. She was watching the doors.

"It's a mean piece of business," complained the mere boy. He explained to her how amazing it was that anybody should treat him in such a manner. "But I'll get square with her, you bet. She won't get far ahead of yours truly, you know," he added, winking. "I'll tell her plainly that it was bloomin' mean business. And she won't come it over me with any of her 'now-Freddie-dears.' She thinks my name is Freddie, you know, but of course it ain't. I always tell these people some name like that, because if they got on to your right name they might use it sometime. Understand? Oh, they don't fool me much."

Maggie was paying no attention, being intent upon the doors. The mere boy relapsed into a period of gloom, during which he exterminated a number of cocktails with a determined air, as if replying defiantly to fate. He occasionally broke forth into sentences composed of invectives joined together in a long chain.

The girl was still staring at the doors. After a time, the mere boy began to see cobwebs just in front of his nose. He spurred himself into being agreeable and insisted upon her having a charlotte russe and a glass of beer.

"They's gone," he remarked, "they's gone." He looked at her through the smoke wreaths. "Shay, lil girl, we mightish well make bes' of it. You ain't such bad-lookin' girl, y' know. Not half bad. Can't come up to Nell, though. No, can't do it! Well, I should shay not! Nell fine-lookin' girl! F-i-n-ine. You look bad longsider her, but by y'self ain't so bad. Have to do, anyhow. Nell gone. O'ny you left. Not half bad, though."

Maggie stood up. "I'm going home," she said.

The mere boy started. "Eh? What? Home!" he cried, struck with amazement. "I beg pardon, did hear say home?"

"I'm going home," she repeated.

"Great heavens! What hav' a struck?" demanded the mere boy of himself, stupefied. In a semicomatose state, he conducted her on board an uptown car, ostentatiously paid her fare, leered kindly at her through the rear window, and fell off the steps.

- *xv* -

A forlorn woman went along a lighted avenue. The street was filled with people desperately bound on missions. An endless crowd darted at the elevated station stairs, and the horsecars were thronged with owners of bundles.

The pace of the forlorn woman was slow. She was apparently searching for someone. She loitered near the doors of saloons and watched men emerge from them. She furtively scanned the faces in the rushing stream of pedestrians. Hurrying men, bent on catching some boat or train, jostled her

elbows, failing to notice her, their thoughts fixed on distant
dinners.

The forlorn woman had a peculiar face. Her smile was no
smile. But when in repose, her features had a shadowy look
that was like a sardonic grin, as if someone had sketched
with cruel forefinger indelible lines about her mouth.

Jimmie came strolling up the avenue. The woman encountered him with an aggrieved air. "Oh, Jimmie, I've been
lookin' all over for yehs—" she began.

Jimmie made an impatient gesture and quickened his pace.
"Ah, don't bodder me!" he said, with the savageness of a man
whose life is pestered.

The woman followed him along the sidewalk in somewhat
the manner of a suppliant. "But, Jimmie," she said, "yehs
told me yehs—"

Jimmie turned upon her fiercely as if resolved to make a last
stand for comfort and peace. "Say, Hattie, don' foller me from
one end of deh city teh deh odder. Let up, will yehs! Give me
a minute's res', can't yehs? Yehs makes me tired, allus taggin'
me. See? Ain' yehs got no sense? Do yehs want people teh
get on to me? Go chase yerself."

The woman stepped closer and laid her fingers on his arm.
"But, look a' here—"

Jimmie snarled. "Oh, go teh blazes!" He darted into the
front door of a convenient saloon and a moment later came
out into the shadows that surrounded the side door. On the
brilliantly lighted avenue, he perceived the forlorn woman
dodging about like a scout. Jimmie laughed with an air of
relief and went away.

When he returned home, he found his mother clamoring.
Maggie had returned. She stood shivering beneath the torrent
of her mother's wrath.

"Well, I'm damned!" said Jimmie in greeting.

His mother, tottering about the room, pointed a quivering
forefinger. "Look ut her, Jimmie, look ut her. Dere's yer sister,
boy. Dere's yer sister. Look ut her! Look ut her!" She screamed
at Maggie with scoffing laughter.

The girl stood in the middle of the room. She edged about as if unable to find a place on the floor to put her feet.

"Ha ha, ha!" bellowed the mother. "Dere she stands! Ain't she purty? Look ut her! Ain' she sweet, deh beast? Look ut her! Ha, ha! Look ut her!" She lurched forward and put her red and seamed hands upon her daughter's face. She bent down and peered keenly up into the eyes of the girl. "Oh, she's jes' dessame as she ever was, ain' she? She's her mudder's putty darlin' yit, ain' she? Look ut her, Jimmie. Come here and look ut her."

The loud, tremendous railing of the mother brought the denizens of the Rum Alley tenement to their doors. Women came in the hallways. Children scurried to and fro.

"What's up? Dat Johnson party on anudder tear?"

"Naw. Young Mag's come home!"

"Git out!"

Through the open doors, curious eyes stared in at Maggie. Children ventured into the room and ogled her as if they formed the front row at a theatre. Women, without, bent toward each other and whispered, nodding their heads with airs of profound philosophy.

A baby, overcome with curiosity concerning this object at which all were looking, sidled forward and touched her dress, cautiously, as if investigating a red-hot stove. Its mother's voice rang out like a warning trumpet. She rushed forward and grabbed her child, casting a terrible look of indignation at the girl.

Maggie's mother paced to and fro, addressing the doorful of eyes, expounding like a glib showman. Her voice rang through the building. "Dere she stands," she cried, wheeling suddenly and pointing with dramatic finger. "Dere she stands! Look ut her! Ain' she a dandy? An' she was so good as to come home teh her mudder, she was! Ain' she a beaut'? Ain't she a dandy?"

The jeering cries ended in another burst of shrill laughter.

The girl seemed to awaken. "Jimmie—"

He drew hastily back from her. "Well, now, yer a t'ing, ain' yeh?" he said, his lips curling in scorn. Radiant virtue sat upon his brow, and his repelling hands expressed horror of contamination.

Maggie turned and went.

The crowd at the door fell back precipitately. A baby falling down in front of the door wrenched a scream like that of a wounded animal from its mother. Another woman sprang forward and picked it up with a chivalrous air, as if rescuing a human being from an oncoming express train.

As the girl passed down through the hall, she went before open doors framing more eyes strangely microscopic, and sending broad beams of inquisitive light into the darkness of her path. On the second floor she met the gnarled old woman who possessed the music box.

"So," she cried, " 'ere yehs are back again, are yehs? An' dey've kicked yehs out? Well, come in an' stay wid me t'night. I ain' got no moral standin'."

From above came an unceasing babble of tongues, over all of which rang the mother's derisive laughter.

- xvi -

Pete did not consider that he had ruined Maggie. If he had thought that her soul could never smile again, he would have believed the mother and brother, who were pyrotechnic over the affair, to be responsible for it. Besides, in his world, souls did not insist upon being able to smile. "What d' hell?"

He felt a trifle entangled. It distressed him. Revelations and scenes might bring upon him the wrath of the owner of the saloon, who insisted upon respectability of an advanced type. "What do dey wanna raise such a smoke about it fer?" demanded he of himself, disgusted with the attitude of the family. He saw no necessity that people should lose their equilibrium merely because their sister or their daughter had stayed away from home. Searching about in his mind for possible reasons for their conduct, he came upon the conclusion that Maggie's motives were cor.ect, but that the two others wished to snare him. He felt pursued.

The woman whom he had met in the hilarious hall showed a disposition to ridicule him. "A little, pale thing with no spirit," she said. "Did you note the expression of her eyes? There was something in them about pumpkin pie and virtue. That is a peculiar way the left corner of her mouth has of twitching, isn't it? Dear, dear, Pete, what are you coming to?"

Pete asserted at once that he never was very much interested in the girl. The woman interrupted him, laughing. "Oh, it's not of the slightest consequence to me, my dear young man. You needn't draw maps for my benefit. Why should I be concerned about it?" But Pete continued with his explanations. If he was laughed at for his tastes in women, he felt obliged to say that they were only temporary or indifferent ones.

The morning after Maggie had departed from home, Pete stood behind the bar. He was immaculate in white jacket and apron, and his hair was plastered over his brow with infinite correctness. No customers were in the place. Pete was twisting his napkined fist slowly in a beer glass, softly whistling to himself, and occasionally holding the object of his attention between his eyes and a few weak beams of sunlight that found their way over the thick screens and into the shaded rooms.

With lingering thoughts of the woman of brilliance and audacity, the bartender raised his head and stared through the varying cracks between the swaying bamboo doors. Suddenly the whistling pucker faded from his lips. He saw Maggie walking slowly past. He gave a great start, fearing for the previously mentioned eminent respectability of the place.

He threw a swift, nervous glance about him, all at once feeling guilty. No one was in the room. He went hastily over to the side door. Opening it and looking out, he perceived Maggie standing, as if undecided, at the corner. She was searching the place with her eyes. As she turned her face toward him, Pete beckoned to her hurriedly, intent upon returning with speed to a position behind the bar, and to the atmosphere of respectability upon which the proprietor insisted.

Maggie came to him, the anxious look disappearing from her face and a smile wreathing her lips. "Oh, Pete—" she began brightly.

The bartender made a violent gesture of impatience. "Oh, say," cried he vehemently. "What d' yeh wanna hang aroun' here fer? Do yer wanna git me inteh trouble?" he demanded with an air of injury.

Astonishment swept over the girl's features. "Why, Pete! Yehs tol' me—"

Pete's glance expressed profound irritation. His countenance reddened with the anger of a man whose respectability is being threatened. "Say, yehs makes me tired! See? What d' yeh wanna tag aroun' atter me fer? Yeh'll do me dirt wid d' ol' man an' dey'll be trouble! If he sees a woman roun' here he'll go crazy an' I'll lose me job! See? Ain' yehs got no sense? Don' be allus bodderin' me. See? Yer brudder came in here an' made trouble an' d' ol' man hadda put up fer it! An' now I'm done! See? I'm done."

The girl's eyes stared into his face. "Pete, don' yeh remem—"

"Oh, go ahn!" interrupted Pete, anticipating.

The girl seemed to have a struggle with herself. She was apparently bewildered and could not find speech. Finally she asked in a low voice, "But where kin I go?"

The question exasperated Pete beyond the powers of endurance. It was a direct attempt to give him some responsibility in a matter that did not concern him. In his indignation, he volunteered information. "Oh, go to hell!" cried he. He slammed the door furiously and returned, with an air of relief, to his respectability.

Maggie went away. She wandered aimlessly for several blocks. She stopped once and asked aloud a question of herself: "Who?" A man who was passing near her shoulder humorously took the questioning word as intended for him. "Eh! What? Who? Nobody! I didn't say anything," he laughingly said, and continued his way.

Soon the girl discovered that if she walked with such apparent aimlessness, some men looked at her with calculating eyes. She quickened her step, frightened. As a protection, she adopted a demeanor of intentness, as if going somewhere.

After a time, she left rattling avenues and passed between rows of houses with sternness, and stolidity stamped upon their features. She hung her head, for she felt their eyes grimly upon her.

Suddenly she came upon a stout gentleman in a silk hat and a chaste black coat, whose decorous row of buttons reached from his chin to his knees. The girl had heard of the grace of God and she decided to approach this man. His beaming, chubby face was a picture of benevolence and kindheartedness. His eyes shone good will.

But as the girl timidly accosted him, he made a convulsive movement and saved his respectability by a vigorous sidestep. He did not risk it to save a soul. For how was he to know that there was a soul before him that needed saving?

- xvii -

Upon a wet evening, several months later, two interminable rows of cars, pulled by slipping horses, jangled along a prominent side street. A dozen cabs, with coat-enshrouded drivers, clattered to and fro. Electric lights, whirring softly, shed a blurred radiance. A flower dealer, his feet tapping impatiently, his nose and his wares glistening with raindrops, stood behind an array of roses and chrysanthemums. Two or three theatres emptied a crowd upon the storm-swept sidewalks. Men pulled their hats over their eyebrows and raised their collars to their ears. Women shrugged impatient shoulders in their warm cloaks and stopped to arrange their skirts for a walk through the storm. People who had been constrained to comparative silence for two hours burst into a roar of conversation, their hearts still kindling from the glowings of the stage.

The sidewalks became tossing seas of umbrellas. Men stepped forth to hail cabs or cars, raising their fingers in varied forms of polite request or imperative demand. An endless procession wended toward elevated stations. An atmosphere of pleasure and prosperity seemed to hang over the throng, born, perhaps, of good clothes and of two hours in a place of forgetfulness.

In the mingled light and gloom of an adjacent park, a handful of wet wanderers, in attitudes of chronic dejection, were scattered among the benches.

A girl of the painted cohorts of the city went along the street. She threw changing glances at men who passed her, giving smiling invitations to those of rural or untaught pattern and usually seeming sedately unconscious of the men with a metropolitan seal upon their faces. Crossing glittering avenues, she went into the throng emerging from the places of forgetfulness. She hurried forward through the crowd as if intent upon reaching a distant home, bending forward in her handsome cloak, daintily lifting her skirts, and picking for her well-shod feet the dryer spots upon the sidewalks.

The restless doors of saloons, clashing to and fro, disclosed animated rows of men before bars and hurrying barkeepers. A concert hall gave to the street faint sounds of swift, machine-like music, as if a group of phantom musicians were hastening.

A tall young man, smoking a cigarette with a sublime air, strolled near the girl. He had on evening dress, a mustache, a chrysanthemum, and a look of *ennui*, all of which he kept carefully under his eye. Seeing the girl walk on as if such a young man as he was not in existence, he looked back, transfixed with interest. He stared glassily for a moment, but gave a slight convulsive start when he discerned that she was neither new, Parisian, nor theatrical. He wheeled about hastily and turned his stare into the air, like a sailor with a searchlight.

A stout gentleman, with pompous and philanthropic whiskers, went stolidly by, the broad of his back sneering at the girl. A belated man in business clothes, and in haste to catch a car, bounced against her shoulder. "Hi, there, Mary, I beg your pardon! Brace up, old girl." He grasped her arm to steady her, and then was away running down the middle of the street.

The girl walked on out of the realm of restaurants and saloons. She passed more glittering avenues and went into darker blocks than those where the crowd traveled.

A young man in light overcoat and Derby hat received a glance shot keenly from the eyes of the girl. He stopped and looked at her, thrusting his hands into his pockets and making a mocking smile curl his lips. "Come, now, old lady," he said, "you don't mean to tell me that you sized me up for a farmer?"

A laboring man marched along with bundles under his arms. To her remarks he replied, "It's a fine evenin', ain't it?"

She smiled squarely into the face of a boy who was hurrying by with his hands buried in his overcoat pockets, his blond locks bobbing on his youthful temples, and a cheery smile of unconcern upon his lips. He turned his head and smiled back at her, waving his hands. "Not this eve—some other eve."

A drunken man, reeling in her pathway, began to roar at her. "I ain' go' no money!" he shouted, in a dismal voice. He lurched on up the street, wailing to himself, "I ain' go' no money. Ba' luck. Ain' go' no more money."

The girl went into gloomy districts near the river, where the tall black factories shut in the street and only occasional broad beams of light fell across the sidewalks from saloons. In front of one of these places, whence came the sound of a violin vigorously scraped, the patter of feet on boards, and the ring of loud laughter, there stood a man with blotched features.

Farther on in the darkness, she met a ragged being with shifting, bloodshot eyes and grimy hands.

She went into the blackness of the final block. The shutters of the tall buildings were closed like grim lips. The structure seemed to have eyes that looked over them, beyond them, at other things. Afar off, the lights of the avenues glittered as if from an impossible distance. Streetcar bells jingled with a sound of merriment.

At the feet of the tall buildings appeared the deathly black hue of the river. Some hidden factory sent up a yellow glare, that lit for a moment the waters lapping oilily against timbers. The varied sounds of life, made joyous by distance and seeming unapproachableness, came faintly and died away to a silence.

- *xviii* -

In a partitioned-off section of a saloon sat a man with a half-dozen women, gleefully laughing, hovering about him. The man had arrived at that stage of drunkenness where affection is felt for the universe. "I'm good f'ler, girls," he said, convincingly. "I'm good f'ler. An'body trea's me right, I allus trea's zem right! See?"

The women nodded their heads approvingly. "To be sure," they cried in hearty chorus. "You're the kind of a man we like, Pete. You're outa sight! What yeh goin' to buy this time, dear?"

"An't'ing yehs wants!" said the man in an abandonment of good will. His countenance shone with the true spirit of benevolence. He was in the proper mood of missionaries. He would have fraternized with obscure Hottentots. And above all, he was overwhelmed in tenderness for his friends, who were all illustrious. "An't'ing yehs wants!" repeated he, waving his hands with beneficent recklessness. "I'm good f'ler, girls, an' if an'body trea's me right, I— Here," called he through an open door to a waiter, "bring girls drinks. What 'ill yehs have, girls? An't'ing yehs want."

The waiter glanced in with the disgusted look of the man who serves intoxicants for the man who takes too much of them. He nodded his head shortly at the order from each individual, and went.

"W' 're havin' great time," said the man. "I like you girls! Yer right sort! See?" He spoke at length and with feeling concerning the excellences of his assembled friends. "Don' try pull man's leg, but have a good time! Dass right! Dass way teh do! Now, if I s'ought yehs tryin' work me fer drinks, wouldn' buy notting! But yer right sort! Yehs know how ter

treat a f'ler, an' I stays by yehs till spen' las' cent! Dass right!
I'm good f'ler an' I knows when an'body trea's me right!"

Between the times of the arrival and departure of the
waiter, the man discoursed to the women on the tender regard he felt for all living things. He laid stress upon the
purity of his motives in all dealings with men in the world,
and spoke of the fervor of his friendship for those who were
amiable. Tears welled slowly from his eyes. His voice quavered when he spoke to his companions.

Once, when the waiter was about to depart with an empty
tray, the man drew a coin from his pocket and held it forth.
"Here," said he, quite magnificently, "here's quar'."

The waiter kept his hands on his tray. "I don't want yer
money," he said.

The other put forth the coin with tearful insistence. "Here's
quar'!" cried he. "Take 't! Yer goo' f'ler an' I wan' yehs
take 't!"

"Come, come, now," said the waiter, with the sullen air
of a man who is forced into giving advice. "Put yer mon'
in yer pocket! Yer loaded an' yehs on'y makes a fool of yerself."

As the waiter passed out of the door, the man turned
pathetically to the women. "He don' know I'm goo' f'ler,"
cried he dismally.

"Never you mind, Pete dear," said the woman of brilliance
and audacity, laying her hand with great affection upon his
arm. "Never you mind, old boy! We'll stay by you, dear!"

"Dass ri'!" cried the man, his face lighting up at the soothing tones of the woman's voice. "Dass ri'; I'm goo' f'ler, an'
w'en anyone trea's me ri', I trea's zem ri'! Shee?"

"Sure!" cried the women. "And we're not goin' back on
you, old man."

The man turned appealing eyes to the woman. He felt
that if he could be convicted of a contemptible action, he
would die. "Shay, Nell, I allus trea's yehs shquare, didn' I? I
allus been goo' f'ler wi' yehs, ain't I, Nell?"

"Sure you have, Pete," assented the woman. She delivered an oration to her companions. "Yessir, that's a fact.

Pete's a square fellah, he is. He never goes back on a friend. He's the right kind an' we stay by him, don't we, girls?"

"Sure!" they exclaimed. Looking lovingly at him, they raised their glasses and drank his health.

"Girlsh," said the man beseechingly, "I allus trea's yehs ri', didn' I? I'm goo' f'ler, ain' I, girlsh?"

"Sure!" again they chorused.

"Well," said he finally, "le's have nozzer drink, zen."

"That's right," hailed a woman, "that's right. Yer no bloomin' jay! Yer spends yer money like a man. Dat's right."

The man pounded the table with his quivering fists. "Yessir," he cried, with deep earnestness, as if someone disputed him. "I'm goo' f'ler, an' w'en anyone trea's me ri', I allus trea's—le's have nozzer drink." He began to beat the wood with his glass. "Shay!" howled he, growing suddenly impatient. As the waiter did not then come, the man swelled with wrath. "Shay!" howled he again. The waiter appeared at the door. "Bringsh drinksh," said the man.

The waiter disappeared with the orders.

"Zat f'ler fool!" cried the man. "He insul' me! I'm ge'man! Can' stan' be insul'! I'm goin' lick 'im when comes!"

"No, no!" cried the women, crowding about and trying to subdue him. "He's all right! He didn't mean anything! Let it go! He's a good fellah!"

"Di'n' he insul' me?" asked the man earnestly.

"No," said they. "Of course he didn't! He's all right!"

"Sure he didn' insul' me?" demanded the man, with deep anxiety in his voice.

"No, no! We know him! He's a good fellah. He didn't mean anything."

"Well, zen," said the man resolutely, "I'm go' 'pol'gize!"

When the waiter came, the man struggled to the middle of the floor. "Girlsh shed you insul' me! I shay—lie! I 'pol'-gize!"

"All right," said the waiter.

The man sat down. He felt a sleepy but strong desire to straighten things out and have a perfect understanding with everybody. "Nell, I allus trea's yeh shquare, di'n' I? Yeh likes me, don' yehs, Nell? I'm goo' f'ler?"

"Sure!" said the woman.

"Yeh knows I'm stuck on yehs, don' yehs, Nell?"

"Sure!" she repeated carelessly.

Overwhelmed by a spasm of drunken adoration, he drew two or three bills from his pocket and, with the trembling fingers of an offering priest, laid them on the table before the woman. "Yehs knows yehs kin have all I got, 'cause I'm stuck on yehs, Nell, I—I'm stuck on yehs, Nell—buy drinksh— we're havin' grea' time—w'en anyone trea's me ri'—I—Nell— we're havin' heluva—time."

Presently he went to sleep with his swollen face fallen forward on his chest.

The women drank and laughed, not heeding the slumbering man in the corner. Finally he lurched forward and fell groaning to the floor.

The women screamed in disgust and drew back their skirts. "Come ahn!" cried one, starting up angrily, "let's get out of here."

The woman of brilliance and audacity stayed behind, taking up the bills and stuffing them into a deep, irregularly shaped pocket. A guttural snore from the recumbent man caused her to turn and look down at him. She laughed. "What a fool!" she said, and went.

The smoke from the lamps settled heavily down in the little compartment, obscuring the way out. The smell of oil, stifling in its intensity, pervaded the air. The wine from an overturned glass dripped softly down upon the blotches on the man's neck.

- *xix* -

In a room a woman sat at a table eating like a fat monk in a picture.

A soiled, unshaven man pushed open the door and entered. "Well," said he, "Mag's dead."

"What?" said the woman, her mouth filled with bread.

"Mag's dead," repeated the man.

"Deh blazes she is!" said the woman. She continued her meal.

When she finished her coffee, she began to weep. "I kin remember when her two feet was no bigger dan yer t'umb, and she weared worsted boots," moaned she.

"Well, what a' dat?" said the man.

"I kin remember when she weared worsted boots," she cried.

The neighbors began to gather in the hall, staring in at the weeping woman as if watching the contortions of a dying dog. A dozen women entered and lamented with her. Under their busy hands, the room took on that appalling appearance of neatness and order with which death is greeted.

Suddenly the door opened and a woman in a black gown rushed in with outstretched arms. "Ah, poor Mary!" she cried, and tenderly embraced the moaning one. "Ah, what ter'ble affliction is dis!" continued she. Her vocabulary was derived from mission churches. "Me poor Mary, how I feel fer yehs! Ah, what a ter'ble affliction is a disobed'ent chile." Her good, motherly face was wet with tears. She trembled in eagerness to express her sympathy.

The mourner sat with bowed head, rocking her body heavily to and fro, and crying out in a high, strained voice that sounded like a dirge on some forlorn pipe. "I kin remember when she weared worsted boots, an' her two feets was no bigger dan yer t'umb, an' she weared worsted boots, Miss Smith," she cried, raising her streaming eyes.

"Ah, me poor Mary!" sobbed the woman in black. With low, coddling cries, she sank on her knees by the mourner's chair, and put her arms about her. The other women began to groan in different keys.

"Yer poor, misguided chil' is gone now, Mary, an' let us hope it's fer deh bes'. Yeh'll fergive her now, Mary, won't yehs, dear, all her disobed'ence? All her t'ankless behavior to her mudder an' all her badness? She's gone where her ter'ble sins will be judged."

The woman in black raised her face and paused. The inevitable sunlight came streaming in at the window and shed a ghastly cheerfulness upon the faded hues of the room. Two or three of the spectators were sniffing, and one was weeping loudly.

The mourner arose and staggered into the other room. In a moment she emerged with a pair of faded baby shoes held in the hollow of her hand. "I kin remember when she used to wear dem!" cried she. The women burst anew into cries as if they had all been stabbed. The mourner turned to the soiled and unshaven man. "Jimmie, boy, go git yer sister! Go git yer sister an' we'll put deh boots on her feets!"

"Dey won't fit her now, yeh fool," said the man.

"Go git yer sister, Jimmie!" shrieked the woman, confronting him fiercely.

The man swore sullenly. He went over to a corner and slowly began to put on his coat. He took his hat and went out, with a dragging, reluctant step.

The woman in black came forward and again besought the mourner. "Yeh'll fergive her, Mary! Yeh'll fergive yer bad, bad chil'! Her life was a curse an' her days were black, an' yeh'll fergive yer bad girl? She's gone where her sins will be judged."

"She's gone where her sins will be judged!" cried the other women, like a choir at a funeral.

"Deh Lord gives and deh Lord takes away," said the woman in black, raising her eyes to the sunbeams.

"Deh Lord gives and deh Lord takes away," responded the others.

"Yeh'll fergive her, Mary?" pleaded the woman in black.

The mourner essayed to speak, but her voice gave way. She shook her great shoulders frantically, in an agony of grief. The tears seemed to scald her face. Finally her voice came and arose in a scream of pain. "Oh, yes, I'll fergive her! I'll fergive her!"

# The Men in the Storm

THE blizzard began to swirl great clouds of snow along the streets, sweeping it down from the roofs, and up from the pavements, until the faces of pedestrians tingled and burned as from a thousand needle-prickings. Those on the walks huddled their necks closely in the collars of their coats, and went along stooping like a race of aged people. The drivers of vehicles hurried their horses furiously on their way. They were made more cruel by the exposure of their position, aloft on high seats. The streetcars, bound uptown, went slowly, the horses slipping and straining in the spongy brown mass that lay between the rails. The drivers, muffled to the eyes, stood erect, facing the wind, models of grim philosophy. Overhead, trains rumbled and roared, and the dark structure of the elevated railroad, stretching over the avenue, dripped little streams and drops of water upon the mud and snow beneath.

All the clatter of the street was softened by the masses that lay upon the cobbles, until, even to one who looked from a window, it became important music, a melody of life made necessary to the ear by the dreariness of the pitiless beat and sweep of the storm. Occasionally one could see black figures of men busily shoveling the white drifts from the walks. The sounds from their labor created new recollections of rural experiences which every man manages to have in a measure. Later, the immense windows of the shops became aglow with light, throwing great beams of orange and yellow upon the pavement. They were infinitely cheerful, yet in a way they accentuated the force and discomfort of the storm, and gave a meaning to the pace of the people and the vehicles, scores of pedestrians and drivers, wretched with cold faces, necks, and feet, speeding for scores of unknown doors and entrances, scattering to an infinite variety of shelters, to places which the imagination made warm with the familiar colors of home.

There was an absolute expression of hot dinners in the pace of the people. If one dared to speculate upon the destination of those who came trooping, he lost himself in a maze of social calculation; he might fling a handful of sand and attempt to follow the flight of each particular grain. But as to the suggestion of hot dinners, he was in firm lines of thought, for it was upon every hurrying face. It is a matter of tradition; it is from the tales of childhood. It comes forth with every storm.

However, in a certain part of a dark west-side street, there was a collection of men to whom these things were as if they were not. In this street was located a charitable house where for five cents the homeless of the city could get a bed at night, and in the morning coffee and bread.

During the afternoon of the storm, the whirling snows acted as drivers, as men with whips, and at half-past three the walk before the closed doors of the house was covered with wanderers of the street, waiting. For some distance on either side of the place they could be seen lurking in the doorways and behind projecting parts of buildings, gathering in close bunches in an effort to get warm. A covered wagon drawn up near the curb sheltered a dozen of them. Under the stairs that led to the elevated-railway station, there were six or eight, their hands stuffed deep in their pockets, their shoulders stooped, jiggling their feet. Others always could be seen coming, a strange procession, some slouching along with the characteristic hopeless gait of professional strays, some coming with hesitating steps, wearing the air of men to whom this sort of thing was new.

It was an afternoon of incredible length. The snow, blowing in twisting clouds, sought out the men in their meager hiding places, and skillfully beat in among them, drenching their persons with showers of fine, stinging flakes. They

crowded together, muttering, and fumbling in their pockets
to get their red, inflamed wrists covered by the cloth.

Newcomers usually halted at one end of the groups and
addressed a question, perhaps much as a matter of form:
"Is it open yet?"

Those who had been waiting inclined to take the ques-
tioner seriously and became contemptuous. "No; do yeh
think we'd be standin' here?"

The gathering swelled in numbers steadily and persistently. One could always see them coming, trudging slowly
through the storm.

Finally, the little snow plains in the street began to as-
sume a leaden hue from the shadows of evening. The buildings upreared gloomily save where various windows became
brilliant figures of light, that made shimmers and splashes
of yellow on the snow. A street lamp on the curb struggled
to illuminate, but it was reduced to impotent blindness by
the swift gusts of sleet crusting its panes.

In this half-darkness, the men began to come from their
shelter places and mass in front of the doors of charity.
They were of all types, but the nationalities were mostly
American, German, and Irish. Many were strong, healthy,
clear-skinned fellows, with that stamp of countenance which
is not frequently seen upon seekers after charity. There were
men of undoubted patience, industry, and temperance, who,
in time of ill fortune, do not habitually turn to rail at the
state of society, snarling at the arrogance of the rich, and
bemoaning the cowardice of the poor, but who at these times
are apt to wear a sudden and singular meekness, as if they
saw the world's progress marching from them, and were
trying to perceive where they had failed, what they had
lacked, to be thus vanquished in the race. Then there were
others, of the shifting Bowery element, who were used to
paying ten cents for a place to sleep, but who now came
here because it was cheaper.

But they were all mixed in one mass so thoroughly that
one could not have discerned the different elements, but
for the fact that the laboring men, for the most part, re-

mained silent and impassive in the blizzard, their eyes fixed on the windows of the house, statues of patience.

The sidewalk soon became completely blocked by the bodies of the men. They pressed close to one another like sheep in a winter's gale, keeping one another warm by the heat of their bodies. The snow came upon this compressed group of men until, directly from above, it might have appeared like a heap of snow-covered merchandise, if it were not for the fact that the crowd swayed gently with a unanimous rhythmical motion. It was wonderful to see how the snow lay upon the heads and shoulders of these men, in little ridges an inch thick perhaps in places, the flakes steadily adding drop and drop, precisely as they fall upon the unresisting grass of the fields. The feet of the men were all wet and cold, and the wish to warm them accounted for the slow, gentle rhythmical motion. Occasionally, some man whose ear or nose tingled acutely from the cold winds would wriggle down until his head was protected by the shoulders of his companions.

There was a continuous murmuring discussion as to the probability of the doors being speedily opened. They persistently lifted their eyes toward the windows. One could hear little combats of opinion.

"There's a light in th' winder!"

"Naw; it's a reflection f'm across th' way."

"Well, didn't I see 'em light it?"

"You did?"

"I did!"

"Well, then, that settles it!"

As the time approached when they expected to be allowed to enter, the men crowded to the doors in an unspeakable crush, jamming and wedging in a way that, it seemed, would crack bones. They surged heavily against the building in a powerful wave of pushing shoulders. Once a rumor flitted among all the tossing heads.

"They can't open th' door! Th' fellers er smack up agin 'em."

Then a dull roar of rage came from the men on the outskirts; but all the time they strained and pushed until it appeared to be impossible for those that they cried out against to do anything but be crushed into pulp.

"Ah, git away f'm th' door!"

"Git outa that!"

"Throw 'em out!"

"Kill 'em!"

"Say, fellers, now, what th' 'ell? G've 'em a chance t' open th' door!"

"Yeh damn pigs, give 'em a chance t' open th' door!"

Men in the outskirts of the crowd occasionally yelled when a boot heel of one of trampling feet crushed on their freezing extremities.

"Git off me feet, yeh clumsy tarrier!"

"Say, don't stand on me feet! Walk on th' ground!"

A man near the doors suddenly shouted, "O-o-oh! Le' me out—le' me out!" And another, a man of infinite valor, once twisted his head so as to half-face those who were pushing behind him. "Quit yer shovin', yeh"—and he delivered a volley of the most powerful and singular invective, straight into the faces of the men behind him. It was as if he was hammering the noses of them with curses of triple brass. His face, red with rage, could be seen, upon it an expression of sublime disregard of consequences. But nobody cared to reply to his imprecations; it was too cold. Many of them snickered, and all continued to push.

In occasional pauses of the crowd's movement, the men had opportunities to make jokes; usually grim things, and no doubt very uncouth. Nevertheless, they were notable—one does not expect to find the quality of humor in a heap of old clothes under a snowdrift.

The winds seemed to grow fiercer as time wore on. Some of the gusts of snow that came down on the close collection of heads cut like knives and needles, and the men huddled, and swore, not like dark assassins, but in a sort of American fashion, grimly and desperately, it is true, but yet with a wondrous undereffect, indefinable and mystic, as if there was some kind of humor in this catastrophe, in this situation in a night of snow-laden winds.

Once the window of the huge dry-goods shop across the street furnished material for a few moments of forgetfulness. In the brilliantly lighted space appeared the figure of a man. He was rather stout and very well clothed. His beard was fashioned charmingly after that of the Prince of Wales. He stood in an attitude of magnificent reflection. He slowly stroked his mustache with a certain grandeur of manner, and looked down at the snow-encrusted mob. From below, there was denoted a supreme complacence in him. It seemed that the sight operated inversely, and enabled him to more clearly regard his own delightful environment.

One of the mob chanced to turn his head, and perceived the figure in the window. "Hello, look-it 'is whiskers," he said genially.

Many of the men turned then, and a shout went up. They called to him in all strange keys. They addressed him in every manner, from familiar and cordial greetings to carefully worded advice concerning changes in his personal appearance. The man presently fled, and the mob chuckled ferociously, like ogres who had just devoured something.

They turned then to serious business. Often they addressed the stolid front of the house.

"Oh, let us in, fer Gawd's sake!"

"Let us in, or we'll all drop dead!"

"Say, what's th' use o' keepin' us poor Indians out in th' cold?"

And always someone was saying, "Keep off my feet."

The crushing of the crowd grew terrific toward the last. The men, in keen pain from the blasts, began almost to fight. With the pitiless whirl of snow upon them, the battle for shelter was going to the strong. It became known that the basement door at the foot of a little steep flight of stairs was the one to be opened, and they jostled and heaved in this direction like laboring fiends. One could hear them panting and groaning in their fierce exertion.

Usually someone in the front ranks was protesting to those

in the rear. "O-o-ow! Oh, say now, fellers, let up, will yeh?
Do yeh wanta kill somebody?"

A policeman arrived and went into the midst of them,
scolding and berating, occasionally theatening, but using no
force but that of his hands and shoulders against these
men who were only struggling to get in out of the storm.
His decisive tones rang out sharply: "Stop that pushin' back
there! Come, boys, don't push! Stop that! Here you, quit
yer shovin'! Cheese that!"

When the door below was opened, a thick stream of men
forced a way down the stairs, which were of an extraordinary
narrowness, and seemed only wide enough for one at a time.
Yet they somehow went down almost three abreast. It was
a difficult and painful operation. The crowd was like a turbu-
lent water forcing itself through one tiny outlet. The men in
the rear, excited by the success of the others, made frantic
exertions, for it seemed that this large band would more than
fill the quarters, and that many would be left upon the pavements. It would be disastrous to be of the last, and accordingly men with the snow biting their faces writhed and
twisted with their might. One expected that, from the tremendous pressure, the narrow passage to the basement door would
be so choked and clogged with human limbs and bodies
that movement would be impossible. Once indeed the crowd
was forced to stop, and a cry went along that a man had
been injured at the foot of the stairs. But presently the slow
movement began again, and the policeman fought at the top
of the flight to ease the pressure of those that were going
down.

A reddish light from a window fell upon the faces of the
men when they, in turn, arrived at the last three steps and
were about to enter. One could then note a change of
expression that had come over their features. As they stood
thus upon the threshold of their hopes, they looked suddenly
contented and complacent. The fire had passed from their
eyes and the snarl had vanished from their lips. The very
force of the crowd in the rear, which had previously vexed
them, was regarded from another point of view, for it now

made it inevitable that they should go through the little doors into the place that was cheery and warm with light.

The tossing crowd on the sidewalk grew smaller and smaller. The snow beat with merciless persistence upon the bowed heads of those who waited. The wind drove it up from the pavements in frantic forms of winding white, and it seethed in circles about the huddled forms passing in one by one, three by three, out of the storm.

~~~~~~~~~~~~~~~~~~~~~~~~~~~~~~~~~~~~~

# *The Monster*

### *- i -*

LITTLE JIM was, for the time, Engine Number 36, and he was making the run between Syracuse and Rochester. He was fourteen minutes behind time, and the throttle was wide open. In consequence, when he swung around the curve at the flower bed, a wheel of his cart destroyed a peony. Number 36 slowed down at once and looked guiltily at his father, who was mowing the lawn. The doctor had his back to this accident, and he continued to pace slowly to and fro, pushing the mower.

Jim dropped the tongue of the cart. He looked at his father and at the broken flower. Finally he went to the peony and tried to stand it on its pins, resuscitated, but the spine of it was hurt, and it would only hang limply from his hand. Jim could do no reparation. He looked again toward his father.

He went onto the lawn, very slowly, and kicking wretchedly at the turf. Presently his father came along with the whirring machine, while the sweet, new grass blades spun from the knives. In a low voice, Jim said, "Pa!"

The doctor was shaving this lawn as if it were a priest's chin. All during the season he had worked at it in the coolness and peace of the evenings after supper. Even in the shadow of the cherry trees the grass was strong and healthy. Jim raised his voice a trifle. "Pa!"

The doctor paused, and with the howl of the machine no longer occupying the sense, one could hear the robins in the cherry trees arranging their affairs. Jim's hands were behind his back, and sometimes his fingers clasped and unclasped. Again he said, "Pa!" The child's fresh and rosy lip was lowered.

The doctor stared down at his son, thrusting his head forward and frowning attentively. "What is it, Jimmie?"

"Pa!" repeated the child at length. Then he raised his finger and pointed at the flower bed. "There!"

"What?" said the doctor, frowning more. "What is it, Jim?"

After a period of silence, during which the child may have undergone a severe mental tumult, he raised his finger and repeated his former word: "There!" The father had respected this silence with perfect courtesy. Afterward, his glance carefully followed the direction indicated by the child's finger, but he could see nothing which explained to him. "I don't understand what you mean, Jimmie," he said.

It seemed that the importance of the whole thing had taken away the boy's vocabulary. He could only reiterate, "There!"

The doctor mused upon the situation, but he could make nothing of it. At last he said, "Come, show me."

Together they crossed the lawn toward the flower bed. At some yards from the broken peony, Jimmie began to lag. "There!" The word came almost breathlessly.

"Where?" said the doctor.

Jimmie kicked at the grass. "There!" he replied.

The doctor was obliged to go forward alone. After some trouble he found the subject of the incident, the broken flower. Turning then, he saw the child lurking at the rear and scanning his countenance.

The father reflected. After a time he said, "Jimmie, come here." With an infinite modesty of demeanor, the child came forward. "Jimmie, how did this happen?"

The child answered, "Now—I was playin' train—and—now —I runned over it."

"You were doing what?"

"I was playin' train."

The father reflected again. "Well, Jimmie," he said slowly, "I guess you had better not play train any more today. Do you think you had better?"

"No, sir," said Jimmie.

During the delivery of the judgment, the child had not faced his father, and afterward he went away, with his head lowered, shuffling his feet.

- *ii* -

It was apparent from Jimmie's manner that he felt some kind of desire to efface himself. He went down to the stable. Henry Johnson, the Negro who cared for the doctor's horses, was sponging the buggy. He grinned fraternally when he saw Jimmie coming. These two were pals. In regard to almost everything in life they seemed to have minds precisely alike. Of course there were points of emphatic divergence. For instance, it was plain from Henry's talk that he was a very handsome Negro, and he was known to be a light, a weight, and an eminence in the suburb of the town where lived the larger number of the Negroes, and obviously this glory was over Jimmie's horizon; but he vaguely appreciated it and paid deference to Henry for it, mainly because Henry appreciated it and deferred to himself. However, on all points of conduct as related to the doctor, who was the moon, they were in complete but unexpressed understanding. Whenever Jimmie became the victim of an eclipse, he went to the stable to solace himself with Henry's crimes. Henry, with the elasticity of his race, could usually provide a sin to place himself on a footing with the disgraced one. Perhaps he would remember that he had forgotten to put the hitching strap in the back of the buggy on some recent occasion, and had been reprimanded by the doctor. Then these two would commune subtly and without words concerning their moon, holding themselves sympathetically as people who had committed similar treasons. On the other hand, Henry would sometimes choose to absolutely repudiate this idea, and when Jimmie appeared in his shame would bully him most virtuously, preaching with assurance the precepts of the doctor's creed, and pointing out to Jimmie all his abominations. Jimmie did not discover that this was odious in his comrade. He accepted it and lived in its shadow with humility, merely trying to conciliate the saintly Henry with acts of deference. Won by this attitude, Henry would sometimes allow the child to enjoy the felicity of squeezing the sponge over a buggy wheel, even when Jimmie was still gory from unspeakable deeds.

Whenever Henry dwelt for a time in sackcloth, Jimmie did not patronize him at all. This was a justice of his age, his condition. He did not know. Besides, Henry could drive a horse, and Jimmie had a full sense of this sublimity. Henry personally conducted the moon during the splendid journeys through the country roads, where farms spread on all sides, with sheep, cows, and other marvels abounding.

"Hello, Jim!" said Henry, poising his sponge. Water was dripping from the buggy. Sometimes the horses in the stalls stamped thunderingly on the pine floor. There was an atmosphere of hay and of harness.

For a minute Jimmie refused to take an interest in anything. He was very downcast. He could not even feel the wonders of wagon-washing. Henry, while at work, narrowly observed him.

"Your pop done wallop yer, didn't he?" he said at last.

"No," said Jimmie defensively, "he didn't."

After this casual remark, Henry continued his labor, with a scowl of occupation. Presently he said, "I done tol' yer many's th' time not to go a-foolin' an' a-projjeckin' with them flowers. Yer pop don't like it nohow." As a matter of fact, Henry had never mentioned flowers to the boy.

Jimmie preserved a gloomy silence, so Henry began to use seductive wiles in this affair of washing a wagon. It was not until he began to spin a wheel on the tree, and the sprinkling water flew everywhere, that the boy was visibly moved. He had been seated on the sill of the carriage-house door, but at the beginning of this ceremony, he arose and circled toward the buggy, with an interest that slowly consumed the remembrance of a late disgrace.

Johnson could then display all the dignity of a man whose duty it was to protect Jimmie from a splashing. "Look out, boy! Look out! You done gwi' spile yer pants. I raikon your mommer don't 'low this foolishness, she know it. I ain't gwi' have you round yere spilin' yer pants, an' have Mis' Trescott light on me pressen'ly. 'Deed I ain't."

He spoke with an air of great irritation, but he was not annoyed at all. This tone was merely a part of his importance. In reality he was always delighted to have the child there to witness the business of the stable. For one thing, Jimmie was invariably overcome with reverence when he was told how beautifully a harness was polished or a horse groomed. Henry explained each detail of this kind with unction, procuring great joy from the child's admiration.

- *iii* -

After Johnson had taken his supper in the kitchen, he went to his loft in the carriage house and dressed himself with much care. No belle of a court circle could bestow more mind on a toilet than did Johnson. On second thought, he was more like a priest arraying himself for some parade of the church. As he emerged from his room and sauntered down the carriage drive, no one would have suspected him of ever having washed a buggy.

It was not altogether a matter of the lavender trousers, nor yet the straw hat with its bright silk band. The change was somewhere far in the interior of Henry. But there was no cakewalk hyperbole in it. He was simply a quiet, well-bred gentleman of position, wealth, and other necessary achievements out for an evening stroll, and he had never washed a wagon in his life.

In the morning, when in his working clothes, he had met a friend—"Hello, Pete!" "Hello, Henry!" Now, in his effulgence, he encountered this same friend. His bow was not at all haughty. If it expressed anything, it expressed consummate generosity—"Good evenin', Misteh Washington." Pete, who was very dirty, being at work in a potato patch, responded in a mixture of abasement and appreciation—"Good evenin', Misteh Johnsing."

The shimmering blue of the electric arc lamps was strong in the main street of the town. At numerous points it was conquered by the orange glare of the outnumbering gaslights in the windows of shops. Through this radiant lane moved a crowd, which culminated in a throng before the post office, awaiting the distribution of the evening mails. Occasionally there came into it a shrill electric streetcar, the motor singing like a cageful of grasshoppers, and possessing a great gong that clanged forth both warnings and simple noise. At the little theatre, which was a varnish-and-red-plush miniature of one of the famous New York theatres, a company of strollers was to play *East Lynne*. The young men of the town were mainly gathered at the corners, in distinctive groups which expressed various shades and lines of chumship, and had little to do with any social gradations. There they discussed everything with critical insight, passing the whole town in review as it swarmed in the street. When the gongs of the electric cars ceased for a moment to harry the ears, there could be heard the sound of the feet of the leisurely crowd on the bluestone pavement, and it was like the peaceful evening lashing at the shore of a lake. At the foot of the hill, where two lines of maples sentineled the way, an electric lamp glowed high among the embowering branches and made most wonderful shadow etchings on the road below it.

When Johnson appeared amid the throng, a member of one of the profane groups at a corner instantly telegraphed news of this extraordinary arrival to his companions. They hailed him. "Hello, Henry! Going to walk for a cake tonight?"

"Ain't he smooth?"

"Why, you've got that cake right in your pocket, Henry!"

"Throw out your chest a little more."

Henry was not ruffled in any way by these quiet admonitions and compliments. In reply, he laughed a supremely good-natured, chuckling laugh, which nevertheless expressed an underground complacency of superior metal.

Young Griscom, the lawyer, was just emerging from Reifsnyder's barber shop, rubbing his chin contentedly. On the steps he dropped his hand and looked with wide eyes into the crowd. Suddenly he bolted back into the shop. "Wow!" he cried to the parliament. "You ought to see the coon that's coming!"

Reifsnyder and his assistant instantly poised their razors high and turned toward the window. Two belathered heads reared from the chairs. The electric shine in the street caused an effect like water to them who looked through the glass from the yellow glamour of Reifsnyder's shop. In fact, the people without resembled the inhabitants of a great aquarium that here had a square pane in it. Presently, into this frame swam the graceful form of Henry Johnson.

"Chee!" said Reifsnyder. He and his assistants with one accord threw their obligations to the winds and, leaving their lathered victims helpless, advanced to the window. "Ain't he a taisy?" said Reifsnyder, marveling.

But the man in the first chair, with a grievance in his mind, had found a weapon. "Why, that's only Henry Johnson, you blamed idiots! Come on now, Reif, and shave me. What do you think I am—a mummy?"

Reifsnyder turned, in a great excitement. "I bait you any money that vas not Henry Johnson! Henry Johnson! Rats!" The scorn put into this last word made it an explosion. "That man was a Pullman-car porter or someding. How could that be Henry Johnson?" he demanded turbulently. "You vas crazy."

The man in the first chair faced the barber in a storm of

indignation. "Didn't I give him those lavender trousers?" he roared.

And young Griscom, who had remained attentively at the window, said, "Yes, I guess that was Henry. It looked like him."

"Oh, vell," said Reifsnyder, returning to his business, "if you think so! Oh, vell!" He implied that he was submitting for the sake of amiability.

Finally the man in the second chair, mumbling from a mouth made timid by adjacent lather, said, "That was Henry Johnson all right. Why, he always dresses like that when he wants to make a front! He's the biggest dude in town—anybody knows that."

"Chinger!" said Reifsnyder.

Henry was not at all oblivious of the wake of wondering ejaculation that streamed out behind him. On other occasions he had reaped this same joy, and he always had an eye for the demonstration. With a face beaming with happiness, he turned away from the scene of his victories into a narrow side street, where the electric light still hung high, but only to exhibit a row of tumbledown houses leaning together like paralytics.

The saffron Miss Bella Farragut, in a calico frock, had been crouched on the front stoop, gossiping at long range, but she espied her approaching caller at a distance. She dashed around the corner of the house, galloping like a horse. Henry saw it all, but he preserved the polite demeanor of a guest when a waiter spills claret down his cuff. In this awkward situation he was simply perfect.

The duty of receiving Mr. Johnson fell upon Mrs. Farragut, because Bella, in another room, was scrambling wildly into her best gown. The fat old woman met him with a great ivory smile, sweeping back with the door, and bowing low. "Walk in, Misteh Johnson, walk in. How is you dis ebenin', Misteh Johnson, how is you?"

Henry's face showed like a reflector as he bowed and bowed, bending almost from his head to his ankles. "Good evenin', Mis' Fa'gut, good evenin'. How is you dis evenin'? Is all you' folks well, Mis' Fa'gut?"

After a great deal of kowtow, they were planted in two chairs opposite each other in the living room. Here they exchanged the most tremendous civilities, until Miss Bella swept into the room, when there was more kowtow on all sides, and a smiling show of teeth that was like an illumination.

The cooking stove was of course in this drawing room, and on the fire was some kind of long-winded stew. Mrs. Farragut was obliged to arise and attend to it from time to time. Also young Sim came in and went to bed on his pallet in the corner. But to all these domesticities the three maintained an absolute dumbness. They bowed and smiled and ignored and imitated until a late hour, and if they had been the occupants of the most gorgeous salon in the world they could not have been more like three monkeys.

After Henry had gone, Bella, who encouraged herself in the appropriation of phrases, said, "Oh, Ma, isn't he divine?"

- *iv* -

A Saturday evening was a sign always for a larger crowd to parade the thoroughfare. In summer the band played until ten o'clock in the little park. Most of the young men of the town affected to be superior to this band, even to despise it; but in the still and fragrant evenings they invariably turned out in force, because the girls were sure to attend this concert, strolling slowly over the grass, linked closely in pairs, or preferably in threes, in the curious public dependence upon one another which was their inheritance. There was no particular social aspect to this gathering, save that group regarded group with interest, but mainly in silence. Perhaps one girl would nudge another girl and suddenly say, "Look! There goes Gertie Hodgson and her sister!" And they would appear to regard this as an event of importance.

On a particular evening, a rather large company of young men were gathered on the sidewalk that edged the park. They remained thus beyond the borders of the festivities because of their dignity, which would not exactly allow them to appear in anything which was so much fun for the younger lads. These latter were careering madly through the crowd, precipitating minor accidents from time to time, but usually fleeing like mist swept by the wind before retribution could lay hands upon them.

The band played a waltz which involved a gift of prominence to the bass horn, and one of the young men on the sidewalk said that the music reminded him of the new engines on the hill pumping water into the reservoir. A similarity of this kind was not inconceivable, but the young man did not say it because he disliked the band's playing. He said it because it was fashionable to say that manner of thing concerning the band. However, over in the stand, Billie Harris, who played the snare drum, was always surrounded by a throng of boys, who adored his every whack.

After the mails from New York and Rochester had been finally distributed, the crowd from the post office added to the mass already in the park. The wind waved the leaves of the maples, and high in the air, the blue-burning globes of the arc lamps caused the wonderful traceries of leaf shadows on the ground. When the light fell upon the upturned face of a girl, it caused it to glow with a wonderful pallor. A policeman came suddenly from the darkness and chased a gang of obstreperous little boys. They hooted him from a distance. The leader of the band had some of the mannerisms of the great musicians, and during a period of silence, the crowd smiled when they saw him raise his hand to his brow, stroke it sentimentally, and glance upward with a look of poetic anguish. In the shivering light, which gave to the park an effect like a great, vaulted hall, the throng swarmed, with a gentle murmur of dresses switching the turf, and with a steady hum of voices.

Suddenly, without preliminary bars, there arose from afar the great, hoarse roar of a factory whistle. It raised and swelled to a sinister note, and then it sang on the night wind one long call that held the crowd in the park immovable, speechless. The bandmaster had been about to vehemently let fall his hand to start the band on a thundering career through a popular march, but, smitten by this giant voice from the night, his hand dropped slowly to his knee, and, his mouth agape, he looked at his men in silence. The cry died away to a wail and then to stillness. It released the muscles of the company of young men on the sidewalk, who had been like statues, posed eagerly, lithely, their ears turned. And then they wheeled upon each other simultaneously, and in a single explosion, they shouted, "One!"

Again the sound swelled in the night and roared its long, ominous cry, and as it died away, the crowd of young men wheeled upon each other and, in chorus, yelled, "Two!"

There was a moment of breathless waiting. Then they bawled, "Second district!" In a flash the company of indolent and cynical young men had vanished like a snowball disrupted by dynamite.

- *v* -

Jake Rogers was the first man to reach the home of Tuscarora Hose Company Number Six. He had wrenched his key from his pocket as he tore down the street, and he jumped at the spring lock like a demon. As the doors flew back before his hands, he leaped and kicked the wedges from a pair of wheels, loosened a tongue from its clasp, and in the glare of the electric light which the town placed before each of its hose houses, the next comers beheld the spectacle of Jake Rogers bent like hickory in the manfulness of his pulling, and the heavy cart was moving slowly toward the doors. Four men joined him at the time, and as they swung with the cart out into the street, dark figures sped toward them from the ponderous shadows in back of the electric lamps. Some set up the inevitable question: "What district?"

"Second," was replied to them in a compact howl. Tuscarora Hose Company Number Six swept on a perilous wheel into Niagara Avenue, and as the men, attached to the cart by the rope which had been payed out from the windlass under the tongue, pulled madly in their fervor and abandon, the gong under the axle clanged incitingly. And sometimes the same cry was heard: "What district?"

"Second."

On a grade, Johnnie Thorpe fell, and exercising a singular muscular ability, rolled out in time from the track of the oncoming wheel, and arose, disheveled and aggrieved, casting a look of mournful disenchantment upon the black crowd that poured after the machine. The cart seemed to be the apex of a dark wave that was whirling as if it had been a broken dam. Behind the lad were stretches of lawn, and in that direction front doors were banged by men who hoarsely shouted out into the clamorous avenue, "What district?"

At one of these houses, a woman came to the door bearing a lamp, shielding her face from its rays with her hands. Across the cropped grass, the avenue represented to her a kind of black torrent, upon which, nevertheless, fled numerous miraculous figures upon bicycles. She did not know that the towering light at the corner was continuing its nightly whine.

Suddenly a little boy somersaulted around the corner of the house as if he had been projected down a flight of stairs by a catapultian boot. He halted himself in front of the house by dint of a rather extraordinary evolution with his legs. "Oh, Ma," he gasped, "can I go? Can I, Ma?"

She straightened with the coldness of the exterior mother judgment, although the hand that held the lamp trembled slightly. "No, Willie; you had better come to bed."

Instantly he began to buck and fume like a mustang. "Oh, Ma," he cried, contorting himself, "oh, Ma, can't I go? Please, Ma, can't I go? Can't I go, Ma?"

"It's half-past nine now, Willie."

He ended by wailing out a compromise: "Well, just down to the corner, Ma? Just down to the corner?"

From the avenue came the sound of rushing men who wildly shouted. Somebody had grappled the bell rope in the Methodist church, and now over the town rang this solemn and terrible voice, speaking from the clouds. Moved from its peaceful business, this bell gained a new spirit in the portentous night, and it swung the heart to and fro, up and down, with each peal of it.

"Just down to the corner, Ma?"

"Willie, it's half-past nine now."

- vi -

The outlines of the house of Dr. Trescott had faded quietly into the evening, hiding a shape such as we call Queen Anne against the pall of the blackened sky. The neighborhood was at this time so quiet, and seemed so devoid of obstructions, that Hannigan's dog thought it a good opportunity to prowl in forbidden precincts, and so came and pawed Trescott's lawn, growling, and considering himself a formidable beast. Later, Peter Washington strolled past the house and whistled, but there was no dim light shining from Henry's loft, and presently Peter went his way. The rays from the street, creeping in silvery waves over the grass, caused the row of shrubs along the drive to throw a clear, bold shade.

A wisp of smoke came from one of the windows at the end of the house and drifted quietly into the branches of a cherry tree. Its companions followed it in slowly increasing numbers, and finally there was a current controlled by invisible banks which poured into the fruit-laden boughs of the cherry tree. It was no more to be noted than if a troop of dim and silent gray monkeys had been climbing a grapevine into the clouds.

After a moment, the window brightened as if the four panes of it had been stained with blood, and a quick ear might have been led to imagine the fire imps calling and calling, clan joining clan, gathering to the colors. From the street, however, the house maintained its dark quiet, insisting to a passer-by that it was the safe dwelling of people who chose to retire early to tranquil dreams. No one could have heard this low droning of the gathering clans.

Suddenly the panes of the red windows tinkled and crashed to the ground, and at other windows there suddenly reared other flames, like bloody specters at the apertures of a haunted house. This outbreak had been well planned, as if by professional revolutionists.

A man's voice suddenly shouted, "Fire! Fire! Fire!" Hannigan had flung his pipe frenziedly from him because his lungs demanded room. He tumbled down from his perch, swung over the fence, and ran shouting toward the front door of the Trescotts'. Then he hammered on the door, using his fists as if they were mallets. Mrs. Trescott instantly came to one of the windows on the second floor. Afterward she knew she had been about to say, "The doctor is not at home, but if you will leave your name, I will let him know as soon as he comes."

Hannigan's bawling was for a minute incoherent, but she understood that it was not about croup.

"What?" she said, raising the window swiftly.

"Your house is on fire! You're all ablaze! Move quick if—" His cries were resounding in the street as if it were a cage of echoes. Many feet pattered swiftly on the stones. There was one man who ran with an almost fabulous speed. He wore lavender trousers. A straw hat with a bright silk band was held half crumpled in his hand.

As Henry reached the front door, Hannigan had just broken the lock with a kick. A thick cloud of smoke poured over them, and Henry, ducking his head, rushed into it. From Hannigan's clamor he knew only one thing, but it turned him blue with horror. In the hall, a lick of flame had found the cord that supported "Signing the Declaration." The engraving slumped suddenly down at one end, and then dropped to the floor, where it burst with the sound of a bomb. The fire was already roaring like a winter wind among the pines.

At the head of the stairs, Mrs. Trescott was waving her arms as if they were two reeds. "Jimmie! Save Jimmie!" she screamed in Henry's face. He plunged past her and disappeared, taking the long-familiar routes among these upper chambers, where he had once held office as a sort of second assistant housemaid.

Hannigan had followed him up the stairs, and grappled

the arm of the maniacal woman there. His face was black with rage. "You must come down," he bellowed.

She would only scream at him in reply, "Jimmie! Jimmie! Save Jimmie!" But he dragged her forth while she babbled at him.

As they swung out into the open air, a man ran across the lawn, and seizing a shutter, pulled it from its hinges and flung it far out upon the grass. Then he frantically attacked the other shutters one by one. It was a kind of temporary insanity.

"Here, you," howled Hannigan, "hold Mrs. Trescott—and stop—"

The news had been telegraphed by a twist of the wrist of a neighbor who had gone to the firebox at the corner, and the time when Hannigan and his charge struggled out of the house was the time when the whistle roared its hoarse night call, smiting the crowd in the park, causing the leader of the band, who was about to order the first triumphal clang of a military march, to let his hand drop slowly to his knees.

- *vii* -

Henry pawed awkwardly through the smoke in the upper halls. He had attempted to guide himself by the walls, but they were too hot. The paper was crimpling, and he expected at any moment to have a flame burst from under his hands.

"Jimmie!"

He did not call very loud, as if in fear that the humming flames below would overhear him.

"Jimmie! Oh, Jimmie!"

Stumbling and panting, he speedily reached the entrance to Jimmie's room and flung open the door. The little chamber had no smoke in it at all. It was faintly illuminated by a beautiful, rosy light reflected circuitously from the flames that were consuming the house. The boy had apparently just been aroused by the noise. He sat in his bed, his lips apart, his eyes wide, while upon his little white-robed figure played caressingly the light from the fire. As the door flew open, he had before him this apparition of his pal, a terror-stricken Negro, all tousled and with wool scorching, who leaped upon him and bore him up in a blanket as if the whole affair were a case of kidnaping by a dreadful robber chief. Without waiting to go through the usual short but complete process of wrinkling up his face, Jimmie let out a gorgeous bawl, which resembled the expression of a calf's deepest terror. As Johnson, bearing him, reeled into the smoke of the hall, he flung his arms about his neck and buried his face in the blanket. He called twice in muffled tones, "Mam-ma! Mam-ma!"

When Johnson came to the top of the stairs with his burden, he took a quick step backward. Through the smoke that rolled to him he could see that the lower hall was all ablaze. He cried out then in a howl that resembled Jimmie's former achievement. His legs gained a frightful faculty of bending sidewise. Swinging about precariously on these reedy legs, he made his way back slowly, back along the upper hall. From the way of him then, he had given up almost all idea of escaping from the burning house, and with it the desire. He was submitting, submitting because of his fathers, bending his mind in a most perfect slavery to this conflagration.

He now clutched Jimmie as unconsciously as when, running toward the house, he had clutched the hat with the bright silk band.

Suddenly he remembered a little private staircase which led from a bedroom to an apartment which the doctor had fitted up as a laboratory and workhouse, where he used some of his leisure, and also hours when he might have been sleeping, in devoting himself to experiments which came in the way of his study and interest.

When Johnson recalled this stairway, the submission to the blaze departed instantly. He had been perfectly familiar with it, but his confusion had destroyed the memory of it.

In his sudden momentary apathy there had been little that resembled fear, but now, as a way of safety came to him, the old frantic terror caught him. He was no longer creature to the flames, and he was afraid of the battle with them. It was a singular and swift set of alterations in which he feared twice without submission, and submitted once without fear.

"Jimmie!" he wailed, as he staggered on his way. He wished this little inanimate body at his breast to participate in his tremblings. But the child had lain limp and still during these headlong charges and countercharges, and no sign came from him.

Johnson passed through two rooms and came to the head of the stairs. As he opened the door, great billows of smoke poured out, but gripping Jimmie closer, he plunged down through them. All manner of odors assailed him during this flight. They seemed to be alive with envy, hatred, and malice. At the entrance to the laboratory he confronted a strange spectacle. The room was like a garden in the region where might be burning flowers. Flames of violet, crimson, green, blue, orange, and purple were blooming everywhere. There was one blaze that was precisely the hue of a delicate coral. In another place was a mass that lay merely in phosphorescent inaction like a pile of emeralds. But all these marvels were to be seen dimly through clouds of heaving, turning, deadly smoke.

Johnson halted for a moment on the threshold. He cried out again in the Negro wail that had in it the sadness of the swamps. Then he rushed across the room. An orange-colored flame leaped like a panther at the lavender trousers. This animal bit deeply into Johnson. There was an explosion at one side, and suddenly before him there reared a delicate, trembling sapphire shape like a fairy lady. With a quiet smile, she blocked his path and doomed him and Jimmie. Johnson shrieked, and then ducked in the manner of his race in flights. He aimed to pass under the left guard of the sapphire lady. But she was swifter than eagles, and her talons caught in him as he plunged past her. Bowing his head as if his neck had been struck, Johnson lurched forward, twisting this way and that way. He fell on his back. The still form in the blanket, flung from his arms, rolled to the edge of the floor and beneath the window.

Johnson had fallen with his head at the base of an old-fashioned desk. There was a row of jars upon the top of this desk. For the most part, they were silent amid this rioting, but there was one which seemed to hold a scintillant and writhing serpent.

Suddenly the glass splintered, and a ruby-red snakelike thing poured its thick length out upon the top of the old desk. It coiled and hesitated, and then began to swim a languorous way down the mahogany slant. At the angle, it waved its sizzling, molten head to and fro over the closed eyes of the man beneath it. Then, in a moment, with a mystic impulse, it moved again, and the red snake flowed directly down into Johnson's upturned face.

Afterward the trail of this creature seemed to reek, and amid flames and low explosions, drops like red-hot jewels pattered softly down it at leisurely intervals.

- *viii* -

Suddenly all roads led to Dr. Trescott's. The whole town flowed toward one point. Chippeway Hose Company Number One toiled desperately up Bridge Street Hill even as the Tuscaroras came in an impetuous sweep down Niagara Avenue. Meanwhile the machine of the hook-and-ladder experts from across the creek was spinning on its way. The chief of the fire department had been playing poker in the rear room of Whiteley's cigar store, but at the first breath of the alarm he sprang through the door like a man escaping with the kitty.

In Whilomville, on these occasions, there was always a number of people who instantly turned their attention to the bells in the churches and schoolhouses. The bells not only emphasized the alarm, but it was the habit to send these sounds rolling across the sky in a stirring, brazen uproar until the flames were practically vanquished. There was also a kind of rivalry as to which bell should be made to produce the greatest din. Even the Valley Church, four miles away among the farms, had heard the voices of its brethren, and immediately added a quaint little yelp.

Dr. Trescott had been driving homeward, slowly smoking a cigar, and feeling glad that this last case was now in complete obedience to him, like a wild animal that he had subdued, when he heard the long whistle, and chirped to his horse under the unlicensed but perfectly distinct impression that a fire had broken out in Oakhurst, a new and rather high-flying suburb of the town which was at least two miles from his own home. But in the second blast and in the ensuing silence he read the designation of his own district. He was then only a few blocks from his house. He took out the whip and laid it lightly on the mare. Surprised and frightened at this extraordinary action, she leaped forward, and as the reins straightened like steel bands, the doctor leaned backward a trifle. When the mare whirled him up to the closed gate, he was wondering whose house could be afire. The man who had rung the signal box yelled something at him, but he already knew. He left the mare to her will.

In front of his door was a maniacal woman in a wrapper. "Ned!" she screamed at sight of him. "Jimmie! Save Jimmie!"

Trescott had grown hard and chill. "Where?" he said. "Where?"

Mrs. Trescott's voice began to bubble. "Up—up—up—" She pointed at the second-story windows.

Hannigan was already shouting, "Don't go in that way! You can't go in that way!"

Trescott ran around the corner of the house and disappeared from them. He knew from the view he had taken of the main hall that it would be impossible to ascend from there. His hopes were fastened now to the stairway which led from the laboratory. The door which opened from this room out upon the lawn was fastened with a bolt and lock, but he kicked close to the lock and then close to the bolt. The door with a loud crash flew back. The doctor recoiled from the roll of smoke, and then, bending low, he stepped into the garden of burning flowers. On the floor his stinging eyes could make out a form in a smoldering blanket near the window. Then, as he carried his son toward the door, he saw that the whole lawn seemed now alive with men and boys, the leaders in the great charge that the whole town was making. They seized him and his burden, and overpowered him in wet blankets and water.

But Hannigan was howling, "Johnson is in there yet! Henry Johnson is in there yet! He went in after the kid! Johnson is in there yet!"

These cries penetrated to the sleepy senses of Trescott, and he struggled with his captors, swearing, unknown to him and to them, all the deep blasphemies of his medical-student days. He rose to his feet and went again toward the door of the laboratory. They endeavored to restrain him, although they were much affrighted at him.

But a young man who was a brakeman on the railway, and lived in one of the rear streets near the Trescotts, had gone into the laboratory and brought forth a thing which he laid on the grass.

- ix -

There were hoarse commands from in front of the house. "Turn on your water, Five!" "Let 'er go, One!" The gathering crowd swayed this way and that way. The flames, towering high, cast a wild red light on their faces. There came the clangor of a gong from along some adjacent street. The crowd exclaimed at it. "Here comes Number Three!" "That's Three a-comin'!" A panting and irregular mob dashed into view, dragging a hose cart. A cry of exultation arose from the little boys. "Here's Three!" The lads welcomed Never-Die Hose Company Number Three as if it was composed of a chariot dragged by a band of gods. The perspiring citizens flung themselves into the fray. The boys danced in impish joy at the displays of prowess. They acclaimed the approach of Number Two. They welcomed Number Four with cheers. They were so deeply moved by this whole affair that they bitterly guyed the late appearance of the hook-and-ladder company, whose heavy apparatus had almost stalled them on the Bridge Street hill. The lads hated and feared a fire, of course. They did not particularly want to have anybody's house burn, but still it was fine to see the gathering of the companies, and amid a great noise to watch their heroes perform all manner of prodigies.

They were divided into parties over the worth of different companies, and supported their creeds with no small violence. For instance, in that part of the little city where Number Four had its home it would be most daring for a boy to contend the superiority of any other company. Likewise, in another quarter, when a strange boy was asked which fire company was the best in Whilomville, he was expected to answer, "Number One." Feuds, which the boys forgot and remembered according to chance or the importance of some recent event, existed all through the town.

They did not care much for John Shipley, the chief of the department. It was true that he went to a fire with the speed of a falling angel, but when there he invariably lapsed into a certain still mood which was almost a preoccupation, moving leisurely around the burning structure and surveying it, puffing meanwhile at a cigar. This quiet man, who even when life was in danger seldom raised his voice, was not much to their fancy. Now old Sykes Huntington, when he was chief, used to bellow continually like a bull and gesticulate in a sort of delirium. He was much finer as a spectacle than this Shipley, who viewed a fire with the same steadiness that he viewed a raise in a large jackpot. The greater number of the boys could never understand why the members of these companies persisted in re-electing Shipley, although they often pretended to understand it, because "My father says" was a very formidable phrase in argument, and the fathers seemed almost unanimous in advocating Shipley.

At this time, there was considerable discussion as to which company had got the first stream of water on the fire. Most of the boys claimed that Number Five owned that distinction, but there was a determined minority who contended for Number One. Boys who were the blood adherents of other companies were obliged to choose between the two on this occasion, and the talk waxed warm.

But a great rumor went among the crowds. It was told with hushed voices. Afterward a reverent silence fell even upon the boys. Jimmie Trescott and Henry Johnson had been burned to death, and Dr. Trescott himself had been most savagely hurt. The crowd did not even feel the police pushing at them. They raised their eyes, shining now with awe, toward the high flames.

The man who had information was at his best. In low tones he described the whole affair. "That was the kid's room—in the corner there. He had measles or somethin', and this coon —Johnson—was a-settin' up with 'im, and Johnson got sleepy or somethin' and upset the lamp, and the doctor he was down in his office, and he came running up, and they all got burned together till they dragged 'em out."

Another man, always preserved for the deliverance of the final judgment, was saying, "Oh, they'll die sure. Burned to flinders. No chance. Hull lot of 'em. Anybody can see." The crowd concentrated its gaze still more closely upon these flags of fire which waved joyfully against the black sky. The bells of the town were clashing unceasingly.

A little procession moved across the lawn and toward the street. There were three cots, borne by twelve of the firemen. The police moved sternly, but it needed no effort of theirs to open a lane for this slow cortege. The men who bore the cots were well known to the crowd, but in this solemn parade, during the ringing of the bells and the shouting, and with the red glare upon the sky, they seemed utterly foreign, and Whilomville paid them a deep respect. Each man in this stretcher party had gained a reflected majesty. They were footmen to death, and the crowd made subtle obeisance to this august dignity derived from three prospective graves. One woman turned away with a shriek at sight of the covered body on the first stretcher, and people faced her suddenly in silent and mournful indignation. Otherwise there was barely a sound as these twelve important men with measured tread carried their burdens through the throng.

The little boys no longer discussed the merits of the different fire companies. For the greater part they had been routed. Only the more courageous viewed closely the three figures veiled in yellow blankets.

- x -

Old Judge Denning Hagenthorpe, who lived nearly opposite the Trescotts, had thrown his door wide open to receive the afflicted family. When it was publicly learned that the doctor and his son and the Negro were still alive, it required a specially detailed policeman to prevent people from scaling the front porch and interviewing these sorely wounded. One old lady appeared with a miraculous poultice, and she quoted most damning Scripture to the officer when he said that she could not pass him. Throughout the night, some lads old enough to be given privileges or to compel them from their mothers remained vigilantly upon the curb in anticipation of a death or some such event. The reporter of the *Morning Tribune* rode thither on his bicycle every hour until three o'clock.

Six of the ten doctors in Whilomville attended at Judge Hagenthorpe's house.

Almost at once they were able to know that Trescott's burns were not vitally important. The child would possibly be scarred badly, but his life was undoubtedly safe. As for the Negro, Henry Johnson, he could not live. His body was frightfully seared, but more than that, he now had no face. His face had simply been burned away.

Trescott was always asking news of the two other patients. In the morning, he seemed fresh and strong, so they told him that Johnson was doomed. They then saw him stir on the bed, and sprang quickly to see if the bandages needed readjusting. In the sudden glance he threw from one to another, he impressed them as being both leonine and impracticable.

The morning paper announced the death of Henry Johnson. It contained a long interview with Edward J. Hannigan, in which the latter described in full the performance of Johnson at the fire. There was also an editorial built from all the best

words in the vocabulary of the staff. The town halted in its
accustomed road of thought, and turned a reverent attention
to the memory of this hostler. In the breasts of many people
was the regret that they had not known enough to give him a
hand and a lift when he was alive, and they judged themselves
stupid and ungenerous for this failure.

The name of Henry Johnson became suddenly the title of
a saint to the little boys. The one who thought of it first
could, by quoting it in an argument, at once overthrow his
antagonist, whether it applied to the subject or whether it
did not.

> "Nigger, nigger, never die,
>     Black face and shiny eye."

Boys who had called this odious couplet in the rear of Johnson's march buried the fact at the bottom of their hearts.

Later in the day, Miss Bella Farragut, of No. 7 Watermelon
Alley, announced that she had been engaged to marry Mr.
Henry Johnson.

- xi -

The old judge had a cane with an ivory head. He could
never think at his best until he was leaning slightly on this
stick and smoothing the white top with slow movements of
his hands. It was also to him a kind of narcotic. If by any
chance he mislaid it, he grew at once very irritable, and was
likely to speak sharply to his sister, whose mental incapacity
he had patiently endured for thirty years in the old mansion
on Ontario Street. She was not at all aware of her brother's
opinion of her endowments, and so it might be said that the
judge had successfully dissembled for more than a quarter of
a century, only risking the truth at the times when his cane
was lost.

On a particular day, the judge sat in his armchair on the
porch. The sunshine sprinkled through the lilac bushes and

poured great coins on the boards. The sparrows disputed in the trees that lined the pavements. The judge mused deeply, while his hands gently caressed the ivory head of his cane.

Finally he arose and entered the house, his brow still furrowed in a thoughtful frown. His stick thumped solemnly in regular beats. On the second floor, he entered a room where Dr. Trescott was working about the bedside of Henry Johnson. The bandages on the Negro's head allowed only one thing to appear—an eye, which unwinkingly stared at the judge. The latter spoke to Trescott on the condition of the patient. Afterward he evidently had something further to say, but he seemed to be kept from it by the scrutiny of the unwinking eye, at which he furtively glanced from time to time.

When Jimmie Trescott was sufficiently recovered, his mother had taken him to pay a visit to his grandparents in Connecticut. The doctor had remained to take care of his patients, but as a matter of truth he spent most of his time at Judge Hagenthorpe's house, where lay Henry Johnson. Here he slept and ate almost every meal in the long nights and days of his vigil.

At dinner, and away from the magic of the unwinking eye, the judge said suddenly, "Trescott, do you think it is—" As Trescott paused expectantly, the judge fingered his knife. He said thoughtfully, "No one wants to advance such ideas, but somehow I think that that poor fellow ought to die."

There was in Trescott's face at once a look of recognition, as if in this tangent of the judge he saw an old problem. He merely sighed and answered, "Who knows?" The words were spoken in a deep tone that gave them an elusive kind of significance.

The judge retreated to the cold manner of the bench. "Perhaps we may not talk with propriety of this kind of action, but I am induced to say that you are performing a questionable charity in preserving this Negro's life. As near as I can understand, he will hereafter be a monster, a perfect monster, and probably with an affected brain. No man can observe you as I have observed you and not know that it was a matter of conscience with you, but I am afraid, my friend, that it is

one of the blunders of virtue." The judge had delivered his
views with his habitual oratory. The last three words he spoke
with a particular emphasis, as if the phrase was his discovery.

The doctor made a weary gesture. "He saved my boy's
life."

"Yes," said the judge, swiftly, "yes, I know!"

"And what am I to do?" said Trescott, his eyes suddenly
lighting like an outburst from smoldering peat. "What am I
to do? He gave himself for—for Jimmie. What am I to do for
him?"

The judge abased himself completely before these words.
He lowered his eyes for a moment. He picked at his cucum-
bers.

Presently he braced himself straightly in his chair. "He
will be your creation, you understand. He is purely your
creation. Nature has very evidently given him up. He is dead.
You are restoring him to life. You are making him, and he
will be a monster, and with no mind."

"He will be what you like, judge," cried Trescott, in sudden
polite fury. "He will be anything, but, by God! he saved my
boy."

The judge interrupted in a voice trembling with emotion:
"Trescott! Trescott! Don't I know?"

Trescott had subsided to a sullen mood. "Yes, you know,"
he answered acidly, "but you don't know all about your own
boy being saved from death." This was a perfectly childish
allusion to the judge's bachelorhood. Trescott knew that
the remark was infantile, but he seemed to take desperate
delight in it.

But it passed the judge completely. It was not his spot.
"I am puzzled," said he, in profound thought. "I don't
know what to say."

Trescott had become repentant. "Don't think I don't ap-
preciate what you say, judge. But—"

"Of course!" responded the judge quickly. "Of course."

"It—" began Trescott.

"Of course," said the judge.

In silence they resumed their dinner.

"Well," said the judge ultimately, "it is hard for a man to know what to do."

"It is," said the doctor fervidly.

There was another silence. It was broken by the judge: "Look here, Trescott; I don't want you to think—"

"No, certainly not," answered the doctor earnestly.

"Well, I don't want you to think I would say anything to— It was only that I thought that I might be able to suggest to you that—perhaps—the affair was a little dubious."

With an appearance of suddenly disclosing his real mental perturbation, the doctor said, "Well, what would you do? Would you kill him?" he asked, abruptly and sternly.

"Trescott, you fool," said the old man gently.

"Oh, well, I know, judge, but then—" He turned red, and spoke with new violence: "Say, he saved my boy—do you see? He saved my boy."

"You bet he did," cried the judge, with enthusiasm. "You bet he did." And they remained for a time gazing at each other, their faces illuminated with memories of a certain deed.

After another silence, the judge said, "It is hard for a man to know what to do."

- *xii* -

Late one evening, Trescott, returning from a professional call, paused his buggy at the Hagenthorpe gate. He tied the mare to the old, tin-covered post, and entered the house. Ultimately he appeared with a companion—a man who walked slowly and carefully, as if he were learning. He was wrapped to the heels in an old-fashioned ulster. They entered the buggy and drove away.

After a silence only broken by the swift and musical humming of the wheels on the smooth road, Trescott spoke. "Henry," he said, "I've got you a home here with old Alek Williams. You will have everything you want to eat and a good place to sleep, and I hope you will get along there all right. I will pay all your expenses, and come to see you as often as I can. If you don't get along, I want you to let me know as soon as possible, and then we will do what we can to make it better."

The dark figure at the doctor's side answered with a cheerful laugh. "These buggy wheels don' look like I washed 'em yestehday, docteh," he said.

Trescott hesitated for a moment, and then went on insistently, "I am taking you to Alek Williams, Henry, and I—"

The figure chuckled again. "No, 'deed! No, seh! Alek Williams don' know a hoss! 'Deed he don't. He don' know a hoss from a pig." The laugh that followed was like the rattle of pebbles.

Trescott turned and looked sternly and coldly at the dim form in the gloom from the buggy top. "Henry," he said, "I didn't say anything about horses. I was saying—"

"Hoss? Hoss?" said the quavering voice from these near shadows. "Hoss? 'Deed I don' know all erbout a hoss! 'Deed I don't." There was a satirical chuckle.

At the end of three miles, the mare slackened and the doctor leaned forward, peering, while holding tight reins. The wheels of the buggy bumped often over outcropping boulders. A window shone forth, a simple square of topaz on a great black hillside. Four dogs charged the buggy with ferocity, and when it did not promptly retreat, they circled courageously around the flanks, baying. A door opened near the window in the hillside, and a man came and stood on a beach of yellow light.

"Yah! Yah! You Roveh! You Susie! Come yah! Come yah this minnet!"

Trescott called across the dark sea of grass, "Hello, Alek!"

"Hello!"

"Come down here and show me where to drive."

The man plunged from the beach into the surf, and Trescott could then only trace his course by the fervid and polite ejaculations of a host who was somewhere approaching. Presently Williams took the mare by the head, and uttering cries of welcome and scolding the swarming dogs, led the equipage toward the lights. When they halted at the door and Trescott was climbing out, Williams cried, "Will she stand, docteh?"

"She'll stand all right, but you better hold her for a minute. Now, Henry." The doctor turned and held both arms to the dark figure. It crawled to him painfully like a man going down a ladder. Williams took the mare away to be tied to a little tree, and when he returned, he found them awaiting him in the gloom beyond the rays from the door.

He burst out then like a siphon pressed by a nervous thumb. "Hennery! Hennery, ma ol' frien'. Well, if I ain' glade. If I ain' glade!"

Trescott had taken the silent shape by the arm and led it forward into the full revelation of the light. "Well, now, Alek, you can take Henry and put him to bed, and in the morning I will—"

Near the end of this sentence, old Williams had come front to front with Johnson. He gasped for a second, and then yelled the yell of a man stabbed in the heart.

For a fraction of a moment, Trescott seemed to be looking for epithets. Then he roared, "You old black chump! You old black— Shut up! Shut up! Do you hear?"

Williams obeyed instantly in the matter of his screams, but he continued in a lowered voice, "Ma Lode a' massy! Who'd ever think? Ma Lode a' massy!"

Trescott spoke again in the manner of a commander of a battalion. "Alek!"

The old Negro again surrendered, but to himself he repeated in a whisper, "Ma Lode!" He was aghast and trembling.

As these three points of widening shadows approached the golden doorway, a hale old Negress appeared there, bowing. "Good evenin', docteh! Good evening'! Come in! Come in!" She had evidently just retired from a tempestuous struggle to place the room in order, but she was now bowing rapidly. She made the effort of a person swimming.

"Don't trouble yourself, Mary," said Trescott, entering. "I've brought Henry for you to take care of, and all you've got to do is to carry out what I tell you." Learning that he was not followed, he faced the door, and said, "Come in, Henry."

Johnson entered. "Wheel" shrieked Mrs. Williams. She almost achieved a back somersault. Six young members of the tribe of Williams made a simultaneous plunge for a position behind the stove, and formed a wailing heap.

- *xiii* -

"You know very well that you and your family lived usually on less than three dollars a week, and now that Dr. Trescott pays you five dollars a week for Johnson's board, you live like millionaires. You haven't done a stroke of work since Johnson began to board with you—everybody knows that—and so what are you kicking about?"

The judge sat in his chair on the porch, fondling his cane, and gazing down at old Williams, who stood under the lilac bushes. "Yes, I know, jedge," said the Negro, wagging his head in a puzzled manner. " 'Tain't like as if I didn't 'preciate what the docteh done, but—but—well, yeh see, jedge," he added, gaining a new impetus, "it's—it's hard wuk. This ol' man nev' did wuk so hard. Lode, no."

"Don't talk such nonsense, Alek," spoke the judge sharply. "You have never really worked in your life—anyhow, enough to support a family of sparrows—and now when you are in a more prosperous condition than ever before, you come around talking like an old fool."

The Negro began to scratch his head. "Yeh see, jedge," he said at last, "my ol' 'ooman she cain't 'ceive no lady callahs, nohow."

"Hang lady callers!" said the judge irascibly. "If you have flour in the barrel and meat in the pot, your wife can get along without receiving lady callers, can't she?"

"But they won't come ainyhow, jedge," replied Williams, with an air of still deeper stupefaction. "Noner ma wife's frien's ner noner ma frien's 'ill come near ma res'dence."

"Well, let them stay home if they are such silly people."

The old Negro seemed to be seeking a way to elude this argument, but evidently finding none, he was about to shuffle meekly off. He halted, however. "Jedge," said he, "ma ol' 'ooman's near driv' abstracted."

"Your old woman is an idiot," responded the judge.

Williams came very close and peered solemnly through a branch of lilac. "Jedge," he whispered, "the chillens."

"What about them?"

Dropping his voice to funereal depths, Williams said, "They —they cain't eat."

"Can't eat!" scoffed the judge loudly. "Can't eat! You must think I am as big an old fool as you are. Can't eat—the little rascals! What's to prevent them from eating?"

In answer, Williams said, with mournful emphasis, "Hennery." Moved with a kind of satisfaction at his tragic use of the name, he remained staring at the judge for a sign of its effect.

The judge made a gesture of irritation. "Come, now, you old scoundrel, don't beat around the bush anymore. What are you up to? What do you want? Speak out like a man, and don't give me any more of this tiresome rigmarole."

"I ain't er-beatin' round 'bout nuffin', jedge," replied Williams indignantly. "No seh; I say whatter got to say right out. 'Deed I do."

"Well, say it, then."

"Jedge," began the Negro, taking off his hat and switching his knee with it, "Lode knows I'd do jes 'bout as much fer five dollehs er week as ainy cul'd man, but—but this yere business is awful, jedge. I raikon ain't been no sleep in—in my house sence docteh done fetch 'im."

"Well, what do you propose to do about it?"

Williams lifted his eyes from the ground and gazed off through the trees. "Raikon I got good appetite, an' sleep jes' like er dog, but he—he's done broke me all up. 'Tain' no good, nohow. I wake up in the night; I hear 'im, mebbe, er-whimperin' an' er-whimperin', an' I sneak an' I sneak until I try th' do' to see if he locked in. An' he keep me er-puzzlin' an' er-quakin' all night long. Don't know how 'll do in th' winter. Can't let 'im out where th' chillen is. He'll done freeze where he is now." Williams spoke these sentences as if he were talking to himself. After a silence of deep reflection, he continued, "Folks go round sayin' he ain't Hennery Johnson at all. They say he's er devill"

"What?" cried the judge.

"Yesseh," repeated Williams, in tones of injury, as if his veracity had been challenged. "Yesseh. I'm er-tellin' it to yeh straight, jedge. Plenty cul'd folks up my way say it is a devil."

"Well, you don't think so yourself, do you?"

"No. 'Tain't no devil. It's Hennery Johnson."

"Well, then, what is the matter with you? You don't care what a lot of foolish people say. Go on 'tending to your business, and pay no attention to such idle nonsense."

" 'Tis nonsense, jedge; but he *looks* like er devil."

"What do you care what he looks like?" demanded the judge.

"Ma rent is two dollehs and er half er month," said Williams slowly.

"It might just as well be ten thousand dollars a month," responded the judge. "You never pay it, anyhow."

"Then, anoth' thing," continued Williams, in his reflective tone. "If he was all right in his haid I could stan' it; but, jedge, he's crazier 'n er loon. Then when he looks like er devil, an' done skears all my frien's away, an' ma chillens cain't eat, an ma ole 'ooman jes' raisin' Cain all the time, an' ma rent two dollehs an' er half er month, an' him not right in his haid, it seems like five dollehs er week—"

The judge's stick came down sharply and suddenly upon the floor of the porch. "There," he said. "I thought that was what you were driving at."

Williams began swinging his head from side to side in the strange racial mannerism. "Now hol' on a minnet, jedge," he said defensively. " 'Tain't like as if I didn't 'preciate what the docteh done. 'Tain't that. Docteh Trescott is er kind man, 'an 'tain't like as if I didn't 'preciate what he done; but—but—"

"But what? You are getting painful, Alek. Now tell me this:

did you ever have five dollars a week regularly before in your life?"

Williams at once drew himself up with great dignity, but in the pause after that question he drooped gradually to another attitude. In the end, he answered, heroically, "No, jedge, I ain't. An' 'tain't like as if I was er-sayin' five dollehs wasn't er lot er money for a man like me. But, jedge, what er man oughter git fer this kinder wuk is er salary. Yesseh, jedge," he repeated, with a great, impressive gesture, "fer this kinder wuk er man oughter git er *salary*." He laid a terrible emphasis upon the final word.

The judge laughed. "I know Dr. Trescott's mind concerning this affair, Alek; and if you are dissatisfied with your boarder, he is quite ready to move him to some other place; so, if you care to leave word with me that you are tired of the arrangement and wish it changed, he will come and take Johnson away."

Williams scratched his head again in deep perplexity. "Five dollehs is er big price fer bo'd, but 'tain't no big price fer the bo'd of er crazy man," he said finally.

"What do you think you ought to get?" asked the judge.

"Well," answered Alek, in the manner of one deep in a balancing of the scales, "he looks like er devil, an' done skears e'rybody, an' ma chillens cain't eat, an' I cain't sleep, an' he ain't right in his haid, an'—"

"You told me all those things."

After scratching his wool, and beating his knee with his hat, and gazing off through the trees and down at the ground, Williams said, as he kicked nervously at the gravel, "Well, jedge, I think it is wuth—" He stuttered.

"Worth what?"

"Six dollehs," answered Williams, in a desperate outburst.

The judge lay back in his great armchair and went through all the motions of a man laughing heartily, but he made no sound save a slight cough. Williams had been watching him with apprehension.

"Well," said the judge, "do you call six dollars a salary?"

"No, seh," promptly responded Williams. " 'Tain't a salary. No, 'deed! 'Tain't a salary." He looked with some anger upon the man who questioned his intelligence in this way.

"Well, supposing your children can't eat?"

"I—"

"And supposing he looks like a devil? And supposing all those things continue? Would you be satisfied with six dollars a week?"

Recollections seemed to throng in Williams's mind at these interrogations, and he answered dubiously. "Of co'se a man who ain't right in his haid, an' looks like er devil— But six dollehs—" After these two attempts at a sentence, Williams suddenly appeared as an orator, with a great, shiny palm waving in the air. "I tell yeh, jedge, six dollehs is six dollehs, but if I git six dollehs fer bo'ding Hennery Johnson, I uhns it! I uhns it!"

"I don't doubt that you earn six dollars for every week's work you do," said the judge.

"Well, if I bo'd Hennery Johnson fer six dollehs er week, I uhns it! I uhns it!" cried Williams wildly.

- xiv -

Reifsnyder's assistant had gone to his supper, and the owner of the shop was trying to placate four men who wished to be shaved at once. Reifsnyder was very garrulous—a fact which made him rather remarkable among barbers, who, as a class, are austerely speechless, having been taught silence by the hammering reiteration of a tradition. It is the customers who talk in the ordinary event.

As Reifsnyder waved his razor down the cheek of a man in the chair, he turned often to cool the impatience of the others with pleasant talk, which they did not particularly heed.

"Oh, he should have let him die," said Bainbridge, a railway engineer, finally replying to one of the barber's orations. "Shut up, Reif, and go on with your business!"

Instead, Reifsnyder paused shaving entirely, and turned to front the speaker. "Let him die?" he demanded. "How vas that? How can you let a man die?"

"By letting him die, you chump," said the engineer. The others laughed a little, and Reifsnyder turned at once to his work, sullenly, as a man overwhelmed by the derision of numbers.

"How vas that?" he grumbled later. "How can you let a man die when he has done so much for you?"

"'When he has done so much for you'?" repeated Bainbridge. "You better shave some people. How vas that? Maybe this ain't a barber shop?"

A man hitherto silent now said, "If I had been the doctor, I would have done the same thing."

"Of course," said Reifsnyder. "Any man vould do it. Any man that vas not like you, you—old—flinthearted—fish." He had sought the final words with painful care, and he delivered the collection triumphantly at Bainbridge. The engineer laughed.

The man in the chair now lifted himself higher, while Reifsnyder began an elaborate ceremony of anointing and combing his hair. Now free to join comfortably in the talk, the man said, "They say he is the most terrible thing in the world. Young Johnnie Bernard—that drives the grocery wagon—saw him up at Alek Williams's shanty, and he says he couldn't eat anything for two days."

"Chee!" said Reifsnyder.

"Well, what makes him so terrible?" asked another.

"Because he hasn't got any face," replied the barber and the engineer in duet.

"Hasn't got any face!" repeated the man. "How can he do without any face?"

> "He has no face in the front of his head,
>    In the place where his face ought to grow."

Bainbridge sang these lines pathetically as he arose and hung his hat on a hook. The man in the chair was about to abdicate in his favor. "Get a gait on you now," he said to Reifsnyder. "I go out at seven thirty-one."

As the barber foamed the lather on the cheeks of the engineer, he seemed to be thinking heavily. Then suddenly he burst out. "How would you like to be with no face?" he cried to the assemblage.

"Oh, if I had to have a face like yours—" answered one customer.

Bainbridge's voice came from a sea of lather. "You're kicking because if losing faces became popular, you'd have to go out of business."

"I don't think it will become so much popular," said Reifsnyder.

"Not if it's got to be taken off in the way his was taken off," said another man. "I'd rather keep mine, if you don't mind."

"I guess so!" cried the barber. "Just think!"

The shaving of Bainbridge had arrived at a time of comparative liberty for him. "I wonder what the doctor says to himself?" he observed. "He may be sorry he made him live."

"It was the only thing he could do," replied a man. The others seemed to agree with him.

"Supposing you were in his place," said one, "and Johnson had saved your kid. What would you do?"

"Certainly!"

"Of course! You would do anything on earth for him. You'd take all the trouble in the world for him. And spend your last dollar on him. Well, then?"

"I wonder how it feels to be without any face?" said Reifsnyder musingly.

The man who had previously spoken, feeling that he had expressed himself well, repeated the whole thing. "You would do anything on earth for him. You'd take all the trouble in the world for him. And spend your last dollar on him. Well, then?"

"No, but look," said Reifsnyder. "Supposing you don't got a face!"

- xv -

As soon as Williams was hidden from the view of the old
judge, he began to gesture and talk to himself. An elation had
evidently penetrated to his vitals, and caused him to dilate
as if he had been filled with gas. He snapped his fingers in
the air, and whistled fragments of triumphal music. At times,
in his progress toward his shanty, he indulged in a shuffling
movement that was really a dance. It was to be learned from
the intermediate monologue that he had emerged from his
trials laureled and proud. He was the unconquerable Alex-
ander Williams. Nothing could exceed the bold self-reliance
of his manner. His kingly stride, his heroic song, the derisive
flourish of his hands—all betokened a man who had successfully defied the world.

On his way he saw Zeke Paterson coming to town. They
hailed each other at a distance of fifty yards.

"How do, Broth' Paterson?"

"How do, Broth' Williams?"

They were both deacons.

"Is you' folks well, Broth' Paterson?"

"Middlin', middlin'. How's you' folks, Broth' Williams?"

Neither of them had slowed his pace in the smallest degree.
They had simply begun this talk when a considerable space
separated them, continued it as they passed, and added polite
questions as they drifted steadily apart. Williams's mind
seemed to be a balloon. He had been so inflated that he had
not noticed that Paterson had definitely shied into the dry
ditch as they came to the point of ordinary contact.

Afterward, as he went a lonely way, he burst out again in
song and pantomimic celebration of his estate. His feet moved
in prancing steps.

When he came in sight of his cabin, the fields were bathed
in a blue dusk, and the light in the window was pale. Cavort-
ing and gesticulating, he gazed joyfully for some moments
upon this light. Then suddenly, another idea seemed to attack
his mind, and he stopped, with an air of being suddenly

dampened. In the end, he approached his home as if it were the fortress of an enemy.

Some dogs disputed his advance for a loud moment, and then, discovering their lord, slunk away embarrassed. His reproaches were addressed to them in muffled tones.

Arriving at the door, he pushed it open with the timidity of a new thief. He thrust his head cautiously sidewise, and his eyes met the eyes of his wife, who sat by the table, the lamp-light defining a half of her face. "Sh!" he said, uselessly. His glance traveled swiftly to the inner door which shielded the one bedchamber. The pickaninnies, strewn upon the floor of the living room, were softly snoring. After a hearty meal, they had promptly dispersed themselves about the place and gone to sleep. "Sh!" said Williams again to his motionless and silent wife. He had allowed only his head to appear. His wife, with one hand upon the edge of the table and the other at her knee, was regarding him with wide eyes and parted lips as if he were a specter. She looked to be one who was living in terror, and even the familiar face at the door had thrilled her because it had come suddenly.

Williams broke the tense silence. "Is he all right?" he whispered, waving his eyes toward the inner door. Following his glance timorously, his wife nodded, and in a low tone answered, "I raikon he's done gone t'sleep."

Williams then slunk noiselessly across his threshold.

He lifted a chair, and with infinite care placed it so that it faced the dreaded inner door. His wife moved slightly, so as to also squarely face it. A silence came upon them in which they seemed to be waiting for a calamity, pealing and deadly.

Williams finally coughed behind his hand. His wife started, and looked upon him in alarm. " 'Pears like he done gwine keep quiet ter-night," he breathed. They continually pointed their speech and their looks at the inner door, paying it the homage due to a corpse or a phantom. Another long stillness followed this sentence. Their eyes shone white and wide. A wagon rattled down the distant road. From their chairs they looked at the window, and the effect of the light in the cabin was a presentation of an intensely black and solemn night.

The old woman adopted the attitude used always in church at funerals. At times she seemed to be upon the point of breaking out in prayer.

"He mighty quiet ter-night," whispered Williams. "Was he good ter-day?" For answer his wife raised her eyes to the ceiling in the supplication of Job. Williams moved restlessly. Finally he tiptoed to the door. He knelt slowly and without a sound, and placed his ear near the keyhole. Hearing a noise behind him, he turned quickly. His wife was staring at him aghast. She stood in front of the stove, and her arms were spread out in the natural movement to protect all her sleeping ducklings.

But Williams arose without having touched the door. "I raikon he er-sleep," he said, fingering his wool. He debated with himself for some time. During this interval, his wife remained, a great, fat statue of a mother shielding her children.

It was plain that his mind was swept suddenly by a wave of temerity. With a sounding step, he moved toward the door. His fingers were almost upon the knob when he swiftly ducked and dodged away, clapping his hands to the back of his head. It was as if the portal had threatened him. There was a little tumult near the stove, where Mrs. Williams's desperate retreat had involved her feet with the prostrate children.

After the panic, Williams bore traces of a feeling of shame. He returned to the charge. He firmly grasped the knob with his left hand, and with his other hand turned the key in the lock. He pushed the door, and as it swung portentously open, he sprang nimbly to one side like the fearful slave liberating the lion. Near the stove a group had formed, the terror-stricken mother with her arms stretched, and the aroused children clinging frenziedly to her skirts.

The light streamed after the swinging door, and disclosed a room six feet one way and six feet the other way. It was small enough to enable the radiance to lay it plain. Williams peered warily around the corner made by the doorpost.

Suddenly he advanced, retired, and advanced again with a

howl. His palsied family had expected him to spring backward, and at his howl they heaped themselves wondrously. But Williams simply stood in the little room emitting his howls before an open window. "He's gone! He's gone! He's gone!" His eye and his hand had speedily proved the fact. He had even thrown open a little cupboard.

Presently he came flying out. He grabbed his hat and hurled the outer door back upon its hinges. Then he tumbled headlong into the night. He was yelling, "Docteh Trescott! Docteh Trescott!" He ran wildly through the fields and galloped in the direction of town. He continued to call to Trescott, as if the latter was within easy hearing. It was as if Trescott was poised in the contemplative sky over the running Negro, and could heed this reaching voice: "Docteh Trescott!"

In the cabin, Mrs. Williams, supported by relays from the battalion of children, stood quaking watch until the truth of daylight came as a reinforcement and made them arrogant, strutting, swashbuckler children and a mother who proclaimed her illimitable courage.

- xvi -

Theresa Page was giving a party. It was the outcome of a long series of arguments addressed to her mother, which had been overheard in part by her father. He had at last said five words, "Oh, let her have it." The mother had then gladly capitulated.

Theresa had written nineteen invitations, and distributed them at recess to her schoolmates. Later her mother had composed five large cakes, and still later a vast amount of lemonade.

So the nine little girls and the ten little boys sat quite primly in the dining room, while Theresa and her mother plied them with cake and lemonade, and also with ice cream. This primness sat now quite strangely upon them. It was owing to the presence of Mrs. Page. Previously, in the parlor alone with their games, they had overturned a chair; the boys had let more or less of their hoodlum spirit shine forth. But when circumstances could be possibly magnified to warrant it, the girls made the boys victims of an insufferable pride, snubbing them mercilessly. So in the dining room they resembled a class at Sunday school, if it were not for the subterranean smiles, gestures, rebuffs, and poutings which stamped the affair as a children's party.

Two little girls of this subdued gathering were planted in a settle with their backs to the broad window. They were beaming lovingly upon each other with an effect of scorning the boys.

Hearing a noise behind her at the window, one little girl turned to face it. Instantly she screamed and sprang away, covering her face with her hands. "What was it? What was it?" cried everyone in a roar. Some slight movement of the eyes of the weeping and shuddering child informed the company that she had been frightened by an appearance at the window. At once they all faced the imperturbable window, and for a moment there was a silence. An astute lad made an immediate census of the other lads. The prank of slipping out and looming spectrally at a window was too venerable. But the little boys were all present and astonished.

As they recovered their minds they uttered warlike cries, and through a side door sallied rapidly out against the terror. They vied with each other in daring.

None wished particularly to encounter a dragon in the darkness of the garden, but there could be no faltering when the fair ones in the dining room were present. Calling to each other in stern voices, they went dragooning over the lawn, attacking the shadows with ferocity, but still with the caution of reasonable beings. They found, however, nothing new to the peace of the night. Of course there was a lad who told a great lie. He described a grim figure, bending low and slinking off along the fence. He gave a number of details, rendering his lie more splendid by a repetition of certain forms which he recalled from romances. For instance, he insisted that he had heard the creature emit a hollow laugh.

Inside the house, the little girl who had raised the alarm

was still shuddering and weeping. With the utmost difficulty
was she brought to a state approximating calmness by Mrs.
Page. Then she wanted to go home at once.

Page entered the house at this time. He had exiled himself
until he concluded that this children's party was finished and
gone. He was obliged to escort the little girl home because
she screamed again when they opened the door and she saw
the night.

She was not coherent even to her mother. Was it a man?
She didn't know. It was simply a thing, a dreadful thing.

- *xvii* -

In Watermelon Alley the Farraguts were spending their
evening as usual on the little, rickety porch. Sometimes they
howled gossip to other people on other rickety porches. The
thin wail of a baby arose from a near house. A man had a
terrific altercation with his wife, to which the alley paid no
attention at all.

There appeared suddenly before the Farraguts a monster
making a low and sweeping bow. There was an instant's
pause, and then occurred something that resembled the effect
of an upheaval of the earth's surface. The old woman hurled
herself backward with a dreadful cry. Young Sim had been
perched gracefully on a railing. At sight of the monster, he
simply fell over it to the ground. He made no sound, his eyes
stuck out, his nerveless hands tried to grapple the rail to prevent a tumble, and then he vanished. Bella, blubbering, and
with her hair suddenly and mysteriously disheveled, was
crawling on her hands and knees fearsomely up the steps.

Standing before this wreck of a family gathering, the
monster continued to bow. It even raised a deprecatory claw.
"Don' make no botheration 'bout me, Miss Fa'gut," it said
politely. "No, 'deed. I jes' drap in ter ax if yer well this
evenin', Miss Fa'gut. Don' make no botheration. No, 'deed. I
gwine ax you to go to er daince with me, Miss Fa'gut. I ax

you if I can have the magnifercent gratitude of you' company
on that 'casion, Miss Fa'gut."

The girl cast a miserable glance behind her. She was still
crawling away. On the ground beside the porch, young Sim
raised a strange bleat, which expressed both his fright and his
lack of wind. Presently the monster, with a fashionable amble,
ascended the steps after the girl.

She groveled in a corner of the room as the creature took a
chair. It seated itself very elegantly on the edge. It held an
old cap in both hands. "Don' make no botheration, Miss
Fa'gut. Don' make no botheration. No, 'deed. I jes' drap in ter
ax you if you won' do me the proud of acceptin' ma humble
invitation to er daince, Miss Fa'gut."

She shielded her eyes with her arms and tried to crawl past
it, but the genial monster blocked the way. "I jes' drap in ter
ax you 'bout er daince, Miss Fa'gut. I ax you if I kin have
the magnifercent gratitude of you' company on that 'casion,
Miss Fa'gut."

In a last outbreak of despair, the girl, shuddering and
wailing, threw herself face downward on the floor, while the
monster sat on the edge of the chair gabbling courteous invitations, and holding the old hat daintily to his stomach.

At the back of the house, Mrs. Farragut, who was of
enormous weight, and who for eight years had done little
more than sit in an armchair and describe her various ail-
ments, had with speed and agility scaled a high board fence.

- *xviii* -

The black mass in the middle of Trescott's property was
hardly allowed to cool before the builders were at work on
another house. It had sprung upward at a fabulous rate. It
was like a magical composition born of the ashes. The doctor's
office was the first part to be completed, and he had already
moved in his new books and instruments and medicines.

Trescott sat before his desk when the chief of police arrived. "Well, we found him," said the latter.

"Did you?" cried the doctor. "Where?"

"Shambling around the streets at daylight this morning. I'll be blamed if I can figure on where he passed the night."

"Where is he now?"

"Oh, we jugged him. I didn't know what else to do with him. That's what I want you to tell me. Of course, we can't keep him. No charge could be made, you know."

"I'll come down and get him."

The official grinned retrospectively. "Must say he had a fine career while he was out. First thing he did was to break up a children's party at Page's. Then he went to Watermelon Alley. Whoo! He stampeded the whole outfit. Men, women, and children running pell-mell, and yelling. They say one old woman broke her leg, or something, shinning over a fence. Then he went right out on the main street, and an Irish girl threw a fit, and there was a sort of a riot. He began to run, and a big crowd chased him, firing rocks. But he gave them the slip somehow down there by the foundry and in the railroad yard. We looked for him all night, but couldn't find him."

"Was he hurt any? Did anybody hit him with a stone?"

"Guess there isn't much of him to hurt any more, is there? Guess he's been hurt up to the limit. No. They never touched him. Of course, nobody really wanted to hit him, but you know how a crowd gets. It's like—it's like—"

"Yes, I know."

For a moment the chief of the police looked reflectively at the floor. Then he spoke hesitatingly. "You know Jake Winter's little girl was the one that he scared at the party. She is pretty sick, they say."

"Is she? Why, they didn't call me. I always attend the Winter family."

"No? Didn't they?" asked the chief slowly. "Well—you know—Winter is—well, Winter has gone clean crazy over this business. He wanted—he wanted to have you arrested."

"Have me arrested? The idiot! What in the name of wonder could he have me arrested for?"

"Of course. He is a fool. I told him to keep his trap shut.

But then you know how he'll go all over town yapping about the thing. I thought I'd better tip you."

"Oh, he is of no consequence; but then, of course, I'm obliged to you, Sam."

"That's all right. Well, you'll be down tonight and take him out, eh? You'll get a good welcome from the jailer. He don't like his job for a cent. He says you can have your man whenever you want him. He's got no use for him."

"But what is this business of Winter's about having me arrested?"

"Oh, it's a lot of chin about your having no right to allow this—this—this man to be at large. But I told him to tend to his own business. Only I thought I'd better let you know. And I might as well say right now, doctor, that there is a good deal of talk about this thing. If I were you, I'd come to the jail pretty late at night, because there is likely to be a crowd around the door, and I'd bring a—er—mask, or some kind of a veil, anyhow."

- xix -

Martha Goodwin was single, and well along into the thin years. She lived with her married sister in Whilomville. She performed nearly all the housework in exchange for the privilege of existence. Everyone tacitly recognized her labor as a form of penance for the early end of her betrothed, who had died of smallpox, which he had not caught from her.

But despite the strenuous and unceasing workaday of her life, she was a woman of great mind. She had adamantine opinions upon the situation in Armenia, the condition of women in China, the flirtation between Mrs. Minster of Niagara Avenue and young Griscom, the conflict in the Bible class of the Baptist Sunday school, the duty of the United States toward the Cuban insurgents, and many other colossal matters. Her fullest experience of violence was gained on an occasion when she had seen a hound clubbed, but in the plan which she had made for the reform of the world, she advocated

drastic measures. For instance, she contended that all the
Turks should be pushed into the sea and drowned, and that
Mrs. Minster and young Griscom should be hanged side by
side on twin gallows. In fact, this woman of peace, who had
seen only peace, argued constantly for a creed of illimitable
ferocity. She was invulnerable on these questions, because
eventually she overrode all opponents with a sniff. This sniff
was an active force. It was to her antagonists like a bang over
the head, and none was known to recover from this expression
of exalted contempt. It left them windless and conquered.
They never again came forward as candidates for suppression.
And Martha walked her kitchen with a stern brow, an invincible being like Napoleon.

Nevertheless her acquaintances, from the pain of their de-
feats, had been long in secret revolt. It was in no wise a
conspiracy, because they did not care to state their open
rebellion, but nevertheless it was understood that any woman
who could not coincide with one of Martha's contentions was
entitled to the support of others in the small circle. It
amounted to an arrangement by which all were required to
disbelieve any theory for which Martha fought. This, however, did not prevent them from speaking of her mind with
profound respect.

Two people bore the brunt of her ability. Her sister Kate
was visibly afraid of her, while Carrie Dungen sailed across
from her kitchen to sit respectfully at Martha's feet and learn
the business of the world. To be sure, afterward, under another sun, she always laughed at Martha and pretended to
deride her ideas, but in the presence of the sovereign, she
always remained silent or admiring. Kate, her sister, was of
no consequence at all. Her principal delusion was that she did
all the work in the upstairs rooms of the house, while Martha
did it downstairs. The truth was seen only by the husband,
who treated Martha with a kindness that was half banter, half
deference. Martha herself had no suspicion that she was the
only pillar of the domestic edifice. The situation was without
definitions. Martha made definitions, but she devoted them
entirely to the Armenians and Griscom and the Chinese and

other subjects. Her dreams, which in early days had been of love, of meadows and the shade of trees, of the face of a man, were now involved otherwise, and they were companioned in the kitchen curiously, Cuba, the hot-water kettle, Armenia, the washing of the dishes, and the whole thing being jumbled. In regard to social misdemeanors, she who was simply the mausoleum of a dead passion was probably the most savage critic in town. This unknown woman, hidden in a kitchen as in a well, was sure to have a considerable effect of the one kind or the other in the life of the town. Every time it moved a yard, she had personally contributed an inch. She could hammer so stoutly upon the door of a proposition that it would break from its hinges and fall upon her, but at any rate it moved. She was an engine, and the fact that she did not know that she was an engine contributed largely to the effect. One reason that she was formidable was that she did not even imagine that she was formidable. She remained a weak, innocent, and pigheaded creature, who alone would defy the universe if she thought the universe merited this proceeding.

One day Carrie Dungen came across from her kitchen with speed. She had a great deal of grist. "Oh," she cried, "Henry Johnson got away from where they was keeping him, and came to town last night, and scared everybody almost to death."

Martha was shining a dishpan, polishing madly. No reasonable person could see cause for this operation, because the pan already glistened like silver. "Well!" she ejaculated. She imparted to the word a deep meaning. "This, my prophecy, has come to pass." It was a habit.

The overplus of information was choking Carrie. Before she could go on, she was obliged to struggle for a moment. "And, oh, little Sadie Winter is awful sick, and they say Jake Winter was around this morning trying to get Doctor Trescott arrested. And poor old Mrs. Farragut sprained her ankle in trying to climb a fence. And there's a crowd around the jail all the time. They put Henry in jail because they didn't know what else to do with him, I guess. They say he is perfectly terrible."

Martha finally released the dishpan and confronted the headlong speaker. "Well!" she said again, poising a great, brown rag. Kate had heard the excited newcomer, and drifted down from the novel in her room. She was a shivery little woman. Her shoulder blades seemed to be two panes of ice, for she was constantly shrugging and shrugging. "Serves him right if he was to lose all his patients," she said suddenly, in bloodthirsty tones. She snipped her words out as if her lips were scissors.

"Well, he's likely to," shouted Carrie Dungen. "Don't a lot of people say that they won't have him any more? If you're sick and nervous, Doctor Trescott would scare the life out of you, wouldn't he? He would me. I'd keep thinking."

Martha, stalking to and fro, sometimes surveyed the two other women with a contemplative frown.

- xx -

After the return from Connecticut, little Jimmie was at first much afraid of the monster who lived in the room over the carriage house. He could not identify it in any way. Gradually, however, his fear dwindled under the influence of a weird fascination. He sidled into closer and closer relations with it.

One time the monster was seated on a box behind the stable, basking in the rays of the afternoon sun. A heavy crepe veil was swathed about its head.

Little Jimmie and many companions came around the corner of the stable. They were all in what was popularly known as the baby class, and consequently escaped from school a half hour before the other children. They halted abruptly at sight of the figure on the box. Jimmie waved his hand with the air of a proprietor.

"There he is," he said.

"O-o-o," murmured all the little boys, "o-o-o!" They shrank back and grouped according to courage or experience, as at the sound the monster slowly turned its head. Jimmie had remained in the van alone. "Don't be afraid! I won't let him hurt you," he said, delighted.

"Huh!" they replied contemptuously. "We ain't afraid."

Jimmie seemed to reap all the joys of the owner and exhibitor of one of the world's marvels, while his audience remained at a distance—awed and entranced, fearful and envious.

One of them addressed Jimmie gloomily. "Bet you dassent walk right up to him." He was an older boy than Jimmie, and habitually oppressed him to a small degree. This new social elevation of the smaller lad probably seemed revolutionary to him.

"Huh!" said Jimmie, with deep scorn. "Dassent I? Dassent I, hey? Dassent I?"

The group was immensely excited. It turned its eyes upon the boy that Jimmie addressed. "No, you dassent," he said stolidly, facing a moral defeat. He could see that Jimmie was resolved. "No, you dassent," he repeated doggedly.

"Ho?" cried Jimmie. "You just watch! You just watch!"

Amid a silence, he turned and marched toward the monster. But possibly the palpable wariness of his companions had an effect upon him that weighed more than his previous experience, for suddenly, when near to the monster, he halted dubiously. But his playmates immediately uttered a derisive shout, and it seemed to force him forward. He went to the monster and laid his hand delicately on its shoulder. "Hello, Henry," he said, in a voice that trembled a trifle. The monster was crooning a weird line of Negro melody that was scarcely more than a thread of sound, and it paid no heed to the boy.

Jimmie strutted back to his companions. They acclaimed him and hooted his opponent. Amid this clamor the larger boy with difficulty preserved a dignified attitude.

"I dassent, dassent I?" said Jimmie to him. "Now, you're so smart, let's see you do it!"

This challenge brought forth renewed taunts from the others. The larger boy puffed out his cheeks. "Well, I ain't afraid," he explained sullenly. He had made a mistake in diplomacy, and now his small enemies were tumbling his

prestige all about his ears. They crowed like roosters and
bleated like lambs, and made many other noises which were
supposed to bury him in ridicule and dishonor. "Well, I ain't
afraid," he continued to explain through the din.

Jimmie, the hero of the mob, was pitiless. "You ain't afraid,
hey?" he sneered. "If you ain't afraid, go do it, then."

"Well, I would if I wanted to," the other retorted. His
eyes wore an expression of profound misery, but he preserved
steadily other portions of a pot-valiant air. He suddenly faced
one of his persecutors. "If you're so smart, why don't you go
do it?" This persecutor sank promptly through the group to
the rear. The incident gave the badgered one a breathing
spell, and for a moment even turned the derision in another
direction. He took advantage of his interval. "I'll do it if anybody else will," he announced, swaggering to and fro.

Candidates for the adventure did not come forward. To
defend themselves from this countercharge, the other boys
again set up their crowing and bleating. For a while they
would hear nothing from him. Each time he opened his lips,
their chorus of noises made oratory impossible. But at last he
was able to repeat that he would volunteer to dare as much
in the affair as any other boy.

"Well, you go first," they shouted.

But Jimmie intervened to once more lead the populace
against the large boy. "You're mighty brave, ain't you?" he said
to him. "You dared me to do it, and I did—didn't I? Now who's
afraid?" The others cheered this view loudly, and they instantly resumed the baiting of the large boy.

He shamefacedly scratched his left shin with his right foot.
"Well, I ain't afraid." He cast an eye at the monster. "Well,
I ain't afraid." With a glare of hatred at his squalling tor-
mentors, he finally announced a grim intention. "Well, I'll do
it, then, since you're so fresh. Now!"

The mob subsided as with a formidable countenance he
turned toward the impassive figure on the box. The advance
was also a regular progression from high daring to craven
hesitation. At last, when some yards from the monster, the
lad came to a full halt, as if he had encountered a stone wall

The observant little boys in the distance promptly hooted. Stung again by these cries, the lad sneaked two yards forward. He was crouched like a young cat ready for a backward spring. The crowd at the rear, beginning to respect this display, uttered some encouraging cries. Suddenly the lad gathered himself together, made a white and desperate rush forward, touched the monster's shoulder with a far-out-stretched finger, and sped away, while his laughter rang out wild, shrill, and exultant.

The crowd of boys reverenced him at once, and began to throng into his camp, and look at him, and be his admirers. Jimmie was discomfited for a moment, but he and the larger boy, without agreement or word of any kind, seemed to recognize a truce, and they swiftly combined and began to parade before the others.

"Why, it's just as easy as nothing," puffed the larger boy. "Ain't it, Jim?"

"Course," blew Jimmie. "Why, it's as e-e-easy."

They were people of another class. If they had been decorated for courage on twelve battlefields, they could not have made the other boys more ashamed of the situation.

Meanwhile they condescended to explain the emotions of the excursion, expressing unqualified contempt for anyone who could hang back. "Why, it ain't nothin'. He won't do nothin' to you," they told the others, in tones of exasperation.

One of the very smallest boys in the party showed signs of a wistful desire to distinguish himself, and they turned their attention to him, pushing at his shoulders while he swung away from them, and hesitated dreamily. He was eventually induced to make furtive expedition, but it was only for a few yards. Then he paused, motionless, gazing with open mouth. The vociferous entreaties of Jimmie and the large boy had no power over him.

Mrs. Hannigan had come out on her back porch with a pail of water. From this coign she had a view of the secluded portion of the Trescott grounds that was behind the stable. She perceived the group of boys, and the monster on the box. She shaded her eyes with her hand to benefit her vision.

She screeched then as if she was being murdered. "Eddie! Eddie! You come home this minute!"

Her son querulously demanded, "Aw, what for?"

"You come home this minute. Do you hear?"

The other boys seemed to think this visitation upon one of their number required them to preserve for a time the hang-dog air of a collection of culprits, and they remained in guilty silence until the little Hannigan, wrathfully protesting, was pushed through the door of his home. Mrs. Hannigan cast a piercing glance over the group, stared with a bitter face at the Trescott house, as if this new and handsome edifice was insulting her, and then followed her son.

There was wavering in the party. An inroad by one mother always caused them to carefully sweep the horizon to see if there were more coming. "This is my yard," said Jimmie proudly. "We don't have to go home."

The monster on the box had turned its black crepe countenance toward the sky, and was waving its arms in time to a religious chant. "Look at him now," cried a little boy. They turned, and were transfixed by the solemnity and mystery of the indefinable gestures. The wail of the melody was mournful and slow. They drew back. It seemed to spellbind them with the power of a funeral. They were so absorbed that they did not hear the doctor's buggy drive up to the stable. Trescott got out, tied his horse, and approached the group. Jimmie saw him first, and at his look of dismay, the others wheeled.

"What's all this, Jimmie?" asked Trescott in surprise.

The lad advanced to the front of his companions, halted, and said nothing. Trescott's face gloomed slightly as he scanned the scene.

"What were you doing, Jimmie?"

"We was playin'," answered Jimmie huskily.

"Playing at what?"

"Just playin'."

Trescott looked gravely at the other boys, and asked them to please go home. They proceeded to the street much in the manner of frustrated and revealed assassins. The crime of trespass on another boy's place was still a crime when they had only accepted the other boy's cordial invitation, and they were used to being sent out of all manner of gardens upon the sudden appearance of a father or a mother. Jimmie had wretchedly watched the departure of his companions. It involved the loss of his position as a lad who controlled the privileges of his father's grounds, but then he knew that in the beginning he had no right to ask so many boys to be his guests.

Once on the sidewalk, however, they speedily forgot their shame as trespassers, and the large boy launched forth in a description of his success in the late trial of courage. As they went rapidly up the street, the little boy who had made the furtive expedition cried out confidently from the rear, "Yes, and I went almost up to him, didn't I, Willie?"

The large boy crushed him in a few words. "Huh!" he scoffed. "You only went a little way. I went clear up to him."

The pace of the other boys was so manly that the tiny thing had to trot, and he remained at the rear, getting entangled in their legs in his attempts to reach the front rank and become of some importance, dodging this way and that way, and always piping out his little claim to glory.

- *xxi* -

"By the way, Grace," said Trescott, looking into the dining room from his office door, "I wish you would send Jimmie to me before schooltime."

When Jimmie came, he advanced so quietly that Trescott did not at first note him. "Oh," he said, wheeling from a cabinet, "here you are, young man."

"Yes, sir."

Trescott dropped into his chair and tapped the desk with a thoughtful finger. "Jimmie, what were you doing in the back garden yesterday—you and the other boys—to Henry?"

"We weren't doing anything, Pa."

Trescott looked sternly into the raised eyes of his son. "Are you sure you were not annoying him in any way? Now what were you doing, exactly?"

"Why, we—why, we—now—Willie Dalzel said I dassent go right up to him, and I did; and then he did; and then—the other boys were 'fraid; and then—you comed."

Trescott groaned deeply. His countenance was so clouded in sorrow that the lad, bewildered by the mystery of it, burst suddenly forth in dismal lamentations. "There, there. Don't cry, Jim," said Trescott, going round the desk. "Only—" He sat in a great leather reading chair, and took the boy on his knee. "Only I want to explain to you—"

After Jimmie had gone to school, and as Trescott was about to start on his round of morning calls, a message arrived from Doctor Moser. It set forth that the latter's sister was dying in the old homestead, twenty miles away up the valley, and asked Trescott to care for his patients for the day at least. There was also in the envelope a little history of each case and of what had already been done. Trescott replied to the messenger that he would gladly assent to the arrangement.

He noted that the first name on Moser's list was Winter, but this did not seem to strike him as an important fact. When its turn came, he rang the Winter bell. "Good morning, Mrs. Winter," he said cheerfully, as the door was opened. "Doctor Moser has been obliged to leave town today, and he has asked me to come in his stead. How is the little girl this morning?"

Mrs. Winter had regarded him in stony surprise. At last she said, "Come in! I'll see my husband." She bolted into the house. Trescott entered the hall, and turned to the left into the sitting room.

Presently Winter shuffled through the door. His eyes flashed toward Trescott. He did not betray any desire to advance far into the room. "What do you want?" he said.

"What do I want? What do I want?" repeated Trescott, lifting his head suddenly. He had heard an utterly new challenge in the night of the jungle.

"Yes, that's what I want to know," snapped Winter. "What do you want?"

Trescott was silent for a moment. He consulted Moser's

memoranda. "I see that your little girl's case is a trifle serious," he remarked. "I would advise you to call a physician soon. I will leave you a copy of Dr. Moser's record to give to anyone you may call." He paused to transcribe the record on a page of his notebook. Tearing out the leaf, he extended it to Winter as he moved toward the door. The latter shrunk against the wall. His head was hanging as he reached for the paper. This caused him to grasp air, and so Trescott simply let the paper flutter to the feet of the other man.

"Good morning," said Trescott from the hall. This placid retreat seemed to suddenly arouse Winter to ferocity. It was as if he had then recalled all the truths which he had formulated to hurl at Trescott. So he followed him into the hall, and down the hall to the door, and through the door to the porch, barking in fiery rage from a respectful distance. As Trescott imperturbably turned the mare's head down the road, Winter stood on the porch, still yelping. He was like a little dog.

- *xxii* -

"Have you heard the news?" cried Carrie Dungen, as she sped toward Martha's kitchen. "Have you heard the news?" Her eyes were shining with delight.

"No," answered Martha's sister Kate, bending forward eagerly. "What was it? What was it?"

Carrie appeared triumphantly in the open door. "Oh, there's been an awful scene between Doctor Trescott and Jake Winter. I never thought that Jake Winter had any pluck at all, but this morning he told the doctor just what he thought of him."

"Well, what did he think of him?" asked Martha.

"Oh, he called him everything. Mrs. Howarth heard it through her front blinds. It was terrible, she says. It's all over town now. Everybody knows it."

"Didn't the doctor answer back?"

"No! Mrs. Howarth—she says he never said a word. He

just walked down to his buggy and got in, and drove off as co-o-o-l. But Jake gave him jinks, by all accounts."

"But what did he say?" cried Kate, shrill and excited. She was evidently at some kind of feast.

"Oh, he told him that Sadie had never been well since that night Henry Johnson frightened her at Theresa Page's party, and he held him responsible, and how dared he cross his threshold—and—and—and—"

"And what?" said Martha.

"Did he swear at him?" said Kate, in fearsome glee.

"No—not much. He did swear at him a little, but not more than a man does anyhow when he is real mad, Mrs. Howarth says."

"O-oh!" breathed Kate. "And did he call him any names?"

Martha, at her work, had been for a time in deep thought. She now interrupted the others. "It don't seem as if Sadie Winter had been sick since that time Henry Johnson got loose. She's been to school almost the whole time since then, hasn't she?"

They combined upon her in immediate indignation. "School? School? I should say not. Don't think for a moment. School!"

Martha wheeled from the sink. She held an iron spoon, and it seemed as if she was going to attack them. "Sadie Winter has passed here many a morning since then carrying her schoolbag. Where was she going? To a wedding?"

The others, long accustomed to a mental tyranny, speedily surrendered.

"Did she?" stammered Kate. "I never saw her."

Carrie Dungen made a weak gesture.

"If I had been Doctor Trescott," exclaimed Martha loudly, "I'd have knocked that miserable Jake Winter's head off."

Kate and Carrie, exchanging glances, made an alliance in the air. "I don't see why you say that, Martha," replied Carrie with considerable boldness, gaining support and sympathy from Kate's smile. "I don't see how anybody can be blamed for getting angry when their little girl gets almost scared to death and gets sick from it, and all that. Besides, everybody says—"

"Oh, I don't care what everybody says," said Martha.

"Well, you can't go against the whole town," answered Carrie, in sudden, sharp defiance.

"No, Martha, you can't go against the whole town," piped Kate, following her leader rapidly.

" 'The whole town,' " cried Martha. "I'd like to know what you call 'the whole town.' Do you call these silly people who are scared of Henry Johnson 'the whole town'?"

"Why, Martha," said Carrie in a reasoning tone, "you talk as if you wouldn't be scared of him!"

"No more would I," retorted Martha.

"O-oh, Martha, how you talk!" said Kate. "Why, the idea! Everybody's afraid of him."

Carrie was grinning. "You've never seen him, have you?" she asked seductively.

"No," admitted Martha.

"Well, then, how do you know that you wouldn't be scared?"

Martha confronted her. "Have you ever seen him? No? Well, then, how do you know you *would* be scared?"

The allied forces broke out in chorus, "But, Martha, everybody says so. Everybody says so."

"Everybody says what?"

"Everybody that's seen him say they were frightened almost to death. 'Tisn't only women, but it's men, too. It's awful."

Martha wagged her head solemnly. "I'd try not to be afraid of him."

"But supposing you could not help it?" said Kate.

"Yes, and look here," cried Carrie. "I'll tell you another thing. The Hannigans are going to move out of the house next door."

"On account of him?" demanded Martha.

Carrie nodded. "Mrs. Hannigan says so herself."

"Well, of all things!" ejaculated Martha. "Going to move, eh? You don't say so! Where they going to move to?"

"Down on Orchard Avenue."

"Well, of all things! Nice house?"

"I don't know about that. I haven't heard. But there's lots of nice houses on Orchard."

"Yes, but they're all taken," said Kate. "There isn't a vacant house on Orchard Avenue."

"Oh, yes, there is," said Martha. "The old Hampstead house is vacant."

"Oh, of course," said Kate. "But then I don't believe Mrs. Hannigan would like it there. I wonder where they can be going to move to?"

"I'm sure I don't know," sighed Martha. "It must be to someplace we don't know about."

"Well," said Carrie Dungen, after a general reflective silence, "it's easy enough to find out, anyhow."

"Who knows—around here?" asked Kate.

"Why, Mrs. Smith, and there she is in her garden," said Carrie, jumping to her feet. As she dashed out of the door, Kate and Martha crowded at the window. Carrie's voice rang out from near the steps. "Mrs. Smith! Mrs. Smith! Do you know where the Hannigans are going to move to?"

- xxiii -

The autumn smote the leaves, and the trees of Whilomville were panoplied in crimson and yellow. The winds grew stronger, and in the melancholy purple of the nights, the home shine of a window became a finer thing. The little boys, watching the sear and sorrowful leaves drifting down from the maples, dreamed of the near time when they could heap bushels in the streets and burn them during the abrupt evenings.

Three men walked down Niagara Avenue. As they approached Judge Hagenthorpe's house, he came down his walk to meet them in the manner of one who has been waiting.

"Are you ready, judge?" one said.

"All ready," he answered.

The four then walked to Trescott's house. He received them in his office, where he had been reading. He seemed surprised at this visit of four very active and influential citizens, but he had nothing to say of it.

After they were all seated, Trescott looked expectantly from one face to another. There was a little silence. It was broken by John Twelve, the wholesale grocer, who was worth four hundred thousand dollars, and reported to be worth over a million.

"Well, doctor," he said with a short laugh, "I suppose we might as well admit at once that we've come to interfere in something which is none of our business."

"Why, what is it?" asked Trescott, again looking from one face to another. He seemed to appeal particularly to Judge Hagenthorpe, but the old man had his chin lowered musingly to his cane, and would not look at him.

"It's about what nobody talks of—much," said Twelve. "It's about Henry Johnson."

Trescott squared himself in his chair. "Yes?" he said.

Having delivered himself of the title, Twelve seemed to become more easy. "Yes," he answered blandly, "we wanted to talk to you about it."

"Yes?" said Trescott.

Twelve abruptly advanced on the main attack. "Now see here, Trescott, we like you, and we have come to talk right out about this business. It may be none of our affairs and all that, and as for me, I don't mind if you tell me so; but I am not going to keep quiet and see you ruin yourself. And that's how we all feel."

"I am not ruining myself," answered Trescott.

"No, maybe you are not exactly ruining yourself," said Twelve slowly, "but you are doing yourself a great deal of harm. You have changed from being the leading doctor in town to about the last one. It is mainly because there are always a large number of people who are very thoughtless fools, of course, but then that doesn't change the condition."

A man who had not heretofore spoken said, solemnly, "It's the women."

"Well, what I want to say is this," resumed Twelve. "Even if there are a lot of fools in the world, we can't see any reason

why you should ruin yourself by opposing them. You can't
teach them anything, you know."

"I am not trying to teach them anything." Trescott smiled
wearily. "I—it is a matter of—well—"

"And there are a good many of us that admire you for it
immensely," interrupted Twelve, "but that isn't going to
change the minds of all those ninnies."

"It's the women," stated the advocate of this view again.

"Well, what I want to say is this," said Twelve. "We want
you to get out of this trouble and strike your old gait again.
You are simply killing your practice through your infernal
pigheadedness. Now this thing is out of the ordinary, but
there must be ways to—to beat the game somehow, you see.
So we've talked it over—about a dozen of us—and, as I say, if
you want to tell us to mind our own business, why, go ahead;
but we've talked it over, and we've come to the conclusion
that the only way to do is to get Johnson a place somewhere
off up the valley, and—"

Trescott wearily gestured. "You don't know, my friend.
Everybody is so afraid of him, they can't even give him good
care. Nobody can attend to him as I do myself."

"But I have a little no-good farm up beyond Clarence
Mountain that I was going to give to Henry," cried Twelve,
aggrieved. "And if you—and if you—if you—through your
house burning down, or anything—why, all the boys were prepared to take him right off your hands, and—and—"

Trescott arose and went to the window. He turned his
back upon them. They sat waiting in silence. When he returned, he kept his face in the shadow. "No, John Twelve,"
he said, "it can't be done."

There was another stillness. Suddenly a man stirred in his
chair.

"Well, then, a public institution—" he began.

"No," said Trescott. "Public institutions are all very good,
but he is not going to one."

In the background of the group, old Judge Hagenthorpe
was thoughtfully smoothing the polished ivory head of his
cane.

## - xxiv -

Trescott loudly stamped the snow from his feet and shook the flakes from his shoulders. When he entered the house he went at once to the dining room, and then to the sitting room. Jimmie was there, reading painfully in a large book concerning giraffes and tigers and crocodiles.

"Where is your mother, Jimmie?" asked Trescott.

"I don't know, Pa," answered the boy. "I think she is upstairs."

Trescott went to the foot of the stairs and called, but there came no answer. Seeing that the door of the little drawing room was open, he entered. The room was bathed in the half-light that came from the four dull panes of mica in the front of the great stove. As his eyes grew used to the shadows, he saw his wife curled in an armchair. He went to her. "Why, Grace," he said, "didn't you hear me calling you?"

She made no answer, and as he bent over the chair, he heard her trying to smother a sob in the cushion.

"Grace!" he cried. "You're crying!"

She raised her face. "I've got a headache, a dreadful headache, Ned."

"A headache?" he repeated, in surprise and incredulity.

He pulled a chair close to hers. Later, as he cast his eye over the zone of light shed by the dull red panes, he saw that a low table had been drawn close to the stove, and that it was burdened with many small cups and plates of uncut tea cake. He remembered that the day was Wednesday, and that his wife received on Wednesdays.

"Who was here today, Gracie?" he asked.

From his shoulder there came a mumble: "Mrs. Twelve."

"Was she—um," he said. "Why—didn't Anna Hagenthorpe come over?"

The mumble from his shoulder continued: "She wasn't well enough."

Glancing down at the cups, Trescott mechanically counted them. There were fifteen of them. "There, there," he said. "Don't cry, Grace. Don't cry."

The wind was whining round the house, and the snow beat aslant upon the windows. Sometimes the coal in the stove settled with a crumbling sound, and the four panes of mica flashed a sudden new crimson. As he sat holding her head on his shoulder, Trescott found himself occasionally trying to count the cups. There were fifteen of them.

~~~~~~~~~~~~~~~~~~~~~~~~~~~~~~~~~~~~~~~~~~~~~~~~~~

# The Angel Child

- i -

ALTHOUGH Whilomville was in no sense a summer resort, the advent of the warm season meant much to it, for then came visitors from the city—people of considerable confidence— alighting upon their country cousins. Moreover, many citizens who could afford to do so escaped at this time to the seaside. The town, with the commercial life quite taken out of it, drawled and drowsed through long months, during which nothing was worse than the white dust which arose behind every vehicle at blinding noon, and nothing was finer than the cool sheen of the hose sprays over the cropped lawns under the many maples in the twilight.

One summer the Trescotts had a visitation. Mrs. Trescott owned a cousin who was a painter of high degree. I had almost said that he was of national reputation, but come to think of it, it is better to say that almost everybody in the United States who knew about art and its travail knew about him. He had picked out a wife, and naturally, looking at him, one wondered how he had done it. She was quick, beautiful, imperious, while he was quiet, slow, and misty. She was a veritable queen of health, while he, apparently, was of a most brittle constitution. When he played tennis, particularly, he looked every minute as if he were going to break.

They lived in New York, in awesome apartments wherein Japan and Persia, and indeed all the world, confounded the observer. At the end was a cathedral-like studio. They had one child. Perhaps it would be better to say that they had one CHILD. It was a girl. When she came to Whilomville with her parents, it was patent that she had an inexhaustible store of white frocks, and that her voice was high and commanding. These things the town knew quickly. Other things it was doomed to discover by a process.

Her effect upon the children of the Trescott neighborhood was singular. They at first feared, then admired, then embraced. In two days she was a begum. All day long her voice could be heard directing, drilling, and compelling those free-born children; and to say that they felt oppression would be wrong, for they really fought for records of loyal obedience.

All went well until one day was her birthday.

On the morning of this day, she walked out into the Trescott garden and said to her father confidently, "Papa, give me some money, because this is my birthday."

He looked dreamily up from his easel. "Your birthday?" he murmured. Her envisioned father was never energetic enough to be irritable unless someone broke through into that place where he lived with the desires of his life. But neither wife nor child ever heeded or even understood the temperamental values, and so some part of him had grown hardened to their inroads. "Money?" he said. "Here." He handed her a five-dollar bill. It was not that he did not at all understand the nature of a five-dollar bill. He was deaf to it. He had it; he gave it; that was all.

She sallied forth to a waiting people—Jimmie Trescott, Dan Earl, Ella Earl, the Margate twins, the three Phelps children, and others. "I've got some pennies now," she cried, waving the bill, "and I am going to buy some candy." They were deeply stirred by this announcement. Most children are penniless three hundred days in the year, and to another possessing

five pennies they pay deference. To little Cora waving a
bright-green note these children paid heathenish homage. In
some disorder they thronged after her to a small shop on
Bridge Street hill. First of all came ice cream. Seated in the
comic little back parlor, they clamored shrilly over plates
of various flavors, and the shopkeeper marveled that cream
could vanish so quickly down throats that seemed wide open,
always, for the making of excited screams.

These children represented the families of most excellent
people. They were all born in whatever purple there was to
be had in the vicinity of Whilomville. The Margate twins, for
example, were out-and-out prize-winners. With their long,
golden curls and their countenances of similar vacuity, they
shone upon the front bench of all Sunday-school functions,
hand in hand, while their uplifted mother felt about her the
envy of a hundred other parents, and less heavenly children
scoffed from near the door.

Then there was little Dan Earl, probably the nicest boy
in the world, gentle, fine-grained, obedient to the point where
he obeyed anybody. Jimmie Trescott himself was, indeed,
the only child who was at all versed in villainy, but in these
particular days he was on his very good behavior. As a matter
of fact, he was in love. The beauty of his regal little cousin
had stolen his manly heart.

Yes, they were all most excellent children, but, loosened
upon this candy shop with five dollars, they resembled, in a
tiny way, drunken, reveling soldiers within the walls of a
stormed city. Upon the heels of ice cream and cake came
chocolate mice, butterscotch, "everlastings," chocolate cigars,
taffy-on-a-stick, taffy-on-a-slate-pencil, and many semitrans-
parent devices resembling lions, tigers, elephants, horses, cats,
dogs, cows, sheep, tables, chairs, engines (both railway and
for the fighting of fire), soldiers, fine ladies, odd-looking men,
clocks, watches, revolvers, rabbits, and bedsteads. A cent
was the price of a single wonder.

Some of the children, going quite daft, soon had thought to
make fight over the spoils, but their queen ruled with an iron
grip. Her first inspiration was to satisfy her own fancies, but

as soon as that was done, she mingled prodigality with a fine justice, dividing, balancing, bestowing, and sometimes taking away from somebody even that which he had.

It was an orgy. In thirty-five minutes, those respectable children looked as if they had been dragged at the tail of a chariot. The sacred Margate twins, blinking and grunting, wished to take seat upon the floor, and even the most durable Jimmie Trescott found occasion to lean against the counter, wearing at the time a solemn and abstracted air, as if he expected something to happen to him shortly.

Of course their belief had been in an unlimited capacity, but they found there was an end. The shopkeeper handed the queen her change.

"Two seventy-three from five leaves two twenty-seven, Miss Cora," he said, looking upon her with admiration.

She turned swiftly to her clan. "O-oh!" she cried, in amazement. "Look how much I have left!" They gazed at the coins in her palm. They knew then that it was not their capacities which were endless; it was the five dollars.

The queen led the way to the street. "We must think up some way of spending more money," she said, frowning. They stood in silence, awaiting her further speech.

Suddenly she clapped her hands and screamed with delight. "Come on!" she cried. "I know what let's do." Now behold, she had discovered the red-and-white pole in front of the shop of one William Neeltje, a barber by trade.

It becomes necessary to say a few words concerning Neeltje. He was new to the town. He had come and opened a dusty little shop on dusty Bridge Street hill, and although the neighborhood knew from the courier winds that his diet was mainly cabbage, they were satisfied with that meager data. Of course Reifsnyder came to investigate him for the local Barbers' Union, but he found in him only sweetness and light, with a willingness to charge any price at all for a shave or a haircut. In fact, the advent of Neeltje would have made barely a ripple upon the placid bosom of Whilomville if it were not that his name was Neeltje.

At first the people looked at his signboard out of the eye

corner, and wondered lazily why anyone should bear the name of Neeltje; but as time went on, men spoke to other men, saying, "How do you pronounce the name of that barber up there on Bridge Street hill?" And then, before any could prevent it, the best minds of the town were splintering their lances against William Neeltje's signboard. If a man had a mental superior, he guided him seductively to this name, and watched with glee his wrecking. The clergy of the town even entered the lists. There was one among them who had taken a collegiate prize in Syriac, as well as in several less opaque languages, and the other clergymen—at one of their weekly meetings—sought to betray him into this ambush. He pronounced the name correctly, but that mattered little, since none of them knew whether he did or did not; and so they took triumph according to their ignorance. Under these arduous circumstances, it was certain that the town should look for a nickname, and at this time the nickname was in process of formation. So William Neeltje lived on with his secret, smiling foolishly towards the world.

"Come on," cried little Cora. "Let's all get our hair cut. That's what let's do. Let's all get our hair cut! Come on! Come on! Come on!" The others were carried off their feet by the fury of this assault. To get their hair cut! What joy! Little did they know if this were fun; they only knew that their small leader said it was fun. Chocolate-stained but confident, the band marched into William Neeltje's barber shop.

"We wish to get our hair cut," said little Cora haughtily.

Neeltje, in his shirt sleeves, stood looking at them with his half-idiot smile.

"Hurry, now!" commanded the queen. A dray horse toiled step by step, step by step, up Bridge Street hill; a far woman's voice arose; there could be heard the ceaseless hammers of shingling carpenters; all was summer peace. "Come on, now. Who's goin' first? Come on, Ella; you go first. Gettin' our hair cut! Oh, what fun!"

Little Ella Earl would not, however, be first in the chair. She was drawn towards it by a singular fascination, but at the same time she was afraid of it, and so she hung back, saying, "No! You go first! No! You go first!" The question was precipitated by the twins and one of the Phelps children. They made a simultaneous rush for the chair, and screamed and kicked, each pair preventing the third child. The queen entered this melee, and decided in favor of the Phelps boy. He ascended the chair. Thereat an awed silence fell upon the band. And always William Neeltje smiled fatuously.

He tucked a cloth in the neck of the Phelps boy, and taking scissors, began to cut his hair. The group of children came closer and closer. Even the queen was deeply moved. "Does it hurt any?" she asked, in a wee voice.

"Naw," said the Phelps boy with dignity. "Anyhow, I've had m' hair cut afore."

When he appeared to them looking very soldierly with his cropped little head, there was a tumult over the chair. The Margate twins howled; Jimmie Trescott was kicking them on the shins. It was a fight.

But the twins could not prevail, being the smallest of all the children. The queen herself took the chair, and ordered Neeltje as if he were a lady's maid. To the floor there fell proud ringlets, blazing even there in their humiliation with a full, fine bronze light. Then Jimmie Trescott, then Ella Earl (two long, ash-colored plaits), then a Phelps girl, then another Phelps girl; and so on from head to head. The ceremony received unexpected check when the turn came to Dan Earl. This lad, usually docile to any rein, had suddenly grown mulishly obstinate. No, he would not, he would not. He himself did not seem to know why he refused to have his hair cut, but despite the shrill derision of the company, he remained obdurate. Anyhow, the twins, long held in check, and now feverishly eager, were already struggling for the chair.

And so to the floor at last came the golden Margate curls, the heart treasure and glory of a mother, three aunts, and some feminine cousins.

All having been finished, the children, highly elate,

thronged out into the street. They crowed and cackled with pride and joy, anon turning to scorn the cowardly Dan Earl.

Ella Earl was an exception. She had been pensive for some time, and now the shorn little maiden began vaguely to weep. In the door of his shop William Neeltje stood watching them, upon his face a grin of almost inhuman idiocy.

- *ii* -

It now becomes the duty of the unfortunate writer to exhibit these children to their fond parents. "Come on, Jimmie," cried little Cora, "let's go show Mamma." And they hurried off, these happy children, to show Mamma.

The Trescotts and their guests were assembled, indolently awaiting the luncheon bell. Jimmie and the angel child burst in upon them. "Oh, Mamma," shrieked little Cora, "see how fine I am! I've had my hair cut! Isn't it splendid? And Jimmie, too!"

The wretched mother took one sight, emitted one yell, and fell into a chair. Mrs. Trescott dropped a large lady's journal and made a nerveless, mechanical clutch at it. The painter gripped the arms of his chair and leaned forward, staring until his eyes were like two little clock faces. Dr. Trescott did not move or speak.

To the children the next moments were chaotic. There was a loudly wailing mother, and a pale-faced, aghast mother; a stammering father, and a grim and terrible father. The angel child did not understand anything of it save the voice of calamity, and in a moment all her little imperialism went to the winds. She ran sobbing to her mother. "Oh, Mamma! Mamma! Mamma!"

The desolate Jimmie heard out of this inexplicable situation a voice which he knew well, a sort of colonel's voice, and he obeyed like any good soldier. "Jimmie!"

He stepped three paces to the front. "Yes, sir."

"How did this—how did this happen?" said Trescott.

Now Jimmie could have explained how had happened

anything which had happened, but he did not know what had happened, so he said, "I—I—nothin'."

"And, oh, look at her frock!" said Mrs. Trescott brokenly. The words turned the mind of the mother of the angel child. She looked up, her eyes blazing. "Frock!" she repeated. "Frock! What do I care for her frock? Frock!" she choked out again from the depths of her bitterness. Then she arose suddenly, and whirled tragically upon her husband. "Look!" she declaimed. "All—her lovely—hair—all her lovely hair—gone—gone!" The painter was apparently in a fit; his jaw was set, his eyes were glazed, his body was stiff and straight. "All gone—all—her lovely hair—all gone—my poor little darlin'—my—poor—little—darlin'!" And the angel child added her heartbroken voice to her mother's wail as they fled into each other's arms.

In the meantime, Trescott was patiently unraveling some skeins of Jimmie's tangled intellect. "And then you went to this barber's on the hill. Yes. And where did you get the money? Yes. I see. And who besides you and Cora had their hair cut? The Margate twi— Oh, Lord!"

Over at the Margate place, old Eldridge Margate, the grandfather of the twins, was in the back garden picking pease and smoking ruminatively to himself. Suddenly he heard from the house great noises. Doors slammed, women rushed upstairs and downstairs calling to each other in voices of agony. And then, full and mellow upon the still air, arose the roar of the twins in pain.

Old Eldridge stepped out of the pea patch and moved towards the house, puzzled, staring, not yet having decided that it was his duty to rush forward. Then around the corner of the house shot his daughter Mollie, her face pale with horror.

"What's the matter?" he cried.

"Oh, Father," she gasped, "the children! They—"

Then around the corner of the house came the twins, howling at the top of their power, their faces flowing with tears. They were still hand in hand, the ruling passion being strong even in this suffering. At sight of them, old Eldridge took his pipe hastily out of his mouth. "Good God!" he said.

And now what befell one William Neeltje, a barber by trade? And what was said by angry parents of the mother of such an angel child? And what was the fate of the angel child herself?

There was surely a tempest. With the exception of the Margate twins, the boys could well be eliminated from the affair. Of course it didn't matter if their hair was cut. Also the two little Phelps girls had had very short hair, anyhow, and their parents were not too greatly incensed. In the case of Ella Earl, it was mainly the pathos of the little girl's own grieving; but her mother played a most generous part, and called upon Mrs. Trescott, and condoled with the mother of the angel child over their equivalent losses. But the Margate contingent! They simply screeched.

Trescott, composed and cool-blooded, was in the middle of a giddy whirl. He was not going to allow the mobbing of his wife's cousins, nor was he going to pretend that the spoliation of the Margate twins was a virtuous and beautiful act. He was elected, gratuitously, to the position of a buffer.

But curiously enough, the one who achieved the bulk of the misery was old Eldridge Margate, who had been picking pease at the time. The feminine Margates stormed his position as individuals, in pairs, in teams, and en masse. In two days they may have aged him seven years. He must destroy the utter Neeltje. He must midnightly massacre the angel child and her mother. He must dip his arms in blood to the elbows.

Trescott took the first opportunity to express to him his concern over the affair, but when the subject of the disaster was mentioned, old Eldridge, to the doctor's great surprise, actually chuckled long and deeply. "Oh, well, look-a-here," he said. "I never was so much in love with them there damn curls. The curls was purty—yes—but then I'd a darn sight rather see boys look more like boys than like two little wax figgers. An', ye know, the little cusses like it them-

selves. *They* never took no stock in all this washin' an'
combin' an' fixin' an' goin' to church an' paradin' an' showin'
off. They stood it because they were told to. That's all. Of
course this here Neel-te-gee, er whatever his name is, is a
plumb dumb ijit, but I don't see what's to be done, now
that the kids is full well cropped. I might go and burn his
shop over his head, but that wouldn't bring no hair back
onto the kids. They're even kicking on sashes now, and that's
all right, 'cause what fer does a boy want a sash?"

Whereupon Trescott perceived that the old man wore his
brains above his shoulders, and Trescott departed from him
rejoicing greatly that it was only women who could not know
that there was finality to most disasters, and that when a
thing was fully done, no amount of door-slammings, rushing
upstairs and downstairs, calls, lamentations, tears, could
bring back a single hair to the heads of twins.

But the rains came and the winds blew in the most biblical
way when a certain fact came to light in the Trescott household. Little Cora, corroborated by Jimmie, innocently remarked that five dollars had been given her by her father on
her birthday, and with this money the evil had been wrought.
Trescott had known it, but he—thoughtful man—had said
nothing. For her part, the mother of the angel child had up
to that moment never reflected that the consummation of the
wickedness must have cost a small sum of money. But now
it was all clear to her. He was the guilty one—he! "My angel
child!"

The scene which ensued was inspiriting. A few days later,
loungers at the railway station saw a lady leading a shorn
and still undaunted lamb. Attached to them was a husband
and father, who was plainly bewildered, but still more plainly
vexed, as if he would be saying: "Damn 'em! Why can't they
leave me alone?"

# The Pace of Youth

## - i -

STIMSON stood in a corner and glowered. He was a fierce man and had indomitable whiskers, albeit he was very small.

"That young tarrier," he whispered to himself. "He wants to quit makin' eyes at Lizzie. This is too much of a good thing. First thing you know, he'll get fired."

His brow creased in a frown, he strode over to the huge open doors and looked at a sign. "Stimson's Mammoth Merry-Go-Round," it read, and the glory of it was great. Stimson stood and contemplated the sign. It was an enormous affair; the letters were as large as men. The glow of it, the grandeur of it was very apparent to Stimson. At the end of his contemplation, he shook his head thoughtfully, determinedly. "No, no," he muttered. "This is too much of a good thing. First thing you know, he'll get fired."

A soft, booming sound of surf, mingled with the cries of bathers, came from the beach. There was a vista of sand and sky and sea that drew to a mystic point far away in the northward. In the mighty angle, a girl in a red dress was crawling slowly like some kind of a spider on the fabric of nature. A few flags hung lazily above where the bathhouses were marshaled in compact squares. Upon the edge of the sea stood a ship with its shadowy sails painted dimly upon the sky, and high overhead in the still, sun-shot air, a great hawk swung and drifted slowly.

Within the merry-go-round there was a whirling circle of ornamental lions, giraffes, camels, ponies, goats, glittering with varnish and metal that caught swift reflections from windows high above them. With stiff, wooden legs, they swept on in a never-ending race, while a great orchestrion clamored in wild speed. The summer sunlight sprinkled its gold upon the garnet canopies carried by the tireless racers and upon all the devices of decoration that made Stimson's machine magnificent and famous. A host of laughing children bestrode the animals, bending forward like charging cavalrymen, and shaking reins and whooping in glee. At intervals they leaned out perilously to clutch at iron rings that were tendered to them by a long, wooden arm. At the intense moment before the swift grab for the rings, one could see their little, nervous bodies quiver with eagerness; the laughter rang shrill and excited. Down in the long rows of benches, crowds of people sat watching the game, while occasionally a father might arise and go near to shout encouragement, cautionary commands, or applause at his flying offspring. Frequently mothers called out, "Be careful, Georgie!" The orchestrion bellowed and thundered on its platform, filling the ears with its long, monotonous song. Over in a corner, a man in a white apron and behind a counter roared above the tumult, "Popcorn! Popcorn!"

A young man stood upon a small, raised platform, erected in a manner of a pulpit, and just without the line of the circling figures. It was his duty to manipulate the wooden arm and affix the rings. When all were gone into the hands of the triumphant children, he held forth a basket, into which they returned all save the coveted brass one, which meant another ride free and made the holder very illustrious. The young man stood all day upon his narrow platform, affixing rings or holding forth the basket. He was a sort of general squire in these lists of childhood. He was very busy.

And yet Stimson, the astute, had noticed that the young man frequently found time to twist about on his platform and smile at a girl who shyly sold tickets behind a silvered netting. This, indeed, was the great reason of Stimson's glowering. The young man upon the raised platform had no manner of license to smile at the girl behind the silvered netting. It was a most gigantic insolence. Stimson was amazed at it. "By jiminy," he said to himself again, "that fellow is smiling at my daughter." Even in this tone of great wrath it could be discerned that Stimson was filled with wonder that any youth should dare smile at the daughter in the presence of the august father.

Often the dark-eyed girl peered between the shining wires, and upon being detected by the young man, she usually turned her head quickly to prove to him that she was not interested. At other times, however, her eyes seemed filled with a tender fear lest he should fall from that exceedingly dangerous platform. As for the young man, it was plain that these glances filled him with valor, and he stood carelessly upon his perch, as if he deemed it of no consequence that he might fall from it. In all the complexities of his daily life and duties he found opportunity to gaze ardently at the vision behind the netting.

This silent courtship was conducted over the heads of the crowd who thronged about the bright machine. The swift, eloquent glances of the young man went noiselessly and unseen with their message. There had finally become established between the two in this manner a subtle understanding and companionship. They communicated accurately all that they felt. The boy told his love, his reverence, his hope in the changes of the future. The girl told him that she loved him, and she did not love him, that she did not know if she loved him. Sometimes a little sign saying "Cashier" in gold letters, and hanging upon the silvered netting, got directly in range and interfered with the tender message.

The love affair had not continued without anger, unhappiness, despair. The girl had once smiled brightly upon a youth who came to buy some tickets for his little sister, and the young man upon the platform, observing this smile, had been filled with gloomy rage. He stood like a dark statue of vengeance upon his pedestal and thrust out the basket to the children with a gesture that was full of scorn for their hollow happiness, for their insecure and temporary joy. For five hours he did not once look at the girl when she was looking at him. He was going to crush her with his indifference; he was going to demonstrate that he had never been serious.

However, when he narrowly observed her in secret, he discovered that she seemed more blithe than was usual with her. When he found that his apparent indifference had not crushed her, he suffered greatly. She did not love him, he concluded. If she had loved him, she would have been crushed. For two days he lived a miserable existence upon his high perch. He consoled himself by thinking of how unhappy he was, and by swift, furtive glances at the loved face. At any rate, he was in her presence, and he could get a good view from his perch when there was no interference by the little sign: "Cashier."

But suddenly, swiftly, these clouds vanished, and under the imperial blue sky of the restored confidence they dwelt in peace, a peace that was satisfaction, a peace that, like a babe, put its trust in the treachery of the future. This confidence endured until the next day, when she, for an unknown cause, suddenly refused to look at him. Mechanically he continued his task, his brain dazed, a tortured victim of doubt, fear, suspicion. With his eyes he supplicated her to telegraph an explanation. She replied with a stony glance that froze his blood. There was a great difference in their respective reasons for becoming angry. His were always foolish, but apparent, plain as the moon. Hers were subtle, feminine, as incomprehensible as the stars, as mysterious as the shadows at night.

They fell and soared and soared and fell in this manner until they knew that to live without each other would be a wandering in deserts. They had grown so intent upon the uncertainties, the variations, the guessings of their affair that the world had become but a huge, immaterial background. In time of peace, their smiles were soft and prayerful, caresses confided to the air. In time of war, their youthful hearts, capable of profound agony, were wrung by the intricate emotions of doubt. They were the victims of the dread angel of affectionate speculation that forces the brain endlessly on roads that lead nowhere.

At night, the problem of whether she loved him confronted the young man like a specter, looming as high as a hill and telling him not to delude himself. Upon the following day, this battle of the night displayed itself in the renewed fervor of his glances and in their increased number. Whenever he thought he could detect that she, too, was suffering, he felt a thrill of joy.

But there came a time when the young man looked back upon these contortions with contempt. He believed then that he had imagined his pain. This came about when the redoubtable Stimson marched forward to participate.

"This has got to stop," Stimson had said to himself, as he stood and watched them. They had grown careless of the light world that clattered about them; they were become so engrossed in their personal drama that the language of their eyes was almost as obvious as gestures. And Stimson, through his keenness, his wonderful, infallible penetration, suddenly came into possession of these obvious facts. "Well, of all the nerves," he said, regarding with a new interest the young man upon the perch.

He was a resolute man. He never hesitated to grapple with a crisis. He decided to overturn everything at once, for, although small, he was very fierce and impetuous. He resolved to crush this dreaming.

He strode over to the silvered netting. "Say, you want to quit your everlasting grinning at that idiot," he said grimly.

The girl cast down her eyes and made a little heap of quarters into a stack. She was unable to withstand the terrible scrutiny of her small and fierce father.

Stimson turned from his daughter and went to a spot beneath the platform. He fixed his eyes upon the young man and said:

"I've been speakin' to Lizzie. You better attend strictly to your own business or there'll be a new man here next week." It was as if he had blazed away with a shotgun. The young man reeled upon his perch. At last he in a measure regained his composure and managed to stammer, "A—all right, sir." He knew that denials would be futile with the terrible Stimson. He agitatedly began to rattle the rings in the basket, and pretend that he was obliged to count them or inspect them in some way. He, too, was unable to face the great Stimson.

For a moment, Stimson stood in fine satisfaction and gloated over the effect of his threat.

"I've fixed them," he said complacently, and went out to smoke a cigar and revel in himself. Through his mind went the proud reflection that people who came in contact with his granite will usually ended in quick and abject submission.

- *ii* -

One evening, a week after Stimson had indulged in the proud reflection that people who came in contact with his granite will usually ended in quick and abject submission, a young feminine friend of the girl behind the silvered netting came to her there and asked her to walk on the beach after Stimson's Mammoth Merry-Go-Round was closed for the night. The girl assented with a nod.

The young man upon the perch holding the rings saw this nod and judged its meaning. Into his mind came an idea of defeating the watchfulness of the redoubtable Stimson.

When the merry-go-round was closed and the two girls started for the beach, he wandered off aimlessly in another direction, but he kept them in view, and as soon as he was assured that he had escaped the vigilance of Stimson, he followed them.

The electric lights on the beach made a broad band of tremoring light, extending parallel to the sea, and upon the wide walk there slowly paraded a great crowd, intermingling, intertwining, sometimes colliding. In the darkness stretched the vast purple expanse of the ocean, and the deep indigo sky above was peopled with yellow stars. Occasionally out upon the water a whirling mass of froth suddenly flashed into view, like a great, ghostly robe appearing, and then vanished, leaving the sea in its darkness, whence came those bass tones of the water's unknown emotion. A wind, cool, reminiscent of the wave wastes, made the women hold their wraps about

their throats, and caused the men to grip the rims of their
straw hats. It carried the noise of the band in the pavilion
in gusts. Sometimes people unable to hear the music glanced
up at the pavilion and were reassured upon beholding the
distant leader still gesticulating and bobbing, and the other
members of the band with their lips glued to their instruments. High in the sky soared an unassuming moon, faintly
silver.

For a time the young man was afraid to approach the two
girls; he followed them at a distance and called himself a
coward. At last, however, he saw them stop on the outer
edge of the crowd and stand silently listening to the voices
of the sea. When he came to where they stood, he was trembling in his agitation. They had not seen him.

"Lizzie," he began. "I—"

The girl wheeled instantly and put her hand to her throat.
"Oh, Frank, how you frightened me," she said—inevitably.

"Well, you know, I—I—" he stuttered.

But the other girl was one of those beings who are born to
attend at tragedies. She had for love a reverence, an admiration that was greater the more that she contemplated
the fact that she knew nothing of it. This couple, with their
emotions, awed her and made her humbly wish that she
might be destined to be of some service to them. She was
very homely.

When the young man faltered before them, she, in her
sympathy, actually overestimated the crisis, and felt that he
might fall dying at their feet. Shyly, but with courage, she
marched to the rescue.

"Won't you come and walk on the beach with us?" she
said.

The young man gave her a glance of deep gratitude which
was not without the patronage which a man in his condition
naturally feels for one who pities it. The three walked on.

Finally, the being who was born to attend at this tragedy
said that she wished to sit down and gaze at the sea, alone.

They politely urged her to walk on with them, but she was
obstinate. She wished to gaze at the sea, alone. The young

man swore to himself that he would be her friend until he
died.

And so the two young lovers went on without her. They
turned once to look at her.

"Jennie's awful nice," said the girl.

"You bet she is," replied the young man ardently.

They were silent for a little time.

At last the girl said:

"You were angry at me yesterday."

"No, I wasn't."

"Yes, you were, too. You wouldn't look at me once all
day."

"No, I wasn't angry. I was only putting on."

Though she had, of course, known it, this confession seemed
to make her very indignant. She flashed a resentful glance
at him.

"Oh, you were, indeed?" she said with a great air.

For a few minutes she was so haughty with him that he
loved her to madness. And directly this poem, which stuck
at his lips, came forth lamely in fragments.

When they walked back toward the other girl and saw the
patience of her attitude, their hearts swelled in a patronizing
and secondary tenderness for her.

They were very happy. If they had been miserable, they
would have charged this fairy scene of the night with a criminal heartlessness; but as they were joyous, they vaguely
wondered how the purple sea, the yellow stars, the changing
crowds under the electric lights could be so phlegmatic and
stolid.

They walked home by the lakeside way, and out upon the
water those gay paper lanterns, flashing, fleeting, and careering, sang to them, sang a chorus of red and violet, and green
and gold; a song of mystic bands of the future.

One day, when business paused during a dull, sultry afternoon, Stimson went uptown. Upon his return, he found
that the popcorn man, from his stand over in a corner, was
keeping an eye upon the cashier's cage, and that nobody at

all was attending to the wooden arm and the iron rings. He strode forward like a sergeant of grenadiers.

"Where in thunder is Lizzie?" he demanded, a cloud of rage in his eyes.

The popcorn man, although associated long with Stimson, had never got over being dazed.

"They've—they've—gone round to th'—th'—house," he said with difficulty, as if he had just been stunned.

"Whose house?" snapped Stimson.

"Your—your house, I s'pose," said the popcorn man.

Stimson marched round to his home. Kingly denunciations surged, already formulated, to the tip of his tongue, and he bided the moment when his anger could fall upon the heads of that pair of children. He found his wife convulsive and in tears.

"Where's Lizzie?"

And then she burst forth, "Oh—John—John—they've run away, I know they have. They drove by here not three minutes ago. They must have done it on purpose to bid me good-by, for Lizzie waved her hand sadlike; and then, before I could get out to ask where they were going or what, Frank whipped up the horse."

Stimson gave vent to a dreadful roar.

"Get my revolver—get a hack—get my revolver, do you hear—what the devil—" His voice became incoherent.

He had always ordered his wife about as if she were a battalion of infantry, and despite her misery, the training of years forced her to spring mechanically to obey; but suddenly she turned to him with a shrill appeal.

"Oh, John—not—the—revolver."

"Confound it, let go of me!" he roared again, and shook her from him.

He ran hatless upon the street. There were a multitude of hacks at the summer resort, but it was ages to him before he could find one. Then he charged it like a bull.

"Uptown!" he yelled, as he tumbled into the rear seat.

The hackman thought of severed arteries. His galloping horse distanced a large number of citizens who had been running to find what caused such contortions by the little hatless man.

It chanced, as the bouncing hack went along near the lake, Stimson gazed across the calm gray expanse and recognized a color in a bonnet and a pose of a head. A buggy was traveling along a highway that led to Sorington. Stimson bellowed, "There—there—there they are—in that buggy."

The hackman became inspired with the full knowledge of the situation. He struck a delirious blow with the whip. His mouth expanded in a grin of excitement and joy. It came to pass that this old vehicle, with its drowsy horse and its dusty-eyed and tranquil driver, seemed suddenly to awaken, to become animated and fleet. The horse ceased to ruminate on his state, his air of reflection vanished. He became intent upon his aged legs and spread them in quaint and ridiculous devices for speed. The driver, his eyes shining, sat critically in his seat. He watched each motion of this rattling machine down before him. He resembled an engineer. He used the whip with judgment and deliberation as the engineer would have used coal or oil. The horse clacked swiftly upon the macadam, the wheels hummed, the body of the vehicle wheezed and groaned.

Stimson, in the rear seat, was erect in that impassive attitude that comes sometimes to the furious man when he is obliged to leave the battle to others. Frequently, however, the tempest in his breast came to his face and he howled: "Go it—go it—you're gaining; pound 'im! Thump the life out of 'im; hit 'im hard, you fool!" His hand grasped the rod that supported the carriage top, and it was clenched so that the nails were faintly blue.

Ahead, that other carriage had been flying with speed, as from realization of the menace in the rear. It bowled away rapidly, drawn by the eager spirit of a young and modern horse. Stimson could see the buggy top bobbing, bobbing. That little pane, like an eye, was a derision to him. Once he leaned forward and bawled angry sentences. He began to feel impotent; his whole expedition was a tottering of an old man upon a trail of birds. A sense of age made him choke again with wrath. That other vehicle, that was youth, with youth's pace; it was swift-flying with the hope of dreams. He began to comprehend those two children ahead of him, and he knew a sudden and strange awe, because he understood the power of their young blood, the power to fly strongly into the future and feel and hope again, even at that time when his bones must be laid in the earth. The dust rose easily from the hot road and stifled the nostrils of Stimson.

The highway vanished far away in a point with a suggestion of intolerable length. The other vehicle was becoming so small that Stimson could no longer see the derisive eye.

At last the hackman drew rein to his horse and turned to look at Stimson.

"No use, I guess," he said.

Stimson made a gesture of acquiescence, rage, despair. As the hackman turned his dripping horse about, Stimson sank back with the astonishment and grief of a man who has been defied by the universe. He had been in a great perspiration, and now his bald head felt cool and uncomfortable. He put up his hand with a sudden recollection that he had forgotten his hat.

At last he made a gesture. It meant that at any rate he was not responsible.

# The Bride Comes to Yellow Sky

### - i -

THE GREAT Pullman was whirling onward with such dignity of motion that a glance from the window seemed simply to prove that the plains of Texas were pouring eastward. Vast flats of green grass, dull-hued spaces of mesquite and cactus, little groups of frame houses, woods of light and tender trees, all were sweeping into the east, sweeping over the horizon, a precipice.

A newly married pair had boarded this coach at San Antonio. The man's face was reddened from many days in the wind and sun, and a direct result of his new black clothes was that his brick-colored hands were constantly performing in a most conscious fashion. From time to time he looked down respectfully at his attire. He sat with a hand on each knee, like a man waiting in a barber's shop. The glances he devoted to other passengers were furtive and shy.

The bride was not pretty, nor was she very young. She wore a dress of blue cashmere, with small reservations of velvet here and there, and with steel buttons abounding. She continually twisted her head to regard her puff sleeves, very stiff, straight, and high. They embarrassed her. It was quite apparent that she had cooked, and that she expected to cook, dutifully. The blushes caused by the careless scrutiny of some passengers as she had entered the car were strange to see upon this plain, underclass countenance, which was drawn in placid, almost emotionless lines.

They were evidently very happy. "Ever been in a parlor car before?" he asked, smiling with delight.

"No," she answered, "I never was. It's fine, ain't it?"

"Great! And then after a while we'll go forward to the

diner, and get a big layout. Finest meal in the world. Charge a dollar."

"Oh, do they?" cried the bride. "Charge a dollar? Why, that's too much—for us—ain't it, Jack?"

"Not this trip, anyhow," he answered bravely. "We're going to go the whole thing."

Later he explained to her about the trains. "You see, it's a thousand miles from one end of Texas to the other; and this train runs right across it, and never stops but four times." He had the pride of an owner. He pointed out to her the dazzling fittings of the coach; and in truth her eyes opened wider as she contemplated the sea-green figured velvet, the shining brass, silver, and glass, the wood that gleamed as darkly brilliant as the surface of a pool of oil. At one end, a bronze figure sturdily held a support for a separated chamber, and at convenient places on the ceiling were frescos in olive and silver.

To the minds of the pair, their surroundings reflected the glory of their marriage that morning in San Antonio; this was the environment of their new estate; and the man's face in particular beamed with an elation that made him appear ridiculous to the Negro porter. This individual at times surveyed them from afar with an amused and superior grin. On other occasions, he bullied them with skill in ways that did not make it exactly plain to them that they were being bullied. He subtly used all the manners of the most unconquerable kind of snobbery. He oppressed them; but of this oppression they had small knowledge, and they speedily forgot that infrequently a number of travelers covered them with stares of derisive enjoyment. Historically there was supposed to be something infinitely humorous in their situation.

"We are due in Yellow Sky at three forty-two," he said, looking tenderly into her eyes.

"Oh, are we?" she said, as if she had not been aware of it. To evince surprise at her husband's statement was part of her wifely amiability. She took from a pocket a little silver watch; and as she held it before her, and stared at it with a frown of attention, the new husband's face shone.

"I bought it in San Anton' from a friend of mine," he told her gleefully.

"It's seventeen minutes past twelve," she said, looking up at him with a kind of shy and clumsy coquetry. A passenger, noting this play, grew excessively sardonic, and winked at himself in one of the numerous mirrors.

At last they went to the dining car. Two rows of Negro waiters, in glowing white suits, surveyed their entrance with the interest, and also the equanimity, of men who had been forewarned. The pair fell to the lot of a waiter who happened to feel pleasure in steering them through their meal. He viewed them with the manner of a fatherly pilot, his countenance radiant with benevolence. The patronage, entwined with the ordinary deference, was not plain to them. And yet, as they returned to their coach, they showed in their faces a sense of escape.

To the left, miles down a long, purple slope, was a little ribbon of mist where moved the keening Rio Grande. The train was approaching it at an angle, and the apex was Yellow Sky. Presently it was apparent that, as the distance from Yellow Sky grew shorter, the husband became commensurately restless. His brick-red hands were more insistent in their prominence. Occasionally he was even rather absent-minded and faraway when the bride leaned forward and addressed him.

As a matter of truth, Jack Potter was beginning to find the shadow of a deed weigh upon him like a leaden slab. He, the town marshal of Yellow Sky, a man known, liked, and feared in his corner, a prominent person, had gone to San Antonio to meet a girl he believed he loved, and there, after the usual prayers, had actually induced her to marry him, without consulting Yellow Sky for any part of the transaction. He was now bringing his bride before an innocent and unsuspecting community.

Of course, people in Yellow Sky married as it pleased them, in accordance with a general custom; but such was Potter's thought of his duty to his friends, or of their idea of his duty, or of an unspoken form which does not control men in these matters, that he felt he was heinous. He had committed an extraordinary crime. Face to face with this girl in San Antonio, and spurred by his sharp impulse, he had gone headlong over all the social hedges. At San Antonio he was like a man hidden in the dark. A knife to sever any friendly duty, any form, was easy to his hand in that remote city. But the hour of Yellow Sky—the hour of daylight—was approaching.

He knew full well that his marriage was an important thing to his town. It could only be exceeded by the burning of the new hotel. His friends could not forgive him. Frequently he had reflected on the advisability of telling them by telegraph, but a new cowardice had been upon him. He feared to do it. And now the train was hurrying him toward a scene of amazement, glee, and reproach. He glanced out of the window at the line of haze swinging slowly in toward the train.

Yellow Sky had a kind of brass band, which played painfully, to the delight of the populace. He laughed without heart as he thought of it. If the citizens could dream of his prospective arrival with his bride, they would parade the band at the station and escort them, amid cheers and laughing congratulations, to his adobe home.

He resolved that he would use all the devices of speed and plainscraft in making the journey from the station to his house. Once within that safe citadel, he could issue some sort of vocal bulletin, and then not go among the citizens until they had time to wear off a little of their enthusiasm.

The bride looked anxiously at him. "What's worrying you, Jack?"

He laughed again. "I'm not worrying, girl; I'm only thinking of Yellow Sky."

She flushed in comprehension.

A sense of mutual guilt invaded their minds and developed a finer tenderness. They looked at each other with eyes softly aglow. But Potter often laughed the same nervous laugh; the flush upon the bride's face seemed quite permanent.

The traitor to the feelings of Yellow Sky narrowly watched the speeding landscape. "We're nearly there," he said.

Presently the porter came and announced the proximity

of Potter's home. He held a brush in his hand, and with all his airy superiority gone, he brushed Potter's new clothes as the latter slowly turned this way and that way. Potter fumbled out a coin and gave it to the porter, as he had seen others do. It was a heavy and muscle-bound business, as that of a man shoeing his first horse.

The porter took their bag, and as the train began to slow, they moved forward to the hooded platform of the car. Presently the two engines and their long string of coaches rushed into the station of Yellow Sky.

"They have to take water here," said Potter, from a constricted throat and in mournful cadence, as one announcing death. Before the train stopped, his eye had swept the length of the platform, and he was glad and astonished to see there was none upon it but the station agent, who, with a slightly hurried and anxious air, was walking toward the water tanks. When the train had halted, the porter alighted first, and placed in position a little temporary step.

"Come on, girl," said Potter hoarsely. As he helped her down, they each laughed on a false note. He took the bag from the Negro, and bade his wife cling to his arm. As they slunk rapidly away, his hangdog glance perceived that they were unloading the two trunks, and also that the station agent, far ahead near the baggage car, had turned and was running toward him, making gestures. He laughed, and groaned as he laughed, when he noted the first effect of his marital bliss upon Yellow Sky. He gripped his wife's arm firmly to his side, and they fled. Behind them the porter stood, chuckling fatuously.

- *ii* -

The California express on the Southern Railway was due at Yellow Sky in twenty-one minutes. There were six men at the bar of the Weary Gentleman saloon. One was a drummer who talked a great deal and rapidly; three were Texans who

did not care to talk at that time; and two were Mexican sheep-
herders, who did not talk as a general practice in the Weary
Gentleman saloon. The barkeeper's dog lay on the boardwalk
that crossed in front of the door. His head was on his paws,
and he glanced drowsily here and there with the constant
vigilance of a dog that is kicked on occasion. Across the sandy
street were some vivid green grass plots, so wonderful in
appearance, amid the sands that burned near them in a
blazing sun, that they caused a doubt in the mind. They
exactly resembled the grass mats used to represent lawns on
the stage. At the cooler end of the railway station, a man
without a coat sat in a tilted chair and smoked his pipe. The
fresh-cut bank of the Rio Grande circled near the town, and
there could be seen beyond it a great, plum-colored plain of
mesquite.

Save for the busy drummer and his companions in the
saloon, Yellow Sky was dozing. The newcomer leaned gracefully upon the bar, and recited many tales with the confidence
of a bard who has come upon a new field.

"—and at the moment that the old man fell downstairs
with the bureau in his arms, the old woman was coming up
with two scuttles of coal, and of course—"

The drummer's tale was interrupted by a young man who
suddenly appeared in the open door. He cried, "Scratchy
Wilson's drunk, and has turned loose with both hands." The
two Mexicans at once set down their glasses and faded out
of the rear entrance of the saloon.

The drummer, innocent and jocular, answered, "All right,
old man. S'pose he has? Come in and have a drink, anyhow."

But the information had made such an obvious cleft in
every skull in the room that the drummer was obliged to see
its importance. All had become instantly solemn. "Say," said
he, mystified, "what is this?" His three companions made the
introductory gesture of eloquent speech; but the young man
at the door forestalled them.

"It means, my friend," he answered, as he came into the
saloon, "that for the next two hours this town won't be a
health resort."

The barkeeper went to the door, and locked and barred it; reaching out of the window, he pulled in heavy wooden shutters, and barred them. Immediately a solemn, chapel-like gloom was upon the place. The drummer was looking from one to another.

"But say," he cried, "what is this, anyhow? You don't mean there is going to be a gun fight?"

"Don't know whether there'll be a fight or not," answered one man grimly, "but there'll be some shootin'—some good shootin'."

The young man who had warned them waved his hand. "Oh, there'll be a fight fast enough, if anyone wants it. Anybody can get a fight out there in the street. There's a fight just waiting."

The drummer seemed to be swayed between the interest of a foreigner and a perception of personal danger.

"What did you say his name was?" he asked.

"Scratchy Wilson," they answered in chorus.

"And will he kill anybody? What are you going to do? Does this happen often? Does he rampage around like this once a week or so? Can he break in that door?"

"No; he can't break down that door," replied the barkeeper. "He's tried it three times. But when he comes, you'd better lay down on the floor, stranger. He's dead sure to shoot at it, and a bullet may come through."

Thereafter the drummer kept a strict eye upon the door. The time had not yet been called for him to hug the floor, but as a minor precaution, he sidled near to the wall. "Will he kill anybody?" he said again.

The men laughed low and scornfully at the question.

"He's out to shoot, and he's out for trouble. Don't see any good in experimentin' with him."

"But what do you do in a case like this? What do you do?"

A man responded, "Why, he and Jack Potter—"

"But," in chorus the other men interrupted, "Jack Potter's in San Anton'."

"Well, who is he? What's he got to do with it?"

"Oh, he's the town marshal. He goes out and fights Scratchy when he gets on one of these tears."

"Wow!" said the drummer, mopping his brow. "Nice job he's got."

The voices had toned away to mere whisperings. The drummer wished to ask further questions, which were born of an increasing anxiety and bewilderment; but when he attempted them, the men merely looked at him in irritation and motioned him to remain silent. A tense, waiting hush was upon them. In the deep shadows of the room, their eyes shone as they listened for sounds from the street. One man made three gestures at the barkeeper; and the latter, moving like a ghost, handed him a glass and a bottle. The man poured a full glass of whisky, and set down the bottle noiselessly. He gulped the whisky in a swallow, and turned again toward the door in immovable silence. The drummer saw that the barkeeper, without a sound, had taken a Winchester from beneath the bar. Later he saw this individual beckoning to him, so he tiptoed across the room.

"You better come with me back of the bar."

"No, thanks," said the drummer, perspiring. "I'd rather be where I can make a break for the back door."

Whereupon the man of bottles made a kindly but peremptory gesture. The drummer obeyed it, and finding himself seated on a box with his head below the level of the bar, balm was laid upon his soul at sight of various zinc and copper fittings that bore a resemblance to armor plate. The barkeeper took a seat comfortably upon an adjacent box.

"You see," he whispered, "this here Scratchy Wilson is a wonder with a gun—a perfect wonder; and when he goes on the war trail, we hunt our holes—naturally. He's about the last one of the old gang that used to hang out along the river here. He's a terror when he's drunk. When he's sober he's all right—kind of simple—wouldn't hurt a fly—nicest fellow in town. But when he's drunk—whoo!"

There were periods of stillness. "I wish Jack Potter was back from San Anton'," said the barkeeper. "He shot Wilson up once—in the leg—and he would sail in and pull out the kinks in this thing."

Presently they heard from a distance the sound of a shot, followed by three wild yowls. It instantly removed a bond from the men in the darkened saloon. There was a shuffling of feet. They looked at each other. "Here he comes," they said.

- *iii* -

A man in a maroon-colored flannel shirt, which had been purchased for purposes of decoration, and made principally by some Jewish women on the East Side of New York, rounded a corner and walked into the middle of the main street of Yellow Sky. In either hand the man held a long, heavy, blue-black revolver. Often he yelled, and these cries rang through a semblance of a deserted village, shrilly flying over the roofs in a volume that seemed to have no relation to the ordinary vocal strength of a man. It was as if the surrounding stillness formed the arch of a tomb over him. These cries of ferocious challenge rang against walls of silence. And his boots had red tops with gilded imprints, of the kind beloved in winter by little sledding boys on the hillsides of New England.

The man's face flamed in a rage begot of whisky. His eyes, rolling, and yet keen for ambush, hunted the still doorways and windows. He walked with the creeping movement of the midnight cat. As it occurred to him, he roared menacing information. The long revolvers in his hands were as easy as straws; they were moved with an electric swiftness. The little fingers of each hand played sometimes in a musician's way. Plain from the low collar of the shirt, the cords of his neck straightened and sank, straightened and sank, as passion moved him. The only sounds were his terrible invitations. The calm adobes preserved their demeanor at the passing of this small thing in the middle of the street.

There was no offer of fight—no offer of fight. The man

called to the sky. There were no attractions. He bellowed and fumed and swayed his revolvers here and everywhere.

The dog of the barkeeper of the Weary Gentleman saloon had not appreciated the advance of events. He yet lay dozing in front of his master's door. At sight of the dog, the man paused and raised his revolver humorously. At sight of the man, the dog sprang up and walked diagonally away, with a sullen head, and growling. The man yelled, and the dog broke into a gallop. As it was about to enter an alley, there was a loud noise, a whistling, and something spat the ground directly before it. The dog screamed, and wheeling in terror, galloped headlong in a new direction. Again there was a noise, a whistling, and sand was kicked viciously before it. Fear-stricken, the dog turned and flurried like an animal in a pen. The man stood laughing, his weapons at his hips.

Ultimately the man was attracted by the closed door of the Weary Gentleman saloon. He went to it, and hammering with a revolver, demanded drink.

The door remaining imperturbable, he picked a bit of paper from the walk, and nailed it to the framework with a knife. He then turned his back contemptuously upon this popular resort, and walking to the opposite side of the street and spinning there on his heel quickly and lithely, fired at the bit of paper. He missed it by a half inch. He swore at himself, and went away. Later he comfortably fusilladed the windows of his most intimate friend. The man was playing with this town; it was a toy for him.

But still there was no offer of fight. The name of Jack Potter, his ancient antagonist, entered his mind, and he concluded that it would be a glad thing if he should go to Potter's house, and by bombardment induce him to come out and fight. He moved in the direction of his desire, chanting Apache scalp music.

When he arrived at it, Potter's house presented the same still front as had the other adobes. Taking up a strategic position, the man howled a challenge. But this house regarded him as might a great stone god. It gave no sign. After a decent wait, the man howled further challenges, mingling with them wonderful epithets.

Presently there came the spectacle of a man churning himself into deepest rage over the immobility of a house. He fumed at it as the winter wind attacks a prairie cabin in the North. To the distance there should have gone the sound of a tumult like the fighting of two hundred Mexicans. As necessity bade him, he paused for breath or to reload his revolvers.

- iv -

Potter and his bride walked sheepishly and with speed. Sometimes they laughed together shamefacedly and low.

"Next corner, dear," he said finally.

They put forth the efforts of a pair walking bowed against a strong wind. Potter was about to raise a finger to point the first appearance of the new home when, as they circled the corner, they came face to face with a man in a maroon-colored shirt, who was feverishly pushing cartridges into a large revolver. Upon the instant the man dropped his revolver to the ground and, like lightning, whipped another from its holster. The second weapon was aimed at the bridegroom's chest.

There was a silence. Potter's mouth seemed to be merely a grave for his tongue. He exhibited an instinct to at once loosen his arm from the woman's grip, and he dropped the bag to the sand. As for the bride, her face had gone as yellow as old cloth. She was a slave to hideous rites, gazing at the apparitional snake.

The two men faced each other at a distance of three paces. He of the revolver smiled with a new and quiet ferocity.

"Tried to sneak up on me," he said. "Tried to sneak up on me!" His eyes grew more baleful. As Potter made a slight movement, the man thrust his revolver venomously forward. "No; don't you do it, Jack Potter. Don't you move a finger toward a gun just yet. Don't you move an eyelash. The time has come for me to settle with you, and I'm goin' to do it my own way, and loaf along with no interferin'. So if you don't want a gun bent on you, just mind what I tell you."

Potter looked at his enemy. "I ain't got a gun on me, Scratchy," he said. "Honest, I ain't." He was stiffening and steadying, but yet somewhere at the back of his mind a vision of the Pullman floated: the sea-green figured velvet, the shining brass, silver, and glass, the wood that gleamed as darkly brilliant as the surface of a pool of oil—all the glory of the marriage, the environment of the new estate. "You know I fight when it comes to fighting, Scratchy Wilson; but I ain't got a gun on me. You'll have to do all the shootin' yourself."

His enemy's face went livid. He stepped forward, and lashed his weapon to and fro before Potter's chest. "Don't you tell me you ain't got no gun on you, you whelp. Don't tell me no lie like that. There ain't a man in Texas ever seen you without no gun. Don't take me for no kid." His eyes blazed with light, and his throat worked like a pump.

"I ain't takin' you for no kid," answered Potter. His heels had not moved an inch backward. "I'm takin' you for a damn fool. I tell you I ain't got a gun, and I ain't. If you're goin' to shoot me up, you better begin now; you'll never get a chance like this again."

So much enforced reasoning had told on Wilson's rage; he was calmer. "If you ain't got a gun, why ain't you got a gun?" he sneered. "Been to Sunday school?"

"I ain't got a gun because I've just come from San Anton' with my wife. I'm married," said Potter. "And if I'd thought there was going to be any galoots like you prowling around when I brought my wife home, I'd had a gun, and don't you forget it."

"Married!" said Scratchy, not at all comprehending.

"Yes, married. I'm married," said Potter distinctly.

"Married?" said Scratchy. Seemingly for the first time, he saw the drooping, drowning woman at the other man's side. "No!" he said. He was like a creature allowed a glimpse of another world. He moved a pace backward, and his arm, with the revolver, dropped to his side. "Is this the lady?" he asked.

"Yes; this is the lady," answered Potter.

There was another period of silence.

"Well," said Wilson at last, slowly, "I s'pose it's all off now."

"It's all off if you say so, Scratchy. You know I didn't make the trouble." Potter lifted his valise.

"Well, I 'low it's off, Jack," said Wilson. He was looking at the ground. "Married!" He was not a student of chivalry; it was merely that in the presence of this foreign condition he was a simple child of the earlier plains. He picked up his starboard revolver, and placing both weapons in their holsters, he went away. His feet made funnel-shaped tracks in the heavy sand.

~~~~~~~~~~~~~~~~~~~~~~~~~~~~~~~~~~~~~~~~~~~~~~~~~~~~~~~~~~~~

# The Blue Hotel

- *i* -

THE PALACE HOTEL at Fort Romper was painted a light blue, a shade that is on the legs of a kind of heron, causing the bird to declare its position against any background. The Palace Hotel, then, was always screaming and howling in a way that made the dazzling winter landscape of Nebraska seem only a gray, swampish hush. It stood alone on the prairie, and when the snow was falling, the town two hundred yards away was not visible. But when the traveler alighted at the railway station, he was obliged to pass the Palace Hotel before he could come upon the company of low, clapboard houses which composed Fort Romper, and it was not to be thought that any traveler could pass the Palace Hotel without looking at it. Pat Scully, the proprietor, had proved himself a master of strategy when he chose his paints. It is true that on clear days, when the great transcontinental expresses, long lines of swaying Pullmans, swept through Fort Romper, passengers were overcome at the sight, and the cult that knows the brown-reds and the subdivisions of the dark greens of the East expressed shame, pity, horror, in a laugh. But to the citizens of this prairie town and to the people who would naturally stop there, Pat Scully had performed a feat. With this opulence and splendor, these creeds, classes, egotisms that streamed through Romper on the rails day after day, they had no color in common.

As if the displayed delights of such a blue hotel were not sufficiently enticing, it was Scully's habit to go every morning and evening to meet the leisurely trains that stopped at Romper and work his seductions upon any man that he might see wavering, gripsack in hand.

One morning, when a snow-crusted engine dragged its long string of freight cars and its one passenger coach to the station, Scully performed the marvel of catching three men. One was a shaky and quick-eyed Swede, with a great, shining, cheap valise; one was a tall, bronzed cowboy, who was on his way to a ranch near the Dakota line; one was a little, silent man from the East, who didn't look it, and didn't announce it. Scully practically made them prisoners. He was so nimble and merry and kindly that each probably felt it would be the height of brutality to try to escape. They trudged off over the creaking board sidewalks in the wake of the eager little Irishman. He wore a heavy fur cap squeezed tightly down on his head. It caused his two red ears to stick out stiffly, as if they were made of tin.

At last, Scully, elaborately, with boisterous hospitality, conducted them through the portals of the blue hotel. The room which they entered was small. It seemed to be merely a proper temple for an enormous stove, which, in the center, was humming with godlike violence. At various points on its surface the iron had become luminous and glowed yellow from the heat. Beside the stove, Scully's son Johnnie was playing high-five with an old farmer who had whiskers both gray and sandy. They were quarreling. Frequently the old farmer turned his face toward a box of sawdust—colored brown from tobacco juice—that was behind the stove, and spat with an air of great impatience and irritation. With a loud flourish of words, Scully destroyed the game of cards, and bustled his son upstairs with part of the baggage of the new guests. He himself conducted them to three basins of the coldest water in the world. The cowboy and the Easterner burnished themselves fiery red with this water, until it seemed to be some kind of metal polish. The Swede, however, merely dipped his fingers gingerly and with trepidation. It was notable that throughout this series of small ceremonies, the three travelers were made to feel that Scully was very benevolent. He was conferring great favors upon them. He handed the towel from one to another with an air of philanthropic impulse.

Afterward they went to the first room, and sitting about the stove, listened to Scully's officious clamor at his daughters, who were preparing the midday meal. They reflected in the silence of experienced men who tread carefully amid new people. Nevertheless, the old farmer, stationary, invincible in his chair near the warmest part of the stove, turned his face from the sawdust box frequently and addressed a glowing commonplace to the strangers. Usually he was answered in short but adequate sentences by either the cowboy or the Easterner. The Swede said nothing. He seemed to be occupied in making furtive estimates of each man in the room. One might have thought that he had the sense of silly suspicion which comes to guilt. He resembled a badly frightened man.

Later, at dinner, he spoke a little, addressing his conversation entirely to Scully. He volunteered that he had come from New York, where for ten years he had worked as a tailor. These facts seemed to strike Scully as fascinating, and afterward he volunteered that he had lived at Romper for fourteen years. The Swede asked about the crops and the price of labor. He seemed barely to listen to Scully's extended replies. His eyes continued to rove from man to man.

Finally, with a laugh and a wink, he said that some of these Western communities were very dangerous; and after his statement, he straightened his legs under the table, tilted his head, and laughed again, loudly. It was plain that the demonstration had no meaning to the others. They looked at him wondering and in silence.

- *ii* -

As the men trooped heavily back into the front room, the two little windows presented views of a turmoiling sea of snow. The huge arms of the wind were making attempts—mighty, circular, futile—to embrace the flakes as they sped. A gatepost like a still man with a blanched face stood aghast amid this profligate fury. In a hearty voice Scully announced the presence of a blizzard. The guests of the blue hotel, lighting their pipes, assented with grunts of lazy, masculine contentment. No island of the sea could be exempt in the degree of this little room with its humming stove. Johnnie, son of Scully, in a tone which defined his opinion of his ability as a card-player, challenged the old farmer of both gray and sandy whiskers to a game of high-five. The farmer agreed with a contemptuous and bitter scoff. They sat close to the stove, and squared their knees under a wide board. The cowboy and the Easterner watched the game with interest. The Swede remained near the window, aloof, but with a countenance that showed signs of an inexplicable excitement.

The play of Johnnie and the graybeard was suddenly ended by another quarrel. The old man arose while casting a look of heated scorn at his adversary. He slowly buttoned his coat, and then stalked with fabulous dignity from the room. In the discreet silence of all the other men, the Swede laughed. His laughter rang somehow childish. Men by this time had begun to look at him askance, as if they wished to inquire what ailed him.

A new game was formed jocosely. The cowboy volunteered to become the partner of Johnnie, and they all then turned to ask the Swede to throw in his lot with the little Easterner. He asked some questions about the game, and learning that it wore many names, and that he had played it when it was

under an alias, he accepted the invitation. He strode toward
the men nervously, as if he expected to be assaulted. Finally,
seated, he gazed from face to face and laughed shrilly. This
laugh was so strange that the Easterner looked up quickly, the
cowboy sat intent and with his mouth open, and Johnnie
paused, holding the cards with still fingers.

Afterward there was a short silence. Then Johnnie said,
"Well, let's get at it. Come on now!" They pulled their chairs
forward until their knees were bunched under the board.
They began to play, and their interest in the game caused
the others to forget the manner of the Swede.

The cowboy was a board-whacker. Each time that he held
superior cards, he whanged them, one by one, with exceeding
force, down upon the improvised table, and took the tricks
with a glowing air of prowess and pride that sent thrills of
indignation into the hearts of his opponents. A game with a
board-whacker in it is sure to become intense. The countenances of the Easterner and the Swede were miserable
whenever the cowboy thundered down his aces and kings,
while Johnnie, his eyes gleaming with joy, chuckled and
chuckled.

Because of the absorbing play, none considered the strange
ways of the Swede. They paid strict heed to the game. Finally,
during a lull caused by a new deal, the Swede suddenly addressed Johnnie: "I suppose there have been a good many
men killed in this room." The jaws of the others dropped and
they looked at him.

"What in hell are you talking about?" said Johnnie.

The Swede laughed again his blatant laugh, full of a kind
of false courage and defiance. "Oh, you know what I mean,
all right," he answered.

"I'm a liar if I do!" Johnnie protested. The card was
halted, and the men stared at the Swede. Johnnie evidently
felt that as the son of the proprietor he should make a direct
inquiry. "Now what might you be drivin' at, mister?" he
asked. The Swede winked at him. It was a wink full of
cunning. His fingers shook on the edge of the board. "Oh,

maybe you think I have been to nowheres. Maybe you think I'm a tenderfoot?"

"I don't know nothin' about you," answered Johnnie, "and I don't give a damn where you've been. All I got to say is that I don't know what you're driving at. There hain't never been nobody killed in this room."

The cowboy, who had been steadily gazing at the Swede, then spoke: "What's wrong with you, mister?"

Apparently it seemed to the Swede that he was formidably menaced. He shivered and turned white near the corners of his mouth. He sent an appealing glance in the direction of the little Easterner. During these moments, he did not forget to wear his air of advanced pot valor. "They say they don't know what I mean," he remarked mockingly to the Easterner.

The latter answered after prolonged and cautious reflection. "I don't understand you," he said impassively.

The Swede made a movement then which announced that he thought he had encountered treachery from the only quarter where he had expected sympathy, if not help. "Oh, I see you are all against me. I see—"

The cowboy was in a state of deep stupefaction. "Say," he cried, as he tumbled the deck violently down upon the board. "Say, what are you gittin' at, hey?"

The Swede sprang up with the celerity of a man escaping from a snake on the floor. "I don't want to fight!" he shouted. "I don't want to fight!"

The cowboy stretched his long legs indolently and deliberately. His hands were in his pockets. He spat into the sawdust box. "Well, who the hell thought you did?" he inquired.

The Swede backed rapidly toward a corner of the room. His hands were out protectingly in front of his chest, but he was making an obvious struggle to control his fright. "Gentlemen," he quavered, "I suppose I am going to be killed before I can leave this house! I suppose I am going to be killed before I can leave this house!" In his eyes was the dying-swan look. Through the windows could be seen the snow turning blue in the shadow of dusk. The wind tore at the house, and some loose thing beat regularly against the clapboards like a spirit tapping.

A door opened, and Scully himself entered. He paused in surprise as he noted the tragic attitude of the Swede. Then he said, "What's the matter here?"

The Swede answered him swiftly and eagerly: "These men are going to kill me."

"Kill you!" ejaculated Scully. "Kill you! What are you talkin'?"

The Swede made the gesture of a martyr.

Scully wheeled sternly upon his son. "What is this, Johnnie?"

The lad had grown sullen. "Damned if I know," he answered. "I can't make no sense to it." He began to shuffle the cards, fluttering them together with an angry snap. "He says a good many men have been killed in this room, or something like that. And he says he's goin' to be killed here, too. I don't know what ails him. He's crazy, I shouldn't wonder."

Scully then looked for explanation to the cowboy, but the cowboy simply shrugged his shoulders.

"Kill you?" said Scully again to the Swede. "Kill you? Man, you're off your nut."

"Oh, I know," burst out the Swede. "I know what will happen. Yes, I'm crazy—yes. Yes, of course, I'm crazy—yes. But I know one thing—" There was a sort of sweat of misery and terror upon his face. "I know I won't get out of here alive."

The cowboy drew a deep breath, as if his mind was passing into the last stages of dissolution. "Well, I'm doggoned," he whispered to himself.

Scully wheeled suddenly and faced his son. "You've been troublin' this man!"

Johnnie's voice was loud with its burden of grievance. "Why, good Gawd, I ain't done nothin' to 'im."

The Swede broke in. "Gentlemen, do not disturb yourselves. I will leave this house. I will go away, because"—he accused them dramatically with his glance—"because I do not want to be killed."

Scully was furious with his son. "Will you tell me what is

the matter, you young divil? What's the matter, anyhow? Speak out!"

"Blame it!" cried Johnnie in despair. "Don't I tell you I don't know? He—he says we want to kill him, and that's all I know. I can't tell what ails him."

The Swede continued to repeat, "Never mind, Mr. Scully; never mind. I will leave this house. I will go away, because I do not wish to be killed. Yes, of course, I am crazy—yes. But I know one thing! I will go away. I will leave this house. Never mind, Mr. Scully; never mind. I will go away."

"You will not go 'way," said Scully. "You will not go 'way until I hear the reason of this business. If anybody has troubled you, I will take care of him. This is my house. You are under my roof, and I will not allow any peaceable man to be troubled here." He cast a terrible eye upon Johnnie, the cowboy, and the Easterner.

"Never mind, Mr. Scully; never mind. I will go away. I do not wish to be killed." The Swede moved toward the door which opened upon the stairs. It was evidently his intention to go at once for his baggage.

"No, no," shouted Scully peremptorily; but the white-faced man slid by him and disappeared. "Now," said Scully severely, "what does this mane?"

Johnnie and the cowboy cried together, "Why, we didn't do nothin' to 'im!"

Scully's eyes were cold. "No," he said, "you didn't?"

Johnnie swore a deep oath. "Why, this is the wildest loon I ever see. We didn't do nothin' at all. We were jest sittin' here playin' cards, and he—"

The father suddenly spoke to the Easterner. "Mr. Blanc," he asked, "what has these boys been doin'?"

The Easterner reflected again. "I didn't see anything wrong at all," he said at last, slowly.

Scully began to howl. "But what does it mane?" He stared ferociously at his son. "I have a mind to lather you for this, me boy."

Johnnie was frantic. "Well, what have I done?" he bawled at his father.

- iii -

"I think you are tongue-tied," said Scully finally to his son, the cowboy, and the Easterner; and at the end of this scornful sentence, he left the room.

Upstairs the Swede was swiftly fastening the straps of his great valise. Once his back happened to be half turned toward the door, and hearing a noise there, he wheeled and sprang up, uttering a loud cry. Scully's wrinkled visage showed grimly in the light of the small lamp he carried. This yellow effulgence, streaming upward, colored only his prominent features, and left his eyes, for instance, in mysterious shadow. He resembled a murderer.

"Man! Man!" he exclaimed. "Have you gone daffy?"

"Oh, no! Oh, no!" rejoined the other. "There are people in this world who know pretty nearly as much as you do—understand?"

For a moment they stood gazing at each other. Upon the Swede's deathly pale cheeks were two spots brightly crimson and sharply edged, as if they had been carefully painted. Scully placed the light on the table and sat himself on the edge of the bed. He spoke ruminatively. "By cracky, I never heard of such a thing in my life. It's a complete muddle. I can't, for the soul of me, think how you ever got this idea into your head." Presently he lifted his eyes and asked, "And did you sure think they were going to kill you?"

The Swede scanned the old man as if he wished to see into his mind. "I did," he said at last. He obviously suspected that this answer might precipitate an outbreak. As he pulled on a strap, his whole arm shook, the elbow wavering like a bit of paper.

Scully banged his hand impressively on the footboard of the bed. "Why, man, we're goin' to have a line of ilictric streetcars in this town next spring."

"'A line of electric streetcars,'" repeated the Swede stupidly.

"And," said Scully, "there's a new railroad goin' to be built down from Broken Arm to here. Not to mintion the four churches and the smashin'-big brick schoolhouse. Then there's the big factory, too. Why, in two years, Romper'll be a met-tro-*pol*-is."

Having finished the preparation of his baggage, the Swede straightened himself. "Mr. Scully," he said, with sudden hardihood, "how much do I owe you?"

"You don't owe me anythin'," said the old man angrily.

"Yes, I do," retorted the Swede. He took seventy-five cents from his pocket and tendered it to Scully; but the latter snapped his fingers in disdainful refusal. However, it happened that they both stood gazing in a strange fashion at three silver pieces on the Swede's open palm.

"I'll not take your money," said Scully at last. "Not after what's been goin' on here." Then a plan seemed to strike him. "Here," he cried, picking up his lamp and moving toward the door. "Here! Come with me a minute."

"No," said the Swede, in overwhelming alarm.

"Yes," urged the old man. "Come on! I want you to come and see a picter—just across the hall—in my room."

The Swede must have concluded that his hour was come. His jaw dropped and his teeth showed like a dead man's. He ultimately followed Scully across the corridor, but he had the step of one hung in chains.

Scully flashed the light high on the wall of his own chamber. There was revealed a ridiculous photograph of a little girl. She was leaning against a balustrade of gorgeous decoration, and the formidable bang to her hair was prominent. The figure was as graceful as an upright sled stake, and, withal, it was of the hue of lead. "There," said Scully tenderly, "that's the picter of my little girl that died. Her name was Carrie. She had the purtiest hair you ever saw! I was that fond of her, she—"

Turning then, he saw that the Swede was not contemplating the picture at all, but instead, was keeping keen watch on the gloom in the rear.

"Look, man!" cried Scully heartily. "That's the picter of my little gal that died. Her name was Carrie. And then here's the picter of my oldest boy, Michael. He's a lawyer in Lincoln, an' doin' well. I gave that boy a grand eddication, and I'm glad for it now. He's a fine boy. Look at 'im now. Ain't he bold as blazes, him there in Lincoln, an honored an' respicted gintleman! An honored and respicted gintleman," concluded Scully with a flourish. And so saying, he smote the Swede jovially on the back.

The Swede faintly smiled.

"Now," said the old man, "there's only one more thing." He dropped suddenly to the floor and thrust his head beneath the bed. The Swede could hear his muffled voice. "I'd keep it under me piller if it wasn't for that boy Johnnie. Then there's the old woman— Where is it now? I never put it twice in the same place. Ah, now come out with you!"

Presently he backed clumsily from under the bed, dragging with him an old coat rolled into a bundle. "I've fetched him," he muttered. Kneeling on the floor, he unrolled the coat and extracted from its heart a large, yellow-brown whisky bottle.

His first maneuver was to hold the bottle up to the light. Reassured, apparently, that nobody had been tampering with it, he thrust it with a generous movement toward the Swede.

The weak-kneed Swede was about to eagerly clutch this element of strength, but he suddenly jerked his hand away and cast a look of horror upon Scully.

"Drink," said the old man affectionately. He had risen to his feet, and now stood facing the Swede.

There was a silence. Then again Scully said, "Drink!"

The Swede laughed wildly. He grabbed the bottle, put it to his mouth; and as his lips curled absurdly around the opening and his throat worked, he kept his glance, burning with hatred, upon the old man's face.

- *iv* -

After the departure of Scully, the three men, with the cardboard still upon their knees, preserved for a long time an astounded silence. Then Johnnie said, "That's the doddangedest Swede I ever see."

"He ain't no Swede," said the cowboy scornfully.

"Well, what is he, then?" cried Johnnie. "What is he then?"

"It's my opinion," replied the cowboy deliberately, "he's some kind of a Dutchman." It was a venerable custom of the country to entitle as Swedes all light-haired men who spoke with a heavy tongue. In consequence, the idea of the cowboy was not without its daring. "Yes, sir," he repeated. "It's my opinion this feller is some kind of a Dutchman."

"Well, he says he's a Swede, anyhow," muttered Johnnie sulkily. He turned to the Easterner: "What do you think, Mr. Blanc?"

"Oh, I don't know," replied the Easterner.

"Well, what do you think makes him act that way?" asked the cowboy.

"Why, he's frightened." The Easterner knocked his pipe against a rim of the stove. "He's clear frightened out of his boots."

"What at?" cried Johnnie and the cowboy together.

The Easterner reflected over his answer.

"What at?" cried the others again.

"Oh, I don't know, but it seems to me this man has been reading dime novels, and he thinks he's right out in the middle of it—the shootin' and stabbin' and all."

"But," said the cowboy, deeply scandalized, "this ain't Wyoming, ner none of them places. This is Nebrasker."

"Yes," added Johnnie, "an' why don't he wait till he gits *out West?*"

The traveled Easterner laughed. "It isn't different there even—not in these days. But he thinks he's right in the middle of hell."

Johnnie and the cowboy mused long.

"It's awful funny," remarked Johnnie at last.

"Yes," said the cowboy. "This is a queer game. I hope we don't git snowed in, because then we'd have to stand this here man bein' around with us all the time. That wouldn't be no good."

"I wish Pop would throw him out," said Johnnie.

Presently they heard a loud stamping on the stairs, accompanied by ringing jokes in the voice of old Scully, and laughter, evidently from the Swede. The men around the stove stared vacantly at each other. "Gosh!" said the cowboy. The door flew open, and old Scully, flushed and anecdotal, came into the room. He was jabbering at the Swede, who followed him, laughing bravely. It was the entry of two roisterers from a banquet hall.

"Come now," said Scully sharply to the three seated men, "move up and give us a chance at the stove." The cowboy and the Easterner obediently sidled their chairs to make room for the newcomers. Johnnie, however, simply arranged himself in a more indolent attitude, and then remained motionless.

"Come! Git over, there," said Scully.

"Plenty of room on the other side of the stove," said Johnnie.

"Do you think we want to sit in the draught?" roared the father.

But the Swede here interposed with a grandeur of confidence. "No, no. Let the boy sit where he likes," he cried in a bullying voice to the father.

"All right! All right!" said Scully deferentially. The cowboy and the Easterner exchanged glances of wonder.

The five chairs were formed in a crescent about one side of the stove. The Swede began to talk; he talked arrogantly, profanely, angrily. Johnnie, the cowboy, and the Easterner maintained a morose silence, while old Scully appeared to be receptive and eager, breaking in constantly with sympathetic ejaculations.

Finally the Swede announced that he was thirsty. He moved in his chair, and said that he would go for a drink of water.

"I'll git it for you," cried Scully at once.

"No," said the Swede contemptuously. "I'll get it for myself." He arose and stalked with the air of an owner off into the executive parts of the hotel.

As soon as the Swede was out of hearing, Scully sprang to his feet and whispered intensely to the others, "Upstairs he thought I was tryin' to poison 'im."

"Say," said Johnnie, "this makes me sick. Why don't you throw 'im out in the snow?"

"Why, he's all right now," declared Scully. "It was only that he was from the East, and he thought this was a tough place. That's all. He's all right now."

The cowboy looked with admiration upon the Easterner. "You were straight," he said. "You were on to that there Dutchman."

"Well," said Johnnie to his father, "he may be all right now, but I don't see it. Other time he was scared, but now he's too fresh."

Scully's speech was always a combination of Irish brogue and idiom, Western twang and idiom, and scraps of curiously formal diction taken from the storybooks and newspapers. He now hurled a strange mass of language at the head of his son. "What do I keep? What do I keep? What do I keep?" he demanded in a voice of thunder. He slapped his knee impressively, to indicate that he himself was going to make reply, and that all should heed. "I keep a hotel," he shouted. "A hotel, do you mind? A guest under my roof has sacred privileges. He is to be intimidated by none. Not one word shall he hear that would prijudice him in favor of goin' away. I'll not have it. There's no place in this here town where they can say they iver took in a guest of mine because he was afraid to stay here." He wheeled suddenly upon the cowboy and the Easterner. "Am I right?"

"Yes, Mr. Scully," said the cowboy, "I think you're right."

"Yes, Mr. Scully," said the Easterner, "I think you're right."

- v -

At six-o'clock supper, the Swede fizzed like a fire wheel. He sometimes seemed on the point of bursting into riotous song, and in all his madness he was encouraged by old Scully. The Easterner was encased in reserve; the cowboy sat in wide-mouthed amazement, forgetting to eat, while Johnnie wrathily demolished great plates of food. The daughters of the house, when they were obliged to replenish the biscuits, approached as warily as Indians, and having succeeded in their purpose, fled with ill-concealed trepidation. The Swede domineered the whole feast, and he gave it the appearance of a cruel bacchanal. He seemed to have grown suddenly taller; he gazed, brutally disdainful, into every face. His voice rang through the room. Once when he jabbed out harpoon-fashion with his fork to pinion a biscuit, the weapon nearly impaled the hand of the Easterner, which had been stretched quietly out for the same biscuit.

After supper, as the men filed toward the other room, the Swede smote Scully ruthlessly on the shoulder. "Well, old boy, that was a good, square meal." Johnnie looked hopefully at his father; he knew that shoulder was tender from an old fall; and indeed, it appeared for a moment as if Scully was going to flame out over the matter, but in the end he smiled a sickly smile and remained silent. The others understood from his manner that he was admitting his responsibility for the Swede's new viewpoint.

Johnnie, however, addressed his parent in an aside. "Why don't you license somebody to kick you downstairs?" Scully scowled darkly by way of reply.

When they were gathered about the stove, the Swede insisted on another game of high-five. Scully gently deprecated the plan at first, but the Swede turned a wolfish glare upon him. The old man subsided, and the Swede canvassed the others. In his tone there was always a great threat. The cowboy and the Easterner both remarked indifferently that they would play. Scully said that he would presently have to go to meet the six fifty-eight train, and so the Swede turned menacingly upon Johnnie. For a moment their glances crossed like blades, and then Johnnie smiled and said, "Yes, I'll play."

They formed a square, with the little board on their knees. The Easterner and the Swede were again partners. As the play went on, it was noticeable that the cowboy was not board-whacking as usual. Meanwhile Scully, near the lamp, had put on his spectacles, and with an appearance curiously like an old priest, was reading a newspaper. In time he went out to meet the six fifty-eight train, and despite his precautions, a gust of polar wind whirled into the room as he opened the door. Besides scattering the cards, it chilled the players to the marrow. The Swede cursed frightfully. When Scully returned, his entrance disturbed a cosy and friendly scene. The Swede again cursed. But presently they were once more intent, their heads bent forward and their hands moving swiftly. The Swede had adopted the fashion of board-whacking.

Scully took up his paper and for a long time remained immersed in matters which were extraordinarily remote from him. The lamp burned badly, and once he stopped to adjust the wick. The newspaper, as he turned from page to page, rustled with a slow and comfortable sound. Then suddenly he heard three terrible words: "You are cheatin'!"

Such scenes often prove that there can be little of dramatic import in environment. Any room can present a tragic front; any room can be comic. This little den was now hideous as a torture chamber. The new faces of the men themselves had changed it upon the instant. The Swede held a huge fist in front of Johnnie's face, while the latter looked steadily over it into the blazing orbs of his accuser. The Easterner had grown pallid; the cowboy's jaw had dropped in that expression of bovine amazement which was one of his important mannerisms. After the three words, the first sound in the room was made by Scully's paper as it floated forgotten to his feet. His spectacles had also fallen from his nose, but by a clutch he had saved them in air. His hand, grasping the spectacles, now remained poised awkwardly and near his shoulder. He stared at the card-players.

Probably the silence was while a second elapsed. Then, if the floor had been suddenly twitched out from under the men, they could not have moved quicker. The five had projected themselves headlong toward a common point. It happened that Johnnie, in rising to hurl himself upon the Swede, had stumbled slightly because of his curiously instinctive care for the cards and the board. The loss of the moment allowed time for the arrival of Scully, and also allowed the cowboy time to give the Swede a great push which sent him staggering back. The men found tongue together, and hoarse shouts of rage, appeal, or fear burst from every throat. The cowboy pushed and jostled feverishly at the Swede, and the Easterner and Scully clung wildly to Johnnie; but through the smoky air, above the swaying bodies of the peace-compellers, the eyes of the two warriors ever sought each other in glances of challenge that were at once hot and steely.

Of course the board had been overturned, and now the whole company of cards was scattered over the floor, where the boots of the men trampled the fat and painted kings and queens as they gazed with their silly eyes at the war that was waging above them.

Scully's voice was dominating the yells. "Stop, now! Stop, I say! Stop, now—"

Johnnie, as he struggled to burst through the rank formed by Scully and the Easterner, was crying, "Well, he says I cheated! He says I cheated! I won't allow no man to say I cheated! If he says I cheated, he's a —— ——!"

The cowboy was telling the Swede, "Quit, now! Quit, d'ye hear—"

The screams of the Swede never ceased: "He did cheat! I saw him! I saw him—"

As for the Easterner, he was importuning in a voice that was not heeded: "Wait a moment, can't you? Oh, wait a moment. What's the good of a fight over a game of cards? Wait a moment—"

In this tumult, no complete sentences were clear. "Cheat" —"Quit"—"He says"—these fragments pierced the uproar and rang out sharply. It was remarkable that, whereas Scully undoubtedly made the most noise, he was the least heard of any of the riotous band.

Then suddenly there was a great cessation. It was as if each man had paused for breath; and although the room was still lighted with the anger of men, it could be seen that there was no danger of immediate conflict, and at once Johnnie, shouldering his way forward, almost succeeded in confronting the

Swede. "What did you say I cheated for? What did you say I cheated for? I don't cheat, and I won't let no man say I do!"

The Swede said, "I saw you! I saw you!"

"Well," cried Johnnie, "I'll fight any man what says I cheat!"

"No, you won't," said the cowboy. "Not here."

"Ah, be still, can't you?" said Scully, coming between them.

The quiet was sufficient to allow the Easterner's voice to be heard. He was repeating, "Oh, wait a moment, can't you? What's the good of a fight over a game of cards? Wait a moment!"

Johnnie, his red face appearing above his father's shoulder, hailed the Swede again. "Did you say I cheated?"

The Swede showed his teeth. "Yes."

"Then," said Johnnie, "we must fight."

"Yes, fight," roared the Swede. He was like a demoniac. "Yes, fight! I'll show you what kind of a man I am! I'll show you who you want to fight! Maybe you think I can't fight! Maybe you think I can't! I'll show you, you skin, you card-sharp! Yes, you cheated! You cheated! You cheated!"

"Well, let's go at it, then, mister," said Johnnie coolly.

The cowboy's brow was beaded with sweat from his efforts in intercepting all sorts of raids. He turned in despair to Scully. "What are you goin' to do now?"

A change had come over the Celtic visage of the old man. He now seemed all eagerness; his eyes glowed.

"We'll let them fight," he answered stalwartly. "I can't put up with it any longer. I've stood this damned Swede till I'm sick. We'll let them fight."

- *vi* -

The men prepared to go out of doors. The Easterner was so nervous that he had great difficulty in getting his arms into the sleeves of his new leather coat. As the cowboy drew his fur cap down over his ears, his hands trembled. In fact, Johnnie and old Scully were the only ones who displayed no agitation. These preliminaries were conducted without words.

Scully threw open the door. "Well, come on," he said. Instantly a terrific wind caused the flame of the lamp to struggle at its wick, while a puff of black smoke sprang from the chimney top. The stove was in midcurrent of the blast, and its voice swelled to equal the roar of the storm. Some of the scarred and bedabbled cards were caught up from the floor and dashed helplessly against the farther wall. The men lowered their heads and plunged into the tempest as into a sea.

No snow was falling, but great whirls and clouds of flakes, swept up from the ground by the frantic winds, were streaming southward with the speed of bullets. The covered land was blue with the sheen of an unearthly satin, and there was no other hue save where, at the low, black railway station—which seemed incredibly distant—one light gleamed like a tiny jewel. As the men floundered into a thigh-deep drift, it was known that the Swede was bawling out something. Scully went to him, put a hand on his shoulder, and projected an ear. "What's that you say?" he shouted.

"I say," bawled the Swede again, "I won't stand much show against this gang. I know you'll all pitch on me."

Scully smote him reproachfully on the arm. "Tut, man!" he yelled. The wind tore the words from Scully's lips and scattered them far alee.

"You are all a gang of—" boomed the Swede, but the storm also seized the remainder of this sentence.

Immediately turning their backs upon the wind, the men had swung around a corner to the sheltered side of the hotel. It was the function of the little house to preserve here, amid this great devastation of snow, an irregular V-shape of heavily encrusted grass, which crackled beneath the feet. One could imagine the great drifts piled against the windward side. When the party reached the comparative peace of this spot, it was found that the Swede was still bellowing.

"Oh, I know what kind of a thing this is! I know you'll all pitch on me. I can't lick you all!"

Scully turned upon him panther-fashion. "You'll not have to whip all of us. You'll have to whip my son Johnnie. An' the man what troubles you durin' that time will have me to dale with."

The arrangements were swiftly made. The two men faced each other, obedient to the harsh commands of Scully, whose face, in the subtly luminous gloom, could be seen set in the austere, impersonal lines that are pictured on the countenances of the Roman veterans. The Easterner's teeth were chattering, and he was hopping up and down like a mechanical toy. The cowboy stood rocklike.

The contestants had not stripped off any clothing. Each was in his ordinary attire. Their fists were up, and they eyed each other in a calm that had the elements of leonine cruelty in it.

During this pause, the Easterner's mind, like a film, took lasting impressions of three men—the iron-nerved master of the ceremony; the Swede, pale, motionless, terrible; and Johnnie, serene yet ferocious, brutish yet heroic. The entire prelude had in it a tragedy greater than the tragedy of action, and this aspect was accentuated by the long, mellow cry of the blizzard, as it sped the tumbling and wailing flakes into the black abyss of the south.

"Now!" said Scully.

The two combatants leaped forward and crashed together like bullocks. There was heard the cushioned sound of blows, and of a curse squeezing out from between the tight teeth of one.

As for the spectators, the Easterner's pent-up breath exploded from him with a pop of relief, absolute relief from the tension of the preliminaries. The cowboy bounded into the air with a yowl. Scully was immovable as from supreme amazement and fear at the fury of the fight which he himself had permitted and arranged.

For a time the encounter in the darkness was such a perplexity of flying arms that it presented no more detail than would a swiftly revolving wheel. Occasionally a face, as if illumined by a flash of light, would shine out, ghastly and marked with pink spots. A moment later, the men might have been known as shadows, if it were not for the involuntary utterance of oaths that came from them in whispers.

Suddenly a holocaust of warlike desire caught the cowboy, and he bolted foward with the speed of a bronco. "Go it, Johnnie! Go it! Kill him! Kill him!"

Scully confronted him. "Kape back," he said; and by his glance the cowboy could tell that this man was Johnnie's father.

To the Easterner there was a monotony of unchangeable fighting that was an abomination. This confused mingling was eternal to his sense, which was concentrated in a longing for the end, the priceless end. Once the fighters lurched near him, and as he scrambled hastily backward, he heard them breathe like men on the rack.

"Kill him, Johnnie! Kill him! Kill him! Kill him!" The cowboy's face was contorted like one of those agony masks in museums.

"Keep still," said Scully icily.

Then there was a sudden loud grunt, incomplete, cut short, and Johnnie's body swung away from the Swede and fell with sickening heaviness to the grass. The cowboy was barely in time to prevent the mad Swede from flinging himself upon his prone adversary. "No, you don't," said the cowboy, inter- posing an arm. "Wait a second."

Scully was at his son's side. "Johnnie! Johnnie, me boy!" His voice had a quality of melancholy tenderness. "Johnnie! Can you go on with it?" He looked anxiously down into the bloody, pulpy face of his son.

There was a moment of silence, and then Johnnie answered in his ordinary voice, "Yes, I—it—yes."

Assisted by his father, he struggled to his feet. "Wait a bit now till you git your wind," said the old man.

A few paces away, the cowboy was lecturing the Swede. "No, you don't! Wait a second!"

The Easterner was plucking at Scully's sleeve. "Oh, this is enough," he pleaded. "This is enough! Let it go as it stands. This is enough!"

"Bill," said Scully, "git out of the road." The cowboy stepped aside. "Now." The combatants were actuated by a new cau- tion as they advanced toward collision. They'd glared at each other, and then the Swede aimed a lightning blow that carried with it his entire weight. Johnnie was evidently half stupid from weakness, but he miraculously dodged, and his fist sent the overbalanced Swede sprawling.

The cowboy, Scully, and the Easterner burst into a cheer that was like a chorus of triumphant soldiery, but before its conclusion the Swede had scuffled agilely to his feet and come in berserk abandon at his foe. There was another perplexity of flying arms, and Johnnie's body again swung away and fell, even as a bundle might fall from a roof. The Swede instantly staggered to a little wind-waved tree and leaned upon it, breathing like an engine, while his savage and flame-lit eyes roamed from face to face as the men bent over Johnnie. There was a splendor of isolation in his situation at this time which the Easterner felt once when, lifting his eyes from the man on the ground, he beheld that mysterious and lonely figure, waiting.

"Are you any good yet, Johnnie?" asked Scully in a broken voice.

The son gasped and opened his eyes languidly. After a moment, he answered, "No—I ain't—any good—any—more." Then, from shame and bodily ill, he began to weep, the tears furrowing down through the bloodstains on his face. "He was too—too—too heavy for me."

Scully straightened and addressed the waiting figure. "Stranger," he said evenly, "it's all up with our side." Then his voice changed into that vibrant huskiness which is commonly the tone of the most simple and deadly announcements. "Johnnie is whipped."

Without replying, the victor moved off on the route to the front door of the hotel.

The cowboy was formulating new and unspellable blasphemies. The Easterner was startled to find that they were out in a wind that seemed to come direct from the shadowed Arctic floes. He heard again the wail of the snow as it was flung to its grave in the south. He knew now that all this time the cold had been sinking into him deeper and deeper, and he wondered that he had not perished. He felt indifferent to the condition of the vanquished man.

"Johnnie, can you walk?" asked Scully.

"Did I hurt—hurt him any?" asked the son.

"Can you walk, boy? Can you walk?"

Johnnie's voice was suddenly strong. There was a robust impatience in it. "I asked you whether I hurt him any!"

"Yes, yes, Johnnie," answered the cowboy consolingly, "he's hurt a good deal."

They raised him from the ground, and as soon as he was on his feet, he went tottering off, rebuffing all attempts at assistance. When the party rounded the corner, they were fairly blinded by the pelting of the snow. It burned their faces like fire. The cowboy carried Johnnie through the drift to the door. As they entered, some cards again rose from the floor and beat against the wall.

The Easterner rushed to the stove. He was so profoundly chilled that he almost dared to embrace the glowing iron. The Swede was not in the room. Johnnie sank into a chair, and folding his arms on his knees, buried his face in them. Scully, warming one foot and then the other at a rim of the stove, muttered to himself with Celtic mournfulness. The cowboy had removed his fur cap, and with a dazed and rueful air, he was running one hand through his tousled locks. From overhead they could hear the creaking of boards, as the Swede tramped here and there in his room.

The sad quiet was broken by the sudden flinging open of a door that led toward the kitchen. It was instantly followed by an inrush of women. They precipitated themselves upon Johnnie amid a chorus of lamentation. Before they carried their prey off to the kitchen, there to be bathed and harangued with that mixture of sympathy and abuse which is a feat of their sex, the mother straightened herself and fixed old Scully with an eye of stern reproach. "Shame be upon you, Patrick Scully!" she cried. "Your own son, too. Shame be upon you!"

"There now! Be quiet now!" said the old man weakly.

"Shame be upon you, Patrick Scully!" The girls, rallying to this slogan, sniffed disdainfully in the direction of those trembling accomplices, the cowboy and the Easterner. Presently they bore Johnnie away, and left the three men to dismal reflection.

- *vii* -

"I'd like to fight this here Dutchman myself," said the cowboy, breaking a long silence.

Scully wagged his head sadly. "No, that wouldn't do. It wouldn't be right. It wouldn't be right."

"Well, why wouldn't it?" argued the cowboy. "I don't see no harm in it."

"No," answered Scully with mournful heroism. "It wouldn't be right. It was Johnnie's fight, and now we mustn't whip the man just because he whipped Johnnie."

"Yes, that's true enough," said the cowboy, "but—he better not get fresh with me, because I couldn't stand no more of it."

"You'll not say a word to him," commanded Scully, and even then they heard the tread of the Swede on the stairs. His entrance was made theatric. He swept the door back with a bang and swaggered to the middle of the room. No one looked at him. "Well," he cried insolently at Scully, "I s'pose you'll tell me now how much I owe you?"

The old man remained stolid. "You don't owe me nothin'."

"Huh!" said the Swede. "Huh! Don't owe 'im nothin'."

The cowboy addressed the Swede. "Stranger, I don't see how you come to be so gay around here."

Old Scully was instantly alert. "Stop!" he shouted, holding his hand forth, fingers upward. "Bill, you shut up!"

The cowboy spat carelessly into the sawdust box. "I didn't say a word, did I?" he asked.

"Mr. Scully," called the Swede, "how much do I owe you?" It was seen that he was attired for departure, and that he had his valise in his hand.

"You don't owe me nothin'," repeated Scully in the same imperturbable way.

"Huh!" said the Swede. "I guess you're right. I guess if it was any way at all, you'd owe me somethin'. That's what I guess." He turned to the cowboy. "'Kill him! Kill him! Kill him!'" he mimicked, and then guffawed victoriously. "'Kill him!'" He was convulsed with ironical humor.

But he might have been jeering the dead. The three men were immovable and silent, staring with glassy eyes at the stove.

The Swede opened the door and passed into the storm, giving one derisive glance backward at the still group.

As soon as the door was closed, Scully and the cowboy leaped to their feet and began to curse. They trampled to and fro, waving their arms and smashing into the air with their fists. "Oh, but that was a hard minute!" wailed Scully. "That was a hard minute! Him there leerin' and scoffin'! One bang at his nose was worth forty dollars to me that minute! How did you stand it, Bill?"

"How did I stand it?" cried the cowboy in a quivering voice. "How did I stand it? Oh!"

The old man burst into sudden brogue. "I'd loike to take that Swede," he wailed, "and hould 'im down on a shtone flure and bate 'im to a jelly wid a shtick!"

The cowboy groaned in sympathy. "I'd like to git him by the neck and ha-ammer him"—he brought his hand down on a chair with a noise like a pistol shot—"hammer that there Dutchman until he couldn't tell himself from a dead coyote!"

"I'd bate 'im until he—"

"I'd show *him* some things—"

And then together they raised a yearning, fanatic cry: "Oh-o-oh! if we only could—"

"Yes!"

"Yes!"

"And then I'd—"

"O-o-oh!"

- *viii* -

The Swede, tightly gripping his valise, tacked across the face of the storm as if he carried sails. He was following a line of little naked, gasping trees which, he knew, must mark the way of the road. His face, fresh from the pounding of Johnnie's fists, felt more pleasure than pain in the wind and the driving snow. A number of square shapes loomed upon him finally, and he knew them as the houses of the main body of the town. He found a street and made travel along it, leaning heavily upon the wind whenever, at a corner, a terrific blast caught him.

He might have been in a deserted village. We picture the world as thick with conquering and elate humanity, but here, with the bugles of the tempest pealing, it was hard to imagine a peopled earth. One viewed the existence of man then as a marvel, and conceded a glamour of wonder to these lice which were caused to cling to a whirling, fire-smitten, ice-locked, disease-stricken, space-lost bulb. The conceit of man was explained by this storm to be the very engine of life. One was a coxcomb not to die in it. However, the Swede found a saloon.

In front of it an indomitable red light was burning, and the snowflakes were made blood color as they flew through the circumscribed territory of the lamp's shining. The Swede pushed open the door of the saloon and entered. A sanded expanse was before him, and at the end of it four men sat about a table drinking. Down one side of the room extended a radiant bar, and its guardian was leaning upon his elbows listening to the talk of the men at the table. The Swede dropped his valise upon the floor, and smiling fraternally upon the barkeeper, said, "Gimme some whisky, will you?" The man placed a bottle, a whisky glass, and a glass of ice-thick water upon the bar. The Swede poured himself an abnormal portion of whisky and drank it in three gulps. "Pretty bad night," remarked the bartender indifferently. He was making the pretension of blindness which is usually a distinction of his class; but it could have been seen that he was furtively studying the half-erased bloodstains on the face of the Swede. "Bad night," he said again.

"Oh, it's good enough for me," replied the Swede hardily, as he poured himself some more whisky. The barkeeper took his coin and maneuvered it through its reception by the highly nickeled cash machine. A bell rang; a card labeled "20 cts." had appeared.

"No," continued the Swede, "this isn't too bad weather. It's good enough for me."

"So?" murmured the barkeeper languidly.

The copious drams made the Swede's eyes swim, and he breathed a trifle heavier. "Yes, I like this weather. I like it. It suits me." It was apparently his design to impart a deep significance to these words.

"So?" murmured the bartender again. He turned to gaze dreamily at the scroll-like birds and birdlike scrolls which had been drawn with soap upon the mirrors in back of the bar.

"Well, I guess I'll take another drink," said the Swede presently. "Have something?"

"No, thanks; I'm not drinkin'," answered the bartender. Afterward he asked, "How did you hurt your face?"

The Swede immediately began to boast loudly. "Why, in a fight. I thumped the soul out of a man down here at Scully's hotel."

The interest of the four men at the table was at last aroused. "Who was it?" said one.

"Johnnie Scully," blustered the Swede. "Son of the man what runs it. He will be pretty near dead for some weeks, I can tell you. I made a nice thing of him, I did. He couldn't get up. They carried him in the house. Have a drink?"

Instantly the men in some subtle way encased themselves in reserve. "No, thanks," said one. The group was of curious formation. Two were prominent local businessmen; one was the district attorney; and one was a professional gambler of the kind known as "square." But a scrutiny of the group would not have enabled an observer to pick the gambler from the men of more reputable pursuits. He was, in fact, a man so delicate in manner, when among people of fair class, and so judicious in his choice of victims, that in the strictly masculine part of the town's life he had come to be explicitly trusted and admired. People called him a thoroughbred. The fear and contempt with which his craft was regarded were undoubtedly the reason why his quiet dignity shone conspicuous above the quiet dignity of men who might be merely hatters, billiard-markers, or grocery clerks. Beyond an occasional unwary traveler who came by rail, this gambler was supposed to prey solely upon reckless and senile farmers, who, when flush with good crops, drove into town in all the pride and confidence of an absolutely invulnerable stupidity. Hearing at times in circuitous fashion of the despoilment of such a farmer, the important men of Romper invariably laughed in contempt of the victim, and if they thought of the wolf at all, it was with a kind of pride at the knowledge that he would never dare think of attacking their wisdom and courage. Besides, it was popular that this gambler had a real wife and two real children in a neat cottage in a suburb, where he led an exemplary home life; and when anyone even suggested a discrepancy in his character, the crowd immediately vociferated descriptions of this virtuous family circle. Then men who led exemplary home lives, and men who did not lead exemplary home lives, all subsided in a bunch, remarking that there was nothing more to be said.

However, when a restriction was placed upon him—as, for instance, when a strong clique of members of the new Pollywog Club refused to permit him, even as a spectator, to appear in the rooms of the organization—the candor and gentleness with which he accepted the judgment disarmed many of his foes and made his friends more desperately partisan. He invariably distinguished between himself and a respectable Romper man so quickly and frankly that his manner actually appeared to be a continual broadcast compliment.

And one must not forget to declare the fundamental fact of his entire position in Romper. It is irrefutable that in all affairs outside his business, in all matters that occur eternally and commonly between man and man, this thieving card-player was so generous, so just, so moral, that in a contest, he could have put to flight the consciences of nine-tenths of the citizens of Romper.

And so it happened that he was seated in this saloon with the two prominent local merchants and the district attorney.

The Swede continued to drink raw whisky, meanwhile babbling at the barkeeper and trying to induce him to indulge in potations. "Come on. Have a drink. Come on. What—no? Well, have a little one, then. By gawd, I've whipped a man tonight, and I want to celebrate. I whipped him good, too. Gentlemen," the Swede cried to the men at the table, "have a drink?"

"Ssh!" said the barkeeper.

The group at the table, although furtively attentive, had been pretending to be deep in talk, but now a man lifted his eyes toward the Swede and said, shortly, "Thanks. We don't want any more."

At this reply, the Swede ruffled out his chest like a rooster. "Well," he exploded, "it seems I can't get anybody to drink with me in this town. Seems so, don't it? Well!"

"Ssh!" said the barkeeper.

"Say," snarled the Swede, "don't you try to shut me up. I won't have it. I'm a gentleman, and I want people to drink with me. And I want 'em to drink with me now. *Now*—do you understand?" He rapped the bar with his knuckles.

Years of experience had calloused the bartender. He merely grew sulky. "I hear you," he answered.

"Well," cried the Swede, "listen hard then. See those men over there? Well, they're going to drink with me, and don't you forget it. Now you watch."

"Hi!" yelled the barkeeper. "This won't do!"

"Why won't it?" demanded the Swede. He stalked over to the table, and by chance laid his hand upon the shoulder of the gambler. "How about this?" he asked wrathfully. "I asked you to drink with me."

The gambler simply twisted his head and spoke over his shoulder. "My friend, I don't know you."

"Oh, hell!" answered the Swede, "come and have a drink."

"Now, my boy," advised the gambler kindly, "take your hand off my shoulder and go 'way and mind your own business." He was a little, slim man, and it seemed strange to hear him use this tone of heroic patronage to the burly Swede. The other men at the table said nothing.

"What! You won't drink with me, you little dude? I'll make you, then! I'll make you!" The Swede had grasped the gambler frenziedly at the throat, and was dragging him from his chair. The other men sprang up. The barkeeper dashed around the corner of his bar. There was a great tumult, and then was seen a long blade in the hand of the gambler. It shot forward, and a human body, this citadel of virtue, wisdom, power, was pierced as easily as if it had been a melon. The Swede fell with a cry of supreme astonishment.

The prominent merchants and the district attorney must have at once tumbled out of the place backward. The bartender found himself hanging limply to the arm of a chair and gazing into the eyes of a murderer.

"Henry," said the latter, as he wiped his knife on one of the towels that hung beneath the bar rail, "you tell 'em where to find me. I'll be home, waiting for 'em." Then he vanished. A moment afterward the barkeeper was in the street dinning through the storm for help and, moreover, companionship.

The corpse of the Swede, alone in the saloon, had its eyes fixed upon a dreadful legend that dwelt atop of the cash machine: "This registers the amount of your purchase."

- *ix* -

Months later, the cowboy was frying pork over the stove of a little ranch near the Dakota line, when there was a quick thud of hoofs outside, and presently the Easterner entered with the letters and the papers.

"Well," said the Easterner at once, "the chap that killed the Swede has got three years. Wasn't much, was it?"

"He has? Three years?" The cowboy poised his pan of pork, while he ruminated upon the news. "Three years. That ain't much."

"No. It was a light sentence," replied the Easterner as he unbuckled his spurs. "Seems there was a good deal of sympathy for him in Romper."

"If the bartender had been any good," observed the cowboy thoughtfully, "he would have gone in and cracked that there Dutchman on the head with a bottle in the beginnin' of it and stopped all this here murderin'."

"Yes, a thousand things might have happened," said the Easterner tartly.

The cowboy returned his pan of pork to the fire, but his philosophy continued. "It's funny, ain't it? If he hadn't said Johnnie was cheatin' he'd be alive this minute. He was an awful fool. Game played for fun, too. Not for money. I believe he was crazy."

"I feel sorry for that gambler," said the Easterner.

"Oh, so do I," said the cowboy. "He don't deserve none of it for killin' who he did."

"The Swede might not have been killed if everything had been square."

"Might not have been killed?" exclaimed the cowboy. "Everythin' square? Why, when he said that Johnnie was cheatin' and acted like such a jackass? And then in the saloon he fairly walked up to git hurt?" With these arguments the cowboy browbeat the Easterner and reduced him to rage.

"You're a fool!" cried the Easterner viciously. "You're a bigger jackass than the Swede by a million majority. Now let me tell you one thing. Let me tell you something. Listen. Johnnie *was* cheating!"

" 'Johnnie,' " said the cowboy blankly. There was a minute of silence, and then he said robustly, "Why, no. The game was only for fun."

"Fun or not," said the Easterner, "Johnnie was cheating. I saw him. I know it. I saw him. And I refused to stand up and be a man. I let the Swede fight it out alone. And you—you were simply puffing around the place and wanting to fight. And then old Scully himself! We are all in it! This poor gambler isn't even a noun. He is kind of an adverb. Every sin is the result of a collaboration. We, five of us, have collaborated in the murder of this Swede. Usually there are from a dozen to forty women really involved in every murder, but in this case it seems to be only five men—you, I, Johnnie, old Scully; and that fool of an unfortunate gambler came merely as a culmination, the apex of a human movement, and gets all the punishment."

The cowboy, injured and rebellious, cried out blindly into this fog of mysterious theory: "Well, I didn't do anythin', did I?"

---

# The Five White Mice

FREDDIE was mixing a cocktail. His hand with the long spoon was whirling swiftly, and the ice in the glass hummed and rattled like a cheap watch. Over by the window, a gambler, a millionaire, a railway conductor, and the agent of a vast American syndicate were playing seven-up. Freddie surveyed them with the ironical glance of a man who is mixing a cocktail.

From time to time, a swarthy Mexican waiter came with his tray from the rooms at the rear, and called his orders across the bar. The sounds of the indolent stir of the city awakening from its siesta floated over the screens which barred the sun and the inquisitive eye. From the faraway kitchen could be heard the roar of the old French chef, driving, herding, and abusing his Mexican helpers.

A string of men came suddenly in from the street. They stormed up to the bar. There were impatient shouts. "Come, now, Freddie, don't stand there like a portrait of yourself. Wiggle!" Drinks of many kinds and colors—amber, green, mahogany, strong and mild—began to swarm upon the bar, with all the attendants of lemon, sugar, mint, and ice. Freddie, with Mexican support, worked like a sailor in the provision of them, sometimes talking with that scorn for drink and admiration for those who drink which is the attribute of a good barkeeper.

At last a man was afflicted with a stroke of dice-shaking. A herculean discussion was waging, and he was deeply engaged in it, but at the same time he lazily flirted the dice. Occasionally he made great combinations. "Look at that, would you?" he cried proudly. The others paid little heed. Then violently the craving took them. It went along the line like an epidemic, and involved them all. In a moment they had arranged a carnival of dice-shaking, with money penalties and liquid prizes. They clamorously made it a point of honor with Freddie that he, too, should play, and take his chance of sometimes providing this large group with free refreshment. With bent heads, like football players, they surged over the tinkling dice, jostling, cheering, and bitterly arguing. One of the quiet company playing seven-up at the corner table said profanely that the row reminded him of a bowling contest at a picnic.

After the regular shower, many carriages rolled over the smooth *calle*, and sent a musical thunder through the Casa Verde. The shop windows became aglow with light, and the walks were crowded with youths, callow and ogling, dressed vainly according to supposititious fashions. The policemen had muffled themselves in their gnomelike cloaks and placed their lanterns as obstacles for the carriages in the middle of the street. The City of Mexico gave forth the deep, mellow organ tones of its evening resurrection.

But still the group at the bar of the Casa Verde were shaking dice. They had passed beyond shaking for drinks for the crowd, for Mexican dollars, for dinner, for the wine at dinner. They had even gone to the trouble of separating the cigars and cigarettes from the dinner's bill, and causing a distinct man to be responsible for them. Finally they were aghast. Nothing remained within sight of their minds which even remotely suggested further gambling. There was a pause for deep consideration.

"Well!"

"Well!"

A man called out in the exuberance of creation, "I know! Let's stake for a box tonight at the circus! A box at the circus!" The group was profoundly edified. "That's it! That's it! Come on, now! Box at the circus!" A dominating voice cried, "Three dashes—high man out!" An American, tall, and with a face of copper red from the rays that flash among the Sierra Madres and burn on the cactus deserts, took the little leathern cup, and spun the dice out upon the polished wood. A fascinated assemblage hung upon the bar rail. Three kings turned their pink faces upward. The tall man flourished the cup, burlesquing, and flung the two other dice. From them he ultimately extracted one more pink king. "There," he said. "Now let's see! Four kings!" He began to swagger in a sort of provisional way.

The next man took the cup, and blew softly on the top of it. Poising it in his hand, he then surveyed the company with a stony eye, and paused. They knew perfectly well that he was applying the magic of deliberation and ostentatious indifference, but they could not wait in tranquillity during the performance of all these rites. They began to call out impatiently, "Come now! Hurry up!" At last the man, with a gesture that was singularly impressive, threw the dice. The others set up a howl of joy. "Not a pair!" There was another solemn pause. The men moved restlessly. "Come now! Go ahead!" In the end, the man, induced and abused, achieved something that was nothing in the presence of four kings. The tall man climbed on the foot rail, and leaned hazardously forward. "Four kings! My four kings are good to go out," he bellowed into the middle of the mob; and although in a moment he did pass into the radiant region of exemption, he continued to bawl advice and scorn.

The mirrors and oiled woods of the Casa Verde were now dancing with blue flashes from a great buzzing electric lamp. A host of quiet members of the Anglo-Saxon colony had come in for their predinner cocktails. An amiable person was exhibiting to some tourists this popular American saloon. It was a very sober and respectable time of day. Freddie reproved courageously the dice-shaking brawlers, and in return, he received the choicest advice in a tumult of seven combined vocabularies. He laughed. He had been compelled to retire from the game, but he was keeping an interested, if furtive, eye upon it.

Down at the end of the line there was a youth at whom everybody railed for his flaming ill luck. At each disaster, Freddie swore from behind the bar, in a sort of affectionate contempt. "Why, this Kid has had no luck for two days. Did you ever see such throwin'?"

The contest narrowed eventually to the New York Kid and an individual who swung about placidly on legs that moved in nefarious circles. He had a grin that resembled a bit of carving. He was obliged to lean down and blink rapidly to ascertain the facts of his venture, but fate presented him with five queens. His smile did not change, but he puffed gently, like a man who has been running.

The others, having emerged scatheless from this part of the conflict, waxed hilarious with the Kid. They smote him on either shoulder. "We've got you stuck for it, Kid! You can't beat that game! Five queens!"

Up to this time, the Kid had displayed only the temper of the gambler; but the cheerful hoots of the players, supplemented now by a ring of guying noncombatants, caused him to feel profoundly that it would be fine to beat the five queens. He addressed a gambler's slogan to the interior of the cup:

> "Oh, five white mice of chance,
> Shirts of wool and corduroy pants,
> Gold and wine, women and sin,
> All for you if you let me come in—
> Into the house of chance."

Flashing the dice sardonically out upon the bar, he displayed three aces. From two dice in the next throw he achieved one more ace. For his last throw he rattled the single dice for a long time. He already had four aces; if he accomplished another one, the five queens were vanquished, and the box at the circus came from the drunken man's pocket. All of the Kid's movements were slow and elaborate. For his last throw, he planted the cup bottom up on the bar, with the one die hidden under it. Then he turned and faced the crowd with the air of a conjuror or a cheat. "Oh, maybe it's an ace," he said in boastful calm, "maybe it's an ace." Instantly he was presiding over a little drama in which every man was absorbed. The Kid leaned with his back against the bar rail and with his elbows upon it. "Maybe it's an ace," he repeated.

A jeering voice in the background said, "Yes, maybe it is, Kid."

The Kid's eyes searched for a moment among the men. "I'll bet fifty dollars it is an ace," he said.

Another voice asked, "American money?"

"Yes," answered the Kid.

"Oh!" There was a general laugh at this discomfiture. However, no one came forward at the Kid's challenge, and presently he turned to the cup. "Now I'll show you." With the manner of a mayor unveiling a statue, he lifted the cup. There was revealed naught but a ten-spot. In the roar which arose could be heard each man ridiculing the cowardice of his neighbor, and above all the din rang the voice of Freddie berating everyone.

"Why, there isn't one liver to every five men in the outfit. That was the greatest cold bluff I ever saw worked. He wouldn't know how to cheat with dice if he wanted to. Don't know the first thing about it. I could hardly keep from laughin' when I seen him drillin' you around. Why, I tell you I had that fifty dollars right in my pocket, if I wanted to be a chump. You're an easy lot!"

Nevertheless, the group who had won in the circus-box game did not relinquish their triumph. They burst like a storm about the head of the Kid, swinging at him with their fists. " 'Five white mice,' " they quoted, choking, " 'five white mice'!"

"Oh, they are not so bad," said the Kid.

Afterward it often occurred that a man would suddenly jeer a finger at the Kid, and derisively say, " 'Five white mice'!"

On the route from the dinner to the circus, others of the party often asked the Kid if he had really intended to make his appeal to mice. They suggested other animals—rabbits, dogs, hedgehogs, snakes, opossums. To this banter the Kid replied with a serious expression of his belief in the fidelity and wisdom of the five white mice. He presented a most eloquent case, decorated with fine language and insults, in which he proved that if one was going to believe in anything at all, one might as well choose the five white mice. His companions, however, at once and unanimously pointed out to him that his recent exploit did not place him in the light of a convincing advocate.

The Kid discerned two figures in the street. They were making imperious signs at him. He waited for them to approach, for he recognized one as the other Kid—the 'Frisco Kid: there were two Kids. With the 'Frisco Kid was Benson. They arrived almost breathless. "Where you been?" cried the 'Frisco Kid. It was an arrangement that, upon meeting, the one that could first ask this question was entitled to use a tone of limitless injury. "What you been doing? Where you going? Come on with us! Benson and I have got a little scheme."

The New York Kid pulled his arm from the grapple of the other. "I can't. I've got to take these sutlers to the circus. They stuck me for it, shaking dice at Freddie's. I can't, I tell you."

The two did not at first attend to his remarks. "Come on; we've got a little scheme."

"I can't. They've stuck me. I've got to take 'm to the circus."

At this time it did not suit the men with the scheme to recognize these objections as important. "Oh, take 'm some other time." "Well, can't you take 'm some other time?" "Let 'm go." "Damn the circus." "Get cold feet!" "What did you get stuck for?" "Get cold feet!"

But despite their fighting, the New York Kid broke away from them. "I can't, I tell you. They stuck me."

As he left them, they yelled with rage. "Well, meet us, now—do you hear?—in the Casa Verde, as soon as the circus quits! Hear?" They threw maledictions after him.

In the City of Mexico a man goes to the circus without descending in any way to infant amusements, because the Circo Teatro Orrin is one of the best in the world, and too easily surpasses anything of the kind in the United States, where it is merely a matter of a number of rings, if possible, and a great professional agreement to lie to the public. Moreover, the American clown who in the Mexican arena prances and gabbles is the clown to whom writers refer as the delight of their childhood and lament that he is dead. At this circus the Kid was not debased by the sight of mournful prisoner elephants and caged animals, forlorn and sickly. He sat in his box until late, and laughed, and swore, when past laughing, at the comic, foolish, wise clown.

When he returned to the Casa Verde, there was no display of the 'Frisco Kid and Benson. Freddie was leaning upon the bar, listening to four men terribly discuss a question that was not plain. There was a card game in the corner, of course. Sounds of revelry pealed from the rear rooms.

When the Kid asked Freddie if he had seen his friend and Benson, Freddie looked bored. "Oh, yes; they were in here just a minute ago; but I don't know where they went. They've got their skates on. Where've they been? Came in here rolling across the floor like two little gilt gods. They wobbled around for a time, and then 'Frisco wanted me to send six bottles of wine around to Benson's rooms; but I didn't have anybody to send this time of night, and so they got mad and went out. Where did they get their loads?"

In the first deep gloom of the street the Kid paused a moment, debating. But presently he heard quavering voices: "Oh, Kid! Kid! Come 'ere!" Peering, he recognized two vague figures against the opposite wall. He crossed the street, and they said, "Hellokid."

"Say, where did you get it?" he demanded sternly. "You

Indians better go home. What did you want to get scragged for?" His face was luminous with virtue.

As they swung to and fro they made angry denials: "We ain' load'. We ain' load'. Big chump! Comonangetadrink."

The sober youth turned then to his friend. "Hadn't you better go home, Kid? Come on; it's late. You'd better break away."

The 'Frisco Kid wagged his head decisively. "Got take Benson home first. He'll be wallowing round in a minute. Don't mind me; I'm all right."

"Cer'ly he's all right," said Benson, arousing from deep thought. "He's all right. But better take 'm home, though. That's ri-right. He's load'. But he's all right. No need go home any more 'n you. But better take 'm home. He's load'." He looked at his companion with compassion. "Kid, you're load'."

The sober Kid spoke abruptly to his friend from San Francisco. "Kid, pull yourself together now. Don't fool. We've got to brace this ass of a Benson all the way home. Get hold of his other arm."

The 'Frisco Kid immediately obeyed his comrade, without a word or a glower. He seized Benson, and came to attention like a soldier. Later, indeed, he meekly ventured, "Can't we take cab?" But when the New York Kid snapped out that there were no convenient cabs, he subsided to an impassive silence. He seemed to be reflecting upon his state without astonishment, dismay, or any particular emotion. He submitted himself woodenly to the direction of his friend.

Benson had protested when they had grasped his arms. "W'asha doing?" he said in a new and guttural voice. "W'asha doing? I ain' load'. Comonangetadrink. I—"

"Oh, come along, you idiot," said the New York Kid. The 'Frisco Kid merely presented the mien of a stoic to the appeal of Benson, and in silence dragged away at one of his arms. Benson's feet came from that particular spot on the pavement with the reluctance of roots, and also with the ultimate suddenness of roots. The three of them lurched out into the street in the abandon of tumbling chimneys. Benson was meanwhile noisily challenging the others to produce any reasons for his being taken home. His toes clashed into the curb when they reached the other side of the *calle,* and for a moment the Kids hauled him along, with the points of his shoes scraping musically on the pavement. He balked formidably as they were about to pass the Casa Verde. "No, no! Leshavanothdrink! Anothdrink! Onemore!"

But the 'Frisco Kid obeyed the voice of his partner in a manner that was blind, but absolute, and they scummed Benson on past the door. Locked together, the three swung into a dark street. The sober Kid's flank was continually careering ahead of the other wing. He harshly admonished the 'Frisco child, and the latter promptly improved in the same manner of unthinking, complete obedience. Benson began to recite the tale of a love affair—a tale that didn't even have a middle. Occasionally the New York Kid swore. They toppled on their way like three comedians playing at it on the stage.

At midnight, a little Mexican street burrowing among the walls of the city is as dark as a whale's throat at deep sea. Upon this occasion, heavy clouds hung over the capital, and the sky was a pall. The projecting balconies could make no shadows.

"Shay," said Benson, breaking away from his escort suddenly, "what want g'ome for? I ain' load'. You got reg'lar spool fact'ry in your head—you N' York Kid there. Thish oth' Kid, he's mos' proper—mos' proper shober. He's drunk, but—but he's shober."

"Ah, shut up, Benson," said the New York Kid. "Come along now. We can't stay here all night." Benson refused to be corralled, but spread his legs and twirled like a dervish, meanwhile under the evident impression that he was conducting himself most handsomely. It was not long before he gained the opinion that he was laughing at the others. "Eight purple dogsh—dogs! Eight purple dogs! Tha's what Kid'll see in the morn'. Look ou' for 'em. They—"

As Benson, describing the canine phenomena, swung wildly across the sidewalk, it chanced that three other pedestrians were passing in shadowy rank. Benson's shoulder jostled one of them.

A Mexican wheeled upon the instant. His hand flashed to his hip. There was a moment of silence, during which Benson's voice was not heard raised in apology. Then an indescribable comment, one burning word, came from between the Mexican's teeth.

Benson, rolling about in a semidetached manner, stared vacantly at the Mexican, who thrust his lean, yellow face forward, while his fingers played nervously at his hip. The New York Kid could not follow Spanish well, but he understood when the Mexican breathed softly, "Does the señor want fight?"

Benson simply gazed in gentle surprise. The woman next to him at dinner had said something inventive—his tailor had presented his bill—something had occurred which was mildly out of the ordinary, and his surcharged brain refused to cope with it. He displayed only the agitation of a smoker temporarily without a light.

The New York Kid had almost instantly grasped Benson's arm, and was about to jerk him away when the other Kid, who up to this time had been an automaton, suddenly projected himself forward, thrust the rubber Benson aside, and said, "Yes."

There was no sound nor light in the world. The wall at the left happened to be of the common prison-like construction—no door, no window, no opening at all. Humanity was enclosed and asleep. Into the mouth of the sober Kid came a wretched, bitter taste, as if it had filled with blood. He was transfixed, as if he was already seeing the lightning ripples on the knife blade.

But the Mexican's hand did not move at that time. His face went still further forward, and he whispered, "So?" The sober Kid saw his face as if he and it were alone in space—a yellow mask, smiling in eager cruelty, in satisfaction, and above all, it was lit with sinister decision. As for the features, they were reminiscent of an unplaced, a forgotten type, which really resembled with precision those of a man who had shaved him three times in Boston in 1888. But the expression burned his mind as sealing wax burns the palm, and fascinated, stupefied, he actually watched the progress of the man's thought toward the point where a knife would be wrenched from its sheath. The emotion, a sort of mechanical fury, a breeze made by electric fans, a rage made by vanity, smote the dark countenance in wave after wave.

Then the New York Kid took a sudden step forward. His hand was also at his hip. He was gripping there a revolver of robust size. He recalled that upon its black handle was stamped a hunting scene in which a sportsman in fine leggings and a peaked cap was taking aim at a stag less than one-eighth of an inch away.

His pace forward caused instant movement of the Mexicans. One immediately took two steps to face him squarely. There was a general adjustment, pair and pair. The opponent of the New York Kid was a tall man and quite stout. His sombrero was drawn low over his eyes; his serape was flung on his left shoulder; his back was bent in the supposed manner of a Spanish grandee. This concave gentleman cut a fine and terrible figure. The lad, moved by the spirits of his modest and perpendicular ancestors, had time to feel his blood roar at sight of the pose.

He was aware that the third Mexican was over on the left, fronting Benson; and he was aware that Benson was leaning against the wall, sleepily and peacefully eyeing the convention. So it happened that these six men stood, side fronting side, five of them with their right hands at their hips, and with their bodies lifted nervously, while the central pair exchanged a crescendo of provocations. The meaning of their words rose and rose. They were traveling in a straight line toward collision.

The New York Kid contemplated his Spanish grandee. He drew his revolver upward until the hammer was surely free of the holster. He waited, immovable and watchful, while the garrulous 'Frisco Kid expended two and a half lexicons on the middle Mexican.

The Eastern lad suddenly decided that he was going to

be killed. His mind leaped forward and studied the aftermath. The story would be a marvel of brevity when first it reached the far New York home, written in a careful hand on a bit of cheap paper, topped and footed and backed by the printed fortifications of the cable company. But they are often as stones flung into mirrors, these bits of paper upon which are laconically written all the most terrible chronicles of the times. He witnessed the uprising of his mother and sister, and the invincible calm of his hard-mouthed old father, who would probably shut himself in his library and smoke alone. Then his father would come, and they would bring him here, and say, "This is the place." Then, very likely, each would remove his hat. They would stand quietly with their hats in their hands for a decent minute. He pitied his old financing father, unyielding and millioned, a man who commonly spoke twenty-two words a year to his beloved son. The Kid understood it at this time. If his fate was not impregnable, he might have turned out to be a man and have been liked by his father.

The other Kid would mourn his death. He would be preternaturally correct for some weeks, and recite the tale without swearing. But it would not bore him. For the sake of his dead comrade, he would be glad to be preternaturally correct and to recite the tale without swearing.

These views were perfectly stereopticon, flashing in and away from his thought with an inconceivable rapidity, until, after all, they were simply one quick, dismal impression. And now, here is the unreal real: Into this Kid's nostrils, at the expectant moment of slaughter, had come the scent of new-mown hay, a fragrance from a field of prostrate grass, a fragrance which contained the sunshine, the bees, the peace of meadows, and the wonder of a distant, crooning stream. It had no right to be supreme, but it was supreme, and he breathed it as he waited for pain and a sight of the unknown.

But in the same instant, it may be, his thought flew to the 'Frisco Kid, and it came upon him like a flicker of lightning that the 'Frisco Kid was not going to be there to perform, for instance, the extraordinary office of respectable mourner. The other Kid's head was muddled, his hand was unsteady, his agility was gone. This other Kid was facing the determined and most ferocious gentleman of the enemy. The New York Kid became convinced that his friend was lost. There was going to be a screaming murder. He was so certain of it that he wanted to shield his eyes from sight of the leaping arm and the knife. It was sickening—utterly sickening. The New York Kid might have been taking his first sea voyage. A combination of honorable manhood and inability prevented him from running away.

He suddenly knew that it was possible to draw his own revolver, and by a swift maneuver face down all three Mexicans. If he was quick enough, he would probably be victor. If any hitch occurred in the draw he would undoubtedly be dead with his friends. It was a new game. He had never been obliged to face a situation of this kind in the Beacon Club in New York. In this test the lungs of the Kid still continued to perform their duty:

> "Oh, five white mice of chance,
> Shirts of wool and corduroy pants,
> Gold and wine, women and sin,
> All for you if you let me come in—
> Into the house of chance."

He thought of the weight and size of his revolver, and dismay pierced him. He feared that in his hands it would be as unwieldy as a sewing machine for this quick work. He imagined, too, that some singular providence might cause him to lose his grip as he raised his weapon; or it might get fatally entangled in the tails of his coat. Some of the eels of despair lay wet and cold against his back.

But at the supreme moment, the revolver came forth as if it were greased, and it arose like a feather. This somnolent machine, after months of repose, was finally looking at the breasts of men.

Perhaps in this one series of movements the Kid had unconsciously used nervous force sufficient to raise a bale of hay. Before he comprehended it, he was standing behind his revolver, glaring over the barrel at the Mexicans, menacing first one and then another. His finger was tremoring on the trigger. The revolver gleamed in the darkness with a fine, silver light.

The fulsome grandee sprang backward with a low cry. The man who had been facing the 'Frisco Kid took a quick step away. The beautiful array of Mexicans was suddenly disorganized.

The cry and the backward steps revealed something of great importance to the New York Kid. He had never dreamed that he did not have a complete monopoly of all possible trepidations. The cry of the grandee was that of a man who suddenly sees a poisonous snake. Thus the Kid was able to understand swiftly that they were all human beings. They were unanimous in not wishing for too bloody a combat. There was a sudden expression of the equality. He had vaguely believed that they were not going to evince much consideration for his dramatic development as an active factor. They even might be exasperated into an onslaught by it. Instead, they had respected his movement with a respect as great even as an ejaculation of fear and backward steps. Upon the instant, he pounced forward, and began to swear, unreeling great English oaths as thick as ropes, and lashing the faces of the Mexicans with them. He was bursting with rage because these men had not previously confided to him that they were vulnerable. The whole thing had been an absurd imposition. He had been seduced into respectful alarm by the concave attitude of the grandee. And after all, there had been an equality of emotion—an equality! He was furious. He wanted to take the serape of the grandee and swaddle him in it.

The Mexicans slunk back, their eyes burning wistfully. The Kid took aim first at one and then at another. After they had achieved a certain distance, they paused and drew up in a rank. They then resumed some of their old splendor of manner. A voice hailed him in a tone of cynical bravado, as if it had come from between high lips of smiling mockery: "Well, señor, it is finished?"

The Kid scowled into the darkness, his revolver drooping at his side. After a moment he answered, "I am willing." He found it strange that he should be able to speak after this silence of years.

"Good night, señor."

"Good night."

When he turned to look at the 'Frisco Kid, he found him in his original position, his hand upon his hip. He was blinking in perplexity at the point where the Mexicans had vanished.

"Well," said the sober Kid crossly, "are you ready to go home now?"

The 'Frisco Kid said, "Where they gone?" His voice was undisturbed, but inquisitive.

Benson suddenly propelled himself from his dreamful position against the wall. " 'Frisco Kid's all right. He's drunk's fool, and he's all right. But you New York Kid, you're shober." He passed into a state of profound investigation. "Kid shober 'cause didn't go with us. Didn't go with us 'cause went to damn circus. Went to damn circus 'cause lose shakin' dice. Lose shakin' dice 'cause—what make lose shakin' dice, Kid?"

The New York Kid eyed the senile youth. "I don't know. The five white mice, maybe?"

Benson puzzled so over this reply that he had to be held erect by his friends. Finally the 'Frisco Kid said, "Let's go home."

Nothing had happened.

# The Open Boat

A Tale Intended to Be After the Fact:
Being the Experience of Four Men
from the Sunk Steamer *Commodore*

- *i* -

NONE of them knew the color of the sky. Their eyes glanced level, and were fastened upon the waves that swept toward them. These waves were of the hue of slate, save for the tops, which were of foaming white, and all of the men knew the colors of the sea. The horizon narrowed and widened, and dipped and rose, and at all times its edge was jagged with waves that seemed thrust up in points like rocks.

Many a man ought to have a bathtub larger than the boat which here rode upon the sea. These waves were most wrongfully and barbarously abrupt and tall, and each froth-top was a problem in small-boat navigation.

The cook squatted in the bottom, and looked with both eyes at the six inches of gunwale which separated him from the ocean. His sleeves were rolled over his fat forearms, and the two flaps of his unbuttoned vest dangled as he bent to bail out the boat. Often he said, "Gawd! That was a narrow clip." As he remarked it, he invariably gazed eastward over the broken sea.

The oiler, steering with one of the two oars in the boat, sometimes raised himself suddenly to keep clear of water that swirled in over the stern. It was a thin little oar, and it seemed often ready to snap.

The correspondent, pulling at the other oar, watched the waves and wondered why he was there.

The injured captain, lying in the bow, was at this time buried in that profound dejection and indifference which comes, temporarily at least, to even the bravest and most enduring when, willy-nilly, the firm fails, the army loses, the ship goes down. The mind of the master of a vessel is rooted deep in the timbers of her, though he command for a day or a decade; and this captain had on him the stern impression of a scene in the grays of dawn of seven turned faces, and later a stump of a topmast with a white ball on it, that slashed to and fro at the waves, went low and lower, and down. Thereafter there was something strange in his voice. Although steady, it was deep with mourning, and of a quality beyond oration or tears.

"Keep 'er a little more south, Billie," said he.

"A little more south, sir," said the oiler in the stern.

A seat in his boat was not unlike a seat upon a bucking bronco, and by the same token a bronco is not much smaller. The craft pranced and reared and plunged like an animal. As each wave came, and she rose for it, she seemed like a horse making at a fence outrageously high. The manner of her scramble over these walls of water is a mystic thing, and moreover, at the top of them were ordinarily these problems in white water, the foam racing down from the summit of each wave requiring a new leap, and a leap from the air. Then, after scornfully bumping a crest, she would slide and race and splash down a long incline, and arrive bobbing and nodding in front of the next menace.

A singular disadvantage of the sea lies in the fact that after successfully surmounting one wave, you discover that there is another behind it just as important and just as nervously anxious to do something effective in the way of swamping boats. In a ten-foot dinghy one can get an idea of the resources of the sea in the line of waves that is not probable to the average experience which is never at sea in a dinghy. As each slaty wall of water approached, it shut all else from the view of the men in the boat, and it was not difficult to imagine that this particular wave was the final outburst of the ocean, the last effort of the grim water. There was a terrible grace in the move of the waves, and they came in silence, save for the snarling of the crests.

In the wan light the faces of the men must have been gray. Their eyes must have glinted in strange ways as they gazed steadily astern. Viewed from a balcony, the whole thing would doubtless have been weirdly picturesque. But the men in the boat had no time to see it, and if they had had leisure, there were other things to occupy their minds. The sun swung steadily up the sky, and they knew it was broad day because the color of the sea changed from slate to emerald green streaked with amber lights, and the foam was like tumbling snow. The process of the breaking day was unknown to them. They were aware only of this effect upon the color of the waves that rolled toward them.

In disjointed sentences the cook and the correspondent argued as to the difference between a lifesaving station and a house of refuge. The cook had said, "There's a house of refuge just north of the Mosquito Inlet Light, and as soon as they see us they'll come off in their boat and pick us up."

"As soon as who see us?" said the correspondent.

"The crew," said the cook.

"Houses of refuge don't have crews," said the correspondent. "As I understand them, they are only places where clothes and grub are stored for the benefit of shipwrecked people. They don't carry crews."

"Oh, yes, they do," said the cook.

"No, they don't," said the correspondent.

"Well, we're not there yet, anyhow," said the oiler, in the stern.

"Well," said the cook, "perhaps it's not a house of refuge that I'm thinking of as being near Mosquito Inlet Light; perhaps it's a lifesaving station."

"We're not there yet," said the oiler in the stern.

- ii -

As the boat bounced from the top of each wave, the wind tore through the hair of the hatless men, and as the craft plopped her stern down again, the spray slashed past them. The crest of each of these waves was a hill, from the top of which the men surveyed for a moment a broad, tumultuous expanse, shining and wind-riven. It was probably splendid, it was probably glorious, this play of the free sea, wild with lights of emerald and white and amber.

"Bully good thing it's an onshore wind," said the cook. "If not, where would we be? Wouldn't have a show."

"That's right," said the correspondent.

The busy oiler nodded his assent.

Then the captain, in the bow, chuckled in a way that expressed humor, contempt, tragedy, all in one. "Do you think we've got much of a show now, boys?" said he.

Whereupon the three were silent, save for a trifle of hemming and hawing. To express any particular optimism at this time they felt to be childish and stupid, but they all doubtless possessed this sense of the situation in their minds. A young man thinks doggedly at such times. On the other hand, the ethics of their condition was decidedly against any open suggestion of hopelessness. So they were silent.

"Oh, well," said the captain, soothing his children, "we'll get ashore all right."

But there was that in his tone which made them think; so the oiler quoth, "Yes! if this wind holds."

The cook was bailing. "Yes! if we don't catch hell in the surf."

Canton-flannel gulls flew near and far. Sometimes they sat down on the sea, near patches of brown seaweed that rolled over the waves with a movement like carpets on a line in a gale. The birds sat comfortably in groups, and they were envied by some in the dinghy, for the wrath of the sea was no more to them than it was to a covey of prairie chickens a thousand miles inland. Often they came very close and stared at the men with black, beadlike eyes. At these times they were uncanny and sinister in their unblinking scrutiny, and the men hooted angrily at them, telling them to be gone. One came, and evidently decided to alight on the top of the captain's head. The bird flew parallel to the boat and did not circle, but made short, sidelong jumps in the air in chicken fashion. His black eyes were wistfully fixed upon the captain's head. "Ugly brute," said the oiler to the bird. "You look as if you were made with a jackknife." The cook and the correspondent swore darkly at the creature. The captain naturally wished to knock it away with the end of the heavy painter, but he did not dare do it, because anything resembling an emphatic gesture would have capsized this freighted boat; and so, with his open hand, the captain gently and carefully waved the gull away. After it had been discouraged from the pursuit, the captain breathed easier on account of his hair, and others breathed easier because the bird struck their minds at this time as being somehow gruesome and ominous.

In the meantime, the oiler and the correspondent rowed. And also they rowed. They sat together in the same seat, and each rowed an oar. Then the oiler took both oars; then the correspondent took both oars; then the oiler; then the correspondent. They rowed and they rowed. The very ticklish part of the business was when the time came for the reclining one in the stern to take his turn at the oars. By the very last star of truth, it is easier to steal eggs from under a hen than it was to change seats in the dinghy. First the man in the stern slid his hand along the thwart and moved with care, as if he were of Sèvres. Then the man in the rowing seat slid his hand along the other thwart. It was all done with the most extraordinary care. As the two sidled past each other, the whole party kept watchful eyes on the coming wave, and the captain cried, "Look out now! Steady there!"

The brown mats of seaweed that appeared from time to time were like islands, bits of earth. They were traveling, apparently, neither one way nor the other. They were, to all intents, stationary. They informed the men in the boat that it was making progress slowly toward the land.

The captain, rearing cautiously in the bow after the dinghy soared on a great swell, said that he had seen the lighthouse at Mosquito Inlet. Presently the cook remarked that he had seen it. The correspondent was at the oars then, and for some reason he, too, wished to look at the lighthouse; but his back was toward the far shore, and the waves were important, and for some time he could not seize an opportunity to turn his head. But at last there came a wave more gentle than the others, and when at the crest of it, he swiftly scoured the western horizon.

"See it?" said the captain.

"No," said the correspondent slowly, "I didn't see anything."

"Look again," said the captain. He pointed. "It's exactly in that direction."

At the top of another wave the correspondent did as he was bid, and this time his eyes chanced on a small, still thing on the edge of the swaying horizon. It was precisely like the point of a pin. It took an anxious eye to find a lighthouse so tiny.

"Think we'll make it, Captain?"

"If this wind holds and the boat don't swamp, we can't do much else," said the captain.

The little boat, lifted by each towering sea and splashed viciously by the crests, made progress that in the absence of seaweed was not apparent to those in her. She seemed just a wee thing wallowing, miraculously top up, at the mercy of five oceans. Occasionally a great spread of water, like white flames, swarmed into her.

"Bail her, cook," said the captain serenely.

"All right, Captain," said the cheerful cook.

- *iii* -

It would be difficult to describe the subtle brotherhood of men that was here established on the seas. No one said that it was so. No one mentioned it. But it dwelt in the boat, and each man felt it warm him. They were a captain, an oiler, a cook, and a correspondent, and they were friends—friends in a more curiously iron-bound degree than may be common. The hurt captain, lying against the water jar in the bow, spoke always in a low voice and calmly; but he could never command a more ready and swiftly obedient crew than the motley three of the dinghy. It was more than a mere recognition of what was best for the common safety. There was surely in it a quality that was personal and heartfelt. And after this devotion to the commander of the boat, there was this comradeship, that the correspondent, for instance, who had been taught to be cynical of men, knew even at the time was the best experience of his life. But no one said that it was so. No one mentioned it.

"I wish we had a sail," remarked the captain. "We might try my overcoat on the end of an oar, and give you two boys a chance to rest." So the cook and the correspondent held the mast and spread wide the overcoat; the oiler steered; and the little boat made good way with her new rig. Sometimes the oiler had to scull sharply to keep a sea from breaking into the boat, but otherwise sailing was a success.

Meanwhile the lighthouse had been growing slowly larger. It had now almost assumed color, and appeared like a little gray shadow on the sky. The man at the oars could not be prevented from turning his head rather often to try for a glimpse of this little gray shadow.

At last, from the top of each wave, the men in the tossing boat could see land. Even as the lighthouse was an upright shadow on the sky, this land seemed but a long black shadow on the sea. It certainly was thinner than paper. "We must be about opposite New Smyrna," said the cook, who had coasted this shore often in schooners. "Captain, by the way, I believe they abandoned that lifesaving station there about a year ago."

"Did they?" said the captain.

The wind slowly died away. The cook and the correspondent were not now obliged to slave in order to hold high the oar. But the waves continued their old impetuous swooping at the dinghy, and the little craft, no longer under way, struggled woundily over them. The oiler or the correspondent took the oars again.

Shipwrecks are apropos of nothing. If men could only train for them and have them occur when the men had reached pink condition, there would be less drowning at sea. Of the four in the dinghy, none had slept any time worth mentioning for two days and two nights previous to embarking in the dinghy, and in the excitement of clambering about the deck of a foundering ship, they had also forgotten to eat heartily.

For these reasons, and for others, neither the oiler nor the correspondent was fond of rowing at this time. The correspondent wondered ingenuously how in the name of all that was sane could there be people who thought it amusing to row a boat. It was not an amusement; it was a diabolical punishment, and even a genius of mental aberrations could never conclude that it was anything but a horror to the muscles and a crime against the back. He mentioned to the boat in general how the amusement of rowing struck him, and the weary-faced oiler smiled in full sympathy. Previously to the foundering, by the way, the oiler had worked a double watch in the engine room of the ship.

"Take her easy now, boys," said the captain. "Don't spend yourselves. If we have to run a surf, you'll need all your strength, because we'll sure have to swim for it. Take your time."

Slowly the land arose from the sea. From a black line it became a line of black and a line of white—trees and sand. Finally the captain said that he could make out a house on the shore. "That's the house of refuge, sure," said the cook. "They'll see us before long, and come out after us."

The distant lighthouse reared high. "The keeper ought to be able to make us out now, if he's looking through a glass," said the captain. "He'll notify the lifesaving people."

"None of those other boats could have got ashore to give word of this wreck," said the oiler, in a low voice, "else the lifeboat would be out hunting us."

Slowly and beautifully the land loomed out of the sea. The wind came again. It had veered from the northeast to the southeast. Finally a new sound struck the ears of the men in the boat. It was the low thunder of the surf on the shore. "We'll never be able to make the lighthouse now," said the captain. "Swing her head a little more north, Billie."

"A little more north, sir," said the oiler.

Whereupon the little boat turned her nose once more down the wind, and all but the oarsman watched the shore grow. Under the influence of this expansion, doubt and direful apprehension were leaving the minds of the men. The management of the boat was still most absorbing, but it could not prevent a quiet cheerfulness. In an hour, perhaps, they would be ashore.

Their backbones had become thoroughly used to balancing in the boat, and they now rode this wild colt of a dinghy like circus men. The correspondent thought that he had been drenched to the skin, but happening to feel in the top pocket of his coat, he found therein eight cigars. Four of them were soaked with sea water; four were perfectly scatheless. After a search, somebody produced three dry matches; and thereupon the four waifs rode impudently in their little boat and, with an assurance of an impending rescue shining in their eyes, puffed at the big cigars, and judged well and ill of all men. Everybody took a drink of water.

- *iv* -

"Cook," remarked the captain, "there don't seem to be any signs of life about your house of refuge."

"No," replied the cook. "Funny they don't see us!"

A broad stretch of lowly coast lay before the eyes of the men. It was of low dunes topped with dark vegetation. The roar of the surf was plain, and sometimes they could see the white lip of a wave as it spun up the beach. A tiny house was blocked out black upon the sky. Southward, the slim lighthouse lifted its little gray length.

Tide, wind, and waves were swinging the dinghy northward. "Funny they don't see us," said the men.

The surf's roar was here dulled, but its tone was nevertheless thunderous and mighty. As the boat swam over the great rollers, the men sat listening to this roar. "We'll swamp sure," said everybody.

It is fair to say here that there was not a lifesaving station within twenty miles in either direction; but the men did not know this fact, and in consequence they made dark and opprobrious remarks concerning the eyesight of the nation's lifesavers. Four scowling men sat in the dinghy and surpassed records in the invention of epithets.

"Funny they don't see us."

The lightheartedness of a former time had completely faded. To their sharpened minds it was easy to conjure pictures of all kinds of incompetency and blindness and, indeed, cowardice. There was the shore of the populous land, and it was bitter and bitter to them that from it came no sign.

"Well," said the captain ultimately, "I suppose we'll have to make a try for ourselves. If we stay out here too long, we'll none of us have strength left to swim after the boat swamps."

And so the oiler, who was at the oars, turned the boat straight for the shore. There was a sudden tightening of muscles. There was some thinking.

"If we don't all get ashore," said the captain, "if we don't all get ashore, I suppose you fellows know where to send news of my finish?"

They then briefly exchanged some addresses and admonitions. As for the reflections of the men, there was a great deal of rage in them. Perchance they might be formulated thus: "If I am going to be drowned—if I am going to be drowned— if I am going to be drowned, why, in the name of the seven mad gods who rule the sea, was I allowed to come thus far and contemplate sand and trees? Was I brought here merely to have my nose dragged away as I was about to nibble the sacred cheese of life? It is preposterous. If this old ninny-woman, Fate, cannot do better than this, she should be deprived of the management of men's fortunes. She is an old hen who knows not her intention. If she has decided to drown me, why did she not do it in the beginning and save me all this trouble? The whole affair is absurd— But no; she cannot mean to drown me. She dare not drown me. She cannot drown me. Not after all this work." Afterward the man might have had an impulse to shake his fist at the clouds. "Just you drown me now, and then hear what I call you!"

The billows that came at this time were more formidable. They seemed always just about to break and roll over the little boat in a turmoil of foam. There was a preparatory and long growl in the speech of them. No mind unused to the sea would have concluded that the dinghy could ascend these sheer heights in time. The shore was still afar. The oiler was a wily surfman. "Boys," he said swiftly, "she won't live three minutes more, and we're too far out to swim. Shall I take her to sea again, Captain?"

"Yes; go ahead!" said the captain.

This oiler, by a series of quick miracles and fast and steady oarsmanship, turned the boat in the middle of the surf and took her safely to sea again.

There was a considerable silence as the boat bumped over the furrowed sea to deeper water. Then somebody in gloom spoke: "Well, anyhow, they must have seen us from the shore by now."

The gulls went in slanting flight up the wind toward the gray, desolate east. A squall, marked by dingy clouds and clouds brick-red like smoke from a burning building, appeared from the southeast.

"What do you think of those lifesaving people? Ain't they peaches?"

"Funny they haven't seen us."

"Maybe they think we're out here for sport! Maybe they think we're fishin'. Maybe they think we're damned fools."

It was a long afternoon. A changed tide tried to force them southward, but wind and wave said northward. Far ahead, where coastline, sea, and sky formed their mighty angle, there were little dots which seemed to indicate a city on the shore.

"St. Augustine?"

The captain shook his head. "Too near Mosquito Inlet."

And the oiler rowed, and then the correspondent rowed; then the oiler rowed. It was a weary business. The human back can become the seat of more aches and pains than are registered in books for the composite anatomy of a regiment. It is a limited area, but it can become the theatre of innumerable muscular conflicts, tangles, wrenches, knots, and other comforts.

"Did you ever like to row, Billie?" asked the correspondent.

"No," said the oiler, "hang it!"

When one exchanged the rowing seat for a place in the bottom of the boat, he suffered a bodily depression that caused him to be careless of everything save an obligation to wiggle one finger. There was cold sea water swashing to and fro in the boat, and he lay in it. His head, pillowed on a thwart, was within an inch of the swirl of a wave crest, and sometimes a particularly obstreperous sea came inboard and drenched him once more. But these matters did not annoy him. It is almost certain that if the boat had capsized he would have tumbled comfortably out upon the ocean as if he felt sure that it was a great, soft mattress.

"Look! There's a man on the shore!"

"Where?"

"There! See 'im? See 'im?"

"Yes, sure! He's walking along."

"Now he's stopped. Look! He's facing us!"

"He's waving at us!"

"So he is! By thunder!"

"Ah, now we're all right! Now we're all right! There'll be a boat out here for us in half an hour."

"He's going on. He's running. He's going up to that house there."

The remote beach seemed lower than the sea, and it required a searching glance to discern the little black figure. The captain saw a floating stick, and they rowed to it. A bath towel was by some weird chance in the boat, and tying this on the stick, the captain waved it. The oarsman did not dare turn his head, so he was obliged to ask questions.

"What's he doing now?"

"He's standing still again. He's looking, I think— There he goes again—toward the house— Now he's stopped again."

"Is he waving at us?"

"No, not now; he was, though."

"Look! There comes another man!"

"He's running."

"Look at him go, would you!"

"Why, he's on a bicycle. Now he's met the other man. They're both waving at us. Look!"

"There comes something up the beach."

"What the devil is that thing?"

"Why, it looks like a boat."

"Why, certainly, it's a boat."

"No; it's on wheels."

"Yes, so it is. Well, that must be the lifeboat. They drag them along shore on a wagon."

"That's the lifeboat, sure."

"No, by God, it's—it's an omnibus."

"I tell you it's a lifeboat."

"It is not! It's an omnibus. I can see it plain. See? One of these big hotel omnibuses."

"By thunder, you're right. It's an omnibus, sure as fate. What do you suppose they are doing with an omnibus? Maybe they are going around collecting the life crew, hey?"

"That's it, likely. Look! There's a fellow waving a little black flag. He's standing on the steps of the omnibus. There come those other two fellows. Now they're all talking together. Look at the fellow with the flag. Maybe he ain't waving it!"

"That ain't a flag, is it? That's his coat. Why, certainly, that's his coat."

"So it is; it's his coat. He's taken it off and is waving it around his head. But would you look at him swing it!"

"Oh, say, there isn't any lifesaving station there. That's

just a winter-resort-hotel omnibus that has brought over some of the boarders to see us drown."

"What's that idiot with the coat mean? What's he signaling, anyhow?"

"It looks as if he were trying to tell us to go north. There must be a lifesaving station up there."

"No; he thinks we're fishing. Just giving us a merry hand. See? Ah, there, Willie!"

"Well, I wish I could make something out of those signals. What do you suppose he means?"

"He don't mean anything; he's just playing."

"Well, if he'd just signal us to try the surf again, or to go to sea and wait, or go north, or go south, or go to hell, there would be some reason in it. But look at him! He just stands there and keeps his coat revolving like a wheel. The ass!"

"There come more people."

"Now there's quite a mob. Look! Isn't that a boat?"

"Where? Oh, I see where you mean. No, that's no boat."

"That fellow is still waving his coat."

"He must think we like to see him do that. Why don't he quit it? It don't mean anything."

"I don't know. I think he is trying to make us go north. It must be that there's a lifesaving station there somewhere."

"Say, he ain't tired yet. Look at 'im wave!"

"Wonder how long he can keep that up. He's been revolving his coat ever since he caught sight of us. He's an idiot. Why aren't they getting men to bring a boat out? A fishing boat—one of those big yawls—could come out here all right. Why don't he do something?"

"Oh, it's all right now."

"They'll have a boat out here for us in less than no time, now that they've seen us."

A faint yellow tone came into the sky over the low land. The shadows on the sea slowly deepened. The wind bore coldness with it, and the men began to shiver.

"Holy smoke!" said one, allowing his voice to express his impious mood, "if we keep on monkeying out here! If we've got to flounder out here all night!"

"Oh, we'll never have to stay here all night! Don't you worry. They've seen us now, and it won't be long before they'll come chasing out after us."

The shore grew dusky. The man waving a coat blended gradually into this gloom, and it swallowed in the same manner the omnibus and the group of people. The spray, when it dashed uproariously over the side, made the voyagers shrink and swear like men who were being branded.

"I'd like to catch the chump who waved the coat. I feel like socking him one, just for luck."

"Why? What did he do?"

"Oh, nothing, but then he seemed so damned cheerful."

In the meantime the oiler rowed, and then the correspondent rowed, and then the oiler rowed. Gray-faced and bowed forward, they mechanically, turn by turn, plied the leaden oars. The form of the lighthouse had vanished from the southern horizon, but finally a pale star appeared, just lifting from the sea. The streaked saffron in the west passed before the all-merging darkness, and the sea to the east was black. The land had vanished, and was expressed only by the low and drear thunder of the surf.

"If I am going to be drowned—if I am going to be drowned —if I am going to be drowned, why, in the name of the seven mad gods who rule the sea, was I allowed to come thus far and contemplate sand and trees? Was I brought here merely to have my nose dragged away as I was about to nibble the sacred cheese of life?"

The patient captain, drooped over the water jar, was sometimes obliged to speak to the oarsman.

"Keep her head up! Keep her head up!"

"Keep her head up, sir." The voices were weary and low.

This was surely a quiet evening. All save the oarsman lay heavily and listlessly in the boat's bottom. As for him, his eyes were just capable of noting the tall black waves that swept forward in a most sinister silence, save for an occasional subdued growl of a crest.

The cook's head was on a thwart, and he looked without interest at the water under his nose. He was deep in other scenes. Finally he spoke. "Billie," he murmured dreamfully, "what kind of pie do you like best?"

- v -

"Pie!" said the oiler and the correspondent agitatedly. "Don't talk about those things, blast you."

"Well," said the cook, "I was just thinking about ham sandwiches, and—"

A night on the sea in an open boat is a long night. As darkness settled finally, the shine of the light, lifting from the sea in the south, changed to full gold. On the northern horizon a new light appeared, a small, bluish gleam on the edge of the waters. These two lights were the furniture of the world. Otherwise there was nothing but waves.

Two men huddled in the stern, and distances were so magnificent in the dinghy that the rower was enabled to keep his feet partly warm by thrusting them under his companions. Their legs indeed extended far under the rowing seat until they touched the feet of the captain, forward. Sometimes, despite the efforts of the tired oarsman, a wave came piling into the boat, an icy wave of the night, and the chilling water soaked them anew. They would twist their bodies for a moment and groan, and sleep the dead sleep once more, while the water in the boat gurgled about them as the craft rocked.

The plan of the oiler and the correspondent was for one to row until he lost the ability, and then arouse the other from his sea-water couch in the bottom of the boat.

The oiler plied the oars until his head drooped forward and the overpowering sleep blinded him; and he rowed yet afterward. Then he touched a man in the bottom of the boat, and called his name. "Will you spell me for a little while?" he said meekly.

"Sure, Billie," said the correspondent, awaking and dragging himself to a sitting position. They exchanged places carefully, and the oiler, cuddling down in the seawater at the cook's side, seemed to go to sleep instantly.

The particular violence of the sea had ceased. The waves came without snarling. The obligation of the man at the oars was to keep the boat headed so that the tilt of the rollers would not capsize her, and to preserve her from filling when the crests rushed past. The black waves were silent and hard to be seen in the darkness. Often one was almost upon the boat before the oarsman was aware.

In a low voice the correspondent addressed the captain. He was not sure that the captain was awake, although this iron man seemed to be always awake. "Captain, shall I keep her making for that light north, sir?"

The same steady voice answered him. "Yes. Keep it about two points off the port bow."

The cook had tied a life belt around himself in order to get even the warmth which this clumsy cork contrivance could donate, and he seemed almost stovelike when a rower, whose teeth invariably chattered wildly as soon as he ceased his labor, dropped down to sleep.

The correspondent, as he rowed, looked down at the two men sleeping underfoot. The cook's arm was around the oiler's shoulders, and with their fragmentary clothing and haggard faces, they were the babes of the sea—a grotesque rendering of the old babes in the wood.

Later he must have grown stupid at his work, for suddenly there was a growling of water, and a crest came with a roar and a swash into the boat, and it was a wonder that it did not set the cook afloat in his life belt. The cook continued to sleep, but the oiler sat up, blinking his eyes and shaking with the new cold.

"Oh, I'm awful sorry, Billie," said the correspondent contritely.

"That's all right, old boy," said the oiler, and lay down again and was asleep.

Presently it seemed that even the captain dozed, and the correspondent thought that he was the one man afloat on all the ocean. The wind had a voice as it came over the waves, and it was sadder than the end.

There was a long, loud swishing astern of the boat, and a

gleaming trail of phosphorescence, like blue flame, was furrowed on the black waters. It might have been made by a monstrous knife.

Then there came a stillness, while the correspondent breathed with open mouth and looked at the sea.

Suddenly there was another swish and another long flash of bluish light, and this time it was alongside the boat, and might almost have been reached with an oar. The correspondent saw an enormous fin speed like a shadow through the water, hurling the crystalline spray and leaving the long, glowing trail.

The correspondent looked over his shoulder at the captain. His face was hidden, and he seemed to be asleep. He looked at the babes of the sea. They certainly were asleep. So, being bereft of sympathy, he leaned a little way to one side and swore softly into the sea.

But the thing did not then leave the vicinity of the boat. Ahead or astern, on one side or the other, at intervals long or short, fled the long, sparkling streak, and there was to be heard the *whirroo* of the dark fin. The speed and power of the thing was greatly to be admired. It cut the water like a gigantic and keen projectile.

The presence of this biding thing did not affect the man with the same horror that it would if he had been a picnicker. He simply looked at the sea dully and swore in an undertone.

Nevertheless, it is true that he did not wish to be alone with the thing. He wished one of his companions to awake by chance and keep him company with it. But the captain hung motionless over the water jar, and the oiler and the cook in the bottom of the boat were plunged in slumber.

- *vi* -

"If I am going to be drowned—if I am going to be drowned —if I am going to be drowned, why, in the name of the seven mad gods who rule the sea, was I allowed to come thus far and contemplate sand and trees?"

During this dismal night, it may be remarked that a man

would conclude that it was really the intention of the seven mad gods to drown him, despite the abominable injustice of it. For it was certainly an abominable injustice to drown a man who had worked so hard, so hard. The man felt it would be a crime most unnatural. Other people had drowned at sea since galleys swarmed with painted sails, but still—

When it occurs to a man that nature does not regard him as important, and that she feels she would not maim the universe by disposing of him, he at first wishes to throw bricks at the temple, and he hates deeply the fact that there are no bricks and no temples. Any visible expression of nature would surely be pelleted with his jeers.

Then, if there be no tangible thing to hoot, he feels, perhaps, the desire to confront a personification and indulge in pleas, bowed to one knee, and with hands supplicant, saying, "Yes, but I love myself."

A high, cold star on a winter's night is the word he feels that she says to him. Thereafter he knows the pathos of his situation.

The men in the dinghy had not discussed these matters, but each had, no doubt, reflected upon them in silence and according to his mind. There was seldom any expression upon their faces save the general one of complete weariness. Speech was devoted to the business of the boat.

To chime the notes of his emotion, a verse mysteriously entered the correspondent's head. He had even forgotten that he had forgotten this verse, but it suddenly was in his mind.

A soldier of the Legion lay dying in Algiers;
There was lack of woman's nursing, there was dearth of woman's tears;
But a comrade stood beside him, and he took that comrade's hand,
And he said, "I never more shall see my own, my native land."

In his childhood, the correspondent had been made acquainted with the fact that a soldier of the Legion lay dying in Algiers, but he had never regarded the fact as important. Myriads of his schoolfellows had informed him of the soldier's plight, but the dinning had naturally ended by making him perfectly indifferent. He had never considered it his affair that a soldier of the Legion lay dying in Algiers, nor had it appeared to him as a matter for sorrow. It was less to him than the breaking of a pencil's point.

Now, however, it quaintly came to him as a human, living thing. It was no longer merely a picture of a few throes in the breast of a poet, meanwhile drinking tea and warming his feet at the grate; it was an actuality—stern, mournful, and fine.

The correspondent plainly saw the soldier. He lay on the sand with his feet out straight and still. While his pale left hand was upon his chest in an attempt to thwart the going of his life, the blood came between his fingers. In the far Algerian distance, a city of low, square forms was set against a sky that was faint with the last sunset hues. The correspondent, plying the oars and dreaming of the slow and slower movements of the lips of the soldier, was moved by a profound and perfectly impersonal comprehension. He was sorry for the soldier of the Legion who lay dying in Algiers.

The thing which had followed the boat and waited had evidently grown bored at the delay. There was no longer to be heard the slash of the cutwater, and there was no longer the flame of the long trail. The light in the north still glimmered, but it was apparently no nearer to the boat. Sometimes the boom of the surf rang in the correspondent's ears, and he turned the craft seaward then and rowed harder. Southward, someone had evidently built a watch fire on the beach. It was too low and too far to be seen, but it made a shimmering, roseate reflection upon the bluff in back of it, and this could be discerned from the boat. The wind came stronger, and sometimes a wave suddenly raged out like a mountain cat, and there was to be seen the sheen and sparkle of a broken crest.

The captain, in the bow, moved on his water jar and sat erect. "Pretty long night," he observed to the correspondent.

He looked at the shore. "Those lifesaving people take their time."

"Did you see that shark playing around?"

"Yes, I saw him. He was a big fellow, all right."

"Wish I had known you were awake."

Later the correspondent spoke into the bottom of the boat. "Billie!" There was a slow and gradual disentanglement. "Billie, will you spell me?"

"Sure," said the oiler.

As soon as the correspondent touched the cold, comfortable sea water in the bottom of the boat and had huddled close to the cook's life belt, he was deep in sleep, despite the fact that his teeth played all the popular airs. This sleep was so good to him that it was but a moment before he heard a voice call his name in a tone that demonstrated the last stages of exhaustion. "Will you spell me?"

"Sure, Billie."

The light in the north had mysteriously vanished, but the correspondent took his course from the wide-awake captain.

Later in the night, they took the boat farther out to sea, and the captain directed the cook to take one oar at the stern and keep the boat facing the seas. He was to call out if he should hear the thunder of the surf. This plan enabled the oiler and the correspondent to get respite together. "We'll give those boys a chance to get into shape again," said the captain. They curled down, and after a few preliminary chatterings and trembles, slept once more the dead sleep. Neither knew they had bequeathed to the cook the company of another shark, or perhaps the same shark.

As the boat caroused on the waves, spray occasionally bumped over the side and gave them a fresh soaking, but this had no power to break their repose. The ominous slash of the wind and the water affected them as it would have affected mummies.

"Boys," said the cook, with the notes of every reluctance in his voice, "she's drifted in pretty close. I guess one of you had better take her to sea again." The correspondent, aroused, heard the crash of the toppled crests.

As he was rowing, the captain gave him some whisky-and-water, and this steadied the chills out of him. "If I ever get ashore and anybody shows me even a photograph of an oar—"

At last there was a short conversation.

"Billie! Billie, will you spell me?"

"Sure," said the oiler.

- *vii* -

When the correspondent again opened his eyes, the sea and the sky were each of the gray hue of the dawning. Later, carmine and gold was painted upon the waters. The morning appeared finally, in its splendor, with a sky of pure blue, and the sunlight flamed on the tips of the waves.

On the distant dunes were set many little black cottages, and a tall, white windmill reared above them. No man, nor dog, nor bicycle appeared on the beach. The cottages might have formed a deserted village.

The voyagers scanned the shore. A conference was held in the boat. "Well," said the captain, "if no help is coming, we might better try a run through the surf right away. If we stay out here much longer we will be too weak to do anything for ourselves at all." The others silently acquiesced in this reasoning. The boat was headed for the beach. The correspondent wondered if none ever ascended the tall wind tower, and if, then, they never looked seaward. This tower was a giant, standing with its back to the plight of the ants. It represented in a degree, to the correspondent, the serenity of nature amid the struggles of the individual—nature in the wind, and nature in the vision of men. She did not seem cruel to him then, nor beneficent, nor treacherous, nor wise. But she was indifferent, flatly indifferent. It is, perhaps, plausible that a man in this situation, impressed with the unconcern of the universe, should see the innumerable flaws of his life, and have them taste wickedly in his mind, and wish for another chance. A distinction between right and wrong seems absurdly clear to him, then, in this new ignorance of the grave edge, and he understands that if he were given another opportunity, he would mend his conduct and his words, and be better and brighter during an introduction or at a tea.

"Now, boys," said the captain, "she is going to swamp sure. All we can do is to work her in as far as possible, and then when she swamps, pile out and scramble for the beach. Keep cool now, and don't jump until she swamps sure."

The oiler took the oars. Over his shoulders he scanned the surf. "Captain," he said, "I think I'd better bring her about and keep her head on to the seas and back her in."

"All right, Billie," said the captain. "Back her in." The oiler swung the boat then, and, seated in the stern, the cook and the correspondent were obliged to look over their shoulders to contemplate the lonely and indifferent shore.

The monstrous inshore rollers heaved the boat high until the men were again enabled to see the white sheets of water scudding up the slanted beach. "We won't get in very close," said the captain. Each time a man could wrest his attention from the rollers, he turned his glance toward the shore, and in the expression of the eyes during this contemplation there was a singular quality. The correspondent, observing the others, knew that they were not afraid, but the full meaning of their glances was shrouded.

As for himself, he was too tired to grapple fundamentally with the fact. He tried to coerce his mind into thinking of it, but the mind was dominated at this time by the muscles, and the muscles said they did not care. It merely occurred to him that if he should drown it would be a shame.

There were no hurried words, no pallor, no plain agitation. The men simply looked at the shore. "Now remember to get well clear of the boat when you jump," said the captain.

Seaward the crest of a roller suddenly fell with a thunderous crash, and the long, white comber came roaring down upon the boat.

"Steady now," said the captain. The men were silent. They turned their eyes from the shore to the comber and waited. The boat slid up the incline, leaped at the furious top, bounced over it, and swung down the long back of the wave. Some water had been shipped, and the cook bailed it out.

But the next crest crashed also. The tumbling, boiling flood of white water caught the boat and whirled it almost perpendicular. Water swarmed in from all sides. The correspondent had his hands on the gunwale at this time, and when the water entered at that place he swiftly withdrew his fingers, as if he objected to wetting them.

The little boat, drunken with this weight of water, reeled and snuggled deeper into the sea.

"Bail her out, cook! Bail her out!" said the captain.

"All right, Captain," said the cook.

"Now, boys, the next one will do for us sure," said the oiler. "Mind to jump clear of the boat."

The third wave moved forward, huge, furious, implacable. It fairly swallowed the dinghy, and almost simultaneously the men tumbled into the sea. A piece of life belt had lain in the bottom of the boat, and as the correspondent went overboard, he held this to his chest with his left hand.

The January water was icy, and he reflected immediately that it was colder than he had expected to find it off the coast of Florida. This appeared to his dazed mind as a fact important enough to be noted at the time. The coldness of the water was sad; it was tragic. This fact was somehow mixed and confused with his opinion of his own situation, so that it seemed almost a proper reason for tears. The water was cold.

When he came to the surface, he was conscious of little but the noisy water. Afterward he saw his companions in the sea. The oiler was ahead in the race. He was swimming strongly and rapidly. Off to the correspondent's left, the cook's great white and corked back bulged out of the water; and in the rear the captain was hanging with his one good hand to the keel of the overturned dinghy.

There is a certain immovable quality to a shore, and the correspondent wondered at it amid the confusion of the sea.

It seemed also very attractive; but the correspondent knew that it was a long journey, and he paddled leisurely. The piece of life preserver lay under him, and sometimes he whirled down the incline of a wave as if he were on a hand sled.

But finally he arrived at a place in the sea where travel was beset with difficulty. He did not pause swimming to inquire what manner of current had caught him, but there his progress ceased. The shore was set before him like a bit of scenery on a stage, and he looked at it and understood with his eyes each detail of it.

As the cook passed, much farther to the left, the captain was calling to him, "Turn over on your back, cook! Turn over on your back and use the oar."

"All right, sir." The cook turned on his back, and paddling with an oar, went ahead as if he were a canoe.

Presently the boat also passed to the left of the correspondent, with the captain clinging with one hand to the keel. He would have appeared like a man raising himself to look over a board fence if it were not for the extraordinary gymnastics of the boat. The correspondent marveled that the captain could still hold to it.

They passed on nearer to shore—the oiler, the cook, the captain—and following them went the water jar, bouncing gaily over the seas.

The correspondent remained in the grip of this strange new enemy—a current. The shore, with its white slope of sand and its green bluff topped with little, silent cottages, was spread like a picture before him. It was very near to him then, but he was impressed as one who, in a gallery, looks at a scene from Brittany or Algiers.

He thought: "I'm going to drown? Can it be possible? Can it be possible? Can it be possible?" Perhaps an individual must consider his own death to be the final phenomenon of nature.

But later a wave perhaps whirled him out of this small, deadly current, for he found suddenly that he could again make progress toward the shore. Later still he was aware that the captain, clinging with one hand to the keel of the dinghy, had his face turned away from the shore and toward him, and was calling his name. "Come to the boat! Come to the boat!"

In his struggle to reach the captain and the boat, he reflected that when one gets properly wearied, drowning must really be a comfortable arrangement—a cessation of hostilities accompanied by a large degree of relief; and he was glad of it, for the main thing in his mind for some moments had been horror of the temporary agony. He did not wish to be hurt.

Presently he saw a man running along the shore. He was undressing with most remarkable speed. Coat, trousers, shirt, everything flew magically off him.

"Come to the boat!" called the captain.

"All right, Captain." As the correspondent paddled, he saw the captain let himself down to bottom and leave the boat. Then the correspondent performed his one little marvel of the voyage. A large wave caught him and flung him with ease and supreme speed completely over the boat and far beyond it. It struck him even then as an event in gymnastics and a true miracle of the sea. An overturned boat in the surf is not a plaything to a swimming man.

The correspondent arrived in water that reached only to his waist, but his condition did not enable him to stand for more than a moment. Each wave knocked him into a heap, and the undertow pulled at him.

Then he saw the man who had been running and undressing, and undressing and running, come bounding into the water. He dragged ashore the cook, and then waded toward the captain; but the captain waved him away and sent him to the correspondent. He was naked—naked as a tree in winter; but a halo was about his head, and he shone like a saint. He gave a strong pull, a long drag, and a bully heave at the correspondent's hand. The correspondent, schooled in the minor formulae, said, "Thanks, old man." But suddenly the man cried, "What's that?" He pointed a swift finger. The correspondent said, "Go."

In the shallows, face downward, lay the oiler. His forehead touched sand that was periodically, between each wave, clear of the sea.

The correspondent did not know all that transpired afterward. When he achieved safe ground he fell, striking the sand with each particular part of his body. It was as if he had dropped from a roof, but the thud was grateful to him.

It seemed that instantly the beach was populated with men with blankets, clothes, and flasks, and women with coffeepots and all the remedies sacred to their minds. The welcome of the land to the men from the sea was warm and generous; but a still and dripping shape was carried slowly up the beach, and the land's welcome for it could only be the different and sinister hospitality of the grave.

When it came night, the white waves paced to and fro in the moonlight, and the wind brought the sound of the great sea's voice to the men on the shore, and they felt that they could then be interpreters.

# Three Miraculous Soldiers

-i-

THE GIRL was in the front room on the second floor, peering through the blinds. It was the "best room." There was a very new rag carpet on the floor. The edges of it had been dyed with alternate stripes of red and green. Upon the wooden mantel there were two little puffy figures in clay—a shepherd and a shepherdess, probably. A triangle of pink-and-white wool hung carefully over the edge of this shelf. Upon the bureau there was nothing at all save a spread newspaper, with edges folded to make it into a mat. The quilts and sheets had been removed from the bed and were stacked upon a chair. The pillows and the great feather mattress were muffled and tumbled until they resembled great dumplings. The picture of a man terribly leaden in complexion hung in an oval frame on one white wall and steadily confronted the bureau.

From between the slats of the blinds she had a view of the road as it wended across the meadows to the woods, and again where it reappeared crossing the hill, half a mile away. It lay yellow and warm in the summer sunshine. From the long grasses of the meadow came the rhythmic click of the insects. Occasional frogs in the hidden brook made a peculiar chug-chug sound, as if somebody throttled them. The leaves of the wood swung in gentle winds. Through the dark green branches of the pines that grew in the front yard could be seen the mountains, far to the southeast, and inexpressibly blue.

Mary's eyes were fastened upon the little streak of road that appeared on the distant hill. Her face was flushed with excitement, and the hand which stretched in a strained pose on the sill trembled because of the nervous shaking of the wrist. The pines whisked their green needles with a soft, hissing sound against the house.

At last the girl turned from the window and went to the head of the stairs. "Well, I just know they're coming, anyhow," she cried argumentatively to the depths.

A voice from below called to her angrily, "They ain't. We've never seen one yet. They never come into this neighborhood. You just come down here and 'tend to your work insteader watching for soldiers."

"Well, Ma, I just know they're coming."

A voice retorted with the shrillness and mechanical violence of occasional housewives. The girl swished her skirts defiantly and returned to the window.

Upon the yellow streak of road that lay across the hillside there now was a handful of black dots—horsemen. A cloud of dust floated away. The girl flew to the head of the stairs and whirled down into the kitchen.

"They're coming! They're coming!"

It was as if she had cried "Fire!" Her mother had been peeling potatoes while seated comfortably at the table. She sprang to her feet. "No—it can't be—how you know it's them—

where?" The stubby knife fell from her hand, and two or three curls of potato skin dropped from her apron to the floor.

The girl turned and dashed upstairs. Her mother followed, gasping for breath, and yet contriving to fill the air with question, reproach, and remonstrance. The girl was already at the window, eagerly pointing. "There! There! See 'em! See 'em!"

Rushing to the window, the mother scanned for an instant the road on the hill. She crouched back with a groan. "It's them, sure as the world! It's them!" She waved her hands in despairing gestures.

The black dots vanished into the wood. The girl at the window was quivering, and her eyes were shining like water when the sun flashes. "Hush! They're in the woods! They'll be here directly." She bent down and intently watched the green archway whence the road emerged. "Hush! I hear 'em coming," she swiftly whispered to her mother, for the elder woman had dropped dolefully upon the mattress and was sobbing. And, indeed, the girl could hear the quick, dull trample of horses. She stepped aside with sudden apprehension, but she bent her head forward in order to still scan the road.

"Here they are!"

There was something very theatrical in the sudden appearance of these men to the eyes of the girl. It was as if a scene had been shifted. The forest suddenly disclosed them—a dozen brown-faced troopers in blue—galloping.

"Oh, look!" breathed the girl. Her mouth was puckered into an expression of strange fascination, as if she had expected to see the troopers change into demons and gloat at her. She was at last looking upon those curious beings who rode down from the North—those men of legend and colossal tale—they who were possessed of such marvelous hallucinations.

The little troop rode in silence. At its head was a youthful fellow with some dim yellow stripes upon his arm. In his right hand he held his carbine, slanting upward, with the stock resting upon his knee. He was absorbed in a scrutiny of the country before him.

At the heels of the sergeant the rest of the squad rode in thin column, with creak of leather and tinkle of steel and tin. The girl scanned the faces of the horsemen, seeming astonished vaguely to find them of the type she knew.

The lad at the head of the troop comprehended the house and its environments in two glances. He did not check the long, swinging stride of his horse. The troopers glanced for a moment like casual tourists, and then returned to their study of the region in front. The heavy thudding of the hoofs became a small noise. The dust, hanging in sheets, slowly sank.

The sobs of the woman on the bed took form in words which, while strong in their note of calamity, yet expressed a querulous mental reaching for some near thing to blame. "And it'll be lucky fer us if we ain't both butchered in our sleep—plundering and running off horses—old Santo's gone—you see if he ain't—plundering—"

"But, Ma," said the girl, perplexed and terrified in the same moment, "they've gone."

"Oh, but they'll come back!" cried the mother, without pausing her wail. "They'll come back—trust them for that—running off horses. Oh, John, John! Why did you, why did you?" She suddenly lifted herself and sat rigid, staring at her daughter. "Mary," she said in a tragic whisper, "the kitchen door isn't locked!" Already she was bended forward to listen, her mouth agape, her eyes fixed upon her daughter.

"Mother," faltered the girl.

Her mother again whispered, "The kitchen door isn't locked."

Motionless and mute, they stared into each other's eyes.

At last the girl quavered, "We better—we better go and lock it." The mother nodded. Hanging arm in arm, they stole across the floor toward the head of the stairs. A board of the floor creaked. They halted and exchanged a look of dumb agony.

At last they reached the head of the stairs. From the kitchen came the bass humming of the kettle and frequent sputterings and cracklings from the fire. These sounds were sinister. The mother and the girl stood incapable of movement. "There's somebody down there!" whispered the elder woman.

Finally the girl made a gesture of resolution. She twisted her arm from her mother's hands and went two steps downward. She addressed the kitchen: "Who's there?" Her tone was intended to be dauntless. It rang so dramatically in the silence that a sudden new panic seized them, as if the suspected presence in the kitchen had cried out to them. But the girl ventured again: "Is there anybody there?" No reply was made save by the kettle and the fire.

With a stealthy tread the girl continued her journey. As she neared the last step, the fire crackled explosively, and the girl screamed. But the mystic presence had not swept around the corner to grab her, so she dropped to a seat on the step and laughed. "It was—was only the—the fire," she said, stammering hysterically.

Then she arose with sudden fortitude and cried, "Why, there isn't anybody there! I know there isn't." She marched down into the kitchen. In her face was dread, as if she half expected to confront something, but the room was empty. She cried joyously, "There's nobody here! Come on down, Ma." She ran to the kitchen door and locked it.

The mother came down to the kitchen. "Oh, dear, what a fright I've had! It's given me the sick headache. I know it has."

"Oh, Ma," said the girl.

"I know it has—I know it. Oh, if your father was only here! He'd settle those Yankees mighty quick—he'd settle 'em! Two poor, helpless women—"

"Why, Ma, what makes you act so? The Yankees haven't—"

"Oh, they'll be back—they'll be back. Two poor, helpless women! Your father and your Uncle Asa and Bill off gallivanting around and fighting when they ought to be protecting their home! That's the kind of men they are. Didn't I say to your father just before he left—"

"Ma," said the girl, coming suddenly from the window, "the barn door is open. I wonder if they took old Santo."

"Oh, of course they have—of course—Mary, I don't see what we are going to do—I don't see what we are going to do."

The girl said, "Ma, I'm going to see if they took old Santo."

"Mary," cried the mother, "don't you dare!"

"But think of poor old Sant, Ma."

"Never you mind old Santo. We're lucky to be safe ourselves, I tell you. Never mind old Santo. Don't you dare to go out there, Mary—Mary!"

The girl had unlocked the door and stepped out upon the porch. The mother cried in despair, "Mary!"

"Why, there isn't anybody out here," the girl called in response. She stood for a moment with a curious smile upon her face, as of gleeful satisfaction at her daring.

The breeze was waving the boughs of the apple trees. A rooster with an air importantly courteous was conducting three hens upon a foraging tour. On the hillside at the rear of the gray, old barn, the red leaves of a creeper flamed amid the summer foliage. High in the sky, clouds rolled toward the north. The girl swung impulsively from the little stoop and ran toward the barn.

The great door was open, and the carved peg which usually performed the office of a catch lay on the ground. The girl could not see into the barn because of the heavy shadows. She paused in a listening attitude and heard a horse munching placidly. She gave a cry of delight and sprang across the threshold. Then she suddenly shrank back and gasped. She had confronted three men in gray seated upon the floor with their legs stretched out and their backs against Santo's manger. Their dust-covered countenances were expanded in grins.

- *ii* -

As Mary sprang backward and screamed, one of the calm men in gray, still grinning, announced, "I knowed you'd holler." Sitting there comfortably, the three surveyed her with amusement.

Mary caught her breath, throwing her hand up to her throat. "Oh!" she said, "you—you frightened me!"

"We're sorry, lady, but couldn't help it no way," cheerfully responded another. "I knowed you'd holler when I seen you coming yere, but I raikoned we couldn't help it no way. We hain't a-troubling this yere barn, I don't guess. We been doing some mighty tall sleeping yere. We done woke when them Yanks loped past."

"Where did you come from? Did—did you escape from the —the Yankees?" The girl still stammered and trembled.

The three soldiers laughed. "No, m'm. No, m'm. They never cotch us. We was in a muss down the road yere about two mile. And Bill yere, they gi'n it to him in the arm, kehplunk. And they pasted me thar, too. Curious. And Sim yere, he didn't get nothing, but they chased us all quite a little piece, and we done lose track of our boys."

"Was it—was it those who passed here just now? Did they chase you?"

The men in gray laughed again. "What—them? No, in-deedee! There was a mighty big swarm of Yanks and a mighty big swarm of our boys, too. What—that little passel? No, m'm."

She became calm enough to scan them more attentively. They were much begrimed and very dusty. Their gray clothes were tattered. Splashed mud had dried upon them in reddish spots. It appeared, too, that the men had not shaved in many days. In the hats there was a singular diversity. One soldier wore the little blue cap of the Northern infantry, with corps emblem and regimental number; one wore a great slouch hat with a wide hole in the crown; and the other wore no hat at all. The left sleeve of one man and the right sleeve of another had been slit, and the arms were neatly bandaged with clean cloths. "These hain't no more than two little cuts," explained one. "We stopped up yere to Mis' Leavitt's—she said her name was—and she bind them for us. Bill yere, he had the thirst come on him. And the fever, too. We—"

"Did you ever see my father in the army?" asked Mary. "John Hinckson—his name is."

The three soldiers grinned again, but they replied kindly,

"No, m'm. No, m'm, we hain't never. What is he—in the cavalry?"

"No," said the girl. "He and my Uncle Asa and my cousin—his name is Bill Parker—they are all with Longstreet—they call him."

"Oh," said the soldiers. "Longstreet? Oh, they're a good smart ways from yere. 'Way off up nawtheast. There hain't nothing but cavalry down yere. They're in the infantry, probably."

"We haven't heard anything from them for days and days," said Mary.

"Oh, they're all right in the infantry," said one man, to be consoling. "The infantry don't do much fighting. They go bellering out in a big swarm and only a few of 'em get hurt. But if they were in the cavalry—the cavalry—"

Mary interrupted him without intention. "Are you hungry?" she asked.

The soldiers looked at each other, struck by some sudden and singular shame. They hung their heads. "No, m'm," replied one at last.

Santo, in his stall, was tranquilly chewing and chewing. Sometimes he looked benevolently over at them. He was an old horse, and there was something about his eyes and his fore-lock which created the impression that he wore spectacles. Mary went and patted his nose. "Well, if you are hungry, I can get you something," she told the men. "Or you might come to the house."

"We wouldn't dast go to the house," said one. "That passel of Yanks was only a scouting crowd, most like. Just an advance. More coming, likely."

"Well, I can bring you something," cried the girl eagerly. "Won't you let me bring you something?"

"Well," said a soldier with embarrassment, "we hain't had much. If you could bring us a little snack like—just a snack—we'd—"

Without waiting for him to cease, the girl turned toward the door. But before she had reached it, she stopped abruptly. "Listen!" she whispered. Her form was bent forward, her head turned and lowered, her hand extended toward the men in a command for silence.

They could faintly hear the thudding of many hoofs, the clank of arms, and frequent calling voices.

"By cracky, it's the Yanks!" The soldiers scrambled to their feet and came toward the door. "I knowed that first crowd was only an advance."

The girl and the three men peered from the shadows of the barn. The view of the road was intersected by tree trunks and a little henhouse. However, they could see many horsemen streaming down the road. The horsemen were in blue. "Oh, hide—hide—hide!" cried the girl, with a sob in her voice.

"Wait a minute," whispered a gray soldier excitedly. "Maybe they're going along by. No, by thunder, they hain't! They're halting. Scoot, boys!"

They made a noiseless dash into the dark end of the barn. The girl, standing by the door, heard them break forth an instant later in clamorous whispers. "Where'll we hide? Where'll we hide? There hain't a place to hide!" The girl turned and glanced wildly about the barn. It seemed true. The stock of hay had grown low under Santo's endless munching, and from occasional levyings by passing troopers in gray. The poles of the mow were barely covered, save in one corner where there was a little bunch.

The girl espied the great feedbox. She ran to it and lifted the lid. "Here! Here!" she called. "Get in here."

They had been tearing noiselessly around the rear part of the barn. At her low call, they came and plunged at the box. They did not all get in at the same moment without a good deal of a tangle. The wounded men gasped and muttered, but they at last were flopped down on the layer of feed which covered the bottom. Swiftly and softly the girl lowered the lid, and then turned like a flash toward the door.

No one appeared there, so she went close to survey the situation. The troopers had dismounted and stood in silence by their horses. A gray-bearded man, whose red cheeks and nose shone vividly above the whiskers, was strolling about with two or three others. They wore double-breasted coats, and faded yellow sashes were wound under their black leather sword belts. The gray-bearded soldier was apparently giving orders, pointing here and there.

Mary tiptoed to the feedbox. "They've all got off their horses," she said to it. A finger projected from a knothole near the top and said to her very plainly, "Come closer." She obeyed, and then a muffled voice could be heard: "Scoot for the house, lady, and if we don't see you again, why, much obliged for what you done."

"Good-by," she said to the feedbox.

She made two attempts to walk dauntlessly from the barn, but each time she faltered and failed just before she reached the point where she could have been seen by the blue-coated troopers. At last, however, she made a sort of rush forward and went out into the bright sunshine.

The group of men in double-breasted coats wheeled in her direction at the instant. The gray-bearded officer forgot to lower his arm, which had been stretched forth in giving an order.

She felt that her feet were touching the ground in a most unnatural manner. Her bearing, she believed, was suddenly grown awkward and ungainly. Upon her face she thought that this sentence was plainly written: "There are three men hidden in the feedbox."

The gray-bearded soldier came toward her. She stopped; she seemed about to run away. But the soldier doffed his little blue cap and looked amiable. "You live here, I presume?" he said.

"Yes," she answered.

"Well, we are obliged to camp here for the night, and as we've got two wounded men with us I don't suppose you'd mind if we put them in the barn."

"In—in the barn?"

He became aware that she was agitated. He smiled assuringly. "You needn't be frightened. We won't hurt anything around here. You'll all be safe enough."

The girl balanced on one foot and swung the other to and

fro in the grass. She was looking down at it. "But—but I don't think Ma would like it if—if you took the barn."

The old officer laughed. "Wouldn't she?" said he. "That's so. Maybe she wouldn't." He reflected for a time and then decided cheerfully, "Well, we will have to go ask her, anyhow. Where is she? In the house?"

"Yes," replied the girl, "she's in the house. She—she'll be scared to death when she sees you!"

"Well, you go and ask her, then," said the soldier, always wearing a benign smile. "You go ask her and then come and tell me."

When the girl pushed open the door and entered the kitchen, she found it empty. "Ma!" she called softly. There was no answer. The kettle still was humming its low song. The knife and the curl of potato skin lay on the floor.

She went to her mother's room and entered timidly. The new, lonely aspect of the house shook her nerves. Upon the bed was a confusion of coverings. "Ma!" called the girl, quaking in fear that her mother was not there to reply. But there was a sudden turmoil of the quilts, and her mother's head was thrust forth. "Mary!" she cried, in what seemed to be a supreme astonishment, "I thought—I thought—"

"Oh, Ma," blurted the girl, "there's over a thousand Yankees in the yard, and I've hidden three of our men in the feedbox!"

The elder woman, however, upon the appearance of her daughter, had begun to thrash hysterically about on the bed and wail.

"Ma," the girl exclaimed, "and now they want to use the barn—and our men in the feedbox! What shall I do, Ma? What shall I do?"

Her mother did not seem to hear, so absorbed was she in her grievous flounderings and tears. "Ma!" appealed the girl. "Ma!"

For a moment Mary stood silently debating, her lips apart, her eyes fixed. Then she went to the kitchen window and peeked.

The old officer and the others were staring up the road. She went to another window in order to get a proper view of the road, and saw that they were gazing at a small body of horsemen approaching at a trot and raising much dust. Presently she recognized them as the squad that had passed the house earlier, for the young man with the dim yellow chevron still rode at their head. An unarmed horseman in gray was receiving their close attention.

As they came very near to the house, she darted to the first window again. The gray-bearded officer was smiling a fine, broad smile of satisfaction. "So you got him?" he called out. The young sergeant sprang from his horse, and his brown hand moved in a salute. The girl could not hear his reply. She saw the unarmed horseman in gray stroking a very black mustache and looking about him coolly and with an interested air. He appeared so indifferent that she did not understand he was a prisoner until she heard the graybeard call out, "Well, put him in the barn. He'll be safe there, I guess." A party of troopers moved with the prisoner toward the barn.

The girl made a sudden gesture of horror, remembering the three men in the feedbox.

- iii -

The busy troopers in blue scurried about the long lines of stamping horses. Men crooked their backs and perspired in order to rub with cloths or bunches of grass these slim equine legs upon whose splendid machinery they depended so greatly. The lips of the horses were still wet and frothy from the steel bars which had wrenched at their mouths all day. Over their backs and about their noses sped the talk of the men.

"Moind where yer plug is steppin', Finerty! Keep 'im aff me!"

"An ould elephant! He shtrides like a schoolhouse."

"Bill's little mar'—she was plum beat when she come in with Crawford's crowd."

"Crawford's the hardest-ridin' cavalryman in the army.

An' he don't use up a horse, neither—much. They stay fresh when the others are most a-droppin'.'"

"Finerty, will yeh moind that cow a' yours?"

Amid a bustle of gossip and banter, the horses retained their air of solemn rumination, twisting their lower jaws from side to side and sometimes rubbing noses dreamfully.

Over in front of the barn, three troopers sat talking comfortably. Their carbines were leaned against the wall. At their side and outlined in the black of the open door stood a sentry, his weapon resting in the hollow of his arm. Four horses, saddled and accoutered, were conferring with their heads close together. The four bridle reins were flung over a post.

Upon the calm green of the land, typical in every way of peace, the hues of war brought thither by the troops shone strangely. Mary, gazing curiously, did not feel that she was contemplating a familiar scene. It was no longer the home acres. The new blue, steel, and faded yellow thoroughly dominated the old green and brown. She could hear the voices of the men, and it seemed from their tone that they had camped there for years. Everything with them was usual. They had taken possession of the landscape in such a way that even the old marks appeared strange and formidable to the girl.

Mary had intended to go and tell the commander in blue that her mother did not wish his men to use the barn at all, but she paused when she heard him speak to the sergeant. She thought she perceived then that it mattered little to him what her mother wished, and that an objection by her or by anybody would be futile. She saw the soldiers conduct the prisoner in gray into the barn, and for a long time she watched the three chatting guards and the pondering sentry. Upon her mind in desolate weight was the recollection of the three men in the feedbox.

It seemed to her that in a case of this description, it was her duty to be a heroine. In all the stories she had read when at boarding school in Pennsylvania, the girl characters, confronted with such difficulties, invariably did hairbreadth things. True, they were usually bent upon rescuing and recovering their lovers, and neither the calm man in gray nor any of the three in the feedbox was lover of hers; but then, a real heroine would not pause over this minor question. Plainly a heroine would take measures to rescue the four men. If she did not at least make the attempt, she would be false to those carefully constructed ideals which were the accumulation of years of dreaming.

But the situation puzzled her. There was the barn with only one door, and with four armed troopers in front of this door, one of them with his back to the rest of the world, engaged, no doubt, in a steadfast contemplation of the calm man and, incidentally, of the feedbox. She knew, too, that even if she should open the kitchen door, three heads and perhaps four would turn casually in her direction. Their ears were real ears.

Heroines, she knew, conducted these matters with infinite precision and dispatch. They severed the hero's bonds, cried a dramatic sentence, and stood between him and his enemies until he had run far enough away. She saw well, however, that even should she achieve all things up to the point where she might take glorious stand between the escaping and the pursuers, those grim troopers in blue would not pause. They would run around her, make a circuit. One by one she saw the gorgeous contrivances and expedients of fiction fall before the plain, homely difficulties of this situation. They were of no service. Sadly, ruefully, she thought of the calm man and of the contents of the feedbox.

The sum of her invention was that she could sally forth to the commander of the blue cavalry, and confessing to him that there were three of her friends and his enemies secreted in the feedbox, pray him to let them depart unmolested. But she was beginning to believe the old graybeard to be a bear. It was hardly probable that he would give this plan his support. It was more probable that he and some of his men would at once descend upon the feedbox and confiscate her three friends. The difficulty with her idea was that she could not learn its value without trying it, and then in case of failure it would be too late for remedies and other plans. She reflected that war made men very unreasonable.

All that she could do was to stand at the window and

mournfully regard the barn. She admitted this to herself with a sense of deep humiliation. She was not, then, made of that fine stuff, that mental satin, which enabled some other beings to be of such mighty service to the distressed. She was defeated by a barn with one door, by four men with eight eyes and eight ears—trivialities that would not impede the real heroine.

The vivid white light of broad day began slowly to fade. Tones of gray came upon the fields, and the shadows were of lead. In this more somber atmosphere, the fires built by the troops down in the far end of the orchard grew more brilliant, becoming spots of crimson color in the dark grove.

The girl heard a fretting voice from her mother's room. "Mary!" She hastily obeyed the call. She perceived that she had quite forgotten her mother's existence in this time of excitement.

The elder woman still lay upon the bed. Her face was flushed, and perspiration stood amid new wrinkles upon her forehead. Weaving wild glances from side to side, she began to whimper. "Oh, I'm just sick—I'm just sick! Have those men gone yet? Have they gone?"

The girl smoothed a pillow carefully for her mother's head. "No, Ma. They're here yet. But they haven't hurt anything— it doesn't seem. Will I get you something to eat?"

Her mother gestured her away with the impatience of the ill. "No—no—just don't bother me. My head is splitting, and you know very well that nothing can be done for me when I get one of these spells. It's trouble—that's what makes them. When are those men going? Look here, don't you go 'way. You stick close to the house now."

"I'll stay right here," said the girl. She sat in the gloom and listened to her mother's incessant moaning. When she attempted to move, her mother cried out at her. When she desired to ask if she might try to alleviate the pain, she was interrupted shortly. Somehow her sitting in passive silence within hearing of this illness seemed to contribute to her mother's relief. She assumed a posture of submission. Sometimes her mother projected questions concerning the local condition, and although she labored to be graphic and at the same time soothing, unalarming, her form of reply was always displeasing to the sick woman, and brought forth ejaculations of angry impatience.

Eventually the woman slept in the manner of one worn from terrible labor. The girl went slowly and softly to the kitchen. When she looked from the window, she saw the four soldiers still at the barn door. In the west, the sky was yellow. Some tree trunks intersecting it appeared black as streaks of ink. Soldiers hovered in blue clouds about the bright splendor of the fires in the orchard. There were glimmers of steel.

The girl sat in the new gloom of the kitchen and watched. The soldiers lit a lantern and hung it in the barn. Its rays made the form of the sentry seem gigantic. Horses whinnied from the orchard. There was a low hum of human voices. Sometimes small detachments of troopers rode past the front of the house. The girl heard the abrupt calls of sentries. She fetched some food and ate it from her hand, standing by the window. She was so afraid that something would occur that she barely left her post for an instant.

A picture of the interior of the barn hung vividly in her mind. She recalled the knotholes in the boards at the rear, but she admitted that the prisoners could not escape through them. She remembered some inadequacies of the roof, but these also counted for nothing. When confronting the problem, she felt her ambitions, her ideals, tumbling headlong like cottages of straw.

Once she felt that she had decided to reconnoiter, at any rate. It was night; the lantern at the barn and the campfires made everything without their circle into masses of heavy, mystic blackness. She took two steps toward the door. But there she paused. Innumerable possibilities of danger had assailed her mind. She returned to the window and stood wavering. At last, she went swiftly to the door, opened it, and slid noiselessly into the darkness.

For a moment she regarded the shadows. Down in the orchard the campfires of the troops appeared precisely like a great painting, all in reds upon a black cloth. The voices of the troopers still hummed. The girl started slowly off in the opposite direction. Her eyes were fixed in a stare; she studied the darkness in front for a moment, before she ventured upon a forward step. Unconsciously, her throat was arranged for a sudden shrill scream. High in the tree branches she could hear the voice of the wind, a melody of the night, low and sad, the plaint of an endless, incommunicable sorrow. Her own distress, the plight of the men in gray—these near matters as well as all she had known or imagined of grief—everything was expressed in this soft mourning of the wind in the trees. At first she felt like weeping. This sound told her of human impotency and doom. Then later the trees and the wind breathed strength to her, sang of sacrifice, of dauntless effort, of hard, carven faces that did not blanch when Duty came at midnight or at noon.

She turned often to scan the shadowy figures that moved from time to time in the light at the barn door. Once she trod upon a stick, and it flopped, crackling in the intolerable manner of all sticks. At this noise, however, the guards at the barn made no sign. Finally she was where she could see the knotholes in the rear of the structure gleaming like pieces of metal from the effect of the light within. Scarcely breathing in her excitement, she glided close and applied an eye to a knothole. She had barely achieved one glance at the interior before she sprang back shuddering.

For the unconscious and cheerful sentry at the door was swearing away in flaming sentences, heaping one gorgeous oath upon another, making a conflagration of his description of his troop horse.

"Why," he was declaring to the calm prisoner in gray, "you ain't got a horse in your hull damned army that can run forty rod with that there little mar'l"

As in the outer darkness Mary cautiously returned to the knothole, the three guards in front suddenly called in low tones: "S-s-s-h! Quit, Pete; here comes the lieutenant." The sentry had apparently been about to resume his declamation, but at these warnings, he suddenly posed in a soldierly manner.

A tall and lean officer with a smooth face entered the barn. The sentry saluted primly. The officer flashed a comprehensive glance about him. "Everything all right?"

"All right, sir."

This officer had eyes like the points of stilettos. The lines from his nose to the corners of his mouth were deep and gave him a slightly disagreeable aspect, but somewhere in his face there was a quality of singular thoughtfulness, as of the absorbed student dealing in generalities, which was utterly in opposition to the rapacious keenness of the eyes, which saw everything.

Suddenly he lifted a long finger and pointed. "What's that?"

"That? That's a feedbox, I suppose."

"What's in it?"

"I don't know. I—"

"You ought to know," said the officer sharply. He walked over to the feedbox and flung up the lid. With a sweeping gesture, he reached down and scooped a handful of feed. "You ought to know what's in everything when you have prisoners in your care," he added, scowling.

During the time of this incident, the girl had nearly swooned. Her hands searched weakly over the boards for something to which to cling. With the pallor of the dying, she had watched the downward sweep of the officer's arm, which after all had only brought forth a handful of feed. The result was a stupefaction of her mind. She was astonished out of her senses at this spectacle of three large men metamorphosed into a handful of feed.

- iv -

It is perhaps a singular thing that this absence of the three men from the feedbox at the time of the sharp lieutenant's investigation should terrify the girl more than it should joy her. That for which she had prayed had come to pass. Apparently the escape of these men in the face of every improbability had been granted her, but her dominating emotion was fright. The feedbox was a mystic and terrible machine, like some dark magician's trap. She felt it almost possible that she should see the three weird men floating spectrally away through the air. She glanced with swift apprehension behind her, and when the dazzle from the lantern's light had left her eyes, saw only the dim hillside stretched in solemn silence.

The interior of the barn possessed for her another fascination because it was now uncanny. It contained that extraordinary feedbox. When she peeped again at the knothole, the calm, gray prisoner was seated upon the feedbox, thumping it with his dangling, careless heels as if it were in no wise his conception of a remarkable feedbox. The sentry also stood facing it. His carbine he held in the hollow of his arm. His legs were spread apart, and he mused. From without came the low mumble of the three other troopers. The sharp lieutenant had vanished.

The trembling yellow light of the lantern caused the figures of the men to cast monstrous, wavering shadows. There were spaces of gloom which shrouded ordinary things in impressive garb. The roof presented an inscrutable blackness, save where small rifts in the shingles glowed phosphorescently. Frequently old Santo put down a thunderous hoof. The heels of the prisoner made a sound like the booming of a wild kind of drum. When the men moved their heads, their eyes shone with ghoulish whiteness, and their complexions were always waxen and unreal. And there was that profoundly strange feedbox, imperturbable with its burden of fantastic mystery.

Suddenly from down near her feet the girl heard a crunching sound, a sort of nibbling, as if some silent and very discreet terrier was at work upon the turf. She faltered back; here was, no doubt, another grotesque detail of this most unnatural episode. She did not run, because physically she was in the power of these events. Her feet chained her to the ground in submission to this march of terror after terror. As she stared at the spot from which this sound seemed to come, there floated through her mind a vague, sweet vision—a vision of her safe little room, in which at this hour she usually was sleeping.

The scratching continued faintly and with frequent pauses, as if the terrier was then listening. When the girl first removed her eyes from the knothole, the scene appeared of one velvet blackness; then gradually objects loomed with a dim luster. She could see now where the tops of the trees joined the sky, and the form of the barn was before her, dyed in heavy purple. She was ever about to shriek, but no sound came from her constricted throat. She gazed at the ground with the expression of countenance of one who watches the sinister-moving grass where a serpent approaches.

Dimly she saw a piece of sod wrenched free and drawn under the great foundation beam of the barn. Once she imagined that she saw human hands, not outlined at all, but sufficient in color, form, or movement to make subtle suggestion.

Then suddenly a thought that illuminated the entire situation flashed in her mind like a light. The three men, late of the feedbox, were beneath the floor of the barn and were now scraping their way under this beam. She did not consider for a moment how they could come there. They were marvelous creatures. The supernatural was to be expected of them. She no longer trembled, for she was possessed upon this instant of the most unchangeable species of conviction. The evidence before her amounted to no evidence at all, but nevertheless her opinion grew in an instant from an irresponsible acorn to a rooted and immovable tree. It was as if she was on a jury.

She stooped down hastily and scanned the ground. There she indeed saw a pair of hands hauling at the dirt where the sod had been displaced. Softly, in a whisper like a breath, she said, "Hey!"

The dim hands were drawn hastily under the barn. The girl reflected for a moment. Then she stooped and whispered, "Hey! It's me!"

After a time there was a resumption of the digging. The ghostly hands began once more their cautious mining. She waited. In hollow reverberations from the interior of the barn came the frequent sounds of old Santo's lazy movements. The sentry conversed with the prisoner.

At last the girl saw a head thrust slowly from under the beam. She perceived the face of one of the miraculous soldiers from the feedbox. A pair of eyes glintered and wavered, then finally settled upon her, a pale statue of a girl. The eyes became lit with a kind of humorous greeting. An arm gestured at her.

Stooping, she breathed, "All right." The man drew himself silently back under the beam. A moment later the pair of hands resumed their cautious task. Ultimately the head and arms of the man were thrust strangely from the earth. He was lying on his back. The girl thought of the dirt in his hair. Wriggling slowly and pushing at the beam above him, he forced his way out of the curious little passage. He twisted his body and raised himself upon his hands. He grinned at the girl and drew his feet carefully from under the beam. When he at last stood erect beside her, he at once began mechanically to brush the dirt from his clothes with his hands. In the barn the sentry and his prisoner were evidently engaged in an argument.

The girl and the first miraculous soldier signaled warily. It seemed that they feared that their arms would make noises in passing through the air. Their lips moved, conveying dim meanings.

In this sign language the girl described the situation in the barn. With guarded motions, she told him of the importance of absolute stillness. He nodded, and then in the same manner he told her of his two companions under the barn floor. He informed her again of their wounded state, and wagged his head to express his despair. He contorted his face, to tell how sore were their arms; and jabbed the air mournfully, to express their remote geographical position.

This signaling was interrupted by the sound of a body being dragged or dragging itself with slow, swishing sound under the barn. The sound was too loud for safety. They rushed to the hole and began to semaphore until a shaggy head appeared with rolling eyes and quick grin.

With frantic downward motions of their arms they suppressed this grin and with it the swishing noise. In dramatic pantomime they informed this head of the terrible consequences of so much noise. The head nodded, and painfully, but with extreme care, the second man pushed and pulled himself from the hole.

In a faint whisper the first man said, "Where's Sim?"

The second man made low reply: "He's right here." He motioned reassuringly toward the hole.

When the third head appeared, a soft smile of glee came upon each face, and the mute group exchanged expressive glances.

When they all stood together, free from this tragic barn, they breathed a long sigh that was contemporaneous with another smile and another exchange of glances.

One of the men tiptoed to a knothole and peered into the barn. The sentry was at that moment speaking. "Yes, we know 'em all. There isn't a house in this region that we don't know who is in it most of the time. We collar 'em once in a while—like we did you. Now that house out yonder, we—"

The man suddenly left the knothole and returned to the others. Upon his face, dimly discerned, there was an indication that he had made an astonishing discovery. The others questioned him with their eyes, but he simply waved an arm to express his inability to speak at that spot. He led them back toward the hill, prowling carefully. At a safe distance from the barn he halted, and as they grouped eagerly about him, he exploded in an intense undertone: "Why, that—that's Cap'n Sawyer they got in yonder."

"Cap'n Sawyer!" incredulously whispered the other men.

But the girl had something to ask. "How did you get out of that feedbox?"

He smiled. "Well, when you put us in there, we was just in a minute when we allowed it wasn't a mighty safe place, and we allowed we'd get out. And we did. We skedaddled round and round until it 'peared like we was going to get cotched, and then we flung ourselves down in the cow stalls where it's low like—just dirt floor—and then we just naturally went a-whooping under the barn floor when the Yanks come. And we didn't know Cap'n Sawyer by his voice nohow. We heard 'im discoursing, and we allowed it was a mighty pert man, but we didn't know that it was him. No, m'm."

These three men, so recently from a situation of peril, seemed suddenly to have dropped all thought of it. They stood with sad faces looking at the barn. They seemed to be making no plans at all to reach a place of more complete safety. They were halted and stupefied by some unknown calamity.

"How do you raikon they cotch him, Sim?" one whispered mournfully.

"I don't know," replied another in the same tone.

Another with a low snarl expressed in two words his opinion of the methods of Fate: "Oh, hell!"

The three men started then as if simultaneously stung, and gazed at the young girl who stood silently near them. The man who had sworn began to make agitated apology: "Pardon, miss! 'Pon my soul, I clean forgot you was by. 'Deed, and I wouldn't swear like that if I had knowed. 'Deed, I wouldn't."

The girl did not seem to hear him. She was staring at the barn. Suddenly she turned and whispered, "Who is he?"

"He's Cap'n Sawyer, m'm," they told her sorrowfully. "He's our own cap'n. He's been in command of us yere since a long time. He's got folks about yere. Raikon they cotch him while he was a-visiting."

She was still for a time, and then, awed, she said, "Will they—will they hang him?"

"No, m'm. Oh, no, m'm. Don't raikon no such thing. No, m'm."

The group became absorbed in a contemplation of the barn. For a time no one moved or spoke. At last the girl was aroused by slight sounds, and turning, she perceived that the three men who had so recently escaped from the barn were now advancing toward it.

- v -

The girl, waiting in the darkness, expected to hear the sudden crash and uproar of a fight as soon as the three creeping men should reach the barn. She reflected in an agony upon the swift disaster that would befall any enterprise so desperate. She had an impulse to beg them to come away. The grass rustled in silken movements as she sped toward the barn.

When she arrived, however, she gazed about her, bewildered. The men were gone. She searched with her eyes, trying to detect some moving thing, but she could see nothing.

Left alone again, she began to be afraid of the night. The great stretches of darkness could hide crawling dangers. From sheer desire to see a human, she was obliged to peep again at the knothole. The sentry had apparently wearied of talking. Instead, he was reflecting. The prisoner still sat on the feedbox, moodily staring at the floor. The girl felt in one way that she was looking at a ghastly group in wax. She started when the old horse put down an echoing hoof. She wished the men would speak; their silence reinforced the strange aspect. They might have been two dead men.

The girl felt impelled to look at the corner of the interior where were the cow stalls. There was no light there save the appearance of peculiar gray haze which marked the track of the dimming rays of the lantern. All else was somber shadow. At last she saw something move there. It might have been as small as a rat, or it might have been a part of something as large as a man. At any rate, it proclaimed that something in that spot was alive. At one time she saw it plainly, and at other times it vanished, because her fixture of gaze caused her occasionally to greatly tangle and blur those peculiar shadows and faint lights. At last, however, she perceived a human head. It was monstrously disheveled and wild. It moved slowly forward until its glance could fall upon the prisoner and then upon the sentry. The wandering rays caused the eyes to glitter like silver. The girl's heart pounded so that she put her hand over it.

The sentry and the prisoner remained immovably waxen,

and over in the gloom the head thrust from the floor watched them with its silver eyes.

Finally, the prisoner slipped from the feedbox, and raising his arms, yawned at great length. "Oh, well," he remarked, "you boys will get a good licking if you fool around here much longer. That's some satisfaction, anyhow, even if you did bag me. You'll get a good walloping." He reflected for a moment, and decided, "I'm sort of willing to be captured if you fellows only get a damned good licking for being so smart."

The sentry looked up and smiled a superior smile. "Licking, hey? Nixey!" He winked exasperatingly at the prisoner. "You fellows are not fast enough, my boy. Why didn't you lick us at——? and at——? and at——?" He named some of the great battles.

To this the captive officer blurted in angry astonishment, "Why, we did!"

The sentry winked again in profound irony: "Yes—I know you did. Of course. You whipped us, didn't you? Fine kind of whipping that was! Why, we—"

He suddenly ceased, smitten mute by a sound that broke the stillness of the night. It was the sharp crack of a distant shot that made wild echoes among the hills. It was instantly followed by the hoarse cry of a human voice, a faraway yell of warning, singing of surprise, peril, fear of death. A moment later there was a distant fierce spattering of shots. The sentry and the prisoner stood facing each other, their lips apart, listening.

The orchard at that instant awoke to sudden tumult. There were the thud and scramble and scamper of feet, the mellow, swift clash of arms, men's voices in question, oath, command, hurried and unhurried, resolute and frantic. A horse sped along the road at a raging gallop. A loud voice shouted, "What is it, Ferguson?" Another voice yelled something incoherent. There was a sharp, discordant chorus of command. An uproarious volley suddenly rang from the orchard. The prisoner in gray moved from his intent, listening attitude. Instantly the eyes of the sentry blazed, and he said with a new and terrible sternness, "Stand where you are!"

The prisoner trembled in his excitement. Expressions of delight and triumph bubbled to his lips. "A surprise, by Gawd! Now—now, you'll see!"

The sentry stolidly swung his carbine to his shoulder. He sighted carefully along the barrel until it pointed at the prisoner's head, about at his nose. "Well, I've got you, anyhow. Remember that! Don't move!"

The prisoner could not keep his arms from nervously gesturing. "I won't; but—"

"And shut your mouth!"

The three comrades of the sentry flung themselves into view. "Pete—devil of a rowl—can you—"

"I've got him," said the sentry calmly and without moving. It was as if the barrel of the carbine rested on piers of stone. The three comrades turned and plunged into the darkness.

In the orchard it seemed as if two gigantic animals were engaged in a mad, floundering encounter, snarling, howling in a whirling chaos of noise and motion. In the barn the prisoner and his guard faced each other in silence.

As for the girl at the knothole, the sky had fallen at the beginning of this clamor. She would not have been astonished to see the stars swinging from their abodes, and the vegetation, the barn, all blow away. It was the end of everything, the grand, universal murder. When two of the three miraculous soldiers who formed the original feedbox corps emerged in detail from the hole under the beam and slid away into the darkness, she did no more than glance at them.

Suddenly she recollected the head with silver eyes. She started forward and again applied her eyes to the knothole. Even with the din resounding from the orchard, from up the road and down the road, from the heavens and from the deep earth, the central fascination was this mystic head. There, to her, was the dark god of the tragedy.

The prisoner in gray at this moment burst into a laugh that was no more than a hysterical gurgle. "Well, you can't hold that gun out forever! Pretty soon you'll have to lower it."

The sentry's voice sounded slightly muffled, for his cheek was pressed against the weapon. "I won't be tired for some time yet."

The girl saw the head slowly rise, the eyes fixed upon the sentry's face. A tall, black figure slunk across the cow stalls and vanished in back of old Santo's quarters. She knew what was to come to pass. She knew this grim thing was upon a terrible mission, and that it would reappear again at the head of the little passage between Santo's stall and the wall, almost at the sentry's elbow; and yet when she saw a faint indication as of a form crouching there, a scream from an utterly new alarm almost escaped her.

The sentry's arms, after all, were not of granite. He moved restively. At last he spoke in his even, unchanging tone: "Well, I guess you'll have to climb into that feedbox. Step back and lift the lid."

"Why, you don't mean—"

"Step back!"

The girl felt a cry of warning arising to her lips as she gazed at this sentry. She noted every detail of his facial expression. She saw, moreover, his mass of brown hair bunching disgracefully about his ears, his clear eyes lit now with a hard, cold light, his forehead puckered in a mighty scowl, the ring upon the third finger of the left hand. "Oh, they won't kill him! Surely they won't kill him!" The noise of the fight in the orchard was the loud music, the thunder and lightning, the rioting of the tempest which people love during the critical scene of a tragedy.

When the prisoner moved back in reluctant obedience, he faced for an instant the entrance of the little passage, and what he saw there must have been written swiftly, graphically in his eyes. And the sentry read it and knew then that he was upon the threshold of his death. In a fraction of time, certain information went from the grim thing in the passage to the prisoner, and from the prisoner to the sentry. But at that instant the black, formidable figure arose, towered, and made its leap. A new shadow flashed across the floor when the blow was struck.

As for the girl at the knothole, when she returned to sense, she found herself standing with clenched hands and screaming with her might.

As if her reason had again departed from her, she ran around the barn, in at the door, and flung herself sobbing beside the body of the soldier in blue.

The uproar of the fight became at last coherent, inasmuch as one party was giving shouts of supreme exultation. The firing no longer sounded in crashes; it was now expressed in spiteful crackles, the last words of the combat, spoken with feminine vindictiveness.

Presently there was a thud of flying feet. A grimy, panting, red-faced mob of troopers in blue plunged into the barn, became instantly frozen to attitudes of amazement and rage, and then roared in one great chorus: "He's gone!"

The girl who knelt beside the body upon the floor turned toward them her lamenting eyes and cried, "He's not dead, is he? He can't be dead?"

They thronged forward. The sharp lieutenant who had been so particular about the feedbox knelt by the side of the girl and laid his head against the chest of the prostrate soldier. "Why, no," he said, rising and looking at the man. "He's all right. Some of you boys throw some water on him."

"Are you sure?" demanded the girl feverishly.

"Of course! He'll be better after a while."

"Oh!" said she softly, and then looked down at the sentry. She started to arise, and the lieutenant reached down and hoisted rather awkwardly at her arm.

"Don't you worry about him. He's all right."

She turned her face with its curving lips and shining eyes once more toward the unconscious soldier upon the floor. The troopers made a lane to the door, the lieutenant bowed, the girl vanished.

"Queer," said a young officer. "Girl very clearly worst kind of rebel, and yet she falls to weeping and wailing like mad over one of her enemies. Be around in the morning with all sorts of doctoring—you see if she ain't. Queer."

The sharp lieutenant shrugged his shoulders. After reflection he shrugged his shoulders again. He said, "War changes many things; but it doesn't change everything, thank God!"

---

# A Mystery of Heroism

THE DARK uniforms of the men were so coated with dust from the incessant wrestling of the two armies that the regiment almost seemed a part of the clay bank which shielded them from the shells. On the top of the hill a battery was arguing in tremendous roars with some other guns, and to the eye of the infantry the artillerymen, the guns, the caissons, the horses, were distinctly outlined upon the blue sky. When a piece was fired, a red streak as round as a log flashed low in the heavens, like a monstrous bolt of lightning. The men of the battery wore white duck trousers, which somehow emphasized their legs; and when they ran and crowded in little groups at the bidding of the shouting officers, it was more impressive than usual to the infantry.

Fred Collins, of A Company, was saying, "Thunder! I wisht I had a drink. Ain't there any water round here?" Then somebody yelled, "There goes th' bugler!"

As the eyes of half the regiment swept in one machine-like movement, there was an instant's picture of a horse in a great, convulsive leap of a death wound and a rider leaning back with a crooked arm and spread fingers before his face. On the ground was the crimson terror of an exploding shell, with fibers of flame that seemed like lances. A glittering bugle swung clear of the rider's back as fell headlong the horse and the man. In the air was an odor as from a conflagration.

Sometimes they of the infantry looked down at a fair little meadow which spread at their feet. Its long, green grass was rippling gently in a breeze. Beyond it was the gray form of a house half torn to pieces by shells and by the busy axes of soldiers who had pursued firewood. The line of an old fence was now dimly marked by long weeds and by an occasional post. A shell had blown the well house to fragments. Little lines of gray smoke ribboning upward from some embers indicated the place where had stood the barn.

From beyond a curtain of green woods there came the sound of some stupendous scuffle, as if two animals of the size of islands were fighting. At a distance there were occasional appearances of swift-moving men, horses, batteries, flags, and with the crashing of infantry volleys were heard, often, wild and frenzied cheers. In the midst of it all Smith and Ferguson, two privates of A Company, were engaged in a heated discussion which involved the greatest questions of the national existence.

The battery on the hill presently engaged in a frightful duel. The white legs of the gunners scampered this way and that way, and the officers redoubled their shouts. The guns, with their demeanors of stolidity and courage, were typical of something infinitely self-possessed in this clamor of death that swirled around the hill.

One of a "swing" team was suddenly smitten quivering to the ground, and his maddened brethren dragged his torn body in their struggle to escape from this turmoil and danger. A young soldier astride one of the leaders swore and fumed in his saddle and furiously jerked at the bridle. An officer screamed out an order so violently that his voice broke and ended the sentence in a falsetto shriek.

The leading company of the infantry regiment was somewhat exposed, and the colonel ordered it moved more fully under the shelter of the hill. There was the clank of steel against steel.

A lieutenant of the battery rode down and passed them, holding his right arm carefully in his left hand. And it was as if this arm was not at all a part of him, but belonged to another man. His sober and reflective charger went slowly. The officer's face was grimy and perspiring, and his uniform was tousled as if he had been in direct grapple with an enemy. He smiled grimly when the men stared at him. He turned his horse toward the meadow.

Collins, of A Company, said, "I wisht I had a drink. I bet there's water in that there ol' well yonder!"

"Yes; but how you goin' to git it?"

For the little meadow which intervened was now suffering a terrible onslaught of shells. Its green and beautiful calm had vanished utterly. Brown earth was being flung in monstrous handfuls. And there was a massacre of the young blades of grass. They were being torn, burned, obliterated. Some curious fortune of the battle had made this gentle little meadow the object of the red hate of the shells, and each one as it exploded seemed like an imprecation in the face of a maiden.

The wounded officer who was riding across this expanse said to himself: "Why, they couldn't shoot any harder if the whole army was massed here!"

A shell struck the gray ruins of the house, and as, after the roar, the shattered wall fell in fragments, there was a noise which resembled the flapping of shutters during a wild gale of winter. Indeed, the infantry paused in the shelter of the bank appeared as men standing upon a shore contemplating a madness of the sea. The angel of calamity had under its glance the battery upon the hill. Fewer white-legged men labored about the guns. A shell had smitten one of the pieces, and after the flare, the smoke, the dust, the wrath of this blow were gone, it was possible to see white legs stretched horizontally upon the ground. And at that interval, to the rear, where it is the business of battery horses to stand with their noses to the fight, awaiting the command to drag their guns out of the destruction, or into it, or wheresoever these incomprehensible humans demanded with whip and spur—in this line of passive and dumb spectators, whose fluttering hearts yet would not let them forget the iron laws of man's control of them—in this rank of brute-soldiers there had been relentless and hideous carnage. From the ruck of bleeding and prostrate horses, the men of the infantry could see one animal raising its stricken body with its forelegs and turning its nose with mystic and profound eloquence toward the sky.

Some comrades joked Collins about his thirst. "Well, if yeh want a drink so bad, why don't yeh go git it?"

"Well, I will in a minnet, if yeh don't shut up!"

A lieutenant of artillery floundered his horse straight down the hill with as little concern as if it were level ground. As he galloped past the colonel of the infantry, he threw up his hand in swift salute. "We've got to get out of that," he roared angrily. He was a black-bearded officer, and his eyes, which resembled beads, sparkled like those of an insane man. His jumping horse sped along the column of infantry.

The fat major, standing carelessly with his sword held horizontally behind him and with his legs far apart, looked after the receding horseman and laughed. "He wants to get back with orders pretty quick, or there'll be no batt'ry left," he observed.

The wise young captain of the second company hazarded to the lieutenant colonel that the enemy's infantry would probably soon attack the hill, and the lieutenant colonel snubbed him.

A private in one of the rear companies looked out over the meadow, and then turned to a companion and said, "Look there, Jim!" It was the wounded officer from the battery, who some time before had started to ride across the meadow, supporting his right arm carefully with his left hand. This man had encountered a shell, apparently, at a time when no one perceived him, and he could now be seen lying face downward with a stirruped foot stretched across the body of his dead horse. A leg of the charger extended slantingly upward, precisely as stiff as a stake. Around this motionless pair the shells still howled.

There was a quarrel in A Company. Collins was shaking his fist in the faces of some laughing comrades. "Dern yeh! I ain't afraid t' go. If yeh say much, I will go!"

"Of course, yeh will! You'll run through that there medder, won't yeh?"

Collins said, in a terrible voice, "You see now!"

At this ominous threat, his comrades broke into renewed jeers.

Collins gave them a dark scowl, and went to find his captain. The latter was conversing with the colonel of the regiment.

"Captain," said Collins, saluting and standing at attention—in those days all trousers bagged at the knees—"Captain, I want t' get permission to go git some water from that there well over yonder!"

The colonel and the captain swung about simultaneously and stared across the meadow. The captain laughed. "You must be pretty thirsty, Collins?"

"Yes, sir, I am."

"Well—ah," said the captain. After a moment, he asked, "Can't you wait?"

"No, sir."

The colonel was watching Collins's face. "Look here, my lad," he said, in a pious sort of voice, "look here, my lad"—Collins was not a lad—"don't you think that's taking pretty big risks for a little drink of water?"

"I dunno," said Collins uncomfortably. Some of the resentment toward his companions, which perhaps had forced him into this affair, was beginning to fade. "I dunno w'ether 'tis."

The colonel and the captain contemplated him for a time.

"Well," said the captain finally.

"Well," said the colonel, "if you want to go, why, go."

Collins saluted. "Much obliged t' yeh."

As he moved away, the colonel called after him. "Take some of the other boys' canteens with you, an' hurry back, now."

"Yes, sir, I will."

The colonel and the captain looked at each other then, for it had suddenly occurred that they could not for the life of them tell whether Collins wanted to go or whether he did not.

They turned to regard Collins, and as they perceived him surrounded by gesticulating comrades, the colonel said, "Well, by thunder! I guess he's going."

Collins appeared as a man dreaming. In the midst of the questions, the advice, the warnings, all the excited talk of his company mates, he maintained a curious silence.

They were very busy in preparing him for his ordeal. When they inspected him carefully, it was somewhat like the examination that grooms give a horse before a race; and they were amazed, staggered, by the whole affair. Their astonishment found vent in strange repetitions.

"Are yeh sure a-goin'?" they demanded again and again.

"Certainly I am," cried Collins at last, furiously.

He strode sullenly away from them. He was swinging five or six canteens by their cords. It seemed that his cap would not remain firmly on his head, and often he reached and pulled it down over his brow.

There was a general movement in the compact column. The long animal-like thing moved slightly. Its four hundred eyes were turned upon the figure of Collins.

"Well, sir, if that ain't th' derndest thing! I never thought Fred Collins had the blood in him for that kind of business."

"What's he goin' to do, anyhow?"

"He's goin' to that well there after water."

"We ain't dyin' of thirst, are we? That's foolishness."

"Well, somebody put him up to it, an' he's doin' it."

"Say, he must be a desperate cuss."

When Collins faced the meadow and walked away from the regiment, he was vaguely conscious that a chasm, the deep valley of all prides, was suddenly between him and his comrades. It was provisional, but the provision was that he return as a victor. He had blindly been led by quaint emotions, and laid himself under an obligation to walk squarely up to the face of death.

But he was not sure that he wished to make a retraction,

even if he could do so without shame. As a matter of truth, he was sure of very little. He was mainly surprised.

It seemed to him supernaturally strange that he had allowed his mind to maneuver his body into such a situation. He understood that it might be called dramatically great.

However, he had no full appreciation of anything, excepting that he was actually conscious of being dazed. He could feel his dulled mind groping after the form and color of this incident. He wondered why he did not feel some keen agony of fear cutting his sense like a knife. He wondered at this, because human expression had said loudly for centuries that men should feel afraid of certain things, and that all men who did not feel this fear were phenomena—heroes.

He was, then, a hero. He suffered that disappointment which we would all have if we discovered that we were ourselves capable of those deeds which we most admire in history and legend. This, then, was a hero. After all, heroes were not much.

No, it could not be true. He was not a hero. Heroes had no shames in their lives, and as for him, he remembered borrowing fifteen dollars from a friend and promising to pay it back the next day, and then avoiding that friend for ten months. When, at home, his mother had aroused him for the early labor of his life on the farm, it had often been his fashion to be irritable, childish, diabolical; and his mother had died since he had come to the war.

He saw that in this matter of the well, the canteens, the shells, he was an intruder in the land of fine deeds.

He was now about thirty paces from his comrades. The regiment had just turned its many faces toward him.

From the forest of terrific noises there suddenly emerged a little uneven line of men. They fired fiercely and rapidly at distant foliage on which appeared little puffs of white smoke. The spatter of skirmish firing was added to the thunder of the guns on the hill. The little line of men ran forward. A color sergeant fell flat with his flag as if he had slipped on ice. There was hoarse cheering from this distant field.

Collins suddenly felt that two demon fingers were pressed into his ears. He could see nothing but flying arrows, flaming red. He lurched from the shock of this explosion, but he made a mad rush for the house, which he viewed as a man submerged to the neck in a boiling surf might view the shore. In the air little pieces of shell howled, and the earthquake explosions drove him insane with the menace of their roar. As he ran, the canteens knocked together with a rhythmical tinkling.

As he neared the house, each detail of the scene became vivid to him. He was aware of some bricks of the vanished chimney lying on the sod. There was a door which hung by one hinge.

Rifle bullets called forth by the insistent skirmishers came from the far-off bank of foliage. They mingled with the shells and the pieces of shells until the air was torn in all directions by hootings, yells, howls. The sky was full of fiends who directed all their wild rage at his head.

When he came to the well, he flung himself face downward and peered into its darkness. There were furtive silver glintings some feet from the surface. He grabbed one of the canteens, and unfastening its cap, swung it down by the cord. The water flowed slowly in with an indolent gurgle.

And now, as he lay with his face turned away, he was suddenly smitten with the terror. It came upon his heart like the grasp of claws. All the power faded from his muscles. For an instant he was no more than a dead man.

The canteen filled with a maddening slowness, in the manner of all bottles. Presently he recovered his strength and addressed a screaming oath to it. He leaned over until it seemed as if he intended to try to push water into it with his hands. His eyes as he gazed down into the well shone like two pieces of metal, and in their expression was a great appeal and a great curse. The stupid water derided him.

There was the blaring thunder of a shell. Crimson light shone through the swift-boiling smoke and made a pink reflection on part of the wall of the well. Collins jerked out his arm and canteen with the same motion that a man would use in withdrawing his head from a furnace.

He scrambled erect and glared and hesitated. On the ground near him lay the old well bucket, with a length of rusty chain. He lowered it swiftly into the well. The bucket struck the water and then, turning lazily over, sank. When, with hand reaching tremblingly over hand, he hauled it out, it knocked often against the walls of the well and spilled some of its contents.

In running with a filled bucket, a man can adopt but one kind of gait. So, through this terrible field over which screamed practical angels of death, Collins ran in the manner of a farmer chased out of a dairy by a bull.

His face went staring white with anticipation—anticipation of a blow that would whirl him around and down. He would fall as he had seen other men fall, the life knocked out of them so suddenly that their knees were no more quick to touch the ground than their heads. He saw the long blue line of the regiment, but his comrades were standing looking at him from the edge of an impossible star. He was aware of some deep wheel ruts and hoofprints in the sod beneath his feet.

The artillery officer who had fallen in this meadow had been making groans in the teeth of the tempest of sound. These futile cries, wrenched from him by his agony, were heard only by shells, bullets. When wild-eyed Collins came running, this officer raised himself. His face contorted and blanched from pain, he was about to utter some great beseeching cry. But suddenly his face straightened, and he called, "Say, young man, give me a drink of water, will you?"

Collins had no room amid his emotions for surprise. He was mad from the threats of destruction.

"I can't!" he screamed, and in his reply was a full description of his quaking apprehension. His cap was gone and his hair was riotous. His clothes made it appear that he had been dragged over the ground by the heels. He ran on.

The officer's head sank down, and one elbow crooked.

His foot in its brass-bound stirrup still stretched over the body of his horse, and the other leg was under the steed.

But Collins turned. He came dashing back. His face had now turned gray, and in his eyes was all terror. "Here it is! Here it is!"

The officer was as a man gone in drink. His arm bent like a twig. His head drooped as if his neck were of willow. He was sinking to the ground, to lie face downward.

Collins grabbed him by the shoulder. "Here it is. Here's your drink. Turn over. Turn over, man, for God's sake!"

With Collins hauling at his shoulder, the officer twisted his body and fell with his face turned toward that region where lived the unspeakable noises of the swirling missiles. There was the faintest shadow of a smile on his lips as he looked at Collins. He gave a sigh, a little primitive breath like that from a child.

Collins tried to hold the bucket steadily, but his shaking hands caused the water to splash all over the face of the dying man. Then he jerked it away and ran on.

The regiment gave him a welcoming roar. The grimed faces were wrinkled in laughter.

His captain waved the bucket away. "Give it to the men!"

The two genial, skylarking young lieutenants were the first to gain possession of it. They played over it in their fashion.

When one tried to drink, the other teasingly knocked his elbow. "Don't, Billie! You'll make me spill it," said the one. The other laughed.

Suddenly there was an oath, the thud of wood on the ground, and a swift murmur of astonishment among the ranks. The two lieutenants glared at each other. The bucket lay on the ground, empty.

# An Episode of War

THE LIEUTENANT'S rubber blanket lay on the ground, and upon it he had poured the company's supply of coffee. Corporals and other representatives of the grimy and hot-throated men who lined the breastwork had come for each squad's portion.

The lieutenant was frowning and serious at this task of division. His lips pursed as he drew with his sword various crevices in the heap, until brown squares of coffee, astoundingly equal in size, appeared on the blanket. He was on the verge of a great triumph in mathematics, and the corporals were thronging forward, each to reap a little square, when suddenly the lieutenant cried out and looked quickly at a man near him as if he suspected it was a case of personal assault. The others cried out also when they saw blood upon the lieutenant's sleeve.

He had winced like a man stung, swayed dangerously, and then straightened. The sound of his hoarse breathing was plainly audible. He looked sadly, mystically, over the breastwork at the green face of a wood, where now were many little puffs of white smoke. During this moment the men about him gazed statue-like and silent, astonished and awed by this catastrophe which happened when catastrophes were not expected—when they had leisure to observe it.

As the lieutenant stared at the wood, they, too, swung their heads, so that for another instant, all hands, still silent, contemplated the distant forest as if their minds were fixed upon the mystery of a bullet's journey.

The officer had, of course, been compelled to take his sword into his left hand. He did not hold it by the hilt. He gripped it at the middle of the blade, awkwardly. Turning his eyes from the hostile wood, he looked at the sword as he held it there, and seemed puzzled as to what to do with it, where to put it. In short, this weapon had of a sudden become a strange thing to him. He looked at it in a kind of stupefaction, as if he had been endowed with a trident, a scepter, or a spade.

Finally he tried to sheathe it. To sheathe a sword held by the left hand, at the middle of the blade, in a scabbard hung at the left hip, is a feat worthy of a sawdust ring. This wounded officer engaged in a desperate struggle with the sword and the wobbling scabbard, and during the time of it he breathed like a wrestler.

But at this instant the men, the spectators, awoke from their stonelike poses and crowded forward sympathetically. The orderly sergeant took the sword and tenderly placed it in the scabbard. At the time, he leaned nervously backward, and did not allow even his finger to brush the body of the lieutenant. A wound gives strange dignity to him who bears it. Well men shy from this new and terrible majesty. It is as if the wounded man's hand is upon the curtain which hangs before the revelations of all existence—the meaning of ants; potentates, wars, cities, sunshine, snow, a feather dropped from a bird's wing; and the power of it sheds radiance upon a bloody form, and makes the other men understand sometimes that they are little. His comrades look at him with large eyes thoughtfully. Moreover, they fear vaguely that the weight of a finger upon him might send him headlong, precipitate the tragedy, hurl him at once into the dim, gray unknown. And so the orderly sergeant, while sheathing the sword, leaned nervously backward.

There were others who proffered assistance. One timidly presented his shoulder and asked the lieutenant if he cared to lean upon it, but the latter waved him away mournfully. He wore the look of one who knows he is the victim of a terrible disease and understands his helplessness. He again stared over the breastwork at the forest, and then, turning, went slowly rearward. He held his right wrist tenderly in his

left hand as if the wounded arm was made of very brittle
glass.

And the men in silence stared at the wood, then at the departing lieutenant; then at the wood, then at the lieutenant.

As the wounded officer passed from the line of battle, he
was enabled to see many things which as a participant in
the fight were unknown to him. He saw a general on a black
horse gazing over the lines of blue infantry at the green
woods which veiled his problems. An aide galloped furiously,
dragged his horse suddenly to a halt, saluted, and presented
a paper. It was, for a wonder, precisely like a historical
painting.

To the rear of the general and his staff, a group, composed
of a bugler, two or three orderlies, and the bearer of the
corps standard, all upon maniacal horses, were working like
slaves to hold their ground, preserve their respectful interval,
while the shells boomed in the air about them, and caused
their chargers to make furious, quivering leaps.

A battery, a tumultuous and shining mass, was swirling
toward the right. The wild thud of hoofs, the cries of the
riders shouting blame and praise, menace and encouragement, and, last, the roar of the wheels, the slant of the
glistening guns, brought the lieutenant to an intent pause.
The battery swept in curves that stirred the heart; it made
halts as dramatic as the crash of a wave on the rocks, and
when it fled onward, this aggregation of wheels, levers, mo-
tors had a beautiful unity, as if it were a missile. The sound
of it was a war chorus that reached into the depths of man's
emotion.

The lieutenant, still holding his arm as if it were of glass,
stood watching this battery until all detail of it was lost, save
the figures of the riders, which rose and fell and waved
lashes over the black mass.

Later he turned his eyes toward the battle, where the
shooting sometimes crackled like bush fires, sometimes sputtered with exasperating irregularity, and sometimes rever-
berated like the thunder. He saw the smoke rolling upward

and saw crowds of men who ran and cheered, or stood and blazed away at the inscrutable distance.

He came upon some stragglers, and they told him how to find the field hospital. They described its exact location. In fact, these men, no longer having part in the battle, knew more of it than others. They told the performance of every corps, every division, the opinion of every general. The lieutenant, carrying his wounded arm rearward, looked upon them with wonder.

At the roadside, a brigade was making coffee and buzzing with talk like a girls' boarding school. Several officers came out to him and inquired concerning things of which he knew nothing. One, seeing his arm, began to scold. "Why, man, that's no way to do. You want to fix that thing." He appropriated the lieutenant and the lieutenant's wound. He cut the sleeve and laid bare the arm, every nerve of which softly fluttered under his touch. He bound his handkerchief over the wound, scolding away in the meantime. His tone allowed one to think that he was in the habit of being wounded every day. The lieutenant hung his head, feeling, in this presence, that he did not know how to be correctly wounded.

The low, white tents of the hospital were grouped around an old schoolhouse. There was here a singular commotion. In the foreground, two ambulances interlocked wheels in the deep mud. The drivers were tossing the blame of it back and forth, gesticulating and berating, while from the ambulances, both crammed with wounded, there came an occasional groan. An interminable crowd of bandaged men were coming and going. Great numbers sat under the trees nursing heads or arms or legs. There was a dispute of some kind raging on the steps of the schoolhouse. Sitting with his back against a tree, a man with a face as gray as a new army blanket was serenely smoking a corncob pipe. The lieutenant wished to rush forward and inform him that he was dying.

A busy surgeon was passing near the lieutenant. "Good morning," he said, with a friendly smile. Then he caught sight of the lieutenant's arm, and his face at once changed.

"Well, let's have a look at it." He seemed possessed suddenly of a great contempt for the lieutenant. This wound evidently placed the latter on a very low social plane. The doctor cried out impatiently, "What muttonhead had tied it up that way anyhow?" The lieutenant answered, "Oh, a man."

When the wound was disclosed, the doctor fingered it disdainfully. "Humph," he said. "You come along with me and I'll 'tend to you." His voice contained the same scorn as if he were saying: "You will have to go to jail."

The lieutenant had been very meek, but now his face flushed, and he looked into the doctor's eyes. "I guess I won't have it amputated," he said.

"Nonsense, man! Nonsense! Nonsense!" cried the doctor. "Come along, now. I won't amputate it. Come along. Don't be a baby."

"Let go of me," said the lieutenant, holding back wrathfully, his glance fixed upon the door of the old schoolhouse, as sinister to him as the portals of death.

And this is the story of how the lieutenant lost his arm. When he reached home, his sisters, his mother, his wife, sobbed for a long time at the sight of the flat sleeve. "Oh, well," he said, standing shamefaced amid these tears, "I don't suppose it matters so much as all that."

---

# The Price of the Harness

## - i -

TWENTY-FIVE men were making a road out of a path up the hillside. The light batteries in the rear were impatient to advance, but first must be done all that digging and smoothing which gains no encrusted medals from war. The men worked like gardeners, and a road was growing from the old pack-animal trail.

Trees arched from a field of guinea grass which resembled young wild corn. The day was still and dry. The men working were dressed in the consistent blue of United States regulars. They looked indifferent, almost stolid, despite the heat and the labor. There was little talking. From time to time a government pack train, led by a sleek-sided, tender bell mare, came from one way or the other way, and the men stood aside as the strong, hard, black-and-tan animals crowded eagerly after their curious little feminine leader.

A volunteer staff officer appeared, and sitting on his horse in the middle of the work, asked the sergeant in command some questions which were apparently not relevant to any military business. Men straggling along on various duties almost invariably spun some kind of joke as they passed.

A corporal and four men were guarding boxes of spare ammunition at the top of the hill, and one of the number often went to the foot of the hill, swinging canteens.

The day wore down to the Cuban dusk, in which the shadows are all grim and of ghostly shape. The men began to lift their eyes from the shovels and picks, and glance in the direction of their camp. The sun threw his last lance through the foliage. The steep mountain range on the right turned blue and as without detail as a curtain. The tiny ruby of light ahead meant that the ammunition guard were cooking their supper. From somewhere in the world came a single rifle shot.

Figures appeared, dim in the shadow of the trees. A murmur, a sigh of quiet relief, arose from the working party. Later, they swung up the hill in an unformed formation, being always like soldiers, and unable even to carry a spade save like United States regular soldiers. As they passed through some fields, the bland, white light of the end of the day feebly touched each hard, bronze profile.

"Wonder if we'll git anythin' to eat," said Watkins, in a low voice.

"Should think so," said Nolan, in the same tone. They

betrayed no impatience; they seemed to feel a kind of awe of the situation.

The sergeant turned. One could see the cool gray eye flashing under the brim of the campaign hat. "What in hell you fellers kickin' about?" he asked. They made no reply, understanding that they were being suppressed.

As they moved on, a murmur arose from the tall grass on either hand. It was the noise from the bivouac of ten thousand men, although one saw practically nothing from the low-cart roadway. The sergeant led his party up a wet clay bank and into a trampled field. Here were scattered tiny white shelter tents, and in the darkness they were luminous like the rearing stones in a graveyard. A few fires burned blood-red, and the shadowy figures of men moved with no more expression of detail than there is in the swaying of foliage on a windy night.

The working party felt their way to where their tents were pitched. A man suddenly cursed; he had mislaid something, and he knew he was not going to find it that night. Watkins spoke again with the monotony of a clock: "Wonder if we'll git anythin' to eat."

Martin, with eyes turned pensively to the stars, began a treatise. "Them Spaniards—"

"Oh, quit it," cried Nolan. "What th' piper do you know about th' Spaniards, you fat-headed Dutchman? Better think of your belly, you blunderin' swine, an' what you're goin' to put in it, grass or dirt."

A laugh, a sort of deep growl, arose from the prostrate men. In the meantime, the sergeant had reappeared and was standing over them. "No rations tonight," he said gruffly, and turning on his heel, walked away.

This announcement was received in silence. But Watkins had flung himself face downward, and putting his lips close to a tuft of grass, he formulated oaths. Martin arose, and going to his shelter, crawled in sulkily. After a long interval, Nolan said aloud, "Hell!" Grierson, enlisted for the war, raised a querulous voice. "Well, I wonder when we *will* git fed?"

From the ground about him came a low chuckle, full of ironical comment upon Grierson's lack of certain qualities which the other men felt themselves to possess.

- *ii* -

In the cold light of dawn the men were on their knees, packing, strapping, and buckling. The comic toy hamlet of shelter tents had been wiped out as if by a cyclone. Through the trees could be seen the crimson of a light battery's blankets, and the wheels creaked like the sound of a musketry fight. Nolan, well gripped by his shelter tent, his blanket, and his cartridge belt, and bearing his rifle, advanced upon a small group of men who were hastily finishing a can of coffee.

"Say, give us a drink, will yeh?" he asked wistfully. He was as sad-eyed as an orphan beggar.

Every man in the group turned to look him straight in the face. He had asked for the principal ruby out of each one's crown. There was a grim silence. Then one said, "What fer?" Nolan cast his glance to the ground, and went away abashed.

But he espied Watkins and Martin surrounding Grierson, who had gained three pieces of hardtack by mere force of his audacious inexperience. Grierson was fending his comrades off tearfully.

"Now don't be damn pigs," he cried. "Hold on a minute." Here Nolan asserted a claim. Grierson groaned. Kneeling piously, he divided the hardtack with minute care into four portions. The men, who had had their heads together like players watching a wheel of fortune, arose suddenly, each chewing. Nolan interpolated a drink of water, and sighed contentedly.

The whole forest seemed to be moving. From the field on the other side of the road a column of men in blue was slowly pouring; the battery had creaked on ahead; from the rear came a hum of advancing regiments. Then from a mile away rang the noise of a shot; then another shot; in a moment the rifles there were drumming, drumming, drumming. The artillery boomed out suddenly. A day of battle was begun.

The men made no exclamations. They rolled their eyes in the direction of the sound, and then swept with a calm glance the forests and the hills which surrounded them, implacably mysterious forests and hills which lent to every rifle shot the ominous quality which belongs to secret assassination. The whole scene would have spoken to the private soldiers of ambushes, sudden flank attacks, terrible disasters, if it were not for those cool gentlemen with shoulder straps and swords who, the private soldiers knew, were of another world and omnipotent for the business.

The battalions moved out into the mud and began a leisurely march in the damp shade of the trees. The advance of two batteries had churned the black soil into a formidable paste. The brown leggings of the men, stained with the mud of other days, took on a deeper color. Perspiration broke gently out on the reddish faces. With his heavy roll of blanket and the half of a shelter tent crossing his right shoulder and under his left arm, each man presented the appearance of being clasped from behind, wrestler-fashion, by a pair of thick, white arms.

There was something distinctive in the way they carried their rifles. There was the grace of an old hunter somewhere in it, the grace of a man whose rifle has become absolutely a part of himself. Furthermore, almost every blue shirt sleeve was rolled to the elbow, disclosing forearms of almost incredible brawn. The rifles seemed light, almost fragile, in the hands that were at the end of these arms, never fat but always with rolling muscles and veins that seemed on the point of bursting. And another thing was the silence and the marvelous impassivity of the faces as the column made its slow way toward where the whole forest spluttered and fluttered with battle.

Opportunely, the battalion was halted astraddle of a stream, and before it again moved, most of the men had filled their canteens. The firing increased. Ahead and to the left, a battery was booming at methodical intervals, while the infantry racket was that continual drumming which, after all, often sounds like rain on a roof. Directly ahead one could hear the deep voices of fieldpieces.

Some wounded Cubans were carried by in litters improvised from hammocks swung on poles. One had a ghastly cut in the throat, probably from a fragment of shell, and his head was turned as if Providence particularly wished to display this wide and lapping gash to the long column that was winding toward the front. And another Cuban, shot through the groin, kept up a continual wail as he swung from the tread of his bearers. "Ay—ee! Ay—ee! *Madre mía! Madre mía!*" He sang this bitter ballad into the ears of at least three thousand men as they slowly made way for his bearers on the narrow wood path. These wounded insurgents were, then, to a large part of the advancing army, the visible messengers of bloodshed and death, and the men regarded them with thoughtful awe. This doleful, sobbing cry—"*Madre mía*"—was a tangible consequent misery of all that firing on in front into which the men knew they were soon to be plunged. Some of them wished to inquire of the bearers the details of what had happened; but they could not speak Spanish, and so it was as if fate had intentionally sealed the lips of all in order that even meager information might not leak out concerning this mystery—battle. On the other hand, many unversed private soldiers looked upon the unfortunate as men who had seen thousands maimed and bleeding, and absolutely could not conjure any further interest in such scenes.

A young staff officer passed on horseback. The vocal Cuban was always wailing, but the officer wheeled past the bearers without heeding anything. And yet he never before had seen such a sight. His case was different from that of the private soldiers. He heeded nothing because he was busy—immensely busy and hurried with a multitude of reasons and desires for doing his duty perfectly. His whole life had been a mere period of preliminary reflection for this situation, and he had no clear idea of anything save his obligation as an officer. A man of this kind might be stupid; it is conceivable that in remote cases certain bumps on his head might be composed entirely of wood; but those traditions of fidelity and courage which have been handed to him from generation to generation, and which he has tenaciously preserved despite the persecution of legislators and the indifference of his country, make it incredible that in battle he should ever fail to give his best blood and his best thought for his general, for his men, and for himself. And so this young officer in the shapeless hat and the torn and dirty shirt failed to heed the wails of the wounded man, even as the pilgrim fails to heed the world as he raises his illumined face toward his purpose—rightly or wrongly, his purpose—his sky of the ideal of duty; the wonderful part of it is that he is guided by an ideal which he has himself created, and has alone protected from attack. The young man was merely an officer in the United States regular army.

The column swung across a shallow ford and took a road which passed the right flank of one of the American batteries. On a hill it was booming and belching great clouds of white smoke. The infantry looked up with interest. Arrayed below the hill and behind the battery were the horses and limbers, the riders checking their pawing mounts, and behind each rider a red blanket flamed against the fervent green of the bushes. As the infantry moved along the road, some of the battery horses turned at the noise of the trampling feet and surveyed the men with eyes as deep as wells, serene, mournful, generous eyes, lit heartbreakingly with something that was akin to a philosophy, a religion of self-sacrifice—oh, gallant, gallant horses!

"I know a feller in that battery," said Nolan musingly. "A driver."

"Damn sight rather be a gunner," said Martin.

"Why would ye?" said Nolan opposingly.

"Well, I'd take my chances as a gunner b'fore I'd sit way up in th' air on a rawboned plug an' git shot at."

"Aw—" began Nolan.

"They've had some losses t'day all right," interrupted Grierson.

"Horses?" asked Watkins.

"Horses and men, too," said Grierson.

"How d'yeh know?"

"A feller told me there by the ford."

They kept only a part of their minds bearing on this discussion because they could already hear high in the air the wire-string note of the enemy's bullets.

- iii -

The road taken by this battalion as it followed other battalions is something less than a mile long in its journey across a heavily wooded plain. It is greatly changed now—in fact it was metamorphosed in two days; but at that time it was a mere track through dense shrubbery, from which rose great dignified, arching trees. It was, in fact, a path through a jungle.

The battalion had no sooner left the battery in the rear than bullets began to drive overhead. They made several different sounds, but as these were mainly high shots, it was usual for them to make the faint note of a vibrant string, touched elusively, half-dreamily.

The military balloon, a fat, wavering, yellow thing, was leading the advance like some new conception of war god. Its bloated mass shone above the trees, and served incidentally to indicate to the men at the rear that comrades were in advance. The track itself exhibited for all its visible length a closely knit procession of soldiers in blue with breasts crossed with white shelter tents. The first ominous order of battle came down the line. "Use the cutoff. Don't use the magazine until you're ordered." Noncommissioned officers repeated the command gruffly. A sound of clicking locks rattled along the columns. All men knew that the time had come.

The front had burst out with a roar like a brush fire. The balloon was dying, dying a gigantic and public death before the eyes of two armies. It quivered, sank, faded into the trees amid the flurry of a battle that was suddenly and tremendously like a storm.

The American battery thundered behind the men with a shock that seemed likely to tear the backs of their heads off. The Spanish shrapnel fled on a line to their left, swirling and swishing in supernatural velocity. The noise of the rifle bullets broke in their faces like the noise of so many lamp chimneys or sped overhead in swift, cruel spitting. And at the front, the battle sound, as if it were simply music, was beginning to swell and swell until the volleys rolled like a surf.

The officers shouted hoarsely, "Come on, men! Hurry up, boys! Come on now! Hurry up!" The soldiers, running heavily in their accouterments, dashed forward. A baggage guard was swiftly detailed; the men tore their rolls from their shoulders as if the things were afire. The battalion, stripped for action, again dashed forward.

"Come on, men! Come on!" To them the battle was as yet merely a road through the woods, crowded with troops who lowered their heads anxiously as the bullets fled high. But a moment later, the column wheeled abruptly to the left and entered a field of tall, green grass. The line scattered to a skirmish formation. In front was a series of knolls treed sparsely like orchards; and although no enemy was visible, these knolls were all popping and spitting with rifle fire. In some places there were to be seen long, gray lines of dirt, entrenchments. The American shells were kicking up reddish clouds of dust from the brow of one of the knolls, where stood a pagoda-like house. It was not much like a battle with men; it was a battle with a bit of charming scenery, enigmatically potent for death.

Nolan knew that Martin had suddenly fallen. "What—" he began.

"They've hit me," said Martin.

"Jesus!" said Nolan.

Martin lay on the ground, clutching his left forearm just

below the elbow with all the strength of his right hand. His lips were pursed ruefully. He did not seem to know what to do. He continued to stare at his arm.

Then suddenly the bullets drove at them low and hard. The men flung themselves face downward in the grass. Nolan lost all thought of his friend. Oddly enough, he felt somewhat like a man hiding under a bed, and he was just as sure that he could not raise his head high without being shot as a man hiding under a bed is sure that he cannot raise his head without bumping it.

A lieutenant was seated in the grass just behind him. He was in the careless and yet rigid pose of a man balancing a loaded plate on his knee at a picnic. He was talking in soothing, paternal tones.

"Now don't get rattled. We're all right here. Just as safe as being in church. . . . They're all going high. Don't mind them. . . . Don't mind them. . . . They're all going high. We've got them rattled and they can't shoot straight. Don't mind them."

The sun burned down steadily from a pale-blue sky upon the crackling woods and knolls and fields. From the roar of musketry, it might have been that the celestial heat was frying this part of the world.

Nolan snuggled close to the grass. He watched a gray line of entrenchments, above which floated the veriest gossamer of smoke. A flag lolled on a staff behind it. The men in the trench volleyed whenever an American shell exploded near them. It was some kind of infantile defiance. Frequently a bullet came from the woods directly behind Nolan and his comrades. They thought at the time that these bullets were from the rifle of some incompetent soldier of their own side.

There was no cheering. The men would have looked about them, wondering where was the army, if it were not that the crash of the fighting for the distance of a mile denoted plainly enough where was the army.

Officially the battalion had not yet fired a shot; there had been merely some irresponsible popping by men on the extreme left flank. But it was known that the lieutenant colonel

who had been in command was dead—shot through the heart—
and that the captains were thinned down to two. At the rear
went on a long tragedy, in which men, bent and hasty, hurried
to shelter with other men, helpless, dazed, and bloody. Nolan
knew of it all from the hoarse and affrighted voices which he
heard as he lay flattened in the grass. There came to him a
sense of exultation. Here, then, was one of those dread and
lurid situations which, in a nation's history, stand out in
crimson letters, becoming a tale of blood to stir generation
after generation. And he was in it, and unharmed. If he lived
through the battle, he would be a hero of the desperate fight
at—and here he wondered for a second what fate would be
pleased to bestow as a name for this battle.

But it is quite sure that hardly another man in the battalion
was engaged in any thoughts concerning the historic. On the
contrary, they deemed it ill that they were being badly cut
up on a most unimportant occasion. It would have benefited
the conduct of whoever were weak if they had known that
they were engaged in a battle that would be famous forever.

- *iv* -

Martin had picked himself up from where the bullet had
knocked him and addressed the lieutenant. "I'm hit, sir," he
said.

The lieutenant was very busy. "All right, all right," he said,
just heeding the man enough to learn where he was wounded.
"Go over that way. You ought to see a dressing station under
those trees."

Martin found himself dizzy and sick. The sensation in his
arm was distinctly galvanic. The feeling was so strange that
he could wonder at times if a wound was really what ailed
him. Once, in this dazed way, he examined his arm; he saw
the hole. Yes, he was shot; that was it. And more than in any
other way, it affected him with a profound sadness.

As directed by the lieutenant, he went to the clump of
trees, but he found no dressing station there. He found only

a dead soldier lying with his face buried in his arms and with his shoulders humped high as if he were convulsively sobbing. Martin decided to make his way to the road, deeming that he thus would better his chances of getting to a surgeon. But he suddenly found his way blocked by a fence of barbed wire. Such was his mental condition that he brought up at a rigid halt before this fence, and stared stupidly at it. It did not seem to him possible that this obstacle could be defeated by any means. The fence was there, and it stopped his progress. He could not go in that direction.

But as he turned, he espied that procession of wounded men, strange pilgrims, that had already worn a path in the tall grass. They were passing through a gap in the fence. Martin joined them. The bullets were flying over them in sheets, but many of them bore themselves as men who had now exacted from fate a singular immunity. Generally there were no outcries, no kicking, no talk at all. They, too, like Martin, seemed buried in a vague but profound melancholy.

But there was one who cried out loudly. A man shot in the head was being carried arduously by four comrades, and he continually yelled one word that was terrible in its primitive strength: "Bread! Bread! Bread!" Following him and his bearers were a limping crowd of men less cruelly wounded, who kept their eyes always fixed on him, as if they gained from his extreme agony some balm for their own sufferings.

"Bread! Give me bread!"

Martin plucked a man by the sleeve. The man had been shot in the foot, and was making his way with the help of a curved, incompetent stick. It is an axiom of war that wounded men can never find straight sticks.

"What's the matter with that feller?" asked Martin.

"Nutty," said the man.

"Why is he?"

"Shot in th' head," answered the other impatiently.

The wail of the sufferer arose in the field amid the swift rasp of bullets and the boom and shatter of shrapnel. "Bread! Bread! Oh, God, can't you give me bread? Bread!" The bearers of him were suffering exquisite agony, and often they exchanged glances which exhibited their despair of ever getting free of this tragedy. It seemed endless.

"Bread! Bread! Bread!"

But despite the fact that there was always in the way of this crowd a wistful melancholy, one must know that there were plenty of men who laughed, laughed at their wounds whimsically, quaintly inventing odd humors concerning bicycles and cabs, extracting from this shedding of their blood a wonderful amount of material for cheerful badinage, and with their faces twisted from pain as they stepped, they often joked like music-hall stars. And perhaps this was the most tearful part of all.

They trudged along a road until they reached a ford. Here under the eave of the bank lay a dismal company. In the mud and in the damp shade of some bushes were a half-hundred pale-faced men prostrate. Two or three surgeons were working there. Also, there was a chaplain, grim-mouthed, resolute, his surtout discarded. Overhead always was that incessant maddening wail of bullets.

Martin was standing gazing drowsily at the scene when a surgeon grabbed him. "Here, what's the matter with you?" Martin was daunted. He wondered what he had done that the surgeon should be so angry with him.

"In the arm," he muttered, half shamefacedly.

After the surgeon had hastily and irritably bandaged the injured member, he glared at Martin and said, "You can walk all right, can't you?"

"Yes, sir," said Martin.

"Well, now, you just make tracks down that road."

"Yes, sir." Martin went meekly off. The doctor had seemed exasperated almost to the point of madness.

The road was at this time swept with the fire of a body of Spanish sharpshooters who had come cunningly around the flanks of the American army, and were now hidden in the dense foliage that lined both sides of the road. They were shooting at everything. The road was as crowded as a street in a city, and at an absurdly short range they emptied their rifles at the passing people. They were aided always by the oversweep from the regular Spanish line of battle.

Martin was sleepy from his wound. He saw tragedy follow tragedy, but they created in him no feeling of horror.

A man with a red cross on his arm was leaning against a great tree. Suddenly he tumbled to the ground, and writhed for a moment in the way of a child oppressed with colic. A comrade immediately began to bustle importantly. "Here," he called to Martin, "help me carry this man, will you?"

Martin looked at him with dull scorn. "I'll be damned if I do," he said. "Can't carry myself, let alone somebody else."

This answer, which rings now so inhuman, pitiless, did not affect the other man. "Well, all right," he said. "Here comes some other fellers." The wounded man had now turned blue-gray; his eyes were closed; his body shook in a gentle, persistent chill.

Occasionally Martin came upon dead horses, their limbs sticking out and up like stakes. One beast, mortally shot, was besieged by three or four men who were trying to push it into the bushes, where it could live its brief time of anguish without thrashing to death any of the wounded men in the gloomy procession.

The mule train, with extra ammunition, charged toward the front, still led by the tinkling bell mare.

An ambulance was stuck momentarily in the mud, and above the crack of battle one could hear the familiar objurgations of the driver as he whirled his lash.

Two privates were having a hard time with a wounded captain, whom they were supporting to the rear. He was half cursing, half wailing out the information that he not only would not go another step toward the rear, but that he was certainly going to return at once to the front. They begged, pleaded at great length as they continually headed him off. They were not unlike two nurses with an exceptionally bad and headstrong little duke.

The wounded soldiers paused to look impassively upon this struggle. They were always like men who could not be aroused by anything further.

The visible hospital was mainly straggling thickets intersected with narrow paths, the ground being covered with men. Martin saw a busy person with a book and a pencil, but he did not approach him to become officially a member of the hospital. All he desired was rest and immunity from nagging. He took seat painfully under a bush and leaned his back upon the trunk. There he remained thinking, his face wooden.

- v -

"My gawd," said Nolan, squirming on his belly in the grass, "I can't stand this much longer."

Then suddenly every rifle in the firing line seemed to go off of its own accord. It was the result of an order, but few men heard the order; in the main they had fired because they heard others fire, and their sense was so quick that the volley did not sound too ragged. These marksmen had been lying for nearly an hour in stony silence, their sights adjusted, their fingers fondling their rifles, their eyes staring at the entrenchments of the enemy. The battalion had suffered heavy losses, and these losses had been hard to bear, for a soldier always reasons that men lost during a period of inaction are men badly lost.

The line now sounded like a great machine set to running frantically in the open air, the bright sunshine of a green field. To the *prut* of the magazine rifles was added the underchorus of the clicking mechanism, steady and swift, as if the hand of one operator was controlling it all. It reminds one always of a loom, a great, grand steel loom, clinking, clanking, plunking, plinking, to weave a woof of thin red threads, the cloth of death. By the men's shoulders under their eager hands dropped continually the yellow, empty shells, spinning into the crushed grass blades to remain there and mark for the belated eye the line of a battalion's fight.

All impatience, all rebellious feeling, had passed out of the men as soon as they had been allowed to use their weapons against the enemy. They now were absorbed in this business of hitting something, and all the long training at the rifle ranges, all the pride of the marksman which had been so long alive in them, made them forget for the time everything but shooting. They were as deliberate and exact as so many watchmakers.

A new sense of safety was rightfully upon them. They knew that those mysterious men in the high, far trenches in front were having the bullets spring in their faces with relentless and remarkable precision; they knew, in fact, that they were now doing the thing which they had been trained endlessly to do, and they knew they were doing it well. Nolan, for instance, was overjoyed. "Plug 'em," he said. "Plug 'em." He laid his face to his rifle as if it were his mistress. He was aiming under the shadow of a certain portico of a fortified house: there he could faintly see a long, black line which he knew to be a loophole cut for riflemen, and he knew that every shot of his was 'going there under the portico, mayhap through the loophole to the brain of another man like himself. He loaded the awkward magazine of his rifle again and again. He was so intent that he did not know of new orders until he saw the men about him scrambling to their feet and running forward, crouching low as they ran.

He heard a shout. "Come on, boys! We can't be last! We're going up! We're going up." He sprang to his feet, and stooping, ran with the others. Something fine, soft, gentle, touched his heart as he ran. He had loved the regiment, the army, because the regiment, the army, was his life—he had no other outlook; and now these men, his comrades, were performing his dream scenes for him; they were doing as he had ordained in his visions. It is curious that in this charge he considered himself as rather unworthy. Although he himself was in the assault with the rest of them, it seemed to him that his comrades were dazzlingly courageous. His part, to his mind, was merely that of a man who was going along with the crowd.

He saw Grierson biting madly with his pincers at a barbed-wire fence. They were halfway up the beautiful sylvan slope; there was no enemy to be seen, and yet the landscape rained bullets. Somebody punched him violently in the stomach. He thought dully to lie down and rest, but instead he fell with a crash.

The sparse line of men in blue shirts and dirty slouch hats swept on up the hill. He decided to shut his eyes for a moment because he felt very dreamy and peaceful. It seemed only a minute before he heard a voice say, "There he is." Grierson and Watkins had come to look for him. He searched their faces at once and keenly, for he had a thought that the line might be driven down the hill and leave him in Spanish hands. But he saw that everything was secure, and he prepared no questions.

"Nolan," said Grierson clumsily, "do you know me?"

The man on the ground smiled softly. "Of course I know you, you chowder-faced monkey. Why wouldn't I know you?"

Watkins knelt beside him. "Where did they plug you, old boy?"

Nolan was somewhat dubious. "It ain't much, I don't think, but it's somewheres there." He laid a finger on the pit of his stomach. They lifted his shirt, and then privately they exchanged a glance of horror.

"Does it hurt, Jimmie?" said Grierson hoarsely.

"No," said Nolan, "it don't hurt any, but I feel sort of dead to the world and numb all over. I don't think it's very bad."

"Oh, it's all right," said Watkins.

"What I need is a drink," said Nolan, grinning at them. "I'm chilly, lying on this damp ground."

"It ain't very damp, Jimmie," said Grierson.

"Well, it is damp," said Nolan, with sudden irritability. "I can feel it. I'm wet, I tell you—wet through—just from lying here."

They answered hastily. "Yes, that's so, Jimmie. It *is* damp. That's so."

"Just put your hand under my back and see how wet the ground is," he said.

"No," they answered. "That's all right, Jimmie. We know it's wet."

"Well, put your hand under and see," he cried stubbornly.

"Oh, never mind, Jimmie."

"No," he said, in a temper. "See for yourself." Grierson seemed to be afraid of Nolan's agitation, and so he slipped a hand under the prostrate man, and presently withdrew it covered with blood. "Yes," he said, hiding his hand carefully from Nolan's eyes, "you were right, Jimmie."

"Of course I was," said Nolan, contentedly closing his eyes. "This hillside holds water like a swamp." After a moment, he said, "Guess I ought to know. I'm flat here on it, and you fellers are standing up."

He did not know he was dying. He thought he was holding an argument on the condition of the turf.

- vi -

"Cover his face," said Grierson in a low and husky voice afterwards.

"What'll I cover it with?" said Watkins.

They looked at themselves. They stood in their shirts, trousers, leggings, shoes; they had nothing.

"Oh," said Grierson, "here's his hat." He brought it and laid it on the face of the dead man. They stood for a time. It was apparent that they thought it essential and decent to say or do something. Finally Watkins said in a broken voice, "Aw, it's a damn shame." They moved slowly off toward the firing line.

In the blue gloom of evening, in one of the fever tents, the two rows of still figures became hideous, charnel. The languid movement of a hand was surrounded with spectral mystery, and the occasional painful twisting of a body under a blanket was terrifying, as if dead men were moving in their graves under the sod. A heavy odor of sickness and medicine hung in the air.

"What regiment are you in?" said a feeble voice.

"Twenty-ninth Infantry," answered another voice.

"Twenty-ninth! Why, the man on the other side of me is in the Twenty-ninth."

"He is? Hey, there, partner, are you in the Twenty-ninth?"

A third voice merely answered wearily, "Martin, of C Company."

"What? Jack, is that you?"

"It's part of me. Who are you?"

"Grierson, you fathead. I thought you were wounded."

There was the noise of a man gulping a great drink of water, and at its conclusion Martin said, "I am."

"Well, what you doin' in the fever place, then?"

Martin replied with drowsy impatience. "Got the fever, too."

"Gee!" said Grierson.

Thereafter there was silence in the fever tent, save for the noise made by a man over in a corner—a kind of man always found in an American crowd—a heroic, implacable comedian and patriot, of a humor that has bitterness and ferocity and love in it, and he was wringing from the situation a grim meaning by singing "The Star-Spangled Banner" with all the ardor which could be procured from his fever-stricken body.

"Billie," called Martin in a low voice, "where's Jimmy Nolan?"

"He's dead," said Grierson.

A triangle of raw, gold light shone on a side of the tent. Somewhere in the valley an engine's bell was ringing, and it sounded of peace and home as if it hung on a cow's neck.

"And where's Ike Watkins?"

"Well, he ain't dead, but he got shot through the lungs. They say he ain't got much show."

Through the clouded odors of sickness and medicine rang the dauntless voice of the man in the corner.

# Virtue in War

## - i -

GATES had left the regular army in 1890, those parts of him which had not been frozen having been well fried. He took with him nothing but an oaken constitution and a knowledge of the plains and the best wishes of his fellow officers. The Standard Oil Company differs from the United States Government in that it understands the value of the loyal and intelligent services of good men and is almost certain to reward them at the expense of incapable men. This curious practice emanates from no beneficent emotion of the Standard Oil Company, on whose feelings you could not make a scar with a hammer and chisel. It is simply that the Standard Oil Company knows more than the United States Government and makes use of virtue whenever virtue is to its advantage. In 1890, Gates really felt in his bones that if he lived a rigorously correct life and several score of his classmates and intimate friends died off, he would get command of a troop of horse by the time he was unfitted by age to be an active cavalry leader. He left the service of the United States and entered the service of the Standard Oil Company. In the course of time he knew that if he lived a rigorously correct life, his position and income would develop strictly in parallel with the worth of his wisdom and experience, and he would not have to walk on the corpses of his friends.

But he was not happier. Part of his heart was in a barracks, and it was not enough to discourse of the old regiment over the port and cigars to ears which were polite enough to betray a languid ignorance. Finally came the year 1898, and Gates dropped the Standard Oil Company as if it were hot. He hit the steel trail to Washington and there fought the first serious action of the war. Like most Americans, he had a native state, and one morning he found himself major in a volunteer infantry regiment whose voice had a peculiar, sharp twang to it which he could remember from childhood. The colonel welcomed the West Pointer with loud cries of joy; the lieutenant colonel looked at him with the pebbly eye of distrust; and the senior major, having had up to this time the best battalion in the regiment, strongly disapproved of him. There were only two majors, so the lieutenant colonel commanded the first battalion, which gave him an occupation. Lieutenant colonels under the new rules do not always have occupations. Gates got the third battalion—four companies commanded by intelligent officers who could gauge the opinions of their men at two thousand yards and govern themselves accordingly. The battalion was immensely interested in the new major. It thought it ought to develop views about him. It thought it was its blankety-blank business to find out immediately if it liked him personally. In the company streets the talk was nothing else. Among the noncommissioned officers there were eleven old soldiers of the regular army, and they knew—and cared—that Gates had held commission in the "Sixteenth Cavalry"—as *Harper's Weekly* says. Over this fact they rejoiced and were glad, and they stood by to jump lively when he took command. He would know his work and he would know *their* work, and then in battle there would be killed only what men were absolutely necessary and the sick list would be comparatively free of fools.

The commander of the second battalion had been called by an Atlanta paper: "Major Rickets C. Carmony, the commander of the second battalion of the 307th ——, is when at home one of the biggest wholesale hardware dealers in his state. Last evening he had ice cream, at his own expense, served out at the regular mess of the battalion, and after dinner the men gathered about his tent where three hearty cheers for the popular major were given." Carmony had bought twelve copies of this newspaper and mailed them home to his friends.

In Gates's battalion there were more kicks than ice cream,

and there was no ice cream at all. Indignation ran high at the
rapid manner in which he proceeded to make soldiers of
them. Some of his officers hinted finally that the men wouldn't
stand it. They were saying that they had enlisted to fight for
their country—yes, but they weren't going to be bullied day
in and day out by a perfect stranger. They were patriots, they
were, and just as good men as ever stepped—just as good as
Gates or anybody like him. But gradually, despite itself, the
battalion progressed. The men were not altogether conscious
of it. They evolved rather blindly. Presently there were fights
with Carmony's crowd as to which was the better battalion at
drills, and at last there was no argument. It was generally
admitted that Gates commanded the crack battalion. The men,
believing that the beginning and the end of all soldiering was
in these drills of precision, were somewhat reconciled to their
major when they began to understand more of what he was
trying to do for them, but they were still fiery, untamed
patriots of lofty pride and they resented his manner toward
them. It was abrupt and sharp.

The time came when everybody knew that the Fifth Army
Corps was the corps designated for the first active service in
Cuba. The officers and men of the 307th observed with despair
that their regiment was not in the Fifth Army Corps. The
colonel was a strategist. He understood everything in a flash.
Without a moment's hesitation, he obtained leave and mounted
the night express for Washington. There he drove senators
and congressmen in span, tandem, and four-in-hand. With
the telegraph he stirred so deeply the governor, the people,
and the newspapers of his state that whenever on a quiet
night the President put his head out of the White House he
could hear the distant vast commonwealth humming with
indignation. And as it is well known that the Chief Executive
listens to the voice of the people, the 307th was transferred
to the Fifth Army Corps. It was sent at once to Tampa, where
it was brigaded with two dusty regiments of regulars, who
looked at it calmly and said nothing. The brigade commander
happened to be no less a person than Gates's old colonel in
the "Sixteenth Cavalry"—as *Harper's Weekly* says—and Gates

was cheered. The old man's rather solemn look brightened when he saw Gates in the 307th. There was a great deal of battering and pounding and banging for the 307th at Tampa, but the men stood it more in wonder than in anger. The two regular regiments carried them along when they could, and when they couldn't waited impatiently for them to come up. Undoubtedly the regulars wished the volunteers were in garrison at Sitka, but they said practically nothing. They minded their own regiments. The colonel was an invaluable man in a telegraph office. When came the scramble for transports, the colonel retired to a telegraph office and talked so ably to Washington that the authorities pushed a number of corps aside and made way for the 307th, as if on it depended everything. The regiment got one of the best transports, and after a series of delays and some starts, and an equal number of returns, they finally sailed for Cuba.

- *ii* -

Now Gates had a singular adventure on the second morning after his arrival at Atlanta to take his post as a major in the 307th.

He was in his tent, writing, when suddenly the flap was flung away and a tall young private stepped inside.

"Well, Maje," said the newcomer genially, "how goes it?"

The major's head flashed up, but he spoke without heat.

"Come to attention and salute."

"Huh!" said the private.

"Come to attention and salute."

The private looked at him in resentful amazement, and then inquired:

"Ye ain't mad, are ye? Ain't nothin' to get huffy about, is there?"

"I— Come to attention and salute."

"Well," drawled the private, as he stared, "seein' as ye are so darn perticular, I don't care if I do—if it'll make yer meals set on yer stomick any better."

Drawing a long breath and grinning ironically, he lazily pulled his heels together and saluted with a flourish.

"There," he said, with a return to his earlier genial manner. "How's that suit ye, Maje?"

There was a silence which to an impartial observer would have seemed pregnant with dynamite and bloody death. Then the major cleared his throat and coldly said:

"And now, what is your business?"

"Who—me?" asked the private. "Oh, I just sorter dropped in." With a deeper meaning, he added, "Sorter dropped in in a friendly way, thinkin' ye was mebbe a different kind of a feller from what ye be."

The inference was clearly marked.

It was now Gates's turn to stare, and stare he unfeignedly did.

"Go back to your quarters," he said at length.

The volunteer became very angry.

"Oh, ye needn't be so up-in-th'-air, need ye? Don't know's I'm dead anxious to inflict my company on yer since I've had a good look at ye. There may be men in this here battalion what's had just as much edjewcation as you have, and I'm damned if they ain't got better *manners*. Good mornin'," he said with dignity; and passing out of the tent, he flung the flap back in place with an air of slamming it as if it had been a door. He made his way back to his company street, striding high. He was furious. He met a large crowd of his comrades.

"What's the matter, Lige?" asked one, who noted his temper.

"Oh, nothin'," answered Lige with terrible feeling. "Nothin'. I jest been lookin' over the new major—that's all."

"What's he like?" asked another.

"Like?" cried Lige. "He's like nothin'. He ain't out'n the same kittle as us. No. Gawd made him all by himself—sep'rate. He's a speshul produc', he is, an' he won't have no truck with jest common—*men*, like you be."

He made a venomous gesture which included them all.

"Did he set on ye?" asked the soldier.

"Set on me? No," replied Lige with contempt. "I set on

*him.* I sized 'im up in a minute. 'Oh, I don't know,' I says, as I was comin' out, 'guess you ain't the only man in the world,' I says."

For a time Lige Wigram was quite a hero. He endlessly repeated the tale of his adventure, and men admired him for so soon taking the conceit out of the new officer. Lige was proud to think of himself as a plain and simple patriot who had refused to endure any high-soaring nonsense.

But he came to believe that he had not disturbed the singular composure of the major, and this concreted his hatred. He hated Gates, not as a soldier sometimes hates an officer, a hatred half of fear. Lige hated as man to man. And he was enraged to see that so far from gaining any hatred in return, he seemed incapable of making Gates have any thought of him save as a unit in a body of three hundred men. Lige might just as well have gone and grimaced at the obelisk in Central Park.

When the battalion became the best in the regiment, he had no part in the pride of the companies. He was sorry when men began to speak well of Gates. He was really a very consistent hater.

- *iii* -

The transport occupied by the 307th was commanded by some sort of a Scandinavian, who was afraid of the shadows of his own topmasts. He would have run his steamer away from a floating Gainsborough hat, and in fact, he ran her away from less on some occasions. The officers, wishing to arrive with the other transports, sometimes remonstrated, and to them he talked of his owners. Every officer in the convoying warships loathed him, for in case any hostile vessel should appear, they did not see how they were going to protect this rabbit, who would probably manage during a fight to be in about a hundred places on the broad, broad sea, and all of them offensive to the Navy's plan. When he was not talking of his owners, he was remarking to the officers of the regiment that a steamer really was not like a valise, and that he was unable to take his ship under his arm and climb trees with it. He further said that "them Naval fellows" were not near so smart as they thought they were.

From an indigo sea arose the lonely shore of Cuba. Ultimately, the fleet was near Santiago, and most of the transports were bidden to wait a minute while the leaders found out their minds. The skipper, to whom the 307th were prisoners, waited for thirty hours halfway between Jamaica and Cuba. He explained that the Spanish fleet might emerge from Santiago Harbor at any time, and he did not propose to be caught. His owners— Whereupon the colonel arose as one having nine hundred men at his back, and he passed up to the bridge and he spake with the captain. He explained indirectly that each individual of his nine hundred men had decided to be the first American soldier to land for this campaign, and that in order to accomplish the marvel, it was necessary for the transport to be nearer than forty-five miles from the Cuban coast. If the skipper would only land the regiment, the colonel would consent to his then taking his interesting old ship and going to h—— with it. And the skipper spake with the colonel. He pointed out that as far as he officially was concerned, the United States Government did not exist. He was responsible solely to his owners. The colonel pondered these sayings. He perceived that the skipper meant that he was running his ship as he deemed best, in consideration of the capital invested by his owners, and that he was not at all concerned with the feelings of a certain American military expedition to Cuba. He was a free son of the sea—he was a sovereign citizen of the republic of the waves. He was like Lige.

However, the skipper ultimately incurred the danger of taking his ship under the terrible guns of the *New York, Iowa, Oregon, Massachusetts, Indiana, Brooklyn, Texas,* and a score of cruisers and gunboats. It was a brave act for the captain of a United States transport, and he was visibly nervous until he could again get to sea, where he offered praises that the accursed 307th was no longer sitting on his head. For almost a week he rambled at his cheerful will over the adjacent high seas, having in his hold a great quantity of military stores as successfully secreted as if they had been buried in a copper box in the cornerstone of a new public building in Boston. He had had his master's certificate for twenty-one years, and those people couldn't tell a marlin spike from the starboard side of the ship.

The 307th was landed in Cuba, but to their disgust they found that about ten thousand regulars were ahead of them. They got immediate orders to move out from the base on the road to Santiago. Gates was interested to note that the only delay was caused by the fact that many men of the other battalions strayed off sight-seeing. In time, the long regiment wound slowly among hills that shut them from sight of the sea.

For the men to admire there were palm trees, little brown huts, passive, uninterested Cuban soldiers much worn from carrying American rations inside and outside. The weather was not oppressively warm, and the journey was said to be only about seven miles. There were no rumors save that there had been one short fight and the army had advanced to within sight of Santiago. Having a peculiar faculty for the derision of the romantic, the 307th began to laugh. Actually there was not *anything* in the world which turned out to be as books describe it. Here they had landed from the transport expecting to be at once flung into line of battle and sent on some kind of furious charge, and now they were trudging along a quiet trail lined with somnolent trees and grass. The whole business so far struck them as being a highly tedious burlesque.

After a time, they came to where the camps of regular regiments marked the sides of the road—little villages of tents no higher than a man's waist. The colonel found his brigade commander and the 307th was sent off into a field of long grass, where the men grew suddenly solemn with the importance of getting their supper.

In the early evening, some regulars told one of Gates's companies that at daybreak this division would move to an attack upon something.

"How d'you know?" said the company, deeply awed.

"Heard it."

"Well, what are we to attack?"

"Dunno."

The 307th was not at all afraid, but each man began to imagine the morrow. The regulars seemed to have as much interest in the morrow as they did in the last Christmas. It was none of their affair, apparently.

"Look here," said Lige Wigram to a man in the 17th Regular Infantry, "whereabouts are we goin' termorrow an' who do we run up against—do ye know?"

The 17th soldier replied truculently, "If I ketch 'th' —— —— —— what stole my terbaccer, I'll whirl in an' break every —— —— bone in his body."

Gates's friends in the regular regiments asked him numerous questions as to the reliability of his organization. Would the 307th stand the racket? They were certainly not contemptuous; they simply did not seem to consider it important whether the 307th would or whether it would not.

"Well," said Gates, "they won't run the length of a tent peg if they can gain any idea of what they're fighting; they won't bunch if they've about six acres of open ground to move in; they won't get rattled at all if they see you fellows taking it easy, and they'll fight like the devil as long as they thoroughly, completely, absolutely, satisfactorily, exhaustively understand what the business is. They're lawyers. All excepting my battalion."

- *iv* -

Lige awakened into a world obscured by blue fog. Somebody was gently shaking him. "Git up; we're going to move." The regiment was buckling up itself. From the trail came the loud creak of a light battery moving ahead. The tones of all men were low; the faces of the officers were composed, serious. The regiment found itself moving along behind the battery before it had time to ask itself more than a hundred questions.

The trail wound through a dense, tall jungle, dark, heavy with dew.

The battle broke with a snap—far ahead. Presently Lige heard from the air above him a faint, low note as if somebody were blowing softly in the mouth of a bottle. It was a stray bullet which had wandered a mile to tell him that war was before him. He nearly broke his neck looking upward. "Did ye hear that?" But the men were fretting to get out of this gloomy jungle. They wanted to see something. The faint rup-rup-rrrrup-rup on in the front told them that the fight had begun; death was abroad, and so the mystery of this wilderness excited them. This wilderness was portentously still and dark.

They passed the battery aligned on a hill above the trail, and they had not gone far when the gruff guns began to roar and they could hear the rocket-like swish of the flying shells. Presently everybody must have called out for the assistance of the 307th. Aides and couriers came flying back to them.

"Is this the 307th? Hurry up your men, please, Colonel. You're needed more every minute."

Oh, they were, were they? Then the regulars were not going to do *all* the fighting? The old 307th was bitterly proud or proudly bitter. They left their blanket rolls under the guard of God and pushed on, which is one of the reasons why the Cubans of that part of the country were, later, so well equipped. There began to appear fields, hot, golden-green in the sun. On some palm-dotted knolls before them they could see little lines of black dots—the American advance. A few men fell, struck down by other men who, perhaps half a mile away, were aiming at somebody else. The loss was wholly in Carmony's battalion, which immediately bunched and backed away, coming with a shock against Gates's advance company. This shock sent a tremor through all of Gates's battalion until men in the very last files cried out nervously, "Well, what in hell is up now?" There came an order to deploy and advance. An occasional hoarse yell from the regulars could be heard. The deploying made Gates's heart bleed for the colonel. The old man stood there directing the movement, straight, fearless, somberly defiant of—everything. Carmony's four companies were like four herds. And all the time the bullets from no living man knows where kept pecking at them and pecking at them. Gates, the excellent Gates, the highly educated and strictly military Gates, grew rankly insubordinate. He knew that the regiment was suffering from nothing but the deadly range and oversweep of the modern rifle, of which many proud and confident nations know noththing save that they have killed savages with it, which is the least of all informations.

Gates rushed upon Carmony.

"—— —— it, man, if you can't get your people to deploy, for —— sake give me a chance! I'm stuck in the woods!"

Carmony gave nothing, but Gates took all he could get and his battalion deployed and advanced like men. The old colonel almost burst into tears, and he cast one quick glance of gratitude at Gates, which the younger officer wore on his heart like a secret decoration.

There was a wild scramble up hill, down dale, through thorny thickets. Death smote them with a kind of slow rhythm, leisurely taking a man now here, now there, but the cat-spit sound of the bullets was always. A large number of the men of Carmony's battalion came on with Gates. They were willing to do anything, anything. They had no real fault, unless it was that early conclusion that any brave, high-minded youth was necessarily a good soldier immediately, from the beginning. In them had been born a swift feeling that the unpopular Gates knew everything, and they followed the trained soldier.

If they followed him, he certainly took them into it. As they swung heavily up one steep hill, like so many windblown horses, they came suddenly out into the real advance. Little blue groups of men were making frantic rushes forward and then flopping down on their bellies to fire volleys while other groups made rushes. Ahead they could see a heavy, houselike fort, which was inadequate to explain from whence came the myriad bullets. The remainder of the scene was landscape. Pale men, yellow men, blue men came out of this landscape quiet and sad-eyed with wounds. Often they were grimly facetious. There is nothing in the American regular so amazing as his conduct when he is wounded—his apologetic limp, his deprecatory arm sling, his embarrassed and ashamed shot hole through the lungs. The men of the 307th looked at calm creatures who had divers punctures and they were made better. These men told them that it was only necessary to keep a-going. They of the 307th lay on their bellies, red, sweating, and panting, and heeded the voice of the elder brother.

Gates walked back of his line, very white of face, but hard and stern past anything his men knew of him. After they had violently adjured him to lie down and he had given weak backs a cold, stiff touch, the 307th charged by rushes. The hatless colonel made frenzied speech, but the man of the time was Gates. The men seemed to feel that this was his business. Some of the regular officers said afterward that the advance of the 307th was very respectable indeed. They were rather surprised, they said. At least five of the crack regiments of the regular army were in this division, and the 307th could win no more than a feeling of kindly appreciation.

Yes, it was very good, very good indeed, but did you notice what was being done at the same moment by the 12th, the 17th, the 7th, the 8th, the 25th, the—

Gates felt that his charge was being a success. He was carrying out a successful function. Two captains fell bang on the grass and a lieutenant slumped quietly down with a death wound. Many men sprawled suddenly. Gates was keeping his men almost even with the regulars, who were charging on his flanks. Suddenly he thought that he must have come close to the fort and that a Spaniard had tumbled a great stone block down upon his leg. Twelve hands reached out to help him, but he cried:

"No, d—— your souls—go on—go on!"

He closed his eyes for a moment, and it really was only for a moment. When he opened them, he found himself alone with Lige Wigram, who lay on the ground near him.

"Maje," said Lige, "yer a good man. I've been a-follerin' ye all day an' I want to say yer a good man."

The major turned a coldly scornful eye upon the private.

"Where are you wounded? Can you walk? Well, if you can, go to the rear and leave me alone. I'm bleeding to death, and you bother me."

Lige, despite the pain in his wounded shoulder, grew indignant.

"Well," he mumbled, "you and me have been on th' outs fer a long time, an' I only wanted to tell ye that what I seen of ye t'day has made me feel mighty different."

"Go to the rear—if you can walk," said the major.

"Now, Maje, look here. A little thing like that—"

"Go to the rear."

Lige gulped with sobs.

"Maje, I know I didn't understand ye at first, but ruther'n let a little thing like that come between us, I'd—I'd—"

"Go to the rear."

In this reiteration Lige discovered a resemblance to that first old offensive phrase. "Come to attention and salute." He pondered over the resemblance and he saw that nothing had changed. The man bleeding to death was the same man to whom he had once paid a friendly visit with unfriendly results. He thought now that he perceived a certain hopeless gulf, a gulf which is real or unreal, according to circumstances. Sometimes all men are equal; occasionally they are not. If Gates had ever criticized Lige's manipulation of a hay fork on the farm at home, Lige would have furiously disdained his hate or blame. He saw now that he must not openly approve the major's conduct in war. The major's pride was in his business, and his, Lige's congratulations, were beyond all enduring.

The place where they were lying suddenly fell under a new, heavy rain of bullets. They sputtered about the men, making the noise of large grasshoppers.

"Major!" cried Lige. "Major Gates! It won't do for ye to be left here, sir. Ye'll be killed."

"But you can't help it, lad. You take care of yourself."

"I'm damned if I do," said the private vehemently. "If I can't git *you* out, I'll stay and wait."

The officer gazed at his man with that same icy, contemptuous gaze.

"I'm—I'm a dead man anyhow. You go to the rear, do you hear?"

"No."

The dying major drew his revolver, cocked it, and aimed it unsteadily at Lige's head.

"Will you obey orders?"

"No."

"One?"

"No."

"Two?"

"No."

Gates weakly dropped his revolver.

"Go to the devil, then. You're no soldier, but"—he tried to add something—"but—" He heaved a long moan. "But—you—you—oh, I'm so-o-o tired."

- *v* -

After the battle, three correspondents happened to meet on the trail. They were hot, dusty, weary, hungry, and thirsty, and they repaired to the shade of a mango tree and sprawled luxuriously. Among them they mustered twoscore friends who on that day had gone to the far shore of the hereafter, but their senses were no longer resonant. Shackles was babbling plaintively about mint juleps, and the others were bidding him to have done.

"By the way," said one at last, "it's too bad about poor old Gates of the 307th. He bled to death. His men were crazy. They were blubbering and cursing around there like wild people. It seems that when they got back there to look for him, they found him just about gone, and another wounded man was trying to stop the flow with his hat! His hat, mind you. Poor old Gatesie!"

"Oh, no, Shackles!" said the third man of the party. "Oh,

no, you're wrong. The best mint juleps in the world are made right in New York, Philadelphia, or Boston. That Kentucky idea is only a tradition."

A wounded man approached them. He had been shot through the shoulder and his shirt had been diagonally cut away, leaving much bare skin. Over the bullet's point of entry there was a kind of a white spider, shaped from pieces of adhesive plaster. Over the point of departure there was a bloody bulb of cotton strapped to the flesh by other pieces of adhesive plaster. His eyes were dreamy, wistful, sad. "Say, gents, have any of ye got a bottle?" he asked.

A correspondent raised himself suddenly and looked with bright eyes at the soldier.

"Well, you have got a nerve," he said, grinning. "Have we got a bottle, eh! Who in h—— do you think we are? If we had a bottle of good licker, do you suppose we could let the whole army drink out of it? You have too much faith in the generosity of men, my friend!"

The soldier stared, oxlike, and finally said, "Huh?"

"I say," continued the correspondent, somewhat more loudly, "that if we had had a bottle we would have probably finished it ourselves by this time."

"But," said the other, dazed, "I *meant* an empty bottle. I didn't mean no *full* bottle."

The correspondent was humorously irascible.

"An empty bottle! You must be crazy! Who ever heard of a man looking for an empty bottle? It isn't sense! I've seen a million men looking for full bottles, but you're the first man I ever saw who insisted on the bottle's being empty. What in the world do you want it for?"

"Well, ye see, mister," explained Lige slowly, "our major he was killed this mornin' an' we're jes' goin' to bury him, an' I thought I'd jest take a look 'round an' see if I couldn't borry an empty bottle, an' then I'd take an' write his name an' reg'ment on a paper an' put it in th' bottle an' bury it with him, so's when they come fer to dig him up sometime an' take him home, there sure wouldn't be no mistake."

"Oh!"

# The Second Generation

CASPAR CADOGAN resolved to go to the tropic wars and do something. The air was blue and gold with the pomp of soldiering, and in every ear rang the music of military glory. Caspar's father was a United States Senator from the great state of Skowmulligan, where the war fever ran very high. Chill is the blood of many of the sons of millionaires, but Caspar took the fever and posted to Washington. His father had never denied him anything, and this time all that Caspar wanted was a little captaincy in the Army—just a simple little captaincy.

The old man had been entertaining a delegation of respectable bunco-steerers from Skowmulligan who had come to him on a matter which is none of the public's business.

Bottles of whisky and boxes of cigars were still on the table in the sumptuous private parlor. The Senator had said, "Well, gentlemen, I'll do what I can for you." By this sentence he meant whatever he meant.

Then he turned to his eager son. "Well, Caspar?" The youth poured out his modest desires. It was not altogether his fault. Life had taught him a generous faith in his own abilities. If anyone had told him that he was simply an ordinary d——d fool, he would have opened his eyes wide at the person's lack of judgment. All his life people had admired him.

The Skowmulligan war horse looked with quick disapproval into the eyes of his son. "Well, Caspar," he said slowly, "I am of the opinion that they've got all the golf experts and tennis champions and cotillion leaders and piano tuners and billiard markers that they really need as officers. Now, if you were a soldier—"

"I know," said the young man with a gesture, "but I'm not exactly a fool, I hope, and I think if I get a chance I can do something. I'd like to try. I would, indeed."

The Senator lit a cigar. He assumed an attitude of ponderous reflection. "Y—yes, but this country is full of young men who are fools. Full of 'em."

Caspar fidgeted in the desire to answer that while he admitted the profusion of young men who were not fools, he felt that he himself possessed interesting and peculiar qualifications which would allow him to make his mark in any field of effort which he seriously challenged. But he did not make this graceful statement, for he sometimes detected something ironic in his father's temperament. The Skowmulligan war horse had not thought of expressing an opinion of his own ability since the year 1865, when he was young, like Caspar.

"Well, well," said the Senator finally. "I'll see about it. I'll see about it." The young man was obliged to await the end of his father's characteristic method of thought. The war horse never gave a quick answer, and if people tried to hurry him, they seemed able to arouse only a feeling of irritation against making a decision at all. His mind moved like the wind, but practice had placed a Mexican bit in the mouth of his judgment. This old man of light, quick thought had taught himself to move like an ox cart. Caspar said, "Yes, sir." He withdrew to his club, where, to the affectionate inquiries of some envious friends, he replied, "The old man is letting the idea soak."

The mind of the war horse was decided far sooner than Caspar expected. In Washington, a large number of well-bred, handsome young men were receiving appointments as lieutenants, as captains, and occasionally as majors. They were a strong, healthy, clean-eyed, educated collection. They were a prime lot. A German field marshal would have beamed with joy if he could have had them—to send to school. Anywhere in the world they would have made a grand show as material, but intrinsically they were not lieutenants, captains, and majors. They were fine men, though manhood is only an essential part of a lieutenant, a captain, or a major. But at any rate, this arrangement had all the logic of going to sea in a bathing machine.

The Senator found himself reasoning that Caspar was as good as any of them, and better than many. Presently he was bleating here and there that his boy should have a chance. "The boy's all right, I tell you, Henry. He's wild to go, and I don't see why they shouldn't give him a show. He's got plenty of nerve, and he's keen as a whiplash. I'm going to get him an appointment, and if you can do anything to help it along, I wish you would."

Then he betook himself to the White House and the War Department and made a stir. People think that Administrations are always slavishly, abominably anxious to please the Machine. They are not; they wish the Machine sunk in red fire, for by the power of ten thousand past words, looks, gestures, writings, the Machine comes along and takes the Administration by the nose and twists it, and the Administration dare not even yell. The huge force which carries an election to success looks reproachfully at the Administration and says, "Give me a bun." That is a very small thing with which to reward a Colossus.

The Skowmulligan war horse got his bun and took it to his hotel, where Caspar was moodily reading war rumors. "Well, my boy, here you are." Caspar was a captain and commissary on the staff of Brigadier General Reilly, commander of the Second Brigade of the First Division of the Thirtieth Army Corps.

"I had to work for it," said the Senator grimly. "They talked to me as if they thought you were some sort of empty-headed idiot. None of 'em seemed to know you personally. They just sort of took it for granted. Finally I got pretty hot in the collar." He paused a moment; his heavy, grooved face set hard; his blue eyes shone. He clapped a hand down upon the handle of his chair.

"Caspar, I've got you into this thing, and I believe you'll do all right, and I'm not saying this because I distrust either your sense or your grit. But I want you to understand you've *got to make a go of it*. I'm not going to talk any twaddle about your country and your country's flag. You understand all about that. But now you're a soldier, and there'll be this to do and that to do, and fighting to do, and you've got to do *every d——d one of 'em* right up to the handle. I don't know how much of a shindy this thing is going to be, but any shindy is enough to show how much there is in a man. You've got your appointment, and that's all I can do for you; but I'll thrash you with my own hands if when the Army gets back, the other fellows say my son is 'nothing but a good-looking dude.'"

He ceased, breathing heavily. Caspar looked bravely and frankly at his father, and answered in a voice which was not very tremulous. "I'll do my best. This is my chance. I'll do my best with it."

The Senator had a marvelous ability of transition from one manner to another. Suddenly he seemed very kind. "Well, that's all right, then. I guess you'll get along all right with Reilly. I know him well, and he'll see you through. I helped him along once. And now about this commissary business. As I understand it, a commissary is a sort of caterer in a big way—that is, he looks out for a good many more things than a caterer has to bother his head about. Reilly's brigade has probably from two to three thousand men in it, and in regard to certain things you've got to look out for every man of 'em every day. I know perfectly well you couldn't successfully run a boardinghouse in Ocean Grove. How are you going to manage for all these soldiers, hey? Thought about it?"

"No," said Caspar, injured. "I didn't want to be a commissary. I wanted to be a captain in the line."

"They wouldn't hear of it. They said you would have to take a staff appointment where people could look after you."

"Well, let them look after me," cried Caspar resentfully, "but when there's any fighting to be done, I guess I won't necessarily be the last man."

"That's it," responded the Senator. "That's the spirit." They both thought that the problem of war would eliminate to an equation of actual battle.

Ultimately Caspar departed into the South to an encampment in salty grass under pine trees. Here lay an Army corps twenty thousand strong. Caspar passed into the dusty sunshine of it, and for many weeks he was lost to view.

- ii -

"Of course, I don't know a blamed thing about it," said Caspar frankly and modestly to a circle of his fellow staff officers. He was referring to the duties of his office.

Their faces became expressionless; they looked at him with eyes in which he could fathom nothing. After a pause, one politely said, "Don't you?" It was the inevitable two words of convention.

"Why," cried Caspar, "I didn't know what a commissary officer was until I *was* one. My old guv'nor told me. He'd looked it up in a book somewhere, I suppose; but *I* didn't know."

"Didn't you?"

The young man's face glowed with sudden humor. "Do you know, the word was intimately associated in my mind with camels. Funny, eh? I think it came from reading that rhyme of Kipling's about the commissariat camel."

"Did it?"

"Yes. Funny, isn't it? Camels!"

The brigade was ultimately landed at Siboney as part of an army to attack Santiago. The scene at the landing sometimes resembled the inspiriting daily drama at the approach to the Brooklyn Bridge. There was a great bustle, during which the wise man kept his property gripped in his hands lest it might march off into the wilderness in the pocket of one of the striding regiments. Truthfully, Caspar should have had frantic occupation, but men saw him wandering bootlessly here and there crying, "Has anyone seen my saddlebags? Why, if I lose them, I'm ruined. I've got everything packed away in 'em. Everything!"

They looked at him gloomily and without attention. "No," they said. It was to intimate that they would not give a rip if he had lost his nose, his teeth, and his self-respect. Reilly's brigade collected itself from the boats and went off, each regiment's soul burning with anger because some other regiment was in advance of it. Moving along through the scrub and under the palms, men talked mostly of things that did not pertain to the business in hand.

General Reilly finally planted his headquarters in some tall grass under a mango tree. "Where's Cadogan?" he said suddenly as he took off his hat and smoothed the wet, gray hair from his brow. Nobody knew. "I saw him looking for his saddlebags down at the landing," said an officer dubiously. "Bother him," said the general contemptuously. "Let him stay there."

Three venerable regimental commanders came, saluted stiffly and sat in the grass. There was a powwow, during which Reilly explained much that the division commander had told him. The venerable colonels nodded; they understood. Everything was smooth and clear to their minds. But still, the colonel of the Forty-fourth Regular Infantry murmured about the commissariat. His men—and then he launched forth in a sentiment concerning the privations of his men in which you were confronted with his feeling that his men—his men were the only creatures of importance in the universe, which feeling was entirely correct for him. Reilly grunted. He did what most commanders did. He set the competent line to doing the work of the incompetent part of the staff.

In time Caspar came trudging along the road merrily swinging his saddlebags. "Well, General," he cried as he saluted, "I found 'em."

"Did you?" said Reilly. Later an officer rushed to him tragically: "General, Cadogan is off there in the bushes eatin' potted ham and crackers all by himself." The officer was sent back into the bushes for Caspar, and the general sent Caspar with an order. Then Reilly and the three venerable colonels, grinning, partook of potted ham and crackers. "Tashe a' right," said Reilly with his mouth full. "Dorsey, see if 'e got some'n else."

"Mush be selfish young pig," said one of the colonels, with his mouth full. "Who's he, General?"

"Son—Sen'tor Cad'gan—ol' frien' mine—dash 'im."

Caspar wrote a letter:

DEAR FATHER: I am sitting under a tree using the flattest part of my canteen for a desk. Even as I write, the division ahead of us is moving forward and we don't know what moment the storm of battle may break out. I don't know what the plans are. General Reilly knows, but he is so good as to give me very little of his confidence. In fact, I might be part of a forlorn hope, from all to the contrary I've heard from him. I understood you to say in Washington that you at one time had been of some service to him, but if that is true I can assure you he has completely forgotten it. At times his manner to me is little short of being offensive, but of course I understand that it is only the way of a crusty old soldier who has been made boorish and bearish by a long life among the Indians. I dare say I shall manage it all right without a row.

When you hear that we have captured Santiago, please send me by first steamer a box of provisions and clothing, particularly sardines, pickles, and lightweight underwear. The other men on the staff are nice, quiet chaps, but they seem a bit crude. There has been no fighting yet save the skirmish by Young's brigade. Reilly was furious because we couldn't get in it. I met General Peel yesterday. He was very nice. He said he knew you well when he was in Congress. Young Jack May is on Peel's staff. I knew him well in college. We spent an hour talking over old times. Give my love to all at home.

The march was leisurely. Reilly and his staff strolled out to the head of the long, sinuous column and entered the sultry gloom of the forest. Some less fortunate regiments had to wait among the trees at the side of the trail, and as Reilly's brigade passed them, officer called to officer, classmate to classmate, and in these greetings rang a note of everything, from West Point to Alaska. They were going into an action in which they, the officers, would lose over a hundred in killed and wounded—officers alone—and these greetings, in which many nicknames occurred, were in many cases farewells such as one pictures being given with ostentation, solemnity, fervor. "There goes Gory Widgeon! Hello, Gory! Where you starting for? Hey, Gory!"

Caspar communed with himself and decided that he was not frightened. He was eager and alert; he thought that now his obligation to his country, or himself, was to be faced, and he was mad to prove to old Reilly and the others that after all he was a very capable soldier.

- iii -

Old Reilly was stumping along the line of his brigade and mumbling like a man with a mouthful of grass. The fire from the enemy's position was incredible in its swift fury, and Reilly's brigade was getting its share of a very bad ordeal. The old man's face was of the color of a tomato, and in his rage he mouthed and sputtered strangely. As he pranced along his thin line, scornfully erect, voices arose from the grass beseeching him to take care of himself. At his heels scrambled a bugler with pallid skin and clenched teeth, a chalky, trembling youth, who kept his eye on old Reilly's back and followed it.

The old gentleman was quite mad. Apparently he thought the whole thing a dreadful mess, but now that his brigade was irrevocably in it he was full-tilting here and everywhere to establish some irreproachable, immaculate kind of behavior on the part of every man Jack in his brigade. The intentions of the three venerable colonels were the same. They stood behind their lines, quiet, stern, courteous old fellows, admonishing their regiments to be very pretty in the face of such a hail of magazine-rifle and machine-gun fire as has never in this world been confronted save by beardless savages when the white man has found occasion to take his burden to some new place.

And the regiments were pretty. The men lay on their little stomachs and got peppered according to the law and said nothing, as the good blood pumped out into the grass, and even if a solitary rookie tried to get a decent reason to move to some haven of rational men, the cold voice of an officer made him look criminal with a shame that was a credit to his regimental education. Behind Reilly's command was a bullet-torn jungle through which it could not move as a brigade; ahead of it were Spanish trenches on hills. Reilly considered that he was in a fix, no doubt, but he said this only to himself. Suddenly he saw on the right a little point of blue-shirted men already halfway up the hill. It was some pathetic fragment of the Sixth United States Infantry. Chagrined, shocked, horrified, Reilly bellowed to his bugler, and the chalk-faced youth unlocked his teeth and sounded the charge by rushes.

The men formed hastily and grimly, and rushed. Apparently there awaited them only the fate of respectable soldiers. But they went because—of the opinions of others, perhaps. They went because—no loud-mouthed lot of jailbirds such as the Twenty-Seventh Infantry could do anything that they could not do better. They went because Reilly ordered it. They went because they went.

And yet not a man of them to this day has made a public speech explaining precisely how he did the whole thing and detailing with what initiative and ability he comprehended and defeated a situation which he did not comprehend at all.

Reilly never saw the top of the hill. He was heroically striving to keep up with his men when a bullet ripped quietly through his left lung, and he fell back into the arms of the bugler, who received him as he would have received a Christmas present. The three venerable colonels inherited the brigade in swift succession. The senior commanded for about fifty seconds, at the end of which he was mortally shot. Before they could get the news to the next in rank he, too, was shot. The junior colonel ultimately arrived wih a lean and puffing little brigade at the top of the hill. The men lay down and fired volleys at whatever was practicable.

In and out of the ditchlike trenches lay the Spanish dead, lemon-faced corpses dressed in shabby, blue-and-white ticking. Some were huddled down comfortably like sleeping children; one had died in the attitude of a man flung back in a dentist's chair; one sat in the trench with his chin sunk despondently to his breast; few preserved a record of the agitation of battle. With the greater number it was as if death had touched them so gently, so lightly, that they had not known of it. Death had come to them rather in the form of an opiate than of a bloody blow.

But the arrived men in the blue shirts had no thought of the sallow corpses. They were eagerly exchanging a hail of shots with the Spanish second line, whose ash-colored entrenchments barred the way to a city white amid trees. In the pauses, the men talked.

"We done the best. Old E Company got there. Why, one time the hull of B Company was *behind* us."

"Jones, he was the first man up. I saw 'im."

"Which Jones?"

"Did you see ol' Two-bars runnin' like a land crab? Made good time, too. He hit only in the high places. He's all right."

"The lootenant is all right, too. He was a good ten yards ahead of the best of us. I hated him at the post, but for this here active service there's none of 'em can touch him."

"This is mighty different from being at the post."

"Well, we done it, an' it wasn't b'cause *I* thought it could be done. When we started, I ses to m'self: 'Well, here goes a lot o' d——d fools.' "

" 'Tain't over yet."

"Oh, they'll never git us back from here. If they start to chase us back from here, we'll pile 'em up so high the last ones can't climb over. We've come this far, an' we'll stay here. I ain't done pantin'."

"Anything is better than packin' through that jungle an' gettin' blistered from front, rear, an' both flanks. I'd rather tackle another hill than go trailin' in them woods, so thick you can't tell whether you are one man or a division of cav'lry."

"Where's that young kitchen soldier, Cadogan, or whatever his name is. Ain't seen him today."

"Well, *I* seen him. He was right in with it. He got shot, too, about half up the hill, in the leg. I seen it. He's all right. Don't worry about him. He's all right."

"I seen 'im, too. He done his stunt. As soon as I can git this piece of barbed-wire entanglement out o' me throat I'll give 'm a cheer."

"He ain't shot at all, b'cause there he stands, there. See 'im?"

Rearward, the grassy slope was populous with little groups of men searching for the wounded. Reilly's brigade began to dig with its bayonets and shovel with its meat-ration cans.

- *iv* -

Senator Cadogan paced to and fro in his private parlor and smoked small, brown, weak cigars. These little wisps seemed utterly inadequate to console such a ponderous satrap.

It was the evening of the 1st of July, 1898, and the Senator was immensely excited, as could be seen from the superlatively calm way in which he called out to his private secretary, who was in an adjoining room. The voice was serene, gentle, affectionate, low.

"Baker, I wish you'd go over again to the War Department and see if they've heard anything about Caspar."

A very bright-eyed, hatchet-faced young man appeared in a doorway, pen still in hand. He was hiding a nettle-like irritation behind all the finished audacity of a smirk, sharp, lying, trustworthy young politician. "I've just got back from there, sir," he suggested.

The Skowmulligan war horse lifted his eyes and looked for a short second into the eyes of his private secretary. It was not a glare or an eagle glance; it was something beyond the practice of an actor; it was simply meaning. The clever private secretary grabbed his hat and was at once enthusiastically away. "All right, sir," he cried. "I'll find out."

The War Department was ablaze with light, and messengers were running. With the assurance of a retainer of an old house, Baker made his way through much small-caliber vociferation. There was rumor of a big victory; there was rumor of a big defeat. In the corridors various watchdogs arose from their armchairs and asked him of his business in tones of uncertainty which in no wise compared with their previous habitual deference to the private secretary of the war horse of Skowmulligan.

Ultimately Baker arrived in a room where some kind of head clerk sat writing feverishly at a roll-top desk. Baker asked a question, and the head clerk mumbled profanely without lifting his head. Apparently he said, "How in the blankety-blank blazes do I know?"

The private secretary let his jaw fall. Surely some new spirit had come suddenly upon the heart of Washington—a spirit which Baker understood to be almost defiantly indifferent to the wishes of Senator Cadogan, a spirit which was not courteously oily. What could it mean? Baker's foxlike mind sprang wildly to a conception of overturned factions, changed friends, new combinations. The assurance which had come from experience of a broad political situation suddenly left him, and he would not have been amazed if someone had told him that Senator Cadogan now controlled only six votes in the state of Skowmulligan. "Well," he stammered in his bewilderment, "well—there isn't any news of the old man's son, hey?" Again the head clerk replied blasphemously.

Eventually Baker retreated in disorder from the presence of this head clerk, having learned that the latter did not give a —— if Casper Cadogan were sailing through Hades on an ice yacht.

Baker stormed other and more formidable officials. In fact, he struck as high as he dared. They one and all flung him short, hard words, even as men pelt an annoying cur with pebbles. He emerged from the brilliant light, from the groups of men with anxious, puzzled faces, and as he walked back to the hotel he did not know if his name were Baker or Cholmondeley.

However, as he walked up the stairs to the Senator's rooms, he contrived to concentrate his intellect upon a manner of speaking.

The war horse was still pacing his parlor and smoking. He paused at Baker's entrance. "Well?"

"Mr. Cadogan," said the private secretary coolly, "they told me at the Department that they did not give a cuss whether your son was alive or dead."

The Senator looked at Baker and smiled gently. "What's that, my boy?" he asked in a soft and considerate voice.

"They said—" gulped Baker, with a certain tenacity. "They said that they didn't give a cuss whether your son was alive or dead."

There was a silence for the space of three seconds. Baker stood like an image; he had no machinery for balancing the issues of this kind of a situation, and he seemed to feel that if he stood as still as a stone frog he would escape the ravages of a terrible senatorial wrath which was about to break forth in a hurricane speech which would snap off trees and sweep away barns.

"Well," drawled the Senator lazily, "who did you see, Baker?"

The private secretary resumed a certain usual manner of breathing. He told the names of the men whom he had seen.

"Ye—e—es," remarked the Senator. He took another little brown cigar and held it with a thumb and first finger, staring at it with the calm and steady scrutiny of a scientist investigating a new thing. "So they don't care whether Caspar is alive or dead, eh? Well—maybe they don't— That's all right— However—I think I'll just look in on 'em and state my views."

When the Senator had gone, the private secretary ran to the window and leaned afar out. Pennsylvania Avenue was gleaming silver blue in the light of many arc lamps; the cable trains groaned along to the clangor of gongs; from the window, the walks presented a hardly diversified aspect of shirtwaists and straw hats. Sometimes a newsboy screeched.

Baker watched the tall, heavy figure of the Senator moving out to intercept a cable train. "Great Scott!" cried the private secretary to himself. "There'll be three distinct kinds of grand, plain, practical fireworks. The old man is going for 'em. I wouldn't be in Lascum's boots. Ye gods, what a row there'll be."

In due time, the Senator was closeted with some kind of deputy-third-assistant battery horse in the offices of the War Department. The official obviously had been told off to make a supreme effort to pacify Cadogan, and he certainly was acting according to his instructions. He was almost in tears; he spread out his hands in supplication, and his voice whined and wheedled.

"Why, really, you know, Senator, we can only beg you to look at the circumstances. Two scant divisions at the top of that hill; over a thousand men killed and wounded; the line so thin that any strong attack would smash our Army to flinders. The Spaniards have probably received reinforcements under Pando; Shafter seems to be too ill to be actively in command of our troops; Lawton can't get up with his division before tomorrow. We are actually expecting—no, I won't say expecting—but we would not be surprised—nobody in the department would be surprised if before daybreak we were compelled to give to the country the news of a disaster which would be the worst blow the national pride has ever suffered. Don't you see? Can't you see our position, Senator?"

The Senator, with a pale but composed face, contemplated the official with eyes that gleamed in a way not usual with the big, self-controlled politician.

"I'll tell you frankly, sir," continued the other. "I'll tell you frankly that at this moment we don't know whether we are afoot or a-horseback. Everything is in the air. We don't know whether we have won a glorious victory or simply got ourselves in a deuce of a fix."

The Senator coughed. "I suppose my boy is with the two divisions at the top of that hill? He's with Reilly."

"Yes; Reilly's brigade is up there."

"And when do you suppose the War Department can tell me if he is all right. I want to know."

"My dear Senator, frankly, I don't know. Again I beg you

to think of our position. The Army is in a muddle; it's a general thinking that he must fall back, and yet not sure that he *can* fall back without losing the Army. Why, we're worrying about the lives of sixteen thousand men and the self-respect of the nation, Senator."

"I see," observed the Senator, nodding his head slowly. "And naturally the welfare of one man's son doesn't—how do they say it—doesn't cut any ice."

- v -

And in Cuba it rained. In a few days, Reilly's brigade discovered that by their successful charge they had gained the inestimable privilege of sitting in a wet trench and slowly but surely starving to death. Men's tempers crumbled like dry bread. The soldiers who so cheerfully, quietly, and decently had captured positions which the foreign experts had said were impregnable now in turn underwent an attack which was furious as well as insidious. The heat of the sun alternated with rains which boomed and roared in their falling like mountain cataracts. It seemed as if men took the fever through sheer lack of other occupation. During the days of battle, none had had time to get even a tropic headache, but no sooner was that brisk period over than men began to shiver and shudder by squads and platoons. Rations were scarce enough to make a little fat strip of bacon seem of the size of a corner lot, and coffee grains were pearls. There would have been godless quarreling over fragments if it were not that with these fevers came a great listlessness, so that men were almost content to die, if death required no exertion.

It was an occasion which distinctly separated the sheep from the goats. The goats were few enough, but their qualities glared out like crimson spots.

One morning Jameson and Ripley, two captains in the Forty-fourth Foot, lay under a flimsy shelter of sticks and palm branches. Their dreamy, dull eyes contemplated the men in the trench which went to left and right. To them came

Caspar Cadogan, moaning. "By Jove," he said, as he flung himself wearily on the ground, "I can't stand much more of this, you know. It's killing me." A bristly beard sprouted through the grime on his face; his eyelids were crimson; an indescribably dirty shirt fell away from his roughened neck; and at the same time, various lines of evil and greed were deepened on his face, until he practically stood forth as a revelation, a confession. "I can't stand it. By Jove, I can't."

Stanford, a lieutenant under Jameson, came stumbling along toward them. He was a lad of the class of ninety-eight at West Point. It could be seen that he was flaming with fever. He rolled a calm eye at them. "Have you any water, sir?" he said to his captain. Jameson got upon his feet and helped Stanford to lay his shaking length under the shelter. "No, boy," he answered gloomily. "Not a drop. You got any, Rip?"

"No," answered Ripley, looking with anxiety upon the young officer. "Not a drop."

"You, Cadogan?"

Here Caspar hesitated oddly for a second, and then in a tone of deep regret made answer: "No, Captain; not a mouthful."

Jameson moved off weakly. "You lay quietly, Stanford, and I'll see what I can rustle."

Presently Caspar felt that Ripley was steadily regarding him. He returned the look with one of half-guilty questioning.

"God forgive you, Cadogan," said Ripley, "but you are a damned beast. Your canteen is full of water."

Even then the apathy in their veins prevented the scene from becoming as sharp as the words sounded. Caspar sputtered like a child, and at length merely said, "No, it isn't." Stanford lifted his head to shoot a keen, proud glance at Caspar, and then turned away his face.

"You lie," said Ripley. "I can tell the sound of a full canteen as far as I can hear it."

"Well, if it is, I—I must have forgotten it."

"You lie; no man in this army just now forgets whether his canteen is full or empty. Hand it over."

Fever is the physical counterpart of shame, and when a man

has the one, he accepts the other with an ease which would revolt his healthy self. However, Caspar made a desperate struggle to preserve the forms. He arose, and taking the string from his shoulder, passed the canteen to Ripley. But after all there was a whine in his voice, and the assumption of dignity was really a farce. "I think I had better go, Captain. You can have the water if you want it, I'm sure. But—but I fail to see—I fail to see what reason you have for insulting me."

"Do you?" said Ripley stolidly. "That's all right."

Caspar stood for a terrible moment. He simply did not have the strength to turn his back on this—this affair. It seemed to him that he must stand forever and face it. But when he found the audacity to look again at Ripley, he saw the latter was not at all concerned with the situation. Ripley, too, had the fever. The fever changes all laws of proportion. Caspar went away.

"Here, youngster; here is your drink."

Stanford made a weak gesture. "I wouldn't touch a drop from his blamed canteen if it was the last water in the world," he murmured in his high, boyish voice.

"Don't you be a young jackass," quoth Ripley tenderly.

The boy stole a glance at the canteen. He felt the propriety of arising and hurling it after Caspar, but—he, too, had the fever.

"Don't you be a young jackass," said Ripley again.

- *vi* -

Senator Cadogan was happy. His son had returned from Cuba, and the eight thirty train that evening would bring him to the station nearest to the stone-and-red-shingle villa which the Senator and his family occupied on the shores of Long Island Sound. The Senator's steam yacht lay some hundred yards from the beach. She had just returned from a trip to Montauk Point, where the Senator had made a gallant attempt to gain his son from the transport on which he was coming from Cuba. He had fought a brave sea fight with sundry petty

little doctors and ship's officers, who had raked him with
broadsides describing the laws of quarantine and had used
inelegant speech to a United States Senator as he stood on
the bridge of his own steam yacht. These men had grimly
asked him to tell exactly how much better was Caspar than
any other returning soldier.

But the Senator had not given them a long fight. In fact,
the truth came to him quickly, and with almost a blush he
had ordered the yacht back to her anchorage off the villa. As
a matter of fact, the trip to Montauk Point had been under-
taken largely from impulse. Long ago the Senator had decided
that when his boy returned the greeting should have something Spartan in it. He would make a welcome such as most
soldiers get. There should be no flowers and carriages when
the other poor fellows got none. He should consider Caspar
as a soldier. That was the way to treat a man. But in the end,
a sharp acid of anxiety had worked upon the iron old man,
until he had ordered the yacht to take him out and make a fool
of him. The result filled him with a chagrin which caused
him to delegate to the mother and sisters the entire business
of succoring Caspar at Montauk Point Camp. He had remained at home conducting the huge correspondence of an
active National politician and waiting for this son whom he so
loved and whom he so wished to be a man of a certain strong,
taciturn, shrewd ideal. The recent yacht voyage he now looked
upon as a kind of confession of his weakness, and he was
resolved that no more signs should escape him.

But yet his boy had been down there against the enemy
and among the fevers. There had been grave perils, and his
boy must have faced them. And he could not prevent himself
from dreaming through the poetry of fine actions in which
visions his son's face shone out manly and generous. During
these periods, the people about him, accustomed as they were
to his silence and calm in time of stress, considered that affairs
in Skowmulligan might be most critical. In no other way
could they account for this exaggerated phlegm.

On the night of Caspar's return, he did not go to dinner,
but had a tray sent to his library, where he remained writing.

At last he heard the spin of the dog cart's wheels on the gravel of the drive, and a moment later there penetrated to him the sound of joyful feminine cries. He lit another cigar; he knew that it was now his part to bide with dignity the moment when his son should shake off that other welcome and come to him. He could still hear them; in their exuberance they seemed to be capering like schoolchildren. He was impatient, but this impatience took the form of a polar stolidity.

Presently there were quick steps and a jubilant knock at his door. "Come in," he said.

In came Caspar, thin, yellow, and in soiled khaki. "They almost tore me to pieces," he cried, laughing. "They danced around like wild things." Then, as they shook hands, he dutifully said, "How are you, sir?"

"How are you, my boy?" answered the Senator casually but kindly.

"Better than I might expect, sir," cried Caspar cheerfully. "We had a pretty hard time, you know."

"You look as if they'd given you a hard run," observed the father in a tone of slight interest.

Caspar was eager to tell. "Yes, sir," he said rapidly. "We did, indeed. Why, it was awful. We—any of us—were lucky to get out of it alive. It wasn't so much the Spaniards, you know. The Army took care of them all right. It was the fever and the—you know, we couldn't get anything to eat. And the mismanagement. Why, it was frightful."

"Yes, I've heard," said the Senator. A certain wistful look came into his eyes, and he did not allow it to become prominent. Indeed, he suppressed it. "And you, Caspar? I suppose you did your duty?"

Caspar answered with becoming modesty. "Well, I didn't do more than anybody else, I don't suppose, but—well, I got along all right, I guess."

"And this great charge up San Juan Hill?" asked the father slowly. "Were you in that?"

"Well—yes; I was in it," replied the son.

The Senator brightened a trifle. "You were, eh? In the front of it, or just sort of going along?"

"Well—I don't know. I couldn't tell exactly. Sometimes I was in front of a lot of them, and sometimes I was—just sort of going along."

This time the Senator emphatically brightened. "That's all right, then. And of course—of course you performed your commissary duties correctly?"

The question seemed to make Caspar uncommunicative and sulky. "I did when there was anything to do," he answered. "But the whole thing was on the most unbusinesslike basis you can imagine. And they wouldn't tell you anything. Nobody would take time to instruct you in your duties, and of course, if you didn't know a thing, your superior officer would swoop down on you and ask you why in the deuce such and such a thing wasn't done in such and such a way. Of course, I did the best I could."

The Senator's countenance had again become somberly indifferent. "I see. But you weren't directly rebuked for incapacity, were you? No; of course you weren't. But—I mean— did any of your superior officers suggest that you were 'no good,' or anything of that sort? I mean—did you come off with a clean slate?"

Caspar took a small time to digest his father's meaning. "Oh, yes, sir," he cried at the end of his reflection. "The commissary was in such a hopeless mess anyhow that nobody thought of doing anything but curse Washington."

"Of course," rejoined the Senator harshly. "But supposing that you had been a competent and well-trained commissary officer. What then?"

Again the son took time for consideration, and in the end deliberately replied. "Well, if I had been a competent and well-trained commissary, I would have sat there and eaten up my heart and cursed Washington."

"Well, then, that's all right. And now about this charge up San Juan? Did any of the generals speak to you afterward and say that you had done well? Didn't any of them see you?"

"Why, n—n—no, I don't suppose they did—any more than I did them. You see, this charge was a big thing and covered lots of ground, and I hardly saw anybody excepting a lot of the men."

"Well, but didn't any of the men see you? Weren't you ahead some of the time leading them on and waving your sword?"

Caspar burst into laughter. "Why, no. I had all I could do to scramble along and try to keep up. And I didn't want to go up at all."

"Why?" demanded the Senator.

"Because—because the Spaniards were shooting so much. And you could see men falling, and the bullets rushed around you in—by the bushel. And then at last it seemed that if we once drove them away from the top of the hill, there would be less danger. So we all went up."

The Senator chuckled over this description. "And you didn't flinch at all?"

"Well," rejoined Caspar humorously, "I won't say I wasn't frightened."

"No, of course not. But then you did not let anybody know it?"

"Of course not."

"You understand, naturally, that I am bothering you with all these questions because I desire to hear how my only son behaved in the crisis. I don't want to worry you with it. But if you went through the San Juan charge with credit, I'll have you made a major."

"Well," said Caspar, "I wouldn't say I went through that charge with credit. I went through it all good enough, but the enlisted men around went through in the same way."

"But weren't you encouraging them and leading them on by your example?"

Caspar smirked. He began to see a point. "Well, sir," he said with a charming hesitation. "Aw—er—I—well, I dare say I was doing my share of it."

The perfect form of the reply delighted the father. He could not endure blatancy; his admiration was to be won only by a bashful hero. Now he beat his hand impulsively down upon the table. "That's what I wanted to know. That's it exactly. I'll have you made a major next week. You've found your proper field at last. You stick to the Army, Caspar, and I'll back you up. That's the thing. In a few years, it will be a great career. The United States is pretty sure to have an Army of about a hundred and fifty thousand men. And starting in when you did and with me to back you up—why, we'll make you a general in seven or eight years. That's the ticket. You stay in the Army." The Senator's cheek was flushed with enthusiasm, and he looked eagerly and confidently at his son.

But Caspar had pulled a long face. "The Army?" he said. "Stay in the Army?"

The Senator continued to outline quite rapturously his idea of the future. "The Army, evidently, is just the place for you. You know as well as I do that you have not been a howling success, exactly, in anything else which you have tried. But now the Army just suits you. It is the kind of career which especially suits you. Well, then, go in, and go at it hard. Go in to win. Go at it."

"But—" began Caspar.

The Senator interrupted swiftly. "Oh, don't worry about that part of it. I'll take care of all that. You won't get jailed in some Arizona adobe for the rest of your natural life. There won't be much more of that, anyhow; and besides, as I say, I'll look after all that end of it. The chance is splendid. A young, healthy, and intelligent man, with the start you've already got, and with my backing, can do anything—anything! There will be a lot of active service—oh, yes, I'm sure of it—and everybody who—"

"But," said Caspar, wan, desperate, heroic, "Father, I don't care to stay in the Army."

The Senator lifted his eyes and darkened. "What?" he said. "What's that?" He looked at Caspar.

The son became tightened and wizened like an old miser trying to withhold gold. He replied with a sort of idiot obstinacy, "I don't care to stay in the Army."

The Senator's jaw clinched down, and he was dangerous. But, after all, there was something mournful somewhere. "Why, what do you mean?" he asked gruffly.

"Why, I couldn't get along, you know. The—the—"

"The what?" demanded the father, suddenly uplifted with thunderous anger. "The what?"

Caspar's pain found a sort of outlet in mere irresponsible talk. "Well, you know—the other men, you know. I couldn't get along with them, you know. They're peculiar, somehow; odd; I didn't understand them, and they didn't understand me. We—we didn't hitch, somehow. They're a queer lot. They've got funny ideas. I don't know how to explain it exactly, but—somehow—I don't like 'em. That's all there is to it. They're good fellows enough, I know, but—"

"Oh, well, Caspar," interrupted the Senator. Then he seemed to weigh a great fact in his mind. "I guess—" He paused again in profound consideration. "I guess—" He lit a small, brown cigar. "I guess you are no damn good."

~~~~~~~~~~~~~~~~~~~~~~~~~~~~~~~~~~~~~~~~~

# Death and the Child

## - i -

THE PEASANTS who were streaming down the mountain trail had, in their sharp terror, evidently lost their ability to count. The cattle and the huge, round bundles seemed to suffice to the minds of the crowd if there were now two in each case where there had been three. This brown stream poured on with a constant wastage of goods and beasts. A goat fell behind to scout the dried grass, and its owner, howling, flogging his donkeys, passed far ahead. A colt, suddenly frightened, made a stumbling charge up the hillside. The expenditure was always profligate, and always unnamed, unnoted. It was as if fear was a river, and this horde had simply been caught in the torrent, man tumbling over beast, beast over man, as helpless in it as the logs that fall and shoulder grindingly through the gorges of a lumber country. It was a freshet that might sear the face of the tall, quiet mountain; it might draw a livid line across the land, this downpour of fear with a thousand homes adrift in the current—men, women, babes, animals. From it there arose a constant babble of tongues, shrill, broken, and sometimes choking, as from men drowning. Many made gestures, painting their agonies on the air with fingers that twirled swiftly.

The blue bay, with its pointed ships, and the white town lay below them, distant, flat, serene. There was upon this vista a peace that a bird knows when, high in air, it surveys the world, a great, calm thing rolling noiselessly toward the end of the mystery. Here on the height one felt the existence of the universe scornfully defining the pain in ten thousand minds. The sky was an arch of stolid sapphire. Even to the mountains, raising their mighty shapes from the valley, this headlong rush of the fugitives was too minute. The sea, the sky, and the hills combined in their grandeur to term this misery inconsequent. Then, too, it sometimes happened that a face seen as it passed on the flood reflected curiously the spirit of them all, and still more. One saw then a woman of the opinion of the vaults above the clouds. When a child cried, it cried always because of some adjacent misfortune— some discomfort of a pack saddle or rudeness of an encircling arm. In the dismal melody of this flight there were often sounding chords of apathy. Into these preoccupied countenances one felt that needles could be thrust without purchasing a scream. The trail wound here and there, as the sheep had willed in the making of it.

Although this throng seemed to prove that the whole of humanity was fleeing in one direction—with every tie severed that binds us to the soil—a young man was walking rapidly up the mountain, hastening to a side of the path from time to time to avoid some particularly wide rush of people and cattle. He looked at everything in agitation and pity. Frequently he called admonitions to maniacal fugitives, and at other times he exchanged strange stares with the imperturbable ones. They seemed to him to wear merely the expressions of so many boulders rolling down the hill. He exhibited wonder and awe with his pitying glances.

Turning once toward the rear, he saw a man in the uniform of a lieutenant of infantry marching the same way. He waited then, subconsciously elate at a prospect of being able to make into words the emotion which heretofore had been expressed only in the flash of eyes and sensitive movements of his flexible mouth. He spoke to the officer in rapid French, waving his arms wildly, and often pointing with a dramatic finger. "Ah, this is too cruel, too cruel, too cruel! Is it not? I did not think it would be as bad as this. I did not think—God's mercy! —I did not think at all. And yet, I am a Greek; or at least, my father was a Greek. I did not come here to fight; I am really a correspondent; you see? I was to write for an Italian paper. I have been educated in Italy; I have spent nearly all my life in Italy—at the schools and universities. I knew nothing of war! I was a student—a student. I came here merely because my father was a Greek, and for his sake I thought of Greece. I loved Greece; but I did not dream—"

He paused, breathing heavily. His eyes glistened from that soft overflow which comes on occasion to the glance of a young woman. Eager, passionate, profoundly moved, his first words while facing the procession of fugitives had been an active definition of his own dimension, his personal relation to men, geography, life. Throughout he had preserved the fiery dignity of a tragedian.

The officer's manner at once deferred to this outburst. "Yes," he said, polite but mournful, "these poor people—these poor people! I do not know what is to become of these poor people."

The young man deckamed again, "I had no dream—I had no dream that it would be like this! This is too cruel—too cruel! Now I want to be a soldier. Now I want to fight. Now I want to do battle for the land of my father." He made a sweeping gesture into the northwest.

The officer was also a young man, but he was bronzed and steady. Above his high military collar of crimson cloth with one silver star upon it appeared a profile stern, quiet, and confident, respecting fate, fearing only opinion. His clothes were covered with dust; the only bright spot was the flame of the crimson collar. At the violent cries of his companion he smiled as if to himself, meanwhile keeping his eyes fixed in a glance ahead.

From a land toward which their faces were bent came a continuous boom of artillery fire. It was sounding in regular measures, like the beating of a colossal clock—a clock that was counting the seconds in the lives of the stars, and men had time to die between the ticks. Solemn, oracular, inexorable, the great seconds tolled over the hills as if God fronted this dial rimmed by the horizon. The soldier and the correspondent found themselves silent. The latter in particular was sunk in a great mournfulness, as if he had resolved willy-nilly to swing to the bottom of the abyss where dwelt secrets of this kind, and had learned beforehand that all to be met there was cruelty and hopelessness. A strap of his bright new leather leggings came unfastened, and he bowed over it slowly, impressively, as one bending over the grave of a child.

Then, suddenly, the reverberations mingled until one could not separate one explosion from another, and into the hubbub came the drawling sound of a leisurely musketry fire. Instantly, for some reason of cadence, the noise was irritating, silly, infantile. This uproar was childish. It forced the nerves to object, to protest against this racket, which was as idle as the din of a lad with a drum.

The lieutenant lifted his finger and pointed. He spoke in vexed tones, as if he held the other man personally responsible for the noise. "Well, there!" he said. "If you wish for war, you now have an opportunity magnificent."

The correspondent raised himself upon his toes. He tapped his chest with gloomy pride. "Yes! There is war! There is the war I wish to enter. I fling myself in. I am a Greek—a Greek, you understand. I wish to fight for my country. You know the way. Lead me! I offer myself." Struck with a sudden thought, he brought a case from his pocket, and extracting a card, handed it to the officer with a bow. "My name is Peza," he said simply.

A strange smile passed over the soldier's face. There was pity and pride—the vanity of experience—and contempt in it. "Very well," he said, returning the bow. "If my company is in the middle of the fight, I shall be glad for the honor of your companionship. If my company is not in the middle of the fight, I will make other arrangements for you."

Peza bowed once more, very stiffly, and correctly spoke his thanks. On the edge of what he took to be a great venture toward death, he discovered that he was annoyed at something in the lieutenant's tone. Things immediately assumed new and extraordinary proportions. The battle, the great carnival of woe, was sunk at once to an equation with a vexation by a stranger. He wanted to ask the lieutenant what was his meaning. He bowed again majestically. The lieutenant bowed. They flung a shadow of manners, of capering, tinsel ceremony, across a land that groaned, and it satisfied something within themselves completely.

In the meantime, the river of fleeing villagers was changed to simply a last drooping of belated creatures who fled past stammering and flinging their hands high. The two men had come to the top of the great hill. Before them was a green plain as level as an inland sea. It swept northward, and merged finally into a length of silvery mist. Upon the near part of this plain, and upon two gray, treeless mountains at the sides of it, were little black lines from which floated slanting sheets of smoke. It was not a battle, to the nerves; one could survey it with equanimity, as if it were a tea table. But upon Peza's mind it struck a loud, clanging blow. It was war. Edified, aghast, triumphant, he paused suddenly, his lips apart. He remembered the pageants of carnage that had marched through the dreams of his childhood. Love he knew; that he had confronted alone, isolated, wondering, an individual, an atom taking the hand of a titanic principle. Like the faintest breeze on his forehead, he felt here the vibration from the hearts of forty thousand men.

The lieutenant's nostrils were moving. "I must go at once," he said. "I must go at once."

"I will go with you, wherever you go," shouted Peza loudly.

A primitive track wound down the side of the mountain, and in their rush they bounded from here to there, choosing risks which in the ordinary caution of man would surely have seemed of remarkable danger. The ardor of the correspondent surpassed the full energy of the soldier. Several times he turned and shouted, "Come on! Come on!"

At the foot of the path they came to a wide road which extended toward the battle in a yellow and straight line. Some men were trudging wearily to the rear. They were without rifles; their clumsy uniforms were dirty and all awry. They turned eyes dully aglow with fever upon the pair striding toward the battle. Others were bandaged with the triangular kerchief, upon which one could still see, through bloodstains, the little explanatory pictures illustrating the ways to bind various wounds—"Fig. 1," "Fig. 2," "Fig. 7." Mingled with the pacing soldiers were peasants, indifferent, capable of smiling, gibbering about the battle, which was to them an ulterior drama. A man was leading a string of three donkeys to the rear, and at intervals he was accosted by wounded or fevered soldiers, from whom he defended his animals with apelike cries and mad gesticulations. After much chattering, they usually subsided gloomily, and allowed him to go with his sleek little beasts unburdened. Finally he encountered a soldier who walked slowly, with the assistance of a staff. His head was bound with a wide bandage, grimy from blood and mud. He made application to the peasant, and immediately they were involved in a hideous Levantine discussion. The peasant whined and clamored, sometimes spitting like a kitten. The wounded soldier jawed on thunderously, his great hands stretched in clawlike graspings over the peasant's head. Once he raised his staff and made threat with it. Then suddenly the row was at an end. The other sick men saw their comrade mount the leading donkey, and at once begin to drum with his heels. None attempted to gain the backs of the remaining animals. They gazed after him dully. Finally they saw the caravan outlined for a moment against the sky. The soldier was still waving his arms passionately, having it out with the peasant.

Peza was alive with despair for these men who looked at him with such doleful, quiet eyes. "Ah, my God!" he cried to the lieutenant. "These poor souls! These poor souls!"

The officer faced about angrily. "If you are coming with me, there is no time for this." Peza obeyed instantly and with a sudden meekness. In the moment, some portion of egotism left him, and he modestly wondered if the universe took cognizance of him to an important degree. This theatre for slaughter, built by the inscrutable needs of the earth, was an enormous affair, and he reflected that the accidental destruction of an individual, Peza by name, would perhaps be nothing at all.

With the lieutenant, he was soon walking along behind a series of little crescent-shaped trenches, in which were soldiers tranquilly interested, gossiping with the hum of a tea party. Although these men were not at this time under fire, he concluded that they were fabulously brave, else they would not be so comfortable, so at home, in their sticky brown trenches. They were certain to be heavily attacked before the day was old. The universities had not taught him to understand this attitude. At the passing of the young man in very nice tweed, with his new leggings, his new white helmet, his new field-glass case, his new revolver holster, the soiled soldiers turned with the same curiosity which a being in strange garb meets at the corners of streets. He might as well have been promenading a populous avenue. The soldiers volubly discussed his identity.

To Peza there was something awful in the absolute familiarity of each tone, expression, gesture. These men, menaced with battle, displayed the curiosity of the café. Then, on the verge of his great encounter toward death, he found himself extremely embarrassed, composing his face with difficulty, wondering what to do with his hands, like a gawk at a levee.

344 STEPHEN CRANE

He felt ridiculous, and also he felt awed, aghast at these men who could turn their faces from the ominous front and debate his clothes, his business. There was an element which was newborn into his theory of war.

He was not averse to the brisk pace at which the lieutenant moved along the line. The roar of fighting was always in Peza's ears. It came from some short hills ahead and to the left. The road curved suddenly and entered a wood. The trees stretched their luxuriant and graceful branches over grassy slopes. A breeze made all this verdure gently rustle and speak in long, silken sighs. Absorbed in listening to the hurricane racket from the front, he still remembered that these trees were growing, the grass blades were extending, according to their process. He inhaled a deep breath of moisture and fragrance from the grove, a wet odor which expressed the opulent fecundity of unmoved nature, marching on with her million plans for multiple life, multiple death.

Farther on, they came to a place where the Turkish shells were landing. There was a long, hurtling sound in the air, and then one had sight of a shell. To Peza it was of the conical missiles which friendly officers had displayed to him on board warships. Curiously enough, too, this first shell smacked of the foundry—of men with smudged faces, of the blare of furnace fires. It brought machinery immediately into his mind. He thought that if he was killed there at that time, it would be as romantic to the old standards as death by a bit of falling iron in a factory.

- ii -

A child was playing on a mountain, and disregarding a battle that was waging on the plain. Behind him was the little cobbled hut of his fled parents. It was now occupied by a pearl-colored cow, that stared out from the darkness, thoughtful and tender-eyed. The child ran to and fro, fumbling with sticks, and making great machinations with pebbles. By a striking exercise of artistic license, the sticks were ponies, cows, and dogs, and the pebbles were sheep. He was managing large agricultural and herding affairs. He was too intent on them to pay much heed to the fight four miles away, which at that distance resembled in sound the beating of surf upon rocks. However, there were occasions when some louder outbreak of that thunder stirred him from his serious occupation, and he turned then a questioning eye upon the battle, a small stick poised in his hand, interrupted in the act of sending his dog after his sheep. His tranquillity in regard to the death on the plain was as invincible as that of the mountain on which he stood.

It was evident that fear had swept the parents away from their home in a manner that could make them forget this child, the first-born. Nevertheless, the hut was cleaned bare. The cow had committed no impropriety in billeting herself at the domicile of her masters. This smoke-colored and odorous interior contained nothing as large as a hummingbird. Terror had operated on these runaway people in its sinister fashion—elevating details to enormous heights, causing a man to remember a button while he forgot a coat, overpowering everyone with recollections of a broken coffee cup, deluging them with fears for the safety of an old pipe, and causing them to forget their first-born. Meanwhile the child played soberly with his trinkets.

He was solitary. Engrossed in his own pursuits, it was seldom that he lifted his head to inquire of the world why it made so much noise. The stick in his hand was much larger to him than was an army corps of the distance. It was too childish for the mind of the child. He was dealing with sticks.

The battle lines writhed at times in the agony of a sea creature on the sands. These tentacles flung and waved in a supreme excitement of pain, and the struggles of the great outlined body brought it near and nearer to the child. Once he looked at the plain, and saw some men running wildly across a field. He had seen people chasing obdurate beasts in such fashion, and it struck him immediately that it was a manly thing, which he would incorporate in his game. Con-

sequently he raced furiously at his stone sheep, flourishing a
cudgel, crying the shepherd calls. He paused frequently to
get a cue of manner from the soldiers fighting on the plain.
He reproduced, to a degree, any movements which he accounted rational to his theory of sheepherding, the business
of men, the traditional and exalted living of his father.

- *iii* -

It was as if Peza was a corpse walking on the bottom of the
sea, and finding there fields of grain, groves, weeds, the
faces of men, voices. War, a strange employment of the
race, presented to him a scene crowded with familiar objects which wore the livery of their commonness placidly, un-
dauntedly. He was smitten with keen astonishment; a spread
of green grass, lit with the flames of poppies, was too old for
the company of this new ogre. If he had been devoting the
full lens of his mind to this phase, he would have known
that he was amazed that the trees, the flowers, the grass, all
tender and peaceful nature, had not taken to heels at once
upon the outbreak of battle. He venerated the immovable
poppies.

The road seemed to lead into the apex of an angle formed
by the two defensive lines of the Greeks. There was a struggle of wounded men, and of gunless and jaded men. These
latter did not seem to be frightened. They remained very
cool, walking with unhurried steps, and busy in gossip. Peza
tried to define them. Perhaps during the fight they had
reached the limit of their mental storage, their capacity for
excitement, for tragedy, and had then simply come away.
Peza remembered his visit to a certain place of pictures,
where he had found himself amid heavenly skies and diabolic
midnights—the sunshine beating red upon desert sands,
nude bodies flung to the shore in the green moonglow,
ghastly and starving men clawing at a wall in darkness, a girl
at her bath, with screened rays falling upon her pearly shoulders, a dance, a funeral, a review, an execution—all the
strength of Argus-eyed art; and he had whirled and whirled

amid this universe, with cries of woe and joy, sin and beauty, piercing his ears until he had been obliged to simply come away. He remembered that as he had emerged, he had lit a cigarette with unction, and advanced promptly to a café. A great, hollow quiet seemed to be upon the earth.

This was a different case, but in his thoughts he conceded the same causes to many of these gunless wanderers. They, too, may have dreamed at lightning speed, until the capacity for it was overwhelmed. As he watched them, he again saw himself walking toward the café, puffing upon his cigarette. As if to reinforce his theory, a soldier stopped him with an eager but polite inquiry for a match. He watched the man light his little roll of tobacco and paper and begin to smoke ravenously.

Peza no longer was torn with sorrow at the sight of wounded men. Evidently he found that pity had a numerical limit, and when this was passed the emotion became another thing. Now, as he viewed them, he merely felt himself very lucky, and beseeched the continuance of his superior fortune. At the passing of these slouched and stained figures, he now heard a reiteration of warning. A part of himself was appealing through the medium of these grim shapes. It was plucking at his sleeve and pointing, telling him to beware of these soldiers only as he would have cared for the harms of broken dolls. His whole vision was focused upon his own chance.

The lieutenant suddenly halted. "Look," he said, "I find that my duty is in another direction; I must go another way. But if you wish to fight, you have only to go forward, and any officer of the fighting line will give you opportunity." He raised his cap ceremoniously. Peza raised his new white helmet. The stranger to battles uttered thanks to his chaperon, the one who had presented him. They bowed punctiliously, staring at each other with civil eyes.

The lieutenant moved quietly away through a field. In an instant it flashed upon Peza's mind that this desertion was perfidious. He had been subjected to a criminal discourtesy. The officer had fetched him into the middle of the thing, and then left him to wander helplessly toward death. At one time he was upon the point of shouting at the officer.

In the vale there was an effect as if one was then beneath the battle. It was going on above, somewhere. Alone, unguided, Peza felt like a man groping in a cellar. He reflected, too, that one should always see the beginning of a fight. It was too difficult to thus approach it when the affair was in full swing. The trees hid all the movements of troops from him, and he thought he might be walking out to the very spot which chance had provided for the reception of a fool. He asked eager questions of passing soldiers. Some paid no heed to him; others shook their heads mournfully. They knew nothing, save that war was hard work. If they talked at all, it was in testimony of having fought well, savagely. They did not know if the army was going to advance, hold its ground, or retreat. They were weary.

A long, pointed shell flashed through the air, and struck near the base of a tree with a fierce upheaval, compounded of earth and flames. Looking back, Peza could see the shattered tree quivering from head to foot. Its whole being underwent a convulsive tremor which was an exhibition of pain and, furthermore, deep amazement. As he advanced through the vale, the shells continued to hiss and hurtle in long, low flights, and the bullets purred in the air. The missiles were flying into the breast of an astounded nature. The landscape, bewildered, agonized, was suffering a rain of infamous shots, and Peza imagined a million eyes gazing at him with the gaze of startled antelopes.

There was a resolute crashing of musketry from the tall hill on the left, and from directly in front there was a mingled din of artillery and musketry firing. Peza felt that his pride was playing a great trick in forcing him forward in this manner under conditions of strangeness, isolation, and ignorance; but he recalled the manner of the lieutenant, the smile on the hilltop among the flying peasants. Peza blushed, and pulled the peak of his helmet down on his forehead. He strode on firmly. Nevertheless, he hated the lieutenant, and he resolved that on some future occasion he would take much trouble to arrange a stinging social revenge upon that grinning jackanapes. It did not occur to him, until later, that he was now going to battle mainly because at a previous time a certain man had smiled.

- *iv* -

The road moved around the base of a little hill, and on this hill a battery of mountain guns was leisurely shelling something unseen. In the lee of the height, the mules, contented under their heavy saddles, were quietly browsing the long grass. Peza ascended the hill by a slanting path. He felt his heart beat swiftly. Once at the top of the hill, he would be obliged to look this phenomenon in the face. He hurried with a mysterious idea of preventing by this strategy the battle from making his appearance a signal for some tremendous renewal. This vague thought seemed logical at the time. Certainly this living thing had knowledge of his coming. He endowed it with the intelligence of a barbaric deity. And so he hurried. He wished to surprise war, this terrible emperor, when it was only growling on its throne. The ferocious and horrible sovereign was not to be allowed to make the arrival a pretext for some fit of smoky rage and blood. In this half-lull, Peza had distinctly the sense of stealing upon the battle unawares.

The soldiers watching the mules did not seem to be impressed by anything august. Two of them sat side by side and talked comfortably; another lay flat upon his back, staring dreamily at the sky; another cursed a mule for certain refractions. Despite their uniforms, their bandoleers and rifles, they were dwelling in the peace of hostlers. However, the long shells were whooping from time to time over the brow of the hill, and swirling in almost straight lines toward the vale of trees, flowers, and grass. Peza, hearing and seeing the shells, and seeing the pensive guardians of the mules, felt reassured. They were accepting the conditions of war as easily as an old sailor accepts the chair behind the counter of a tobacco shop. Or it was merely that the farm boy had gone to sea, and he had adjusted himself to the circumstances immediately, and with only the usual first misadventures in conduct. Peza was proud and ashamed that he was not of them—these stupid peasants who, throughout the world, hold potentates on their thrones, make statesmen illustrious, provide generals with lasting victories, all with ignorance, indifference, or half-witted hatred, moving the world with the strength of their arms, and getting their heads knocked together, in the name of God, the king, or the stock exchange—immortal, dreaming, hopeless asses who surrender their reason to the care of a shining puppet, and persuade some toy to carry their lives in his purse. Peza mentally abased himself before them, and wished to stir them with furious kicks.

As his eyes ranged above the rim of the plateau, he saw a group of artillery officers talking busily. They turned at once, and regarded his ascent. A moment later, a row of infantry soldiers, in a trench beyond the little guns, all faced him. Peza bowed to the officers. He understood at the time that he had made a good and cool bow, and he wondered at it; for his breath was coming in gasps—he was stifling from sheer excitement. He felt like a tipsy man trying to conceal his muscular uncertainty from the people in the street. But the officers did not display any knowledge. They bowed. Behind them Peza saw the plain, glittering green, with three lines of black marked upon it heavily. The front of the first of these lines was frothy with smoke. To the left of this hill was a craggy mountain, from which came a continual dull rattle of musketry. Its summit was ringed with the white smoke. The black lines on the plain slowly moved. The shells that came from there passed overhead, with the sound of great birds frantically flapping their wings. Peza thought of the first sight of the sea during a storm. He seemed to feel against his face the wind that races over the tops of cold and tumultuous billows.

He heard a voice afar off: "Sir, what would you?" He turned, and saw the dapper captain of the battery standing beside him. Only a moment had elapsed.

"Pardon me, sir," said Peza, bowing again.

The officer was evidently reserving his bows. He scanned the newcomer attentively. "Are you a correspondent?" he asked.

Peza produced a card. "Yes; I came as a correspondent," he replied. "But now, sir, I have other thoughts. I wish to help. You see? I wish to help."

"What do you mean?" said the captain. "Are you a Greek? Do you wish to fight?"

"Yes; I am a Greek; I wish to fight." Peza's voice surprised him by coming from his lips in even and deliberate tones. He thought with gratification that he was behaving rather well. Another shell, traveling from some unknown point on the plain, whirled close and furiously in the air, pursuing an apparently horizontal course, as if it were never going to touch the earth. The dark shape swished across the sky.

"Ah," cried the captain, now smiling, "I am not sure that we will be able to accommodate you with a fierce affair here just at this time, but—" He walked gaily to and fro behind the guns with Peza, pointing out to him the lines of the Greeks, and describing his opinion of the general plan of defense. He wore the air of an amiable host. Other officers questioned Peza in regard to the politics of the war. The king, the ministry, Germany, England, Russia—all these huge words were continually upon their tongues. "And the people in Athens, were they—?" Amid this vivacious babble, Peza, seated upon an ammunition box, kept his glance high, watching the appearance of shell after shell. These officers were like men who had been lost for days in the forest. They were thirsty for any scrap of news. Nevertheless, one of them would occasionally dispute their informant courteously. What would Servia have to say to that? No, no; France and Russia could never allow it. Peza was elated. The shells killed no one. War was not so bad! He was simply having coffee in the smoking room of some embassy where reverberate the names of nations.

A rumor had passed along the motley line of privates in the trench. The new arrival with the clean white helmet was a famous English cavalry officer, come to assist the army with his counsel. They stared at the figure of him, surrounded by officers. Peza, gaining sense of the glances and whispers, felt that his coming was an event.

Later, he resolved that he could, with temerity, do something finer. He contemplated the mountain where the Greek infantry was engaged, and announced leisurely to the captain of the battery that he thought presently of going in that direction and getting into the fight. He reaffirmed the sentiments of a patriot. The captain seemed surprised. "Oh, there will be fighting here at this knoll in a few minutes," he said orientally. "That will be sufficient. You had better stay with us. Besides, I have been ordered to resume fire." The officers all tried to dissuade him from departing. It was really not worth the trouble. The battery would begin again directly; then it would be amusing for him.

Peza felt that he was wandering, with his protestations of high patriotism, through a desert of sensible men. These officers gave no heed to his exalted declarations. They seemed too jaded. They were fighting the men who were fighting them. Palaver of the particular kind had subsided before their intense preoccupation in war as a craft. Moreover, many men had talked in that manner, and only talked.

Peza believed at first that they were treating him delicately; they were considerate of his inexperience. War had turned out to be such a gentle business that Peza concluded that he could scorn this idea. He bade them an heroic farewell, despite their objections.

However, when he reflected upon their ways afterward, he saw dimly that they were actuated principally by some universal childish desire for a spectator of their fine things. They were going into action, and they wished to be seen at war, precise and fearless.

- v -

Climbing slowly to the high infantry position, Peza was amazed to meet a soldier whose jaw had been half shot away, and who was being helped down the steep track by two tearful comrades. The man's breast was drenched with blood, and from a cloth which he held to the wound drops were splashing wildly upon the stones of the path. He gazed at Peza for a moment. It was a mystic gaze, which Peza withstood with difficulty. He was exchanging looks with a specter; all aspect of the man was somehow gone from this victim. As Peza went on, one of the unwounded soldiers loudly shouted to him to return and assist in this tragic march. But even Peza's fingers revolted. He was afraid of the specter; he would not have dared to touch it. He was surely craven in the movement of refusal he made to them. He scrambled hastily on up the path. He was running away!

At the top of the hill he came immediately upon a part of the line that was in action. Another battery of mountain guns was here, firing at the streaks of black on the plain. There were trenches filled with men lining parts of the crest, and near the base were other trenches, all crashing away mightily. The plain stretched as far as the eye could see, and from where silver mist ended this emerald ocean of grass, a great ridge of snow-topped mountains poised against a fleckless blue sky. Two knolls, green and yellow with grain, sat on the prairie, confronting the dark hills of the Greek position. Between them were the lines of the enemy. A row of trees, a village, a stretch of road showed faintly on this great canvas, this tremendous picture; but men, the Turkish battalions, were emphasized startlingly upon it. The ranks of troops between the knolls and the Greek position were as black as ink. The first line, of course, was muffled in smoke; but at the rear of it, battalions crawled up, and to and fro, plainer than beetles on a plate. Peza had never understood that masses of men were so declarative, so unmistakable, as if nature makes every arrangement to give information of the coming and the presence of destruction, the end, oblivion. The firing was full, complete, a roar of cataracts, and this pealing of concerted volleys was adjusted to the grandeur of the far-off range of snowy mountains. Peza, breathless, pale, felt that he had been set upon a pillar, and was survey-

ing mankind, the world. In the meantime dust had got in his
eye. He took his handkerchief and mechanically administered
to it.

An officer with a double stripe of purple on his trousers
paced in the rear of the battery of howitzers. He waved a
little cane. Sometimes he paused in his promenade to study
the field through his glasses. "A fine scene, sir," he cried
airily, upon the approach of Peza. It was like a blow in the
chest to the wide-eyed volunteer. It revealed to him a point
of view.

"Yes, sir; it is a fine scene," he answered.

They spoke in French. "I am happy to be able to entertain
monsieur with a little fine practice," continued the officer.
"I am firing upon that mass of troops you see there, a little
to the right. They are probably forming for another attack."

Peza smiled. Here again appeared manners—manners erect
by the side of death.

The right-flank gun of the battery thundered; there was
a belch of fire and smoke; the shell, flung swiftly and afar,
was known only to the ear, in which rang a broadening,
hooting wake of sound. The howitzer had thrown itself backward convulsively, and lay with its wheels moving in the air
as a squad of men rushed toward it; and later, it seemed as
if each little gun had made the supreme effort of its being in
each particular shot. They roared with voices far too loud,
and the thunderous effort caused a gun to bound as in a
dying convulsion. And then occasionally one was hurled with
wheels in air. These shuddering howitzers presented an appearance of so many cowards, always longing to bolt to the
rear, but being implacably held up to their business by this
throng of soldiers who ran in squads to drag them up again
to their obligation. The guns were herded and cajoled and
bullied interminably. One by one, in relentless program, they
were dragged forward to contribute a profound vibration of
steel and wood, a flash and a roar, to the important happiness
of men.

The adjacent infantry celebrated a good shot with smiles
and an outburst of gleeful talk.

"Look, sir," cried an officer once to Peza. Thin smoke was drifting lazily before Peza, and dodging impatiently, he brought his eyes to bear upon that part of the plain indicated by the officer's finger. The enemy's infantry was advancing to attack. From the black lines had come forth an inky mass which was shaped much like a human tongue. It advanced slowly, casually, without apparent spirit, but with an insolent confidence that was like a proclamation of the inevitable.

The impetuous part was all played by the defensive side.

Officers called; men plucked each other by the sleeve. There were shouts—motion. All eyes were turned upon the inky mass which was flowing toward the base of the hills, heavily, languorously, as oily and thick as one of the streams that ooze through a swamp.

Peza was chattering a question at everyone. In the way, pushed aside, or in the way again, he continued to repeat it: "Can they take the position? Can they take the position? Can they take the position?" He was apparently addressing an assemblage of deaf men. Every eye was busy watching every hand. The soldiers did not even seem to see the interesting stranger in the white helmet, who was crying out so feverishly.

Finally, however, the hurried captain of the battery espied him, and heeded his question. "No, sir! No, sir! It is impossible!" he shouted angrily. His manner seemed to denote that if he had had sufficient time he would have completely insulted Peza. The latter swallowed the crumb of news without regard to the coating of scorn, and waving his hand in adieu, he began to run along the crest of the hill toward the part of the Greek line against which the attack was directed.

- *vi* -

Peza, as he ran along the crest of the mountain, believed that his action was receiving the wrathful attention of the hosts of the foe. To him, then, it was incredible foolhardiness thus to call to himself the stares of thousands of hateful eyes.

He was like a lad induced by playmates to commit some in-
discretion in a cathedral. He was abashed; perhaps he even
blushed as he ran. It seemed to him that the whole solemn
ceremony of war had paused during this commission. So he
scrambled wildly over the rocks in his haste to end the
embarrassing ordeal. When he came among the crowning
rifle pits, filled with eager soldiers, he wanted to yell with
joy. None noticed him, save a young officer of infantry, who
said, "Sir, what do you want?" It was obvious that people
had devoted some attention to their own affairs.

Peza asserted, in Greek, that he wished above everything
to battle for the fatherland. The officer nodded. With a smile
he pointed to some dead men, covered with blankets, from
which were thrust upturned, dusty shoes.

"Yes; I know, I know," cried Peza. He thought the officer
was poetically alluding to the danger.

"No," said the officer, at once. "I mean cartridges—a
bandoleer. Take a bandoleer from one of them."

Peza went cautiously toward a body. He moved a hand
toward a corner of a blanket. There he hesitated, stuck, as if
his arm had turned to plaster. Hearing a rustle behind him,
he spun quickly. Three soldiers of the close rank in the
trench were regarding him. The officer came again, and
tapped him on the shoulder. "Have you any tobacco?" Peza
looked at him in bewilderment. His hand was still extended
toward the blanket which covered the dead soldier.

"Yes," he said, "I have some tobacco." He gave the officer
his pouch. As if in compensation, the other directed a soldier to strip the bandoleer from the corpse. Peza, having
crossed the long cartridge belt on his breast, felt that the
dead man had flung his two arms around him.

A soldier, with a polite nod and smile, gave Peza a rifle—
a relic of another dead man. Thus he felt, besides the clutch
of a corpse about his neck, that the rifle was as unhumanly
horrible as a snake that lives in a tomb. He heard at his
ear something that was in effect like the voices of those two
dead men, their low voices speaking to him of bloody death,
mutilation. The bandoleer gripped him tighter; he wished

to raise his hands to his throat, like a man who is choking. The rifle was clumsy; upon his palms he felt the movement of the sluggish currents of a serpent's life; it was crawling and frightful.

All about him were these peasants, with their interested countenances, gibbering of the fight. From time to time, a soldier cried out in semihumorous lamentations descriptive of his thirst. One bearded man sat munching a great bit of hard bread. Fat, greasy, squat, he was like an idol made of tallow. Peza felt dimly that there was a distinction between this man and a young student who could write sonnets and play the piano quite well. This old blockhead was coolly gnawing at the bread, while he—Peza—was being throttled by a dead man's arms.

He looked behind him, and saw that a head, by some chance, had been uncovered from its blanket. Two liquid-like eyes were staring into his face. The head was turned a little sideways, as if to get better opportunity for the scrutiny. Peza could feel himself blanch. He was being drawn and drawn by these dead men, slowly, firmly down, as to some mystic chamber under the earth, where they could walk, dreadful figures, swollen and blood-marked. He was bidden; they had commanded him; he was going, going, going.

When the man in the new white helmet bolted for the rear, many of the soldiers in the trench thought that he had been struck. But those who had been nearest to him knew better. Otherwise they would have heard the silken, sliding, tender noise of the bullet, and the thud of its impact. They bawled after him curses, and also outbursts of self-congratulation and vanity. Despite the prominence of the cowardly part, they were enabled to see in this exhibition a fine comment upon their own fortitude. The other soldiers thought that Peza had been wounded somewhere in the neck, because, as he ran, he was tearing madly at the bandoleer—the dead man's arms. The soldier with the bread paused in his eating, and cynically remarked upon the speed of the runaway.

An officer's voice was suddenly heard calling out the calculation of the distance to the enemy, the readjustment of the sights. There was a stirring rattle along the line. The men turned their eyes to the front. Other trenches, beneath them, to the right, were already heavily in action. The smoke was lifting toward the blue sky. The soldier with the bread placed it carefully on a bit of paper beside him as he turned to kneel in the trench.

- vii -

In the late afternoon, the child ceased his play on the mountain with his flocks and his dogs. Part of the battle had whirled very near to the base of his hill, and the noise was great. Sometimes he could see fantastic, smoky shapes, which resembled the curious figures in foam which one sees on the slant of a rough sea. The plain, indeed, was etched in white circles and whirligigs, like the slope of a colossal wave. The child took seat on a stone, and contemplated the fight. He was beginning to be astonished. He had never before seen cattle herded with such uproar. Lines of flame flashed out here and there. It was mystery.

Finally, without any preliminary indication, he began to weep. If the men struggling on the plain had had time, and greater vision, they could have seen this strange, tiny figure seated on a boulder, surveying them while the tears streamed. It was as simple as some powerful symbol.

As the magic clear light of day amid the mountains dimmed the distances, and the plain shone as a pallid blue cloth marked by the red threads of the firing, the child arose and moved off to the unwelcoming door of his home. He called softly for his mother, and complained of his hunger in the familiar formulae. The pearl-colored cow, grinding her jaws thoughtfully, stared at him with her large eyes. The peaceful gloom of evening was slowly draping the hills.

The child heard a rattle of loose stones on the hillside, and facing the sound, saw, a moment later, a man drag himself up to the crest of the hill and fall panting. Forgetting his mother and his hunger, filled with calm interest, the child walked forward, and stood over the heaving form. His eyes, too, were now large and inscrutably wise and sad, like those of the animal in the house.

After a silence, he spoke inquiringly: "Are you a man?"

Peza rolled over quickly, and gazed up into the fearless and cherubic countenance. He did not attempt to reply. He breathed as if life was about to leave his body. He was covered with dust; his face had been cut in some way, and his cheek was ribboned with blood. All the spick of his former appearance had vanished in a general dishevelment, in which he resembled a creature that had been flung to and fro, up and down, by cliffs and prairies during an earthquake. He rolled his eye glassily at the child.

They remained thus until the child repeated his words: "Are you a man?"

Peza gasped in the manner of a fish. Palsied, windless, and abject, he confronted the primitive courage, the sovereign child, the brother of the mountains, the sky, and the sea, and he knew that the definition of his misery could be written on a wee grass blade.

# Look for these popular titles from Washington Square Press at your bookseller now